MONSTER HUNTER

A LIFE IN SEARCH OF UNKNOWN BEASTS AT HOME AND ABROAD

by

Jonathan Downes
(Director, The Centre for Fortean Zoology)

"Sometimes the pursuit of monsters leads to madness"
Dr Bernard Heuvelmans
On the Track of Unknown Animals

Typeset using Word 2000,
Corel Draw v. 11,
Adobe Photoshop v 7

Illustrations by Mark North
Additional image manipulation by Suzy Decodts

DEDICATION

For Toby the CFZ Dog
1985-2000
For fifteen years my constant companion and best friend

*"When I was young I caught a fleeting glimpse out of the corner of my eye,
I looked around and it was gone, I cannot put my finger on it, this is not how I am…"*

Roger Waters *Comfortably Numb*

AUTHOR'S NOTE

Whereas this book was conceived in the early months of 2001, and I wrote a few bits and bobs for it then, I didn't start work on the project proper until February 2003. I continued it on and off for the next fifteen months, finally flying to America in May 2004 to get away from the office long enough to finish the damn thing.

About half way through I realised how long it was going to be and considered putting it out in two volumes. However, I decided that to publish a two-volume work of autobiography aged 45 was too much of a conceit. When I started work on this book I originally envisaged it containing details of all my cryptozoological exploits around the world. However, I soon found out that I had to draw the line somewhere or else the resulting printer's bill would probably bankrupt me.

I therefore made an arbitrary decision to leave most of my New World exploits for a further volume, so my encounters with 'Rods', the 'Starchild Skull', the dog-headed men of Nevada, the Illinois Black Panther, my 1979 hunts for Bigfoot and giant snapping turtles, and my 1998 hunt for the skunk ape, as well as various UK based investigations into Animal Mutilations, mystery otter-like animals, the mystery coypu of Cornwall, the scarlet viper, and the green-faced 'monkey' of Newton Ferrers will have to wait until a future volume.

Jon Downes,
The Centre for Fortean Zoology, Exeter
(and Jessica's house in Marshall, Illinois),
4.46 a.m 24th May 2004

ACKNOWLEDGEMENTS

I will not enumerate everyone who I met whilst writing this book, nor everyone who appears in it, and certainly not everyone who *should* have appeared in it, but I would like to thank:

My late mother who taught me how to love books and my father who taught me how to write them, my brother Richard, his wife Sian and their children Anne-Marie, Christopher, Timothy and Abigail (it can't be easy having me as a brother when you are an Army chaplain), the wonderful Suzy Decodts, The late David Braund, Lorraine Braund, Kaye and Roy Phillips, David, Ross and Greg Phillips, Marjorie and the late Denny Braund, Ian Wright, Davey and Joanne Curtis, Mike Davis, Richard Dawe, Tom Anderson, Graham Inglis, Richard Freeman, John Fuller, Nick and Dana Redfern, Tim Matthews, Dave Sutton, Gail-Nina Anderson, my daughter Lisa, Karena Bryan, the late Jane Bradley, Jessica and Kiernen Dardeen (and their wonderful family), Maxine Pearson with love, Joyce Howarth, Jan Scarff, Kim Avis, Karl Shuker, Tony "Doc" Shiels, Clinton Keeling, Richard Muirhead, Nigel and Sue Wright, my cousin Pene Rowe, Mark North (thanks for the awesome cover dude), my ex-wife Alison, Steve Harley, Simon Wolstencroft, Mark Martin (I miss u dude), Marcus Sims, Dave Penna and Jim Farebrother, Alyson Diffey, Richard Muirhead, Chris Moiser, Ryan Wood, and of course Rueben but for whom and all that jazz.

"We had a torch and I was shining its beam across trunks about fifteen feet off the ground. I am fairly sure that the animal was standing in a large conifer tree and the illustration we made after the sighting (but not till we got home actually) does depict the animal in a conifer tree, but I'm not that sure now".

Gavin and Sally meet the Owlman (Page 123)

PREFACE

It was a Sunday lunchtime in early September 2000, and I found myself in an opulent, if ever so slightly vulgar-looking house in semi-rural Hampshire, in the south of England. I had gone there to meet a literary agent who had intimated to me that he was going to launch me on the path to international stardom by arranging for a major publishing house to release the title that you are now reading.

Initially, I had very high hopes for the meeting. After all, for the best part of a decade I could justifiably boast of being Britain's only full-time "monster hunter." I had spent years travelling the globe in pursuit of lake monsters, Bigfoot, the Yeti, the Loch Ness Monster, big cats, Vampires, ghostly black dogs, daemons, and a veritable menagerie of other, assorted and distinctly mysterious creatures. My adventures were the stuff of legend (at least, *I* thought that they were). I published two magazines, had written a number of critically acclaimed books and was regularly consulted by the media - ever eager for the latest tale of mystery from the depths of Loch Ness or the heart of the Amazon Jungle. The literary agent had other thoughts on his mind, however.

He was a swarthy young man, good looking in a slightly pretty manner. He lived abroad for most of the time but was visiting his parents in the UK, and for some reason I had been invited to discuss business *en famille*. It was, to put things mildly, an excruciating meal. The agent and his family obviously disliked me as much as I disliked them. They were from the yuppie Gin and Jaguar set, and I had just spent the best part of the previous week living semi-rough in South Wales investigating allegations that a young boy had been attacked by a rogue and savage panther that was rumored to be on the loose.

My soon-to-be ex-girlfriend Linda smiled supportively at me and held my hand reassuringly under the table as I tried to explain my vision for this book (and indeed my literary career) to a bunch of *nouveau riche* and horribly superficial scumbags whom I fervently wished would be first up against the wall when the revolution came. It was obvious that they fought together as a family. It was also obvious that they disapproved of me heartily. An overweight, somewhat scruffy man with collar length hair, a certifiably-mad girlfriend and the mud of a Welsh hillside still adhering to his clothing, had no place within the confines of the life of a semi-retired property developer and his family. It was also becoming glaringly obvious to me that my so-called agent was never going to arrange to have this book published in a million years.

"Have you met anyone famous?" the agent inquired eagerly.
"Well, yes" I admitted reluctantly.
"Have you ever slept with anyone famous?" asked his mother.

Now, call me old fashioned, but I am unused to discussing my sex-life with total strangers, and especially when they are matronly females in late middle age. Suddenly my putative agent, both his parents and his excessively slutty girlfriend were all talking at once. I had to name-drop as many celebrities as possible, they told me, and the book needed copious amounts of kinky sex and romance if it was going to sell.

I tried to explain that although I knew various famous people, they were mostly fading rock stars, and had absolutely nothing to do with the book that I wanted to write. And if I had been more successful in matters of sex and romance, perhaps I wouldn't have wasted my life chasing monsters, I quipped. They stared back at me blankly.

Two days later I received a curt and mildly offensive email severing my professional relationship with the agent. There was no way that I could write a book about my adventures chasing mystery animals and monsters around the world if it was not full of saucy vignettes and celebrity scandal of the sexual kind.

I ignored the email, and over the next three years I wrote this book.

PROLOGUE

FEAR AND LOATHING
(100 MILES NORTH OF LAS VEGAS)

Whilst his mother's womb contained the growing Baal
Even then the sky was waiting quiet and pale
Naked, young, immensely marvellous
Like Baal loved it, when he came to us

That same sky remained with him in joy and care
Even when Baal slept peaceful and unaware
At night a lilac sky, a drunken Baal
Turning pious as the sky grows pale

So through hospital, cathedral, whiskey bar
Baal kept moving onwards and just let things go
When Baal's tired, boys, Baal cannot fall far
He will have his sky down there below

Berthold Brecht "Baal's Hymn"

Night falls quickly in the American desert. The sun, which for twelve hours had scoured the baking red earth below, had vanished behind the grim, unyielding mountains. In that strange time of the twilight, which the people in Devonshire call the dimpsey, the desert creatures (that had stayed hidden for the hottest parts of the day) began to stir, and what, to the casual visitor, seemed to be a barren wilderness soon became a haven of activity. The rats, mice and frogs emerged from their holes, secure in the knowledge that for a few hours, at least, they would be relatively safe from the larger animals like racoons and coyotes, and blissfully unaware that in the sky above them circled the night-birds searching for supper!

I am a zoologist. I should by rights have been out in the desert gazing in awe at the miracle of God's creation. But I wasn't. I was sitting in an air-conditioned bar, a few hundred yards away. I was surrounded by scantily-clad showgirls and a group of genial people that ranged from the mildly eccentric to the certifiably insane; but who all exuded that air of expensive bonhomie common to West Coast Americans of a certain class and a certain age. I was very drunk and was expending most of my energy on a fruitless attempt to seduce a plump blonde divorcee in her late forties, who (it was whispered) was the ex-wife of a famous television producer who had been responsible for some of the most tawdry science fiction TV shows of the previous thirty years. It was my fortieth birthday party and congratulations were not necessarily in order.

I'm not a prude. Indeed, far from it. Like the eponymous hero of Berthold Brecht's *Baal,* I have spent a large proportion of my life on a reasonably successful search for fun. The quest for wine, women and song has taken up a large proportion of my life - probably more than the quest for whatever it is that passes as the truth - but there was something about this place that un-nerved me. It was a Pleasure Palace. A place where one could gamble, drink, and chase members of the opposite sex twenty-four hours a day. Drinks were free as long as you at least *pretended* to gamble, and there was a continual smörgåsbord of luscious, indigestible and tempting food there for the taking. It was party city. It was *Si Redd's Oasis,* a casino and golfing resort in the middle of the Nevada desert. It was no coincidence that it was situated in the town of Mesquite - a few miles from the border with the Mormon state of Utah. The worthies of Utah needed somewhere to go and let their hair down after a lifetime of abstemious morality. Si Redd (whoever he had been) had chosen wisely. It was the perfect location and the perfect holiday resort for the people who couldn't afford Las Vegas. This was *BABYLON d000d!*

The constant search for fun was beginning to pale. There is a limit to the amount of free lobster and bourbon that even *I* am able to consume; and whilst the drunken revellers whom I had only known for a few days were partying like it was 1999 (it *was* 1999) and celebrating the birthday of a fat dude from Blighty as if they had known him for years, I slipped away into a dark corner of the bar, where I sat down and tried to decide whether I wanted to go to bed like a gentleman or carry on drinking. I hardly noticed the tall, thin figure in a long black coat that sidled up to me.

"Mind if I sit down?" he drawled.

I could hardly say no, and anyway I didn't want to. He introduced himself as 'Rueben' and sat, staring implacably at me and without blinking. I had seen him around the conference all week but we hadn't exchanged more than a few words. I had been too busy partying, trying to get laid, and doing my best to avoid the constant panic attacks which beset me every time I was sober enough to remember that I was no longer in the safe haven of my own Centre for Fortean Zoology back in suburban Exeter.

Rueben was somebody different from the Flying Saucer-obsessed "true believers" that I had been meeting and partying with all week. Even in conventional UFO circles I am somewhat of a Luddite. By the standards of the International UFO Congress in Nevada during the summer of 1999, what I had to say was tantamount to apostasy. I was in the United States to talk about (and shamelessly plug) my book *The Rising of the Moon* [Domra 1999], that contained the results of some of my researches into the causative links that apparently existed between disparate Fortean phenomena

My hypothesis had very little to do with orthodox UFOlogy; and whilst the punters listened to me politely, I could tell that they thought that I had got it terribly wrong. To them the UFO subject was a new religion. In a society where the President himself was under threat of indictment for having received blow-jobs from a rather cute young intern, it must have been comforting for a small faction of the populace to be faced with a quasi-historical farrago whereby the country was *really* under the control of a sinister cadre of aliens in an uneasy alliance with the might of the military-industrial complex.

But Rueben was different. He had lizard-like eyes that stared at you unblinkingly. During my presentation that morning, out of a packed hall full of ardent punters, I could feel his eyes staring at me and boring into the heart of my soul as I spoke. I had no idea what he was thinking. But I rather wanted to know.

He broke the uneasy silence.

"I liked your talk, man," he said. "I think that you are probably right." He gazed at me silently while rolling a cigarette with one hand. He was the only person I had met in America who smoked roll-ups. "But do *you* believe it? - that was the question I had to ask myself."

I looked away, embarrassed. He was right. By this time I had written three books on the links between mysterious animals (such as lake monsters, Bigfoot and sea serpents), UFOs and other quasi-Fortean phenomena; and whilst I, like Rueben, was convinced that I was broadly correct in my hypothesis, various things which I had included in my three books in good faith had turned out to be spurious, and if the truth is to be told, after five years' solid investigation of the subject I had really had enough. I wanted a break, and the only reason that I had come to America (apart from the free holiday) was essentially to flog as many copies of my books as I could. I knew that my relationship with my then-publisher was in its terminal stages and I wanted to make as much money as I could out of my hard work before it all went belly-up!

But I couldn't say that to Rueben, could I? After all, despite his timeless reptilian visage and gentle southern manners, he was still a total stranger that I had met in a bar half way across the world; and furthermore he was a total stranger who had just shelled out twenty bucks for a copy of my book. What was worse is that he looked like an uncanny cross between an ageing cowboy and the bass player in *Quicksilver Messenger Service.* I tried to bluster my way out of i,t but instead I essentially spluttered incomprehensibly as Rueben interrupted me.

"You need to go back to where you started, man," he said with a smile. "You gave a good talk. It's a good book. You're a nice guy; but until you go back to the beginning and make sure that you believe what you are writing, you'll never be happy". He smiled at me for the first time and I swear that as the flashing lights from the disco at the other end of the room reflected on the mirrored ceiling, they backlit him dramatically and for a split second it appeared that he had a halo!

"It's your birthday, let me buy you a drink," he said and left the table. He returned a few minutes later and we drank in silence. We sat together like this for about ten minutes, neither of us saying anything. I was rather drunk, but then and now Rueben reminded me of the highly fictional Lazarus Long, the time-travelling hero of a series of novels by the late Robert Anson Heinlein. They had the same big nose, the same rugged features and the same wild staring eyes. No matter how you wish to extrapolate pantheistic solipsism, or argue "world as myth," there was no getting away from the fact that Lazarus Long was a fictional character, and that Rueben was *still* a guy who looked like the bass player in *Quicksilver Messenger Service* and who was *still* sitting at a table with me in a Nevada bar drinking whisky.

"I know that you are hurting at the moment" he said, "and you are going to continue to hurt for a long time. It's gonna get worse before you get better, but you'll get there eventually."

He got up as to leave. Slightly taken aback, so did I. I thought for a moment that he was going to give me a hug. He didn't and instead shook my hand in a surprisingly formal way.

"Happy birthday, son," he said, and disappeared into the stygian darkness of the Casino Bar.

I returned to the bustle of my birthday party in the main section of the bar. My "friends" were still dancing and drinking. I don't think that anyone noticed that I had been away. I grabbed another bourbon and started to dance in what I imagined at the time was a highly sexy and sophisticated style, but which probably looked like the ridiculous floundering of a drunken and rather overweight porpoise. Nobody noticed, and the party continued like it was 1999. (Yes, it was *still* 1999). I continued my fruitless attempts to seduce the fat, blonde ex-wife of the famous television producer, and my "friends" and I danced until the dawn broke over the desert.

As I staggered back to my hotel room, the pink rays of the rising sun were just breaking over the red sandstone mesa. As I staggered along I sang:

> *"So through hospital, cathedral, whiskey bar*
> *Baal kept moving onwards and just let things go*
> *When Baal's tired, boys, Baal cannot fall far*
> *He will have his sky down there below"*

I had disturbed a pair of jackrabbits - spindly beasts who looked like the result of an unfortunate act of miscegenation between a stick insect and a domestic bunny. As I watched the frightened lagomorphs scurry away, I took a pull on my cigarette and breathed in the fresh desert air. Truly it was a good time to be alive. I never saw Rueben again, but I knew that he was right. I had to go back to the beginning.

CHAPTER ONE

THE JEWEL IN THE CROWN

In many ways I am the luckiest man I know. I've known what I wanted to do with my life since I was a small child. The downside is that, although I was seven years old when I made this momentous discovery, it took another 25 years before I was able to translate this dream into some sort of objective reality.

I was raised in Hong Kong - the last jewel in the crown of the British Empire on which the sun would never set. In terms of the Imperial timeline it was a few minutes before dusk. I was a member of the last generation of the children of the Empire. Even children only a few years younger than me, say that the old days of Hong Kong as the easternmost pinnacle of the Raj ended in the early 1970s, when the doctrine of a benign and semi autonomous autocracy run under strict Imperial lines was replaced by a policy of *laissez faire* capitalism which essentially held sway for the remainder of the British tenure of power in the region.

During the late spring of 1968 I was eight years old. I was sitting in a geography lesson at Peak School on Hong Kong Island. I was not a good pupil, and my schooldays were far from successful, but for some reason this particular geography lesson remains fresh in my memory thirty-six years later.

My teacher, a Mrs. Alexander, a lady of whom I can remember almost nothing apart from the fact that she hailed from Northern Ireland and lived in the same block of flats as my family at Mount Austin Mansions, was explaining about the geography of Hong Kong. It was only then, after having lived in Hong Kong for the whole of my conscious life, that I realised quite how small it was, and began to be aware of the peculiar nature of the land in which I lived.

"By the time you are my age," said Mrs. Alexander, "Hong Kong as you know it will not exist any longer." This was an extraordinary concept for a nine year old to grasp, and so I missed the next sentence while I grappled with it.

"Hong Kong is not a country in itself," she continued. "It is run by people in England, another island on the other side of the world."

I knew this, of course. My father worked in that unfathomable entity of the "grown-up" world called "The Government", but it was only then, as Mrs. Alexander pointed out, that the relative positions of Hong Kong and the United Kingdom on the map of the world (large portions of which, even then, were still coloured pink) that I began to grasp the distances involved. As the bell rang for the mid-morning break Mrs. Alexander finished her lesson with words that remain fresh in my mind nearly three decades later.

"Hong Kong is not a country, it is a Crown Colony. When you have boys and girls of your own there won't be any colonies left, and you will be able to tell your children how you lived in a little piece of history," Mrs. Alexander added.

For political reasons, although Hong Kong was still legally a Crown Colony, it began to be known as a "Territory" somewhere in the middle of the decade after Mrs. Alexander's lesson. I was not aware of this politically correct nomenclature and managed to mortally offend one correspondent, in a letter about Sea Serpents in the South China Sea, by referring to "The Colony of Hong Kong."

It is of course now a Special Administrative Region [SAR] of the People's Republic of China, but for reasons of etiquette, I use the term "region" except when quoting directly from another source, or referring to Hong Kong's position in Colonial History. The name really doesn't matter a damn because the place itself will always remain. Despite the encroachments of Communism, Urbanisation and Pollution, the bamboo snakes will still live in the thickets and people walking in the hills will still see the scurry of paws as ferret badgers disappear into their holes in the ground. The animals of Hong Kong, who care little for politics, will remain as enigmatic as ever.

From an early age I had been interested in animals. From that point of view, Hong Kong was an ideal place to grow up. Whereas my counterparts in the United Kingdom would have had to make do with foxes, badgers, and hedgehogs, I had the South China Sea as my playground, and the entire Continent of Asia as my hinterland. I could see large swathes of tropical forest from my bedroom window, and I was surrounded by exotic and beautiful, wild creatures. My mother always claimed that the first word I spoke was "zoo." As Gerald Durrell's mother claimed exactly the same thing, I do not know whether to take this piece of information *cum grano salis* or not. Four-and-a-bit decades on, it doesn't really matter. What does matter is that I had a remarkable childhood - from a zoological point of view at least mostly because as far back as I can remember, my mother used to read stories to me, and one of my favorites was the *Jungle Book.*

In those days, Kipling's prose had yet to be perverted and adulterated by the black cloud of Disney, and I revelled in the glorious stories of animals and men in the Indian sub-continent. My mother always encouraged me in my interest in natural history, and when I was five or six years old she acquired a book written by G.A.K. Herklots titled *The Hong Kong Countryside.* I still have it today, and of all the thousands of books in my collection it is probably the one that I have read most over the years. Much to my joy, many of the animals as described by Kipling also lived in my own backyard.

Hooded cobras and kraits lurked in the undergrowth surrounding the playground where I went each day after school. All the way through my schooldays, my mother had a mortal fear that I would be bitten by these poisonous snakes, but luckily, for me at least, this never happened. There were mongooses (not the same species as *Rikki Tikki Tavy*, but close enough), porcupines, wild red dogs or dholes; and every evening, if you went to the right place, you could see the massed hordes of dog-faced fruit bats venturing forth into the gathering dusk. Even *Shere Khan* and *Bagheera* had relatives in Hong Kong; the last leopard was shot in the late 1950s, and there were reports of tigers visiting the wilder parts of the New Territories every winter throughout the 1960s. It was truly a magical place for a young naturalist to grow up.

As I got older, my interest in natural history grew, and I filled every inch of my bedroom with jam-jars, shoeboxes, and fish tanks that all contained a wide variety of the local fauna. Much to the eternal credit of my mother and our servant Ah Tim, I got away with it, and over the years I learnt much about the husbandry of small creatures - something that has stood me in good stead throughout my adult life.

My mother encouraged my interests in natural history and the written word, and, ironically on the same day that Mrs. Alexander had so radically overthrown my worldview, my mother figuratively kicked it into touch. Every Thursday she would go into town to play tennis at a venerable institution known as the Ladies' Recreation Club (LRC). After a game of tennis and a leisurely lunch with her friends she would go to the Central Library and get out library books for my young brother and I. One day she found me a book titled *The Amazing Zoo That Dudley Drew*, about a young boy forced to spend the day in bed with a cold. Mind-numbingly bored, he spent the day drawing pictures of fantastic animals. Although the intricacies of the plot escape me, these wonderful creatures came to life and wandered around his house. I became obsessed with this book, and talked about nothing else for weeks until my parents had to threaten me with having the book banned from the house if I didn't shut up. You would have thought that my mother would have learnt her lesson after that, but no. When I came back from school after my fateful geography lesson with Mrs. Alexander, I found that my mother had got me a book that would literally change my life. It was called *Myth or Monster* and it introduced me to the concept that there were, indeed, monsters living in the world - and furthermore ones which were even more extraordinary than anything that had been drawn by young Dudley. This book introduced me to the Loch Ness monster, to sea serpents, to the Yeti, to its North American cousin, Bigfoot, to the fearsome *Mngwa* - the brindled, grey, killer-cat of East Africa, and to the mystery beasts of the South American jungle.

This was heady stuff for an eight-year-old. I read the book in one sitting, had my tea, went to bed early and read it again. The next morning I woke up, my head and heart filled with a new determination.

"I'm going to be a Monster Hunter when I grow up," I announced at breakfast. And I meant it. I'm not going to rewrite history and pretend that my parents were wholeheartedly supportive of my childish outburst, because they weren't. To be quite honest, I can't remember what they said. I can imagine, however. I was at the age when children want to be astronauts, or train drivers, or soldiers, and my parents can easily be forgiven for not taking this momentous and life changing decision seriously. However, the die was cast, and any chance of me leading a normal life had gone completely out of the window.

For weeks after my new discovery, monsters and mystery animals all types dominated my thoughts; and together with a couple of friends who were equally obsessed with the natural world, I made a map of the immediate area surrounding the block of flats in which we lived. On this map we had plotted the places where birds had nested, where we knew that the local agamas - large, chunky lizards with armoured scales and long tails - lived, and the place in the thick woodland which surrounded the ruins of a hotel that had been bombed out during the Second World War, and where we knew there was a breeding colony of Hodgson's porcupines. To this map was added a fair smidgen of wishful thinking, as we mentally exaggerated a small colony of feral dogs which lived on one of the hillsides into a pack of wolves, and spent our evenings and weekends combing the forested sides of Victoria Peak in search of fearsome tigers and leopards, which we knew from Herklots once lived there, and which we were convinced still did.

Ironically it turned out that Hong-Kong was indeed a hotbed of monster-hunting activity. There were, indeed, mystery animals living there, although my investigations into them would not take concrete form for another 25 years. However, even at the age of eight, my monster-hunting research was starting in earnest.

My earliest investigation was into the foxes of Hong Kong. The local race of the red fox *(Vulpes vulpes hoole),* was - at least, according to accepted disciplines - extinct in the colony. However, one evening some friends of my parents had come around for drinks and I was astounded to hear one of them say that the evening before they had actually seen a fox peering over the low stone wall of their garden perimeter. These people were unusual in Hong Kong "expat" society in that they had a garden. Most of us - including my family - lived in large, opulent and luxurious blocks of flats. These people - and since my mother's death I have no way of finding out who they actually were - lived in one of the few luxury bungalows which had been reserved for higher echelons of the colonial government.

The red fox is an important part of the British zooiconography, and it is perhaps because of their "sporting" connotations that they have been persecuted throughout their range. It has been said, not altogether unfairly, that one of the most peculiar things about the British, is that they will travel for miles and miles through trackless wastes to finally discover a feverish swamp in the middle of nowhere, only to call the place "Piccadilly." Something else notable about the British abroad, is that wherever they go, "the unspeakable" has an unfortunate tendency to pursue "the uneatable" at the slightest possible opportunity, and Hong Kong was no exception. Although their activities have now ceased, the Fanling Hunt was a notable part of life between the wars in the New Territories, and has some reasonably important zoological implications. Herklots wrote:

"The fox of the plains and lower hills of South China is a sub-species of, and is very similar to the European red fox; it is paler in colour and lacks the black spot on each side of the nose. There is more gray on the flanks and thighs, the fore feet have less black, and the red tones are less fulvous and more chestnut than the European Red Fox. Head and body length 26 inches, tail 16.5 inches to the tips of the protecting hairs. Foxes occur both on Hong Kong Island and in the New Territories though they are not often seen. The Chinese name is *hung oo lei,* (Red Fox)."

It was generally accepted, however, that by the mid-1960s, although there may have been a few isolated specimens in the wilder parts of the New Territories or on Lantau Island, there had been no foxes to speak of in the colony since before the Second World War. However, my mother's friend had seen one - and when you are eight years old grown-ups are infallible. *The Mystery of the Mysterious Fox of Victoria Peak* (as I fondly and slightly-absurdly dubbed it) engrossed me for weeks, and I made a complete pain in the arse of myself, interviewing as many residents - and their servants - as I could, and asking all of them the same question: Had they seen a fox? This early experience of mystery animal investigations taught me some valuable lessons. People are, on the whole, idiots. If something doesn't interest them, they don't understand why it should interest anybody else. They will do their best to poke fun, and generally deride anybody who is doing something that they personally perceive as pointless. Sadly, as I discovered at the early age of eight, most people find monster hunting to be completely boring.

The natural world is of no interest to most of the human race. They can only understand it if it is a media-emasculated rainforest, and if the inhabitants are very safe and controllable, as they are on the television screen in the corner of your sitting room. People, on the whole, are just not interested in going out into the wilds to look for strange things themselves. I found as a child, that whereas the adult world - and that included my teachers - were happy to encourage me to collect butterflies, for example (the natural world is perfectly acceptable when it is killed, pinned to a piece of cork, and left to dry), children were supposed to be seen and not heard. When a child takes it upon himself to wander around asking impertinent questions from his elders and betters he has suddenly crossed over from being a genial eccentric to being a threat. Sadly, this attitude is not a characteristic reserved for children.

As an adult monster hunter, I have found that exactly the same thing tends to happen. If I were to confine my zoological researches to creatures such as birds, butterflies, and small mammals, nobody would have a problem with it. It is only when one ventures away from the well-trodden paths of orthodoxy that one encounters a problem. As an adult, even when one is the director of the world's foremost monster-hunting research organization (and, furthermore, one which has as its President a national hero who has been decorated by the monarch), society will hold either deride you, or treat you like a complete lunatic. Truly a monster hunter is without honour in his own land.

The second lesson that I learned, is to respect - and do one's best to understand - cultural differences. Whereas the Europeans that I spoke to on my quest for the South China Fox either made silly remarks or told me in no uncertain terms to go away, the Chinese were much more interested. They told me of their encounters with foxes of many different shapes, sizes and colours. I was too young to understand. I thought that - in some peculiarly inscrutable oriental manner - they were being as annoying as the adults of my own race. It was only when I consulted my bible - Herklots - that I realised how wrong I was being.

Herklots pointed out that in Cantonese, the term "Fox" has a number of different meanings. He noted that several local animals were named foxes by the Chinese. The little spotted civet is known as *t'sat kan lei* (seven striped fox), the Chinese civet, *Sam kan lei* (three striped fox), the masked palm civet, *ng kan lei* (five striped fox), and the ferret badger, *kwoh tse lei* (fruit eating little fox).

It was all beginning to make sense. However, it didn't go anywhere near to explaining what it was that my mother's friend had seen, or the animals that the Chinese people that I had I spoken with had described to me were; and no one apart from my mother's friend had ever seen anything even vaguely resembling a European red fox. Then came my breakthrough. With the innocence of an eight-year-old, I had assumed that Herklots's book was the definitive account of the fauna of Hong Kong. I hadn't realised that the book had been written eight years before I was born, and that a lot had changed over the intervening years.

In 1968, it was 16 years after Herklots had written the book, and, it transpired that Herklots hadn't even been living in Hong Kong when the writing of the book was completed. It was basically compiled from his pre-war nature diaries, and from articles that he had written for the prestigious journal *The Hong Kong Naturalist* that had been published between 1929 and 1941. The information on which I had come to rely was therefore - in some instances - nearly 40 years out of date. This was my third great discovery: just because something is written in a book does not *necessarily* mean that it is accurate.

Armed with these new discoveries and revelations, I pressed on, I like to think, like a junior Sherlock Holmes - albeit perhaps a slightly precocious one. Each afternoon, in the summer of 1968, as I trudged up and down the Peak road, to and from the ruins of what had once been the Governor's summer palace at the summit of Victoria Peak, I revelled in my new-found knowledge. All around me were exciting mysteries just waiting to be solved.

One afternoon I spent over an hour watching a pair of hair-crested drongos - strange crow-like birds with peculiar lyre shaped tails - killing and eating a small King Cobra. Another afternoon, I was sidetracked from my quest for the truth about the Victoria Peak Fox when I saw - for the first and any time on the island - a pair of barking deer running, startled, into the thick undergrowth at the bottom of Mount Austin. I stealthily followed them into the woods as my heart pounded in my eardrums. Sidetracked in their headlong flight to get away from me, the two tiny deer ran into a rotten log with the tiny hooves. It fell apart to reveal an entire universe: peculiar millipedes, like tiny elongate armadillos, came tumbling out. Two local giant centipedes, *scolopendra* and *scutigeria*, bristled at me, waving their antenna menacingly. Most excitingly, there were three small spade-foot toads that glared at me accusingly with bulbous eyes - not unlike those of an elderly alcoholic slouched in a shop doorway.

The slopes of Mount Austin were covered with rhododendron trees - some of which stretched to a height of 20 or 30 feet above me in the forest canopy, and the incessant babble of a family of white-faced laughing thrushes filled the tropical air. Above us all in the azure blue sky, two or three black-tailed kites - best known to generations of Indian Army Expats as "Shite Hawks" because of their habit of circling above rubbish dumps and manure pits in search of small rodents - circled lazily.

Forcing myself into a mode of self-discipline (that I have to admit to I have seldom managed to achieve on a regular basis in the 35 years that have followed), I continued my journey up the winding Peak Road towards the house where the sighting had taken place. I promised my mother that, under no circumstances, would I be so presumptuous as to bother her distinguished friend in person. Even at the age of eight I could understand the logic in that. After all, he had already told me everything that he knew - and he wasn't particularly interested anyway. All he had seen was a very familiar animal - a red fox (a species that, with the benefit of hindsight, I can see he had probably pursued on horseback over the Home Counties during his youth), peering at him over the low stone wall of his garden. He had no idea that there was anything exciting about the incident, and to him I was merely the slightly annoying small boy who used to get in the way and ask pointless questions about something about which he wasn't particularly interested. However, I hadn't promised my mother that I wouldn't do any detective work in the location where the fox had been seen.

I feel so sorry for the youth of today. To them, the Native Americans are people who have fuelled an entire industry of homemade dream-catchers, statuettes of the Great Manitou, and home self-improvement courses in Native American spirituality. To my generation, there was something completely different. We saw them on television at least three nights a week, either killing or being killed by cowboys, or - like my hero Tonto - assisting a slightly inept Lone Ranger behave like a 19th century analogue of Superman. Fuelled by my in-depth knowledge of Indian lore - which I had gathered from watching episode after episode of the aforementioned *Lone Ranger* and *Bat Masterson* - I knew just what to do. As I approached the bungalow (that stood in its own grounds just below the tree line), I assumed the mantle of an expert Native American woodsman, and stealthily began to reconnoitre my surroundings.

Doing my best to get into character, I reached into my school satchel, took out the slightly battered Red Indian headdress that my mother had given me as a Christmas present, and using one of the lipsticks which I had purloined from her dressing table, I carefully applied my war paint; then, suitably garbed, I made my way through the undergrowth on all fours. Stealthily, I crept around the outside of the perimeter wall. By this time, I was in such a heightened state of excitement that I was sure that I would see a fox lurking behind each of the bushes and trees. Sadly, I saw nothing.

As well as Red Indians, other cultural influences were at work upon me. I was an avid reader of Enid Blyton's *Secret Seven* books in which a small band of precocious, upper-middle-class children, ran rings around the police and solved baffling crimes by dint of crafty detective work. In an attempt to emulate this second set of heroes, I did my best to search for clues. However, the clues were spectacular by their absence. I therefore only had one option open to me. I would have to follow in the footsteps of the *Secret Seven* and make a map of the crime scene. The fact that there hadn't been a crime was no particular obstacle to me.

My grandfather had given me a compass that was worn on my wrist like a wristwatch. It had never worked, and I had no real idea how to take a compass bearing, but it was - after all - one of my few items of quasi-scientific equipment, and I was determined to make use of it. I paced the length and breadth of the garden and perimeter wall. Every few yards I consulted my spectacularly useless compass in the vain hope that I would be able to extrapolate some data from it. After about half an hour's work, I had created a crude - and with hindsight a completely useless - map, of which I was very proud, and bore it home in triumph to the corner of my bedroom, which I fondly called my laboratory. Here I kept my microscope, my natural history books, my shell and butterfly collections, and various small creatures imprisoned in a variety of makeshift aquaria.

Sadly, when I looked back over the events of the day, I had to admit to myself that whilst the adventure had been fun, it had not really brought me any closer to the truth.

The next day in school, I confided to my best friend William about my problem. He suggested that we should go and ask his mother for advice. His mother was a slightly remote figure, but one of whom I was in great awe. She was a *real* scientist - albeit an anthropologist - and she was one of the few grown-ups to actively encourage me in my endeavours. After school I went back to William's flat and diffidently approached his mother. I was always fascinated by his mother's study. There were books everywhere, and various niches around the walls contained a variety of archaeological and anthropological specimens. Most of these seemed to be ancient pottery, but also included a few adze heads and shapeless pieces of metal that William and I fondly believed were instruments of torture, but which were, with the benefit of hindsight, compass mountings from eighteenth-century sea-going junks. William's mother was very interested in my quest, and she reached up to one of the voluminous bookshelves and brought down a thin blue paperback that I later found out was entitled *Mammals of Hong Kong* by Patricia Marshall. I took the book and sat cross-legged in the corner of the room.

Once again, I found that my hero - Herklots - was ridiculously out of date. Several of the mammal species that he had listed as being common in the colony were now, in fact, extinct. Moreover, *this* book had only been published the previous year and so it was as up-to-date a tome as it was possible to get. Manfully resisting the temptation to become sidetracked in descriptions of some of the more exotic creatures such as pangolins and civet cats, I turned the section dedicated to the South China red fox. Suddenly my mystery was solved. Marshall wrote:

"Now very rare, a few pairs only living in the New Territories. Of the two foxes released on Hong Kong Island in 1965 one was subsequently killed by a car and the other illegally trapped."

So, there *had* been foxes on Hong Kong Island within the last few years, after all. William's mother showed me how to interpret the references at the end of the book and we discovered that the fox that had been hit by a car only a few hundred yards from the place where my mother's friend had seen one. Furthermore, it had been killed only a few weeks after the sighting had taken place. I had solved what I like to think was my first monster hunting mystery.

The next day at school I went rushing in to tell my teacher and classmates all about it. I shouldn't have bothered. My friends were completely uninterested, and my form teacher told me tartly that if I wanted to amount to anything in life I should concentrate on my nine times table rather than searching for animals that were of no possible interest to anybody. I knew then that most adults were not like William's mother. I made a silent vow that when I grew up I would be like her, rather than like the boorish and unimaginative people that a benevolent colonial administration had entrusted to nurture the growth of a generation of young minds.

But that wasn't my only encounter with an unknown animal during my childhood. I actually encountered a *bona fide* mystery animal when I was about eight years old, and I didn't even realize it! As a child, my two favorite days out were to the P.G Farm (an establishment which had originally been founded to provide fresh fruit, vegetables and meat for an exclusive and expensive restaurant called the *Parisian Grill*, and which was by the late Sixties a rather down-at-heel garden centre, pet shop, and petting zoo), and to the Botanical Gardens. These were gloriously run-down remnants of the colony's imperial past. Stately, and slightly disheveled statues of governors long-forgotten, British monarchs, and luminaries of the East India Company were scattered around an expensive park around which had been carefully terraformed, with the minimum of imagination, to resemble one of the less salubrious municipal boating parks in - say - Croydon, Surbiton, or one of the other backwaters of suburban Surrey. As I sit here at my computer writing this on a Bank Holiday Monday in the spring of 2003, it suddenly occurred to me to find out whether this Mecca of my childhood had survived into the 21st century, and if so whether it had been graced with a website. The answer to both questions was yes. As the website revealed:

"Following the major expansion in the mid-1970s, emphasis were then directed to the techniques in captive breeding and conservation breeding programs. Today, our mission is developed to guide the activities for zoological collection:-

a)   To foster an understanding of and appreciation for all living things through education, conservation, research programs and exhibition

and

b)   To develop appreciation for the interdependence of nature

At present, about half of the Garden's land is dedicated to the keeping of zoological exhibits. Over 600 birds, 70 mammals and 40 reptiles are being housed in about 40 enclosures."

The species list that follows is impressive, and the sub-page which gives the history of the Botanical Gardens carefully glosses over the fact that animals have indeed been kept at the gardens for many years. However, all those they were a constant source of delight to me as a small child. Even the most rosy of rose-coloured spectacles cannot detract from the fact that the animal exhibits at Hong-Kong botanical gardens of the 1960s were smelly and rather nasty disgraces. They consisted of three or four aviaries, some semi-wild monkeys (more about them later), and five or six rather shabby cages about the size of my living room and that contained a variety of not particularly spectacular zoo exhibits. The exhibits changed fairly rapidly. At the time, my mother intimated that this was because the animals went on holiday. Now, it seems perfectly obvious that this shabby and tawdry little menagerie had a high turnover of exhibits *purely* because the cages were so unsuitable that the inhabitants died with monotonous regularity.

The ever-shifting population included, at various times, Celebes crested macaques, an elderly and rather moth eaten Asian black bear, some coatis, an extremely large reticulated python, and a large, greenish-brown monitor lizard. From my earliest years, I have been always been fascinated by reptiles, amphibians and fish. As I write this, I can hear my tree frogs singing away in the corner of my sitting room, there is a Nile Monitor called Roger in an enormous vivarium in my bedroom, and the landing is home to a couple of alligator snapping turtles, a red eared terrapin, and a cane toad named "Little Noodles." This monitor lizard in Hong Kong, however, was the first one that I had seen. I was familiar with Komodo Dragons from programs on television; but seeing a monitor lizard - albeit only three or four feet in length - in the flesh was a true revelation. I remember squatting on my haunches, outside, and gazing at the miserable reptile in awe. It sat there on the bare concrete floor of its cage, motionless for much of the time; though occasionally it would slither unenthusiastically towards the fetid pool of stagnant, green, scummy water that served both as drinking water and its bath.

Having shared a bedroom with a monitor lizard for several years now, I am more conversant with their mores. Roger likes nothing more than to defecate in his water, so it has to be changed on a regular basis to avoid it becoming an open sewer. This knowledge may help one realize why this glorious lizard was only resident at the Botanical Gardens for a brief period before - like so many of its predecessors - going on "holiday."

The upper part of Victoria Peak was encircled with a number of footpaths that partly, or wholly, circumnavigated the mountain. It was my family's practice to go into the countryside for walks on Sunday afternoons; and on one Sunday afternoon in 1967 or 1968, we were walking along the footpath which heads from Magazine Gap into the forested interior of the island.

One of the defining characteristics of the mind of a small child is the way that it accepts everything at face value. Despite having a patchy, but in places surprisingly deep, knowledge of the fauna of Hong Kong I was not particularly surprised, therefore, when during our Sunday afternoon walk, my family was confronted by the very same - or, so I thought, at the time - monitor lizard who had so recently "gone on holiday" from the Botanical Gardens crossing the footpath in front of us. It was greenish brown in color and stared straight at me accusingly, with little beady black eyes, and disappeared into the undergrowth that flanked the tiny footpath.

This incident would probably have been merely consigned to the flotsam and jetsam of my childhood memories if it had not been for another incident that took place a few years later. In the September of 1970, I left the primary school which I had attended since the age of six and began secondary school. I was a pupil at Island School, which had only been founded four years previously, and was - at the time - based in what had been a military hospital on Bowen Road in the Mid-Levels. It was a strange place with a peculiar *zeitgeist*. It was popularly believed to have been haunted and the memoirs of its first headmaster, Geoffrey Speke, include amusing recollections of early pupils who had been fed ghost stories by their amahs and house servants, and who were old enough to remember how the hospital had been the site of some of the worst atrocities of the Second World War. The invading Japanese troops had massacred, tortured, and raped patients and nursing staff in the hospital and it was widely believed that their ghosts remained. I can honestly say that I never saw anything even mildly paranormal there, but the shadow of its macabre past enveloped the school like a shroud.

I *do* remember - during the hot autumn of 1970 - being appalled to find the bodies of dog-faced fruit bats that had been crucified on the trunks of the huge palm trees and that surrounded the school grounds. It appeared that this was the work of local Chinese building contractors who were working on new buildings for the school and who believed that these utterly harmless creatures were possessed of evil spirits. However, on the plus side, Island School had a zoo. It wasn't a very big zoo, but it was undoubtedly a zoo. It was presided over by a lady called Mrs. Maylett and it included several gibbons, at least two of the local species of civet, a rhesus monkey, a long tailed macaque, large numbers of birds, some reptiles and some smaller domestic livestock which was beneath my dignity to take an interest in. Dr. John Romer - the zoologist who took over from Herklots in the early 1950s as the leading authority on Hong Kong animals (especially the Reptiles and Amphibians) - was a frequent visitor, and on at least two occasions he donated beasts from his own collection to the Island School Zoo. One of these was a large Burmese python, and the other was a locally caught Chinese water monitor *(Varanus salvator)*.

I'd been vaguely aware for years that water monitors occasionally were to be found in Hong Kong. If I had thought about it - and I am not going to do a Stalinist rewrite of history and imbue my eight year old alter ego with insights that I certainly didn't have at that time - I probably would have thought that the monitor lizard that my family and I had seen a few years earlier near Magazine Gap had been of the species. However, when I saw Romer's magnificent specimen, it became perfectly obvious that the two species were entirely distinct. The water monitor is a distinctive lizard with a rather beautiful pattern of yellow dots that has given it the alternate name of golden water monitor. It is also a much more delicate creature than the slightly chunky lizard that I had seen both in the botanical gardens and - albeit for a few seconds - in the wild. The water monitor is the only member of its family in Hong Kong, or indeed in most of China. If the animal that I had seen was not a water-monitor, what on earth was it?

Much to my joy, nearly 30 years after my original sighting, I discovered supporting evidence for the existence of a hitherto unknown species of large monitor lizard in Hong Kong. Over the years I have been collecting bound copies of *The Hong Kong Naturalist*. Sadly, it has become prohibitively expensive in recent years. A complete set was sold very recently for over £14,000. However, I have been collecting individual volumes as and when I can, and I have photocopies of many of the more interesting articles from the remaining volumes. One of these - amazingly - contains an account of the capture of a lizard that appears to be an unknown species of monitor, from Victoria Peak.

On the 21st January 1930 a lady walking along Lugard Road was frightened when she saw what she thought was a "miniature crocodile." With the help of a passing policeman, some Chinese coolies, and a "Japanese gentleman who was passing" they cornered the creature. With great presence of mind the unnamed Japanese gentleman took off his coat and threw it over the animal. The lizard later allowed itself to be dumped in a sack and to be taken to a police station and ultimately to the Botanic Gardens where it "was placed in a cage." The creature was examined by Dr Geoffrey Herklots, the most famous naturalist then living in Hong Kong. His description read thus:

Total length - 22¼ inches, head: 6 inches, tail: 1 foot 6¼ inches.

Breadth - At neck 2¼ inches, middle of body 6 inches, in front of hind limbs 2½ inches, middle of tail 1 inch.

Depth - Base of tail 2 inches, groove along back and beginning of tail, ridge along rest of tail.

Colour - Above brown-grey, or deep olive, with yellow spots or hands, below a dirty yellow, neck no distinctive bands,

Eyes - Open and close independently, lower lids move upwards. Iris a marbled pale Vandyke brown with a very narrow white or very faintly yellow circle immediately next to pupil.

Herklots noted that this was only one of several records of strange lizards seen both on Hong Kong Island and on the mainland at the time. It was initially identified as *Varanus bengalensis*, a species that isn't actually found in China. It was also tentatively identified as an African species - *Varanus albiguaris*. The surviving photographs, however, suggest that it was not either of these species. It is also certain that it was not the indigenous *Varanus salvator* so what was it?

Today, exotic animals from all over the world are kept as pets, and escapees undoubtedly can and do become established in the wild; however, the international trade in exotic reptiles was almost non-existent seventy years ago. Therefore, the suggestion that the lizard that died soon after capture was an escaped African species can, I think, be discounted.

Unfortunately, the originals of the photographs were destroyed during the Japanese occupation of Hong Kong during the Second World War, as was the preserved body of the unfortunate reptile. Two rather substandard pictures are all that remain. For what it is worth, however, I am convinced that the animal that I saw, and the creature photographed by Herklots, were of the same species. Precisely what it was remains a mystery.

My family was lucky enough to have a boat. She was a small cabin cruiser that we kept at anchor at Tai Tam Bay on the south side of the island. She was called *The Ailsa* and every weekend we went down to Tai Tam and sailed around the small islands in the vicinity. For my ninth birthday my parents gave me half shares (with my brother) in a rowing boat that we named *The Seahorse*. By that time, I had discovered Arthur Ransome's charming children's adventure stories, and emulating the characters in *Swallows and Amazons,* my brother and I paddled around the bay playing at pirates and explorers. My father - who not only had a history in the Merchant Navy, but had been a keen member of the Hong Kong Royal Naval Reserve - banned us from flying the Jolly Roger. At the time, I thought that he was merely being unfair, but as I now know much of the work of the Hong Kong RNR was conducting anti piracy patrols, his objection to his two young sons crewing a vessel displaying a pirate's flag is easier to understand.

Although I made no monstrous discoveries, as such, whilst on my voyages in these two intrepid ships, I learnt much about the marine life of the colony. On one never-to-be-forgotten occasion, we sailed through the middle of a shoal of hundreds of Portuguese Man o'War. These deadly jellyfish drifted like little toy boats of a virulent blue on the surface of the South China Sea. On another occasion I caught an octopus inside an empty beer bottle, and on another occasion - whilst alone in the *Seahorse,* I drifted silently over a veritable field of enormous starfish lying motionless on the ocean floor two or three fathoms of clear water beneath me.

On my 11th birthday I remember seeing two enormous king crabs - refugees from an impossibly prehistoric past - swimming effortlessly into the shallow water of Tai Tam, looking for somewhere to lay their eggs. My reverie was interrupted by a young Chinese boy with a boathook. He started to try and catch them, and when he didn't succeed, was about to crush them. Appalled, I ran up and punched him on the nose. He ran away screaming and I was soundly chastised by my father. Again, with the benefit of hindsight, this was perfectly understandable. The Cultural Revolution of 1967 had hit Hong Kong like a bombshell. I remember seeing a troupe of Red Guards marching up the Peak Road only a few hundred yards away from where we lived. The Communist Party was, of course, banned in the colony, but the doctrine of global revolution which had politicized students in Paris, the UK, and the US, and which had already produced at least one martyr in Jan Palanck (who had committed suicide by self-immolation in front of the advancing Russian tanks in his home town of Budapest), inspired many young Chinese men to follow their lead and rise up against their imperialist masters.

My father understood the increasing fragility of race relations in the Colony, and was understandably frightened. When his oldest son became involved in an imbroglio that could have been perceived as having racist connotations, he was furious. My true defence - that I was only trying to protect two increasingly rare survivors from the Permian period from an ignominious death - cut no ice with him. Luckily, it appears that the young boy I punched could not have been the scion of a family of hardened revolutionaries because none of us heard anything about the incident again, and British rule in the colony continued for another 30 years.

Just behind Tai Tam bay was a series of reservoirs. The largest of these - Tai Tam Tuk - had been created in the early 20th century when a river was dammed and a steep wooded valley was flooded. At the bottom of the reservoir are the remains of at least one small village (and, according some sources, two) that had been an unfortunate victim of the burgeoning Crown Colony's need for more and more fresh water. Some of my fondest childhood memories are of walking through the winding paths that lead through the thick woodland, as the whole family went for another of our regular Sunday walks. During my researches for this chapter I tried to find some photographs of the P.G. Farm and discovered this account of an encounter with some particularly frightening mystery animals in the heavily wooded hillsides surrounding the reservoir:

"We got to our chosen area and set up camp for the weekend under a concrete bridge that had once been part of a more permanent track around the reservoir. Through the night we heard an animal howling, it was a very strange sort of howl, quite indescribable really. As dawn broke we could see some trees about fifty yards along the bank swaying as something moved through them. The first animal appeared on the bank no more than forty yards form us followed by another half dozen or so, they looked like a cross between an orangutan and a chimpanzee. They stopped dead when they saw us and then very slowly started to walk towards us, one of the lads with us got very nervous and after shouting something quite incoherent, threw a rock at them. This caused the apes to start jumping about, they started to make their weird howling noise and having previously seen my friends reaction to aggressive animals I quickly picked up all my bits and was the first one to leg it up the track, the others no more than a second behind me.

There had been an Irish kid with us called Pat and none of us had noticed that he was asleep when the apes arrived, he had woken up to find himself being watched at close quarters by the apes and his friends all gone. Apparently the apes had spent a couple of hours playing around on the bank and then just wandered off into the trees. When he told us about this I wished I had stayed but was then glad I hadn't as I hadn't been wearing brown trousers. Pat returned to the reservoir on his own several times and the apes always came to see him but as winter approached they stopped coming."

The above-quote is taken from the fishing memoirs of a man named Nick Buss, who lived in Hong Kong during the early 1960s. Despite spending many happy hours in those woods at roughly the same time, I never saw any monkeys there. Indeed, if you discount the semi-tame rhesus macaques that I mentioned earlier when describing the Botanical Gardens, I only ever saw two wild monkeys in Hong Kong. This sighting occurred one afternoon in 1970 when I was on my way home from school. I had to take the Peak Tram from Island School in Bowen Road to the terminus at the top of the Peak that was only a few hundred yards from where my family lived at Peak Mansions. On this particular afternoon, the little green tram-car had to halt its journey for about five minutes to allow a female monkey with at least one infant gripping precariously on to the hair on its back, to make a leisurely crossing (using the masts and cables that propelled the trolley cars up and down the Peak) to traverse the tram line.

The first connection that would be made in the minds of most people between monkeys and Hong Kong is the widespread belief in the Chinese custom of eating raw monkey brains, often out of the trepanned skull of a living monkey. It is interesting to note that whereas some television documentaries shown on British TV during the late 1980's repeated this story with glee, others denied that this was more than a historical curiosity that certainly doesn't happen any more. I am certain that whatever perversity can be dreamed up by the human psyche is catered for somewhere on the globe, and as most human perversities are catered for somewhere in Hong Kong, monkey brains are probably still scooped out and eaten somewhere in the less well traversed areas of the territory.

The living monkey population of Hong Kong is no less mysterious. Although there is no doubt that monkeys have existed in Hong Kong since at least 1918, and probably have always existed here, their status is far less certain. In 1870 Robert Swinhoe - a man who can justifiably be described as the Father of Hong Kong natural history - described a small monkey species which he named *Macacus Sancti-johannis* . He wrote that: "This rock monkey is found in most of the small islands about Hong Kong and is like a Rhesus with a very short tail."

He continued: "Dried bodies of this animal split in two are often exhibited from the ceiling in druggists shops in Canton and Hong Kong; and its bones are used for medicinal purposes."

Writing in 1951 Herklots reported: "There are still monkeys wild on the Lema Islands south of the Colony. On the island of Hong Kong a monkey family was watched early one morning near Tai Tam reservoir in 1947, and I have had occasional accounts of monkeys having been seen on The Peak and in the Deep Water Bay valley. It is possible, but not certain that these are descendants of the original wild stock."

Herklots identified the original wild monkeys as Rhesus Monkeys, that (at least when he was writing), had a range stretching from "India to the whole of China south of the Yangtze." However, when Swinhoe had originally described *M. Sancti-johannis* he specifically said that the Hong Kong monkeys were *like* a rhesus but with a short tail. The rhesus monkey has a long tail, and was first described by Zimmerman in 1780. It is an animal with which Swinhoe was bound to have been familiar, and therefore if he drew a distinction between the "Hong Kong Rock Monkey" and the rhesus then we can safely assume that they were two different animals.

Herklots noted that monkeys were released into the woodland near the Kowloon reservoir during the First World War. During the Japanese occupation of the Colony in the Second World War, and after the trees had been cut down, the surviving animals scattered. Since the war they have been reported from several districts in the New Territories including their own haunts. Patricia Marshall then added a few more pieces to an ever more complicated jigsaw by announcing in 1967 that a second species - the long tailed macaque - had either been released or escaped from captivity during or shortly after the 1939-1945 hostilities. But we still need to consider Swinhoe's original record.

Macacus Sancti-johannis is said to have a very short tail. As we have seen, both of the species that were found in Hong Kong before 1981 have quite noticeable tails. By the end of the 20th Century there were at least four macaque species (and various hybrids) living in the colony. It was claimed that all of these were introduced, and that the indigenous population had died out. But none of these species has anything approaching a "pig tail."

According to my friend, the noted zoologist C.H.Keeling, *Macacus Sancti-johannis* is generally considered as a sub species of the Rhesus Monkey. A female specimen, was presented to London Zoo on the 14th January 1867 by R. Swinhoe.

It had been caught on North Lema Island, just south of Hong Kong territorial waters. It is said to have been found on St. John's Island in the South China Sea and both the monkey and the island were named after Commander St. John R.N.

It is disappointing to discover that *Macacus Sancti-johannis* is not distinct at a specific level, but the mystery still remains. If this subspecies is different enough from the Rhesus Monkey to be accorded sub-specific status, and if the tail is so short that Sketchley claimed it was "pig tailed," then what *actually* happened to the Hong Kong populations?

Even if we ignore the mystery of where the Hong Kong island animals disappeared to between 1947 and 1970, and even if we ignore the fact that some of the later records do not mention monkeys on the island itself, there seems no doubt that Rhesus monkeys are, and have been, resident on Hong Kong island.

Whether or not we are to accept that *Macacus Sancti-johannis* is distinct merely at sub-specific level (and the interbreeding between three of the four species described as being naturalised residents of the Colony in 1992 suggests that there is more to be learned about the genetics of the Macaque family), then the animals were certainly distinct enough morphologically with a pig-tail, (suggesting a curly tail), that they were for a while considered to be a distinct species.

And the animals that frightened the group of young fishermen in 1964? The fact that they were described as apes rather than monkeys suggests that within the past thirty years there were, indeed, pig tailed monkeys living wild in the more remote forests on the south side of Hong Kong island. The fact that they were reported in the very location where Herklots noted them in 1947, suggests that they were a well-established population, and I fervently hope that they are still there!

Even if they are not, it seems likely that the genes which produce this pig-tail are hidden somewhere within the gene pool of the Rhesus monkeys on Hong Kong Island itself. It also seems most probable that these genetic differences may yet assert themselves once more; and even if they no longer exist there, Hong Kong Island will again be the home to a distinctive pig tailed monkey!

Anyone who has known me in later life will probably be surprised to learn that when I was in primary school I was a keen amateur boxer. I have a sneaking suspicion that in these politically correct days at the beginning of the 21st century, young boys of seven and eight are probably not encouraged to beat the living crap out of each other in the name of sportsmanship. As my career as a pugilist only lasted for a couple of years in the mid-1960s, I cannot really comment as to whether it did me any harm or not. I don't think so. However, for a couple of years, I was taught the 'Royal and ancient sport of Kings' by a man called Billy Tingle who ran a sports club for boys in the Colony. He taught me to swim and box and he singularly failed to teach me to play cricket. His wife was the proprietor of the nursery school at which I started my education, and the couple were - as far as I remember - leading lights within the expatriate community on the island. Once again, whilst preparing this chapter, I took recourse to the Internet in a vain attempt to try and find out some biographical information about this man who was such a pivotal influence on generations of young people in Hong Kong. I found one reference - the biography of a local boxing champion - that made a veiled jibe at the "institutional racism" of Tingle's establishment. As my mother is now dead, and it was she who arranged my attendance at the various establishments run by Mr. and Mrs. Tingle, there is nobody left for me to ask.

It was Billy Tingle, however, who first told me about the last great mystery animal story of Hong Kong. During my short career as a pugilist, I attended boxing lessons in the hall of my *alma mater*. One evening I overheard my instructor talking to one of the teachers about tigers. Once again, I had been aware that tigers occasionally visited Hong Kong. One of my earliest memories of Hong Kong natural history was a warning broadcast on the local Rediffusion radio station warning hill-walkers not to venture into the wilds of the Sai Kung Peninsular on that particular weekend because a female tiger-with cubs - had been spotted there. So, when I heard my boxing instructor and his friend mention the great striped cat - the villain of the *Jungle Book* - my ears pricked up, and ignoring the strictures that children were to be seen and not heard, I asked him for some more information.

He told me that during the Second World War, when civilian internees had been incarcerated in what was now the maximum-security prison at Stanley, Japanese soldiers had shot a tiger. I rushed home, and grabbed my figurative bible. As has probably become almost painfully obvious, it is Herklots's book, *The Hong Kong Countryside,* that became the most important book ever written on the natural history of the territory. I believe that large portions of Herklots' book were written whilst he was interned by the Japanese in Stanley Internment Camp. I also believe that he was lucky enough to take his complete set of *The Hong Kong Naturalist* into captivity with him. It was during the war, while all Britons and their allies living in the colony were interned in prison-camps, that the next, and possibly the most intriguing chapter in the story of the tigers of Hong Kong took place. Herklots seemed unsure of what had actually happened:

"During our internment at Stanley a remarkable story filtered into the camp that there was a tiger at large on Hong-Kong Island. Later it was reported to be on Stanley Peninsula. The guards got excited and it was risky walking about in the evening for an excited guard might fire at a prisoner mistaking him for a tiger! Soon pug-marks were seen at the camp: I examined some myself but was by no means convinced. Then the story was spread that the tiger had been shot and finally there came into camp a Chinese or Japanese paper containing a photograph of the dead tiger. This photograph I saw. People said that it was a menagerie animal that had got loose; a likely story! It is strange how loath people are to believe that tigers do visit the Colony and occasionally swim the harbour and visit the island."

Even at the age of eight I felt that there was something rather peculiar about this statement. It was almost as if Herklots didn't believe the story himself. It was almost certain that *something* had happened. But what? At the time I had just discovered Lewis Carroll and I misquoted "Alice" that "someone" had certainly killed "something" and that the "something" was a large tiger. Again, my enquiring young mind was tempered by the prevailing "children are to be seen and not heard" attitudes which were prevalent in Colonial Society forty years ago. So, once again, I had to work by stealth. Over the following years and months I gingerly asked various grown-ups if they had heard of the event, and much to my surprise quite a few of them had.

The Second World War was the defining event of my generation - even though hostilities had ceased fourteen years before I was born. I don't know what it was like in the UK for a young child growing up during the 1960s, but for me growing up in Hong Kong - a British Colony which had suffered four years of intense brutality under Japanese occupation the reminders were everywhere. During our weekend excursions on *The Ailsa* we regularly visited Beaufort Island; a tiny, rocky and uninhabited islet a few miles off the southern coast of Hong Kong Island. There, in the barren centre, was a concrete pillbox in which a lonely Japanese soldier had kept lookout for the incoming American dive-bombers during the last vicious battle for freedom. As a child, this remote outpost of the Imperial Japanese Army fascinated me, and I would lie in it for hours, gazing up at the eggshell blue sky to watch the white tailed sea eagles circling effortlessly above me.

My friends and I played soldiers in the disused gun emplacements that still stood along parts of Lugard Rd., and amongst my parents' friends and acquaintances were several who had been prisoners of war during the years of occupation. There was no shortage of source material for me to draw on. Over the years and months I pieced together the facts of the case from snippets of information that I could glean from those who had been there. About ten years after my quest began - when I was approaching adulthood and living in England I discovered the following passage in a book of reminiscences about the history of Hong Kong written by someone with the pen name of *Thagorus:*

"During the war, a tiger was shot by a party of Japanese Militiamen near Stanley in May 1942. A Mr. E.W.Bradbury, who was once a butcher with the Dairy Farm Company, was brought from the Stanley Internment camp to skin the animal, the meat from which subsequently provided a feast for members of the Hong Kong race club. The animal was three feet high, six feet long, weighed 240lbs and had a nineteen-inch tail. The skin of the tiger was stuffed and mounted in the hall of Government House, from which it was subsequently transferred to Japan in 1944. One theory about its presence on the island was that it had escaped from a menagerie during the Japanese invasion; another and more likely theory was that it had swum over from the mainland."

Unlike my quest for the elusive red fox, I found that my elders and betters were happy to talk about their exploits during the war, and on this occasion evidence was relatively easy to get hold of. However, making sense of it all was far more complicated. My primary school had a small library, and for some reason best known to the Gods of cryptoinvestigative theory it contained several back issues of *The Hong Kong News*, an English language newspaper published by the occupying Japanese. Leafing idly through these one day I hit paydirt. I found a contemporary account of the incident:

Fierce Tiger shot in Stanley Woods! Successful Hong Kong police hunt in early morning.

"Although for some years past, rumours had circulated that there were tigers roaming the Hong Kong hills, it was only yesterday morning that such was shown to be fact, and the feat of shooting the first tiger on the island was accomplished by Nipponese gendarmes and Indian and Chinese police at the back of Stanley village. Early yesterday morning the lowing of wild beasts was heard by many residents in Stanley village and gendarmes and police and military set off fully armed to search the hills. The search party, consisting of Nipponese gendarmes and Indian and Chinese policemen, was headed by Lt. Colonel Hirabayashi. The party was divided into smaller groups and a net was spread around the woods. After going

over the ground for some considerable time, one group of searchers came across the tigers lair. They immediately opened fire but despite all efforts and the use of big wire netting the beast succeeded in evading the hunters. Not discouraged by the failure of the first attempt, the Nipponese police continued their search and a bigger cordon was thrown around the whole area.

Apparently alarmed by the noise the tiger rushed about the forest for some time when it was again encountered by the police party. The police opened fire, and shots from an Indian policeman this time found their mark, causing the tiger to halt. The Indian fired three shots, hitting the tiger in the head, left shoulder and lungs.

Despite its wounds the tiger continued to struggle against the efforts of the policemen to tie it up. In the struggle, one of the Indian police was injured. However, the work of the Nipponese and Indian Police was fully rewarded as the tiger was finally subdued. The dead tiger was then taken to the vacant ground outside the gendarme office at Stanley."

Eventually, in the mid 1990s I obtained a number of books and photocopies which confirmed the story. The day that they arrived in the post I was laid low with the flu, but I eagerly sat up in bed, tore open the packaging and read the documents which finally confirmed the details of the incident which had obsessed me for nearly thirty years. A book about the Japanese occupation included a photograph of the dead beast, credited to Lady May Ride, which is captioned: "The famous Stanley Tiger which was shot by the guards in 1942. This appears to be the only unofficial photograph taken by an inmate at Stanley."

If this is the photograph from the Japanese newspaper, referred to by Herklots, why was it taken by an internee, whoever he or she was? Collaborating with the enemy to the extent of becoming an unofficial press photographer for a newspaper full of propaganda, which was published by the occupying power would have been considered almost treasonable.

However, the photocopy of the original newspaper cutting that I had first read back in the little whitewashed library at Peak School showed that the Lady May Ride photograph was not the one used by the occupying Japanese. This is a far less impressive piece of photography than the Lady May Ride photograph that, despite the claims that it is an unofficial photograph, is obviously posed and well composed. The stringency of Japanese security arrangements, especially earlier on in the War is legendary. Violence, torture, and even executions, were relatively commonplace for what the Japanese considered to be infringements of security. If, indeed, it was taken by an internee and not by a Japanese Press Photographer, then the evidence suggests that it was done so with the connivance, tacit, or overt knowledge of the Japanese Military. The head of the creature is being supported by a man who appears to be an Indian, and presumably the policeman that shot it. If the man in the picture is a guard or policeman, as seems probable, he was certainly aware that he was being photographed. He is even smiling for the camera! It seems almost impossible that the Japanese Security Forces could not have been aware of the photograph.

When one compares it with the crude picture which accompanied the item in *The Hong Kong News* then the whole affair becomes even more unlikely. There may have been three thousand internees, but it seems almost impossible that Herklots, who was after all Hong Kong's leading naturalist and the editor of the *Hong Kong Naturalist* magazine, and a minor celebrity in his own right, would not have known about the tiger incident from more than hearsay and rumours. Dr. Herklots was important enough to be put in charge of revitalising the post war fishing industry for the region, in a successful attempt to restore food stocks as quickly as possible. Another history of the Japanese occupation gives more details of this affair and implies that Herklots, whom he describes as a "Biologist just released from Stanley Internment Camp," was a person of considerable importance. Even if he had not been taken to view the carcass in person, it seems certain that the photographer, who did see the carcass would have spoken to Herklots about it!

We have examined enough evidence from Herklots already in this chapter, to suggest that he is a reliable and indeed an expert witness. His mind may have been vague about minor details, but surely an event as important to the sum total knowledge of the zoo-fauna of Hong Kong as this would have remained fresh in his mind. As a Fortean, I have often been accused of paranoid conspiracy theorising, but in this case, something doesn't add up!

The mounted skin was taken to a place of honour in the newly restored Government House and eventually ended up in a Buddhist Temple in Stanley village.

Back in the late 1960s I remember talking about the affair to my beloved amah - Ah Tim. She told me that according to Chinese belief, the tiger was the King of Beasts and the arrival of a tiger unexpectedly in a neighbourhood was often seen as an omen that a new Emperor or King was about to take the throne. It is certain that some people at the time saw the death of the unfortunate tiger in Stanley Internment Camp as being a signal that the reign of the King-Emperor George VI was nearing an end, and the reign of the God-Emperor Hirohito was about to begin!

It seems likely that the invading Japanese were determined to extract the maximum of publicity from the event by exploiting local folk beliefs. Near the end of the war when it was obvious that they would lose, they were still fermenting Chinese Nationalist feelings, often through the use of cultural motifs, and sometimes by recruiting collaborators, in an attempt to ensure that at least the British would no longer be in power in Hong Kong. They failed, as history has proven, but the different stories I managed to unearth over a period of some thirty years suggested that someone, either wittingly or unwittingly, was not telling the whole truth.

The whole affair is a real mystery, and excitingly it is a mystery that I hope that eventually I shall be able to solve. Although there is no doubt that South China tigers did visit Hong Kong on many occasions, it is very tempting to speculate that the unfortunate creature that was shot in 1941 was, indeed, a captive animal which had been released in the area by the occupying Japanese forces as a crude - but remarkably successful - piece of psychological warfare.

The affair has become somewhat of an obsession with me since I first heard about it from Billy Tingle back in the mid 1960s. The skin of what is *apparently* the Stanley tiger can still be found hanging in a Buddhist temple in Stanley village. One of these days I have every intention of going back to Hong Kong, and somehow obtaining a DNA sample from the pelt. It should then be a reasonably simple job to ascertain whether this was the last verified tiger to visit Hong Kong or whether it was just one of the sadder casualties of the most terrible conflict of the 20th century.

My family left Hong Kong in 1971, and we returned to England, eventually settling in rural north Devon. At the time I was devastated. Hong Kong was the only world that I knew. I had to leave behind all of my animals, and I felt certain that in a country where tigers, pangolins, pythons and giant lizards were to be replaced by foxes, rabbits, and hedgehogs, my career as an amateur naturalist, and even more amateur monster hunter, was doomed to an ignoble and premature ending.

Little did I know that this was only the beginning.

CHAPTER TWO

THE CHILDREN OF THE NIGHT

I was nearly twelve years old when I first came to live in England. Puberty hit me like a series of rather unpleasant thunderbolts within a few months of my arrival as a stranger in a very strange land. I had been brought up in Hong Kong - the jewel in the crown of the Empire - during the very last days when the British Empire could actually have been justified with that name

In many ways Hong Kong was far more English than England itself. Certainly, the people who surrounded me during my privileged Ex-Pat childhood were more fiercely loyal to the crown, and more proudly English than the motley collection of people with whom I found myself surrounded on my return to the motherland. Where, I asked myself in dismay, were the jolly village greens and the smiling tradesmen who always had a cheery word for the village children? Throughout my schooldays in Hong Kong, the hymns we had sung in Assembly promised me a land where children happily "gathered rushes" in their play, and where "the rich man in his castle" and "the poor man at his gate" were quite content with life, and respected each other and all got along jolly happily together. This idyllic world was occasionally disrupted by the japes of people like Billy Bunter or [just] William Brown and his band of Outlaws; but the Famous Five, the Secret Seven, Bulldog Drummond or Rupert Bear were always there to save the day and restore the world to a nice, stable upper-middle class equilibrium.

The England of 1971 was something completely different. Who were these longhaired people with beards who actually dared to stop my father as he was walking down Bideford High Street and offer him a flower? Who were these rough and uncouth youths that I met every day in school who kicked and beat me up because I was "a poof" who "talked posh" and didn't know who or what 'Leeds United' were? Where were Jennings and Biggles when you needed them?

I felt like the character of Doctor Cornelius in C.S. Lewis's *Prince Caspian,* who had dedicated his life to wandering throughout the further reaches of the Kingdom of Narnia, by then civilised and humanised by the conquering (and somewhat melodramatic) humans, in search of a mystical heritage that he knew only from dimly remembered stories. In many ways that is what I am still doing, and I believe that Rueben recognised this fact when he stopped me that night in the

Mesquite casino bar. However, like Doctor Cornelius, I began to realise that although the Arcadian world of the England of my dreams probably didn't exist (and even more disappointingly, probably never had done). Behind both the yobbish, classless, and post-revolutionary facade of the early seventies, and even behind the idyllic world described in my favourite and inspirational children's books, lay a deeper truth. England was still a very strange place indeed.

It was a place where, if you looked hard enough, in all the old and unfamiliar places, naked savages could still be found. Where people still saw fairies. Where feathered birdmen swooped down upon innocent children in haunted woods, and where the lakes, seas and rivers were still haunted by long necked monsters. I had only been in the country for a few hours when I had my first inkling that this might be the case.

Our journey back to England from Hong Kong had been a momentous one. I am sure my parents planned it so that my brother and I would have an experience that we would remember for the rest of our lives, but being the ungrateful little brats that children of seven and eleven are, it didn't really work out like that. The first part of the trip was idyllic. We flew from Hong Kong to Bombay, with a forced stopover in Bangkok due to Engine failure on the plane. After a few days in Bangkok we set sail for Europe on a journey that would last several weeks and that stopped off at Mombasa, Durban, Cape Town, Tenerife, Barcelona and Brindisi, before finally docking at Venice. I am probably one of the last people to have seen the Plaza San Marco when it was not under water; although the romance and intrigue of this beautiful city largely passed me by. At the age of eleven I was far more interested in reaching England, where I would, of course, soon find myself part of a band of stalwart chums who would have thrilling adventures. Of course, it doesn't work like that.

We crossed Europe by train, and by the time we reached Paris I have a sneaking suspicion that the entire family was heartily sick of the journey and just wanted to get back to the UK. My darling mother (God rest her soul) tried to interest me in the sights of cosmopolitan Paris, but the beauties of the Seine left me cold, and the only memory that I have is of trying desperately to mentally subdue a burgeoning erection caused by the proximity of so many pieces of statuary depicting naked women. This was the age of my burgeoning sexuality; and although I was still definitely in the "Girls are Icky" stage, I was desperate to know what they looked like with no clothes on.

We took the ferry for England with a sigh of relief, and although my grounding in Biggles books had prepared me for a feeling of glorious patriotic fervour at the sight of the white cliffs of Dover it was a rough crossing, I had over-eaten at lunchtime and at the first sight of my glorious motherland I was copiously and messily sick in my mother's second best hat. As we disembarked at Dover a seagull shat messily in my brother's eye, and it was two smelly, disgruntled and cross children who were ushered onto the train that was to take us from Dover to London.

At the time, I was obsessed with the Second World War. The cessation of hostilities had been less than three decades before, and in the same way that so many of the children of my contemporaries seem obsessed by *The Beatles* - an ensemble who played their last notes as a group well before they were born, I and my contemporaries were obsessed by the War. It was, after all, the defining event of our lives, even though it had been over for fourteen years before I was born. Our parents had fought in, or at least lived through the war, there were still a surprisingly large number of derelict bomb sites, and as late as 1974 Japanese soldiers who refused to believe that the war was finally over, emerged from the jungles of The Philippines in unbowed triumph.

As our train trundled and ambled through the verdant Kent countryside I gazed rapturously out of the window. Gone was the smell of vomit, and I forgot that my little brother, still snivelling, stank of seagull shit. I could see Oast Houses, I could see hop fields. These were the fields over which The Battle of Britain (as immortalised for me by the eponymous 1969 movie) had been fought. I was finally in England, and I would soon see the land for which we had fought the Hun, not once, but twice in my Grandparent's lifetimes. As the dusk began to gather round, I picked up a newspaper that had been left on the seat of our carriage by a previous passenger.

I leafed through it idly, but my attention was transfixed by one particular story. The headline read "Little Miss Starkers," and told the story of how several motorists driving home late at night along one lonely stretch of road near Sevenoaks had been startled to see the figure of a young teenage girl - completely naked - emerge from a pond by the side of the road and cross the road slowly in front of them paying no attention to the oncoming traffic. One report even described the girl's breasts as being draped in waterweed from the lake. All the witnesses (five in all, I believe, although you must remember that it is over thirty years since I read the story) described how she had disappeared into the undergrowth on the opposite side of the road.

The journalist who had written the story was quick to blame these sightings on drugged skinny-dipping hippies, but I was transfixed. Not only did I find the story almost unbelievably sexually arousing, it was also redolent of my spiritual mentor, Doctor Cornelius's quest for the "Old Narnians". Perhaps "Little Miss Starkers" was a dryad of some sort - a water spirit, a living embodiment of the healing stream. It was a stunning image for an eleven year old with an overactive imagination. When said eleven year old was also within twelve months of the onset of puberty, it gave him a fixation with alfresco sexual encounters that would take him nearly another decade to experience for himself, but that is another story. However, I can truly say that the five minutes that it took me to read that poorly written newspaper story changed my life and set me on the trail of wild men, and unearthly humanoids amongst England's green and pleasant land.

I first visited Devonshire during the summer of 1969. My family was on holiday from Hong-Kong, and we spent the vast majority of our time in the UK staying at a guesthouse near the village of Widecombe in the Moor deep in the heart of Dartmoor. My father was a Devonshire man, and had been born just outside Tavistock in 1925. He was eager to show his young sons what was essentially his homeland. Although I had visited England as a small child in 1963 and had travelled around Scotland in a Dormobile in 1967, this was my first introduction to rural England. It was a revelation. That summer I fell in love - I began a love affair with the English countryside which has continued unabated ever since. The Devonshire countryside in the early summer is possibly one of the most beautiful places in the world, and it was an idyllic location for what - with the benefit of hindsight - was one of the happiest summers of my life. It was the last summer before my father began to succumb to the arthritis which only two years later forced his retirement, and - almost as if he knew what was to come - he enthusiastically showed my brother and me as many of the highways and byways of this most magical part of England has he could.

My father knew many of the local folk legends, and showed us the tower of Widecombe Church, allegedly damaged by a visitation from the devil in the Middle Ages. He took us to Jay's grave - the last resting place of a teenage housemaid who committed suicide when she found she was pregnant by the son of the master of the house. The most peculiar thing about this last monument - a sad roadside tomb in the middle of the moor - is that every day fresh flowers are found on the sad little tombstone. Nobody knows who places the flowers. Thirty-four years later the tomb - and the flowers - are still there. In this way I began to understand that what I would later come to know as Forteana is part of a living, breathing tradition and that paranormal or inexplicable events happen to real people in real places, and are not just the domain of fairy tales or horror comics.

During that enchanted summer I had no idea that two years later the family would be living in north Devon. We arrived in the little village of Woolsery in July 1971 and I soon became friends with the three children who lived next door. David was about the same age as me, and to my great joy I found out that we were soulmates. Like me, he had a voracious appetite for knowledge about the natural world and its denizens, like me he read everything that he could get hold of, and like me he had a surreal and slightly peculiar sense of humour. We soon became very close friends indeed, and were inseparable during our schooldays. He was sceptical - though interested - in my new-found passion for cryptozoology, and together we roamed the fields and woods, and investigated the local streams and ponds in search of the wildlife to be found therein.

His two sisters were younger than me: Lorraine by about two years, and Kaye by about four. David and I used to tease them unmercifully. Whilst they, too, were fond of animals, they found the wriggly things that their brother and I used to keep in jam jars in the garden shed to be uniformly icky. David and I realised this and used to torment the poor girls with biscuit tins full of spiders, and jam jars containing large and ugly horseleeches. It is - I believe - a testament to their good nature, that we are still friends more than 30 years later.

I started school at Bideford Grammar that autumn, and soon found that, whereas I had a few close friends who had the same peculiar outlook on life as me, I cordially disliked most of the people with whom I was forced to associate, and that the feeling was usually reciprocated. I didn't like the teachers much either. This book is intended as the chronicle of my monster hunting investigations over the years, so I will forgo the temptation of bitching about my schooldays to any great degree. This is neither the time nor the place; so apart from saying that my schooldays were not the happiest time of my life, I think I will largely ignore them - for this book at least.

In 1973 I first heard about the legend of the hairy hands. Getting changed after a PE lesson was always difficult. Back in Hong Kong I had the first of three operations on my knees - corrective surgery for a congenital bone disorder. Apart from boxing, and to a lesser extent swimming, I had never shown any interest in sport at school, and following my operations my mobility was severely limited for a time, and what little aptitude I had for the sporting life evaporated. Unlike most of my contemporaries I never had any interest in spectator sports. Coming from Hong Kong where none of my friends had even heard of the FA Cup, I was at somewhat of a disadvantage in a school where if you didn't know who Leeds United were you were treated as some sort of a moral leper. Add to this the fact that I was incredibly self-conscious about my body - not only because of puberty, but because of my unsightly operation scars - and you will understand why most of my school career doing my best to avoid compulsory sports. However, on this occasion - at the age of thirteen - I was fascinated to hear two of the other boys in my class claim that they had encountered a legendary phenomenon whilst on an outward-bound course at the Dartmoor Field Studies Centre.

The phenomenon appears to have started in 1921 on what is now the B3212 near Postbridge, when there were three motoring accidents on the main road close to the gate of Archerton farm on an area known locally as Nine Mile Hill. The only contemporarily published information comes from the *Daily Mail* of the 4th and 5th October that year. The first accident happened in March 1921. Dr E. M. Helby, the prison doctor at the maximum-security prison on the moor, was riding down this well-known slope with two children in his sidecar, when the engine suddenly became detached from the frame. He shouted to the children to jump clear, and they were unhurt, but he himself was thrown off and killed.

A few weeks later, a motor-coach was driving up the slope and abruptly mounted the grassy bank on the higher side of the road. It came to rest at such an angle that several passengers were thrown out, and one woman was severely injured. Afterwards the driver was heard to mutter to a villager that he had felt invisible hands pulling the wheel towards the side of the road. On 26 August, a dull foggy Friday, a young army officer riding a motor bicycle was also thrown into the turf verge and sustained scratches and some shock. As a very experienced rider, he was perplexed. "It was not my fault," he said at last. "Believe it or not, something drove me off the road. A pair of hairy hands closed over mine. I felt them as plainly as ever I felt anything in my life-large, muscular, hairy hands. I fought them for all I was worth, but they were too strong for me. They forced the machine into the turf at the edge of the road, and I knew no more till I came to myself, lying a few feet away on my face on the turf."

In the summer of 1924, the renowned Devon folklorist Theo Brown was a child camping in a caravan with her parents on the eastern side of the ruins, about half a mile from the road and about a mile west of Nine Mile Hill. Her mother had heard a rumour of the accidents and the supposed cause. Brown later wrote:

"I knew there was some power very seriously menacing us near, and I must act very swiftly.... As I looked up to the little window at the end of the caravan, I saw something moving, and as I stared, I saw it was the fingers and palm of a very large hand with many hairs on the joints and back of it, clawing up and up to the top of the window which was a little open. I knew it wished to do harm to my husband sleeping below. I knew that the owner of the hand hated us and wished harm, and I knew it was no ordinary human hand, and that no blow or shot would have any power over it. Almost unconsciously I made the Sign of The Cross and I prayed very much that we might be kept safe. At once the hand slowly sank down out of sight and I knew the danger had gone. I did say a thankful prayer and fell at once into a peaceful sleep.

"We stayed in that spot for several weeks but I never felt the evil influence again near the caravan. But I did not feel happy in some places not far off, and would not for anything have walked alone on the moor at night, or on the Tor above our caravan."

Strange incidents happened occasionally in that vicinity over the next half-century, and it appears that the two schoolboys in my class had been the latest in a long line of people to experience something weird in the area. Details were scant, and to be quite honest when I look back, I can remember nothing of substance in what they said. However, it was enough to enthuse me into inveigling places for me, and two of my closest cronies on the next field studies trip.

One would have imagined that my teachers would have been slightly perturbed at why three confirmed non-sportsmen - indeed three schoolboys who not only made no secret of their antipathy towards sport, community activities and the whole ethos of "mens sano in copore whatsit" school spirit, which even in 1973 was an unfortunate hangover from the era of *Tom Brown's Schooldays* - would want to volunteer for a weekend of hiking, abseiling, football, and all things that they spent their entire school career trying to avoid. Luckily, as I have discovered to my benefit again and again throughout my life, those placed an authority over us are often spectacularly stupid.

The next obstacle that needed to be overcome was that the three of us - Jim, Paul and myself - were supposed to be sharing a heavily supervised dormitory with the cream of the yobbo element from two separate schools. The end was in sight for Bideford Grammar School. Two years hence it would have ceased to exist, and would have been combined with its mortal enemy - the local secondary modern school. In a vain attempt to foster some semblance of community spirit between two schools - who wished each other nothing but ill - a series of events like the outward-bound weekend on Dartmoor had been planned. Before we even got to the Field Studies Centre it was beginning to look as if we'd bitten off more than we could chew. The yobbo element (indeed, everybody on the trip except for the teachers and us three), were making no secret of the fact that they intended to "teach those grammar school poofs a lesson that they would not forget," and luckily the harassed teachers in charge of the expedition decided that it would be more prudent if the three of us slept under a different roof from the rest. Jim, Paul and I were therefore given camp beds and allowed to sleep in an empty laboratory. This was heaven.

It never occurred to the powers-that-be that we had our own agenda for the weekend.

For the record, although both Paul's and my sexuality were in a state of flux for several years during the mid-1970s, our main qualification for being a branded "poofs" was that we spoke with a different accent to everybody else, that we read books, that we were not the slightest bit interested in football, and that our musical tastes veered towards pretentious progressive rock, and the hippie mysticism of George Harrison and *Gong*, rather than the boot-boy football terrace anthems beloved of our contemporaries.

The three of us were particularly happy with our new surroundings. We made ourselves at home very quickly. Even today, I have a knack of being able to convert a sterile hotel room or Travel-Lodge into the sort of place where I like to spend some time. At the age of 14 I was no different. Out came the chocolate, out came the cassette player with our favoured music, out came as essential items of day-to-day living equipment such as our butterfly nets and specimen jars, and within half-an-hour we had converted a purpose-built laboratory into our very own *pied-a-terre*. The biggest advantage from our point of view was not the obvious one: that we would avoid being pulverised by the yobbo element (although that was, of course a very big advantage). No, the main advantage was that unlike the other schoolboys on this rather dull trip we were in the enviable position of being able to come and go as we chose.

Unfortunately, it was the middle of the winter. The main problem that this caused was the weather. Dartmoor in the middle of winter is no picnic. It rained most of the weekend - and the rain turned into sleet every few hours. Occasionally it even threatened to snow. After making ourselves at home, we ambled up to the main building to get a meal and to find out, firstly, what the powers-that-be had organised for us over the following two days; and secondly - how to get out of it in order to carry out our personal objectives for the weekend.

It was much easier than we thought. Our appearance in the main Common Room was greeted by jeers and catcalls. As the sports teacher from the secondary modern school began to list the weekend's itinerary of hiking, abseiling etc, I took one of the junior teachers aside and asked for permission for the three of us to be excused the compulsory activities so we could concentrate on some extra-curricular work for the grammar school biology club. With an unmistakable look of relief, the teacher acceded to our request. By some chicanery that even now I have not got to the bottom of, Paul managed to persuade whoever it was that was in charge of the catering arrangements to allow us to prepare and eat our own food separately. Five minutes later, loaded down with enough provisions to keep us happy for the weekend, the three of us went back to our own little lair and didn't lay eyes on the rest of the party until it was time to leave on the Sunday teatime. Not for the last time my life I discovered that there are some great advantages to being an anti-social pain in the arse, whose world-view is at wild variance to that of his contemporaries.

It was the first time in my life that I was completely free of adult supervision. The glorious world described to me by Arthur Ransome and Enid Blyton was finally upon me. That night we sat up until some dreadful hour earnestly discussing the things that 14 year olds talk about - mostly 14 year old girls - and finally got to sleep a few hours before dawn. After a few hours of surprisingly restless sleep, we woke, washed in a desultory fashion, and went outside to explore our surroundings.

Although I had visited Dartmoor on many occasions, for some reason it had always been in the summertime. This was the first time - or at least the first that I can remember - that I had been there in the middle of the winter. It was a revelation. Although Dartmoor is beautiful at any time of the year, early on a winter's morning when the skeletal trees are silhouetted against the sleet grey skyline and even the sheep huddle together in a conspiratorial cabal, it is the most beautiful place in the world. Laughing, the three of us ran across the frosty meadow towards one of the little granite streams that crisscross the moor. "Look!" whispered Jim, and pointed. There, sitting perched uncomfortably on a knobbly grey rock in the middle of the fast flowing water was a dipper - one of the most singular and slightly bizarre of British birds. We watched in silence. The dipper went about business, dived into the water. We could see it "flying" beneath the crystal surface of the mountain stream. It moved exactly as if it were flying through air. On the far side of the stream a tiny Dartmoor pony with straggly mane and a face that looked a thousand years old stood gazing at us with a slightly belligerent manner. A magpie flew past.

All three of us were well brought-up country boys, and knowing that it would surely bring us good luck, we pulled our forelocks, spat over our left shoulders in what we hopefully believed was the direction of the nearest church, and in unison bade good morning to the handsome black and white corvid.

Just then a minibus pulled into the long, grey, stone driveway. It contained another party of school children - this time they were all girls. They were from a private school somewhere in west Devon. Immediately the testosterone started pumping through our bodies - our reverie was broken. Rare birds and Dartmoor ponies were all very well, but the female of the human species exerted a fascination upon us that was far greater. We nudged each other in the ribs. "Phwoaar look at that!" said Paul, smirking. We gazed at the visions of female pulchritude as they disembarked from their minibus, carrying their rucksacks. Vistas of romance appeared in our collective mind's eye, but we were too shy to do anything about it, and we just stood back and watched as the yobbo element from our party appeared, as if from nowhere, and bore down upon the new arrivals like predatory wolves. It was as if we just didn't exist. Surrendering to another overwhelming bodily need - that of hunger - we went back into our little camp in the disused laboratory and had breakfast.

Thirty years later, I can still remember this meal as one of the most satisfying of my life. Who wants a proper meal, when one can eat corned beef on toast and chocolate off paper plates while sitting on one's haunches in the corner of an empty laboratory? Truly, the shackles of the real world were far away and we were living a glorious free existence untrammelled by the mores of our elders and betters. Surely life doesn't get much better than this? But it does - and did.

After our distractions, and our breakfast, we finally sat down to discussing the really important matter at issue: Our quest for the 'hairy hands'. The first that we had to do - we all agreed - was to go and see the place for ourselves.. Unfortunately, this presented us with a whole new set of problems. Although we had been lucky enough to finagle ourselves into a situation where we had a minimum of adult supervision, we were sensible enough to know that this lax attitude on behalf of the teachers was not going to extend to allowing us free rein to wander over Dartmoor as, when, and where we wished. We were also sensible enough to know that those set in authority over us were not going to look kindly upon our true quest - to experience for ourselves a frightening encounter with a disembodied elemental earth spirit. It was time to manipulate the teachers once again.

We realised that, on the whole, the teaching staff had just as low an opinion of us as did the yobbo element. They, too, had an almost childish belief in school spirit, and three boys who listened to peculiar music and cared nothing for sports fitted not at all into their worldview. We realised - even at such a young age - that whereas if we told the truth about our endeavours our quest would be soon nipped in the bud, if we made up some plausible nonsense about wanting to visit this particular part of Dartmoor, they would probably allow us to go.

So we wandered up to the main building and went in search of the teacher in charge: a man in early middle age - at the time I thought he was ancient, although he was probably younger, than I am now. He had a receding hairline, and what was left of his hair was rapidly going grey. He wore a tatty tweed jacket with leather patches on the elbows and chain-smoked Woodbines. As we arrived, he was in the middle of a heated argument with a member of staff from the newly arrived girls' school. Apparently, one of the yobbo elements had made an indecent suggestion to one of the girls and a major incident was brewing. It was the perfect time for a piece of verbal prestidigitation.

"Excuse me, sir," I muttered sheepishly, "but we were wondering if we could go and look for a hen harrier's nest over on the Princetown Road." As soon as I said it I realised that I'd made a mistake. It was the middle of December, and even the rarest of the British birds of prey would never have been stupid enough to try and nest at this time of year. Luckily, the harassed schoolmaster was too preoccupied with the business at hand to pay any attention to what I had said. "Go away, boy...do what you want," he blustered, and I made a hasty retreat. I had got away with it - by the skin of my teeth - but there was *somebody* who had overheard, and who not only realised that my request was completely nonsensical, but put two and two together to extrapolate the obvious piece of data - that my pals and I had plans, at that we were not prepared to share with the powers-that-be.

We went back to our laboratory to prepare for the quest. As we had no particular idea how we were going to look for the hairy hands, and even less idea what we were going to do with them once we found them, we had very little equipment to take. Being schoolboys, and therefore being always hungry, the procurement of an adequate supply of comestibles was far more in order. We had managed to blag enough food for the morning's breakfast, but the acquisition of a gargantuan packed lunch big enough for three was going to be a far more difficult matter to arrange. We were sitting around in the corner of the laboratory sharing a surreptitious cigarette and pondering on this problem when the door opened - and in walked a girl.

I am going to avoid, once again, the temptation to rewrite history. It would be easy enough to do - I haven't seen Paul or Jim or Katie (for that was her name), for nearly 30 years. I have no idea where they are now, or even if they are alive or dead. However, this memoir is as true as my fading memory will allow it to be, and so I will forgo the temptation of making Katie into a stunningly gorgeous teenage supermodel, or turning me into a suave sophisticated young babe magnet. I wasn't and neither was she. She was a fairly ordinary-looking girl of about 14, wearing a rather grubby *Bay City Rollers* sweatshirt and a pair of shapeless jeans. She had shoulder-length brown hair (of the hue most usually seen in the dregs of British Rail coffee cups), freckles, and sparkling blue eyes. I cannot remember whether I thought she was pretty or not - I was too shocked at the realisation that a member of the fairer sex had invaded our masculine sanctum, and moreover had done so at a time when we were sitting around a smoking a cigarette and looking at girlie mags.

"Who are you?" I stuttered. She looked straight back at me with the confident air that I would come to recognize, in later years, as being one that always appears on a woman's face when she knows perfectly well that she is in complete control of the situation, and that there is nothing anybody else can do to change it. Hoping against hope that she had not noticed our choice of reading material, we kicked our dog-eared copies of *Penthouse* under the table and hopefully out of sight. "My name is Katie," she said with a grin, "and I know perfectly well that you three are not going bird-watching. Hen harriers nests in the middle of December? ... I ask you."

We grinned.

"Your teacher must have been insane to believe that nonsense. Now, what you actually going to do?"

She had such a friendly and disarming grin, that we decided wordlessly to take her into our confidence. After all, we had nothing to lose. If she wanted to, Katie could completely ruin the rest of the weekend for us. So we invited her to join us instead. She sat down on the floor with us and shared the end of our cigarette.

Much to our surprise, she took our quest seriously. We had lived with our plans for so long that even we were beginning to doubt that they made any sense. The problem with our plan was that, quite simply, we didn't have a plan. We told Katie about the legends of the hairy hands, and we told her how a brace of our classmates on a previous trip to the Field Studies Centre had claimed an encounter with the phenomenon. She looked excited at this, but then looked slightly crestfallen as we admitted that not only did we not have any details of the encounter between the schoolboys and the elemental earth spirit (if that is what was), but that we had no plans beyond going to look at the part of the road where the accidents that happened 50 years earlier, and where occasional encounters with a disembodied pair of hairy hands had been reported. For the first time since she appeared in our midst, Katie lost her air of manipulative world-weary womanhood and became a little girl pleading with the bigger children to be allowed to join in their games.

"Can I come too?" she begged with little-girl eyes. "Could I?"

We looked at each other and grinned. All three of us had already assumed that Katie would become the 4th member of our party, and as far as we were concerned, it was a done deal. However, in a display of macho arrogance, we pretended to deliberate amongst ourselves for a few moments before graciously acceding to her request. It was many years before I realised that Katie had every intention of coming along with us, whatever we had decided, and that the little girl act was just that - an act, albeit a very good one. It wasn't until the late 1990s - in the wake of my divorce - that I realised that once a woman has made up her mind about something no power on earth can change it.

It soon became obvious that either Katie was far more adept at manipulating the powers-that-be than we were, or the administration at a girls' private school was far more lax - and civilised - than that which we had become used to. We told Katie of our dilemma regarding the acquisition of a picnic lunch. She looked at us, grinned and said: "leave it to me." She trotted back to the main building and no more than five minutes later she returned with a handsome selection of comestibles which would have put one of the famous picnics as described by Enid Blyton to shame. She told us proudly that she had found no difficulty in persuading the teacher in charge of her group to allow her to accompany us on our expedition "in search of rare birds." With a girlish giggle, she admitted, that she too had been unable to think of a better excuse than we had, and that luckily her teachers were as gullible as ours were.

About half-an-hour later we set off. We looked like a post psychedelic version of one of the groups of children in an Enid Blyton novel. As a gawky adolescent, and admittedly - to a certain extent at least - also as an adult, I have been subject to a bizarre cultural dichotomy. On one hand, I have been drawn towards the lifestyle lived by the upper middle-class children in my favourite adventure stories, but on the other, the trappings of the hippy counter-culture have always somewhat appealed. A few months before the events recounted in this chapter, one of our teachers had lectured to us on the evils of drugs. She made this lecture sound so irresistible that I was determined to get stoned as quickly and as often as possible. Unlike my contemporaries I was already aware of the concept of the drug culture. If there were indeed any hard drugs in Bideford, I had no knowledge of them and never encountered any. As a child in Hong Kong, however, I had seen elderly Chinese opium addicts sitting on street corners where they dreamed their lives away, and a mixture of these childhood memories and the irresistible lure of heroin *chic* as practised by the Rolling Stones became like a siren call forever threatening to lure me onto the rocks.

Like others of my generation, I had been introduced to the concept of what it is broadly and vulgarly known as 'weird shit' by my eager perusal of books by people like Erik von Daniken, Carlos Castenada and Lobsang Rampa. Little did I know that von Daniken and Castaneda were lying toe-rags, and that the émigré Tibetan Lama was actually an unemployed plumber from a small suburb of Plymouth. Add to that the rich - albeit naive - gamut of rock and roll mysticism that I had gleaned from albums by George Harrison and Steve Hillage, and my childhood obsession with monster hunting (which seven years on showed no signs of abating) and you are left with a rich and diverse mental and psychological landscape which could either lead to an adulthood full of severe mental health problems, or to a rich and fulfilling career as Britain's leading monster hunter. In my case it led to both.

The four of us walked the two or three miles towards the notorious bend in the B3212 where the fatal accidents that had kick-started this particular series of quasi-Fortean episodes had taken place over half-a-century before. As we walked along, we chatted, and much to my surprise I began to realise that girls were not a different species after all. Until then, the only females that I had spent any time with were my mother, and Lorraine and Kaye. None of them counted. They weren't girls in the true sense of the word - they were just part of my life, and I couldn't really imagine my life without any of them. Katie was something different. She was a *real* girl - she was cute in a slightly tomboyish way and had come into my life through the mechanism of a social situation about which I had been completely unprepared, and I was very surprised at how easily she had fitted into a little band of brothers. It turned out that she had the same hopes and fears that we did. It turned out that she - like us - didn't really fit in with the social *zeitgeist* of day-to-day school life. Like me, she shunned sport and wrote bad poetry. OK, she had dreadful taste in music, but even with the benefit of thirty years of hindsight, I can't hold that against her.

For some reason - and as an author myself I can only guess that it is because she liked to describe sunny days, and probably found that they made writing her plots easier - whenever that the protagonists in an Enid Blyton novel went for a walk, and especially when they sat down for a picnic lunch, the sun was always shining, there was always a blue sky and all was right with the world. On this day in the middle of December 1973, the weather was lousy. Blustery winds drove intermittent flurries of sleet straight into us, and although the sun occasionally threaten to shine, it invariably thought better of it and retreated behind a bank of unpleasant looking clouds. On at least two occasions passing motor vehicles showered us with muddy water as they drove past, oblivious to our presence. By the time that we sat down in the wholly inadequate shelter of a dry-stone wall all four of us were soaked to the skin.

We eventually reached what we hoped was our destination - at least it looked right on the Ordnance Survey map. We then looked at each other. Okay, we'd found the place. It existed, sure enough, but there were no signs of anything sinister there. What on earth were we going to do next? After a quick confabulation, we decided that as there was obviously nothing of any importance to see there, we should try and find the old Powder Mills where Theo Brown herself had seen a physical manifestation of the disembodied hairy hands. Even at the time, I realised that this was a fairly major mistake. None of us had more than the *vaguest* idea of where they were, but I was intent on proving my manhood in front of Katie so I boldly led the way in a vaguely northerly direction. Half-an-hour later, we were somewhere along the Cherry Brook valley and we were completely lost.

Little did I know that the Cherry Brook valley itself was a location of high Fortean interest. A few years later a number of Dartmoor ponies were found killed under mysterious circumstances there. Twenty years later I would come back to investigate the deaths of the ponies. On this occasion the sun was shining, it was high summer and I was accompanied by my wife, daughter and dog. Even then, under the most auspicious of conditions, the sight of the pretty Dartmoor valley, with its wild flowers and silvery brook, brought a shiver down the back of my neck as I remembered the events of December 1973. By this time it was getting dark. None of us had torches and we were all sensible enough to realise that, if we didn't get back to the road before nightfall, we would be in serious trouble. As self-appointed expedition leader I decided not to communicate my fears to the others, and with a silent prayer I scrutinised the map. To the left of me was Lower White Tor. I realised then that we were going completely in the wrong direction, and by a masterpiece of social engineering which still impresses me today whenever I think of it, I managed to turn our little party around and make towards the road without revealing that our entire dilemma had been my fault all along.

We came within sight of the road when there was still plenty of light to see where we were going. This makes what happened next even more inexcusable. On my earliest visits to Dartmoor, my father had impressed upon me the utmost importance of looking where I was going. In the excitement of the afternoon's events I had completely forgotten this sage advice. Even my father had never warned me of the eventuality that I would be alone on the moor on a monster hunting expedition in the middle of winter with two school friends and a girl that I was beginning to fancy something rotten. He certainly never warned me that whilst on this intrepid quest an explosion from the army firing range a few miles away would disturb all the local wildlife, and that an elderly, grizzled dog fox would be startled from cover and rush across our path only a few feet away, startling said young lady to such an extent that she would fall headlong into a particularly treacherous bog. He certainly never warned me that the bog would turn out to be quick sand!

Katie swore in a most unladylike manner and started to struggle. However, the more she struggled, the more she became enmeshed in the sticky mud. It soon became obvious that she was in quite considerable danger. Paul, Jim and I stood by the side of the marsh helpless. Then one of us - I would like to take the credit but to be quite honest after 30 years has elapsed I cannot remember which of us it was - had the bright idea of knotting our denim jackets and parkas together to form a makeshift rope. Shouting at her not struggle, we threw Katie her lifeline and pulled her to safety where she collapsed into my arms. For a few moments - which felt like an eternity - I held her warm, shivering body close to mine. Then we made our way back to the road, and an hour or so later we arrived, muddy, wet and elated back at the Field Studies Centre.

Katie went straight up to the main block to have a shower and get changed. My two companions and I went back to our makeshift base camp in the empty laboratory to do likewise. Later that evening, as Paul, Jim and I were sitting around eating chocolate and drinking a bottle of cider that we had smuggled along with us, in walked Katie. She looked completely different. Again, exhibiting a facet of female personality with which I was not destined to become familiar until I was much older, she had worked wonders upon herself with clean clothes, make-up and hair brush. Gone was the slightly grubby looking tomboy who had shared our adventure. In her place was a charming, demure, and ever-so-slightly sexy young lady.

We stared at her as she sashayed into the room with the confidence of an attractive young woman who knows that all eyes are upon her. "Stop staring at me and pass the bloody cider," she said, laughing, and the spell was broken. The gallant band that had gone in search of the hairy hands was back together again. Unsurprisingly, the events of the day had dampened our appetite for adventure somewhat. We agreed that in order to truly solve the mystery we would have to go back at night, and perform some unspecified magickal ritual to summon up the demon. However, we were all agreed, that it was too cold and wet and that we wouldn't do it *that* night. We promised each other that at some equally unspecified time in the future, the four of us would meet up and solve the mystery of the hairy hands of Postbridge. Of course, we never did.

Instead, we spent the evening getting mildly pissed on cheap cider, making jokes and boosting each other's egos by telling each other how clever and brave we were. Just before 10 o'clock Katie told us, sadly, that there was a curfew for the girls' dormitory and that she would have to go. As the other two were a little unsteady on their feet, I walked Katie back to the main block, and as I wished her goodnight, she - totally unexpectedly- threw her arms around my neck and kissed me. Gently, she eased my lips apart and slipped her sweet, velvety tongue into my mouth, and we kissed for several minutes before she ran inside.

I walked back to the laboratory feeling about ten feet tall. It had been a pretty good day, I thought. Okay, we hadn't seen the monster, but for the first time in my life, I had kissed a girl. And, like Michael Valentine Smith, I found that kissing girls "beats the hell out of card games!"

Sadly, events after that were somewhat anti-climactic. Katie came to see us the next morning to say goodbye, but the magical intimacy of the previous night was gone. She wrote her telephone number on a cigarette packet for me, but I lost it on the way home and I never saw her again. However, I was more convinced than ever that I knew what I wanted to do with my life apart from kissing girls. I wanted to be a monster hunter.

Soon after these events, Paul lost interest in things cryptozoological, and although we remained friends, our paths drifted apart. Jim and I, however had another - and rather more sinister - monster-hunting adventure to come the following summer.

It is quite strange how Fortean concepts have so quickly become assimilated into the mainstream of western culture and consciousness. The word "teleport," for example, has now become a familiar part of the English language due to television programmes like *Star Trek* but did you know that the term was first coined nearly a century ago by the American Philosopher Charles Fort, who has become the guru of those of us who spend our life studying unsolved mysteries? He came up with the concept to explain how some animals seem to be able to defy logic by turning up in areas where they could not possibly have arrived by any natural means.

This is a phenomenon that occurs throughout the natural world. The Queen of the Termite species, *Macrotermes bellicosus,* is so grotesquely huge that it is practically immobile. However, on innumerable occasions there have been reports of them disappearing from one tiny cell within the termite nest, only to reappear in a different one when the connecting corridors are plainly far too small to allow her to traverse through them.

The annals of Fortean literature are full of stories of ponds and lakes, which though completely artificial, and which have never been stocked by their owners are nevertheless found, overnight, to be stocked with a healthy population of fish of various ages.

Another term that has become synonymous with television science fiction is "Shape Shifter". Once again, this is not just a convenient way of introducing an interesting new plot twist into a science fiction book, but it has its analogues within the annals of Fortean and folkloric research throughout the ages. In this section of the book we shall be looking at a selection of folkloric accounts of animal shape-shifters from over the ages.

It is interesting, however, to note, that the belief in such things was widespread, on Dartmoor at least, well within my lifetime. The folklorist Ruth St Ledger Gordon, writing in 1965 in a book called *Witchcraft and Folklore of Dartmoor* noted that in 1961 (only four decades before this present volume was written):

"...when visiting a small village I was asked quite seriously whether I had heard of animals on the moor not being quite what they seemed. In explanation I was told of old moormen who knew from the behaviour or appearance of some particular sheep, bullock or pony that it was not a true beast but only a semblance of one. The idea seemed to be that some elemental or malignant spirit had temporarily assumed the form of the animal in question and was grazing with the herd or flock."

There is a long history of lycanthropy in Devonshire. Indeed, the Sherlock Holmes Society who, amongst other things, publish stories featuring the fictional detective which have been written by their members, include a short story entitled *The Werewolf of Devon* amongst their archive. This novel, by Paul Boler, is the third of three Holmes novels that he has written that contain Fortean themes. In his words:

"The first novel pits Sherlock Holmes against Jack the Ripper in 1888 London. In writing this narrative, I strove to include two essential elements. First of all, I wanted to speak with Conan Doyle's voice and not my own and secondly, I tried to follow the Ripper's actual agenda as to time, place, circumstances and the persona of each of his victims.

The second story fulfills a promise Sir Arthur once made to one day tell the tale of "The Giant Rat of Sumatra", a story for which the world is not yet prepared ...

The third story finds Holmes and Watson once again on the moors of Devonshire where they had pursued the Hound some 15 years earlier. This time they are after a creature more evil, more demonic and more deadly dangerous than the hound ever was."

I wrote to him:

"Dear Mr Boler,

I was interested to discover that you had written a novel about lycanthropy in Devon. I have been researching the mysterious zoofauna of the County for years and wondered whether you were aware that there is, indeed a long and rather

macabre history of werewolves, as well as other shapeshifting creatures in the county?
Best wishes, Jon Downes (Director, The Centre for Fortean Zoology)."

He wrote back: "No, I wasn't. I sent Holmes & Watson to Devon because that was where they had pursued the Hound of the Baskervilles some 15 years earlier. Paul."

A few days later I wrote asking him of his influences in writing his nu-Holmesian stories. Again, he replied promptly:

"Dear Jon, I have only been to England once--in 1993 with my middle daughter--and we only got as far as Exeter, so unfortunately for both myself & the yarn I wanted to spin, I did not get to see the real moors, but Doyle describes them fairly well in his story. I have been a great fan of Conan Doyle since adolescence. He never got to write the story about the Giant Rat of Sumatra he refers to in one of his tales, and I always wondered what it would have been like. Also, a lot of Holmes's cases take place in the 1880's London of Jack the Ripper, so I decided to write novels on both of those subjects as well as the narrative I sent you. Personally, of the 3, I like the werewolf story the best. However, I think that socially the Ripper's murders had a profound effect on East London because they led to reforms in that part of the city, which might not otherwise have happened for a long time. Paul."

I'm not going to come out with any of the old cliches about life imitating art, but the whole affair is curious because there is a long and sordid history of lycanthropy in Devonshire. A particularly interesting series of accounts took place in the valleys on the northern edge of Exmoor, near Lynton in North Devon. The earliest account comes from the pen of Elliot O'Donnell who wrote:

"A woman I met in Tavistock told me she had seen a ghost which she believed to be that of a werewolf, in the Valley of the Doones, Exmoor. She was walking home alone, late one evening, when she saw on the path directly in front of her the tall grey figure of a man with a wolf's head. Advancing stealthily forward, this creature was preparing to spring on a large rabbit that was crouching on the ground, apparently too terror stricken to move, when the abrupt appearance of a stag bursting through the bushes caused it to vanish."

A strikingly similar account from the same region comes from Devon naturalist and folklorist Trevor Beer writing in 1986:

"Even more macabre is the story received from an Ilfracombe gentleman who gave us his name and address but asked that it was not used. I feel that only publicity of this sad case will resolve this evil horror and bring about a happy ending' he states. In fact the following is merely a shortened version of the full story written but the writer reserved copyright, to use his own words, and thus we respect his wishes on this point. The story goes back to the late fifties when the writer was out rabbiting with his dog. Climbing a hedge he stumbled upon an animal ravaging a flock of sheep and taking careful aim he shot it, knowing that he had wounded the animal, the beast rearing onto its hind legs to run off in this fashion into the woods. The dog followed the animal into the trees where there was much hideous snarling unlike any creature he had ever heard before. Suddenly the dog came dashing out of the woods and bolted past its master who, firing a second shot into the trees, also ran for home in great fear.

"The writer went on to explain his later studies of matters concerning the occult and his realisation that the animal he had shot was a Werewolf and a member of a well known local family. Lycanthropy, a form of madness where humans imagine and fully believe they are animals, was also referred to. The writer states further that he knows the family involved and that they called in help from the church over a decade ago but that they had to withdraw because of the terrible phenomena beyond their comprehension. Now the problem is at a stalemate, the family being aware of the nature of his character and chaining him and locking him behind barred doors every night."

Interestingly enough, when I was at school in Bideford in the early 1970s, a similar story was told about one of the older houses on the outskirts of the village of Abbotsham a few miles outside Bideford. It was very much a friend-of-a-friend tale - everyone knew about the "beast" and its predations, that were supposed to be on sheep; although the creature - whilst in human form - was (according to some versions of the tale) said to have made homosexual advances towards various local schoolboys. Needless to say no one ever admitted to having had first hand experience either of the werewolf or the pederast, but I am certain that the story is still deep in the labyrinthine memories of a whole generation of the scions of Bideford Grammar School.

However, the stories I had heard as a young teenager impressed me enough to want to investigate more. I was twelve or thirteen and at that time and I was convinced that I could outrun any "dirty old man in a mac" (or even a dirty old werewolf). I hadn't any more than the vaguest idea of what homosexuality was, and didn't really care. I was young, brave and intrepid, and Jim, whose aid I had enlisted in this noble expedition, had an air pistol - so I knew everything was going to be quite alright.

At that time I lived in a tiny village called Woolfardisworthy, which was about nine miles from Bideford. However, reasonably regularly I visited my friend Jim for the weekend and on one June weekend Jim and I conspired to go werewolf hunting.

We left Jim's house soon after breakfast and cheerfully walked along Abbotsham Road, past our school gates towards the village where the werewolf was supposed to have his haunt. We walked along the very same lanes that *Stalky and Co.* had explored a century or so before, and although they are very different now, thirty years ago, only the thinnest veneer of tarmacadam made any difference at all to the landscape explored by Kipling and his tearaway friends in the 1880s.

The hedgerows were alight with Mayflowers and honeysuckle, but as we approached the village of Abbotsham, and the coast path that led towards Abbotsham Cliffs these were replaced by gorse and furze, and the silver washed fritillaries which hawked up and down the hedgerows like stealth bombers over Iraq, were replaced by the ethereal fluttering holly blues, and the exotic and slightly sinister beauty of the day flying burnet moths.

Climbing over a field gate at a predetermined point, our expedition became an illegal one, as we shamelessly trespassed across farmer's fields towards our destination. About a mile and a half from the road that we had left was the beginnings of a wood. This was, allegedly at least, the beginning of our destination, and we started to feel a little uneasy.

Sheepishly we entered the wood. Neither of us were boy scouts so our woodcraft was not of the kind of which Baden-Powell would have approved; but we had both read *Swallows and Amazons* so we felt that we vaguely knew what we were doing. In all my life of wandering through woods, forests, thickets, jungles and rain forests across the world I have never come across one that was completely silent. Except for this one.

Here and there one could see the mangled and dilapidated remains of a rhododendron bush, indicating that this had once been a carefully managed piece of woodland. Now it was just abandoned wilderness. It felt to us like we were the only visitors here for decades - if not longer. There was absolutely no sound except for the crunching noise of twigs and dead leaves scrunching beneath our feet. No bird song, no buzzing insects, no tiny scurrying animals.

Then we noticed something else strange. Apart from the occasional dirty grey-green of the sickly rhododendron leaves, there was practically no colour. Although it was midsummer, all the trees and bushes, at eye level anyway, appeared to be dead. If you looked up, you could see the outline of the leafy canopy silhouetted against the blue sky, but down here in the wood itself it was as dead as a morgue.

We carried on in silence. We were both uncomfortable but neither of us wanted to be the first to suggest that discretion should be the better part of valour and that we should get the hell out of there as quickly as possible. So we carried on. After what seemed like a lifetime (but was probably only about half an hour) the undergrowth began to thin out and before us we could see a rusty, three-strand barbed wire fence. Being the intrepid souls that we were, we didn't hesitate to clamber over. I tore the seat of my jeans to blazes and was soundly scolded by my mother when I got home - but that is another, and completely irrelevant story.

We carried on through the wood, and it wasn't long before we realised that we were approaching the edge of what appeared to be a large and completely overgrown garden, which was nearly as badly tended as the wood had been. However, at least here there were signs of life; and the terrible feeling of black oppression that had been the *genius loci* of the wood behind us was gone.

Realising that whereas before we had been trespassing and we could probably have got away with it, there was now no doubt that we were perpetrating a criminal act, and furthermore, perpetrating a criminal act on the property of a rich and influential local landowner who may or may not have been a governor of our school, we became very stealthy indeed. If such a thing as a time machine existed, it would, I am sure, surprise the heck out of any of my friends and colleagues (who have only known me as an overweight, and clumsy middle aged man who often walks with a stick), to have seen me thirty years ago as a very stealthy thirteen year old who had read enough books about Red Indians to know how to glide from bush to bush in a relatively inconspicuous manner.

As we progressed around the perimeter of the dilapidated old garden, we suddenly saw the most wonderful sight of our young lives. The 1960s may have made sexual liberation *de rigueur* amongst certain sections of society, but back in 1972 the thirteen-year-old Jonathan Downes had only the vaguest idea of what a naked woman actually looked like.

By modern standards, the girlie magazines of the era were pretty prudish and I had only ever seen a few of them, and the anything-goes culture of the internet where every conceivable sexual taste can be viewed at the click of a mouse button was a generation in front of us. I had no sisters or any close female relatives, and although I was painfully aware of the theoretical differences between boys and girls, I was far too shy to have ever had a girlfriend. Although Jim had a rather cute sister a year younger than him, they came from a strict Methodist family and I am certain that he was as innocent as me, and was as amazed and overjoyed as I was, when we crept, Red Indian style, around the bushes on the edge of a clearing and saw, lying on a blanket in the middle of the small patch of grass, a naked girl of about our age.

She was obviously sunbathing and was lying on her tummy, blissfully unaware that only a dozen yards or so away two gobsmacked teenaged boys were crouching in the long grass staring at her. She was perfect, like a wood nymph. Even now, three decades later, the memory of her long, muscular legs, dirty blonde shoulder length hair, straight back, and slim, almost boyish buttocks conjures up the classic image of femininity for me. Jim and I crouched in the long grass for at least ten minutes watching her and drinking in every possible aspect to savour in our minds over the years ahead.

Believe it or not, this wasn't a sexually voyeuristic thing. It was more an almost religious experience when for the first time we understood what the immortal and non-existent Lazarus Long had meant when he said "what a wonderful world it is that has girls in it."

Then, joy of joys, she turned over, and for a few brief minutes, as she lay on her back with her eyes shut we grokked in their fullness every detail of her breasts, her belly, and that mysterious dark triangle between her thighs. Then she sat up and opened her eyes.

The spell was broken. We knew that she hadn't seen us, but the probable repercussions if we had been caught not only trespassing in the private garden of one of our school governors; but, spying on someone who was most probably his naked daughter, were too grim to contemplate. Taking one last look at the naked wood nymph, who had managed to destroy her image of Elysian loveliness by hauling on a Donny Osmond T shirt and lighting a cigarette, we decided that discretion was the better part of valour and crept back towards the deserted wood.

By this time we had forgotten that our original quest had been for a werewolf. I don't think either of us had actually fully believed in the legend, and, to be quite honest, we weren't even sure if the garden in which we had spied upon the naked girl, was the one that belonged to the house that reputedly harboured the semi-human beast. Anyway, we were hungry, there were fifty pence pieces burning figurative holes in our pockets, and there was a little shop back on the outskirts of Northam that sold the most delicious pasties known to man. We decided to take what we believed was the most direct path through the wood to get to Northam where we could eat pasties, drink pop and relive our adventure of the morning.

We set off in what we fondly believed was the right direction for Northam. Although we were undoubtedly intrepid, direction finding was not our strong suit and we soon became hopelessly lost. As we went deeper and deeper into the wood the atmosphere became more and more unpleasant.

The wood was still oppressively silent, but now, it seemed to us, that it was not just the absence of birdsong or insects - but the absence of *anything*. The nearest analogy that I can come to this happened to me about seven years later when I was visiting Toronto. I was visiting the Natural Science Museum to see the impressive, though horrific, exhibition of mounted passenger pigeons, when I was sidetracked into a gallery where elementary physics experiments were being demonstrated to High School children. Well, although I wasn't a High School pupil, I wasn't much older, and found the displays both interesting and informative. However, one, in particular, freaked me out completely. It was a room that had been lined with some sort of total sound insulating board so that when you entered it you could hear nothing at all except for the sounds of your own body. Even your footsteps on the ground were silent. The *only* sounds that you could hear were those of your bodily functions and any sounds you happened to utter.

This exhibit freaked me out mightily because, just for a second, I was back in the middle of that evil wood in North Devon, and this time I didn't even have my mate, Jim, there to keep me company.

Back in 1972, we were moving as fast as we could. By this time we had completely lost interest in the Northam bun shop. We just wanted to get the hell out of this accursed wood. Then it hit us. A stench such as I have never encountered before or since rolled up towards us through the shrivelled, blighted, stunted trees. Now, I have examined dead animals in the tropics where corpses are reduced to a putrefying mess within hours. I have observed a human autopsy and have conducted dissections of creatures ranging from a woodlouse to a bottlenosed dolphin. I have seen quite a few dead humans, some in particularly unpleasant conditions. On one occasion I even ended up giving attempted mouth-to-mouth resuscitation to a corpse that had drowned on its own vomit. I am not a squeamish man, and I was an even less squeamish youth, but this smell was the most disgusting that I have ever encountered.

We proceeded gingerly. If it hadn't been that we were acutely aware that it would have been appallingly unmanly, I'm sure that we would have held each other's hands for comfort. In fact, if I'm going to be honest, with the hindsight of thirty years, I'm not certain that we didn't. The stench was all-pervading, and although we did our best to avoid whatever its source was, it felt like we were being inexorably drawn towards the epicentre of the phenomenon.

Then suddenly there it was: a dead roebuck, its head caught in a barbed-wire fence and its tortured body splayed out behind it, bloated with putrefaction. Its intestines were spread out besides it. Two and a half decades later I was to encounter a similar phenomenon. As I wrote in my 1999 book, *The Rising of the Moon,* a similar occurrence took place during the summer of 1997:

"A mutilated roebuck was found at a nature reserve on Woodbury Common during the height of the UFO activity in August. Interestingly, although the animal was too decomposed for any thorough examination of its wounds, it had been dismembered and both its legs and head were detached from its body. There were, however, no teeth marks as one would expect from predation by 'normal' carnivores, nor were there the marks of knives, which would have been found on the bones if the animal had been butchered by a human. Again, although the evidence is not conclusive, and indeed the investigation has not yet been concluded, it appears that this unfortunate beast may have been a genuine UFO related animal mutilation!"

I have no idea whether there had been any strange lights seen in the sky over the Torridge estuary at the time that the poor unfortunate beast we found in 1972 had died; and to be quite honest I don't really care, because to this day I am convinced that I know what killed it. In the half-light we could see an amorphous shadow of what appeared to be an enormous black predatory creature crouching over the carcass of the roebuck. If you looked at it directly there was nothing to see, but out of the corners of our eyes it was clearly visible. That was just too much for our last vestiges of intrepidness and the two of us, explorers no longer but frightened children, ran like hell until we finally found ourselves on the cliff path which traverses the long journey between Abbotsham and Westward Ho!

We were back in the sunshine. We were safe. And we never spoke about what had happened again. Soon afterwards our friendship disintegrated in the way that adolescent friendships often do. We never fell out but simply grew apart. It was as if the burden of our shared experience that day was too much for two adolescents to be able to bear and still remain friends.

Not only did we see our first naked female body that day, but, to this day, I am convinced that that we also encountered the Abbotsham werewolf. With the benefit of hindsight I'm not too sure that the two events weren't somehow interlinked.

The years passed. An elderly relative died and left enough money to send my brother and me to a minor public school on the edges of Exmoor. It was a particularly horrid time in my life. There, I found it even more difficult to avoid the twin spectres of "School Spirit" and compulsory sports. I lasted two and a half terms before being expelled. I left home to work in Exeter, and later moved to Bracknell in Berkshire. After a few misadventures I moved to Canada in the summer of 1979, but after a few months I came back again. I was rootless, shiftless and miserable. I got a job in Bideford as a nurse for the mentally handicapped, I managed a local punk band for a while, and I took a lot of drugs.

Nearly a decade after Jim's and my adventure I was back on Abbotsham Cliffs. It was the autumn of 1981 and I was a young, arty punk rocker with an obsessive interest in exploring alternative realities as a tool to achieving a path of spiritual development. This path, for me and my cronies, at least, took the form of ingesting large amounts of psilocybin mushrooms (often washed down with neat gin), listening to *Metal Box* by *Public Image Limited* and waiting for a spiritual revelation which never arrived. It so happened that the best magic mushrooms in the area grew on Abbotsham Cliffs.

Looking back, I am fairly certain that the mental health problems which have plagued me intermittently ever since started during the beautiful Indian summer of 1981, when, fuelled by Timothy Leary, Carlos Castaneda and other gurus of brain damage, I joined in a series of psychic experiments that certainly precipitated my first, temporary, descent into madness and terror. I am also pretty sure that in some strange way the horrific experiences that I am about to describe are linked, surely and inextricably with Jim's and my innocent hunt for a werewolf during the summer of 1972.

Our psychic drug experiments started innocently enough. Initially, we just wanted to see what all the fuss was about. My first magic mushroom trip took place under the vague supervision of a fey young man called Danny Miles. Years later he turned up again, and the resulting mayhem is described in my book *The Blackdown Mystery*. In that book I describe how we first met, and I make no apologies for repeating the passage here:

"I first met Danny Miles at an obscure North Devon rock festival during the late summer of 1981. In those days I was an innocent and not very streetwise fellow in my early twenties, and I still believed that world peace could be achieved by the ingestion of various noxious substances whilst sitting in muddy fields listening to musical ensembles make whooshing noises on (what seem to me now) to be very primitive synthesisers.

I was, I believe, watching Hawkwind playing a spectacularly inept version of 'Master of the Universe', and like most of the rest of the audience, who were cold, muddy and uncomfortable, pretending that I was enjoying myself whilst in reality I was in dire need of both a lavatory and a nice cup of tea and totally unwilling to avail myself of the horribly rudimentary versions of either facility that had been laid on for our "comfort" by the euphemistically named "organisers" of the event. About a hundred yards to my right were the serried ranks of the local Hells Angel fraternity who were encamped *en masse* like an iron-clad phalanx of doom. It was only twelve years after Altamont, and even in the bucolic wastelands of rural Devon, they felt that they had something to live up to. Unfortunately, for me at least, they had decided to set up camp immediately between the area where I had set up my tiny tent and parked my car and the main exit, and several of the nastiest and meanest looking of them were patrolling the area armed with pool cues and what I think were hollowed-out pickaxe handles that had been filled with molten lead. I was therefore somewhat marooned, and feeling uncomfortable, isolated, alone and more than a little frightened.

Suddenly, in the middle of what appeared to me to be a sea of greasy black leather jackets, emerged a delicate, fey looking figure, wearing an extraordinary array of satins and silks in a variety of peacock colours. It looked for all the world as if one of the gaily coloured inhabitants of one of Arthur Rackham's fairy paintings had suddenly been transported into the middle of a field of leather-clad Neanderthals. The figure tripped gaily towards me, and appeared to my addled brain to be floating like a surreal, and rainbow-hued butterfly above the sea of mud and motorbikes. As it got closer I could see that it was a youth, hardly old enough to shave with an angelic halo of light brown hair surrounding a face that was covered with intricate paintings of butterflies and lotus flowers. He came and sat next to me and my companions.

Much to my amazement everyone else who was with me seemed to take this apparition in their stride. "'Lo Danny", one of them grunted cheerfully, "'ow are y'doing?". Another friend asked him what the hell he had been doing wandering blithely through the middle of the taciturn, unfriendly and potentially dangerous crowd of bikers. "Ahhhhh, they're harmless." he said, in an Irish accent that he seemed to be able to turn on and off at will, "and anyway they wouldn't hurt me...I am legion, I am many".

His name was Danny Miles, and for reasons known best to himself he had recently adopted the *nom-de-guerre* of 'Legion the Cosmic Dancer'. I got to know him reasonably well over the next few years, and he would occasionally drift into my life, causing chaos for a few weeks and then disappear as simply as he had arrived. During the years when fashions were led by *Culture Club* and the New Romantics, Danny was in his element. He paraded his omnisexuality for all to see like some magnificent, (if slightly deranged) bird of paradise and flirted outrageously with boys and girls alike. As the decade of Thatcherism advanced and my life became more normal, and I drifted into my disastrous marriage and the twin pitfalls of a job and a mortgage I saw less of him, but he would still turn up once in a while, and we would sit up long into the night, drinking wine, gazing at the stars and talking about nothing in particular as I dreamed dreams of my lost youth.

But strangely, Danny never seemed to either grow any older or to settle down.

It was Danny, who one night in late August. arrived unannounced on the doorstep of my flat in Northam with a little plastic bag full of dried and shrivelled fungi which he then proceeded to make into the most disgusting "tea" that I have ever tasted. He persuaded me to drink the revolting stuff with him, and sitting side by side we sat back on my sofa, listening to loud rock music and waiting for something to happen.

Nothing did.

Then, there was a knock on the door. It was my new next-door neighbours coming to pay a courtesy call and introduce themselves. I have always noticed in life that the sort of person who has a notice on her office wall saying: "You don't have to be crazy to work here but it helps," is usually the most annoying, pointless and conformist person in the building. If you can imagine a family of people like that you can imagine my new next-door neighbours. They were pleasant, well-meaning people, but I think that they were rather taken aback when they found that they were now living next door to a wild eyed man with spikey hair and a wispy beard and his outrageously camp friend. The fact that we were both beginning what was my first, but by no means my last, experiment with psychedelic drugs was also a definite negative point.

We invited them in, but the thick smell of incense and the strains of *The Grateful Dead* intoning *Anthem of the Sun* out of my hi-fi speakers seemed to phase them somewhat. We gave them cold beers from the fridge, but when I noticed my guest's face beginning to look like he was wearing clown makeup it was definitely time for us to get rid of them. I can't remember how we managed it, but we hustled them out of the door without causing major offence, and I then settled back to experience my first "trip."

It was like nothing I had experienced before: My body felt like it was being bombarded by tiny bubbles and I found myself swimming in a sea of shifting images and glorious glowing colours. Occasionally I would find myself drifting into an ugly or disturbing place where I really didn't want to be, but Danny - to my eternal gratitude - would coax me out of it, and I would continue with the positive, joyous aspects of the experience.

After about five hours I began to come down, and I realised that this alternate reality was something that I wanted to explore further, and so I began a pattern that would last pretty well solidly for the rest of that year.

If I had known that, twenty years later, I would be diagnosed with a serious psychotic disorder, and that during my bad periods I would have similar experiences *every* night, but without the aid of stimulants and more importantly without the aid of someone to talk me out of it, I don't think I would have touched magic mushrooms (or peyote, which I tried soon after) with the proverbial bargepole, but I did, and there is nothing I can do to change it. As my grandmother once said to me when I was a very small boy "if ifs and ands were pots and pans we'd all be travelling tinkers" and this is something I have believed solidly ever since. Once something is done, it's done - and there ain't nothing you can do about it!

Over the next few days Danny introduced me to such books as *The Doors of Perception* by Aldous Huxley and various writings by Timothy Leary. By this time, our nightly trips were taken *en masse* with a group of friends, and after a week or so Danny evolved the ritual of guiding us through the trip by reading excerpts from the *Tibetan Book of the Dead* and other esoteric scriptures.

I can't remember whose idea it was, but at the end of October someone suggested that we should follow in the footsteps of Carlos Castaneda and indulge in a group psychedelic experience out of doors. The idea was to somehow contact the spirit of the sacred mushroom on the psychic plane, although it has to be admitted that most of those present (including me) thought of it more as a groovy and rather daring Halloween party. I was really looking forward to it until I discovered that, in his wisdom, Danny had decided to hold this experiment on Abbotsham Cliffs. In many ways this made a lot of sense. If there actually *was* a sacred mushroom spirit, it stood to reason that he would reside amongst the more tangible proofs of his existence, and as already stated, at the time at least, the best magic mushrooms in the area grew at Abbotsham Cliffs.

I was a little uneasy. Although nine years had passed and I had tried to put the matter out of my mind I had never entirely forgotten the events of June 1972. But, I rationalised wildly displaying a capacity for self-delusion that was remarkable even by my standards. *That* had been in the woodlands several miles along the cliffs. *And* it had been in summer. *And* we had been looking for the werewolf. This time we were engaged on a mystical quest for the spirit of the sacred mushroom. It was *obvious* that nothing nasty could possibly happen.

On Halloween night, seven or eight of us camped out on the flat land just behind Abbotsham Cliffs. There were three girls and four or five guys, all dressed in the punk styles that were then *de rigueur*. Cheerfully, we parked our cars in the lay-by, and in the late afternoon sunshine t was a cheerful party that walked the half-mile or so along the footpath to the cliffs. Although it was the end of October it was surprisingly warm, and the two elderly sheep grazing on the scrubland by the cliffs gave the place a delightfully bucolic air.

We built a large bonfire and as the final rays of the setting sun disappeared into the Bristol Channel, Danny, in his self appointed role of showman and shaman came around and dispensed what he described as his "funky communion." It was a potent mixture of gin, mushroom tea, peyote and LSD and was the precursor to one of the most horrific nights of my life. It was a night that I shall certainly never forget, and which I seriously suspect will be permanently etched on the psyches of everyone involved.

The evening started pleasantly enough, because although the chemical mixture that we had ingested was incredibly powerful, the mixture of the pleasantly sylvan surroundings, and what we hadn't yet learned to call "chill out" music issuing from what we hadn't yet learned to call a "ghetto blaster" kept everyone in a mellow and happy state of mind.

Danny started to read aloud from *The Tibetan Book of the Dead* and then began to recite Aleister Crowley's *Hymn to Pan*. None of us realised at the time, but Danny was (knowingly or unknowingly) manipulating the situation like a master. Although everyone was hallucinating heavily by this time, the three girls in particular seemed heavily affected and, encouraged by Danny, started to behave in a most uncharacteristic manner. Despite their Mohicans and studiously torn clothes they were actually very reserved young ladies on the whole; but coaxed by Danny they started to become very affectionate and sensual. They danced rhythmically to the music and kissed and stroked each other, the guys in the group (including me) and particularly Danny.

One plump girl called "Sarah" [not her real name because I see her around Exeter sometimes, and she is now an eminently respectable, professional lady] who boasted the particularly unpleasant punk soubriquet of "Scab" even started to undress and dance semi naked in the firelight.

It would be easy for me to pretend that some sort of totally far out hippy orgy then ensued, but it didn't. Most of the people who were there were too drunk, too stoned, and far too tripped out to perform sexually. I know I was, but again under coaxing from Danny, "Scab" and one of the guys coupled - I won't say 'made love' because there was no love, emotion or tenderness - just animal rutting in the firelight as Danny chanted lines from Crowley and the rest of us looked on giggling inanely and waving our hands about to the rhythmic beat of the music.

Eventually everyone passed out, and that was when the fear came.

I have spent more of my life than I like to admit in alternate states of consciousness. Once upon a time I believed it was because I was exploring a genuinely alternative route to spiritual self-empowerment. Nowadays I believe that all that is rubbish. If there is such a thing as an interventionist God, and I am pretty damn sure that there is, I am sure that he/she would not wish the objects of his/her creation to perform acts of supplication by poisoning themselves. Although the concept of trying to second guess a deity is a pretty dodgy one, the theories of trying to reach nirvana through substance abuse is *also* a pretty dodgy one. I haven't taken psychedelics since that terrible night in 1981. These days when I go to a different place it is usually with alcohol, or prescribed tranquillisers and occasionally with the fruit of the poppy. And these days, when I take drugs it isn't to reach some magickal and non-existent nirvana - it is purely and simply to blot out the fear.

I am convinced that the fear first came to me on All Hallow's Eve 1981.

I don't know how long we had been lying on the bare cold ground. The fire had all but gone out and all that was left were some feebly glowing embers. I don't know what it was that made me wake up because all was still. The only sound was the sea breaking on the rocky shore a hundred yards or so away. Then, on the other side of the campfire someone or something began to moan. I thought at first that it was one of my companions, suffering a bad dream or a worse trip, but the noise was too steady, too rhythmical and too unearthly to be human.

Unlike some people, I had always known which parts of the psychedelic experience were real, and which were chemically induced hallucinations. However it has to be said, in my defence, that I had never before or since imbibed such a potentially lethal cocktail of psychoactive drugs. At the time I felt that I was entirely awake, completely straight and that whatever it was that was happening to me was part of my own objective reality. However I may have been wrong. I may have been dreaming, I may have been hallucinating, or it may have been the first glimmerings of the madness that was to plague me in later life. Maybe it was a bit of all three - or maybe not.

The dull, thrumming moan continued, and was joined by another and another in a weird unearthly harmony such as I have never heard since. As a musician and composer I have sometimes, in idle moments, tried to recapture the sound using computer generated sound programmes, or old analogue synthesisers which I have lying about the house, but I have never come close. It was like nothing else I have ever experienced, and, I hope against all hope, that it is something that I will never experience again.

Then the sky began to change colour. The deep midnight blue was subtly changed into something else. Something was not quite right. H. P.Lovecraft wrote of a place where "The Angles are Wrong," but that night Abbotsham Cliffs became a place where the colours were wrong. The only time I have ever experienced anything even approximating what I saw that night was during the total solar eclipse of August 1999.

At the time I was working as editor of a magazine called *Quest* that was published by a rampant crook called Roy Bird. His company had an appalling reputation for not paying their debts, not honouring their subscriptions, and not parting with any money whatsoever. Bird was always investing cash in hare-brained schemed and promotions which were usually cancelled before they actually happened, with Bird pocketing whatever money had been sent in advance ticket sales.

One promotion of his that actually *did* come to pass was a cross-channel cruise to coincide with the solar eclipse. The ferry was to sail along the line of totality so that we on board could get the best possible view of what was, at least in the UK, a once in a lifetime experience.

As the disc of the sun slowly disappeared I began to feel a very primal panic. I ceased to be an intelligent and reasonably cultured middle-aged writer and surprisingly quickly reverted to being a primal savage. I clutched my then girlfriend Maxine's hand, and much to my surprise I found that tears were rolling down my cheeks. I looked around, embarrassed. Even more to my surprise I realised that most of the people I could see were crying. This was just something so completely alien to any of our shared life experience. From our earliest days, daytime meant the sun, even if it was hidden behind clouds, and for the first time in any of our lives - and there were about 1500 people on the ferry - the sun had disappeared. The rational part of my brain *knew* perfectly well that this was only an uncommon astronomical phenomenon. The sun (like it says in the song) had been "eclipsed by the moon" and I knew perfectly well that, in a few minutes, everything would be back to normal in the UK for the next seventy-four years.

However, emotionally I knew no such thing. I was like an ancient savage who believed that the celestial sphere had been devoured by the inexorable force of the daemonic serpent-dragon and in my heart of hearts I was convinced that the sun had gone for good, and that within the blink of a cosmic eye, I, together with all life on earth would shrivel and die away forever.

The worst thing about this sunless world was the strange, colourless, half-light. Everything was tinged with a murky and unpleasant shade of puce. It was as if the creator had finally tired of the antics of his unruly and ungrateful servants and vomited back all the collected prayers, hopes and fears of mankind throughout the ages all over the pantheon of his creation. The entire world was the colour of vomit, and for what seemed like a lifetime, although I was in the middle of a crowd of 1500 people together with my then lover and many of my closest friends, I felt utterly desolate in a world which God - or at least the oldest God known to mankind - had deserted.

As I lay on the cold turfs of Abbotsham Cliffs I was filled with the same feeling of isolation. The sky, and indeed the rest of the landscape, didn't have the puce vomit stains of the world in the middle of the Eclipse, but was just as wrong. The colours just didn't make sense. Two decades later I am no nearer to describing the colours I was viewing than I was then. However, the colours were so different from anything I had ever experienced that, although I was still lying on the edge of Abbotsham Cliffs, I was actually in a world completely alien - not only to me but to the rest of the human race.

I felt that this was a world that had never known humans, and where humans were not welcome. The strange moaning continued, and it seemed to blend in inextricably with the sound of the surf breaking on the rocks below. Years later I was to discover that only twenty or so miles along the coast to the east, well within living memory, the people of Lynton believed that they could hear the song of the sea - or perhaps it was the merfolk who live in the sea. And although the song was beautiful, it was also deadly: whenever anyone heard it, a sudden and usually bloody and gruesome death was sure to follow.

The sound wasn't music; at least not in the way that either you or I understand the term music. Like the landscape it was completely alien, and part of a world where human beings were simply not welcome. By this time the sky was surprisingly light, but the full moon, which beamed mercilessly down upon us, is impossible to describe. If you can imagine the dying glimmer in your pet dog's eyes as the lethal injection takes effect, or the sickly glimmer of a streetlight engulfed in the smoke from a house-fire then you might have the beginnings of an idea of the horrible, deathly light which threw the landscape into sharp, two dimensional relief.

I sat up, and looked around me. I could see my companions sitting up also. All except for "Scab" who was lying, still naked, spread-eagled as if crucified on the smooth turf.

We were all silent and completely motionless. The horrid moaning harmonies became louder and louder and as we looked on horrified we could see that we weren't alone. I am using the plural rather than the singular because I assume - indeed I *have* to assume - that the other people there saw the same thing that I did.

We weren't alone: there was a total stranger in our midst. A naked female silhouette, that of a girl and much younger than us, was standing over "Scab's" supine body. She stood erect with her arms outstretched above her and her legs akimbo, perfectly mirroring the pose of the naked, plump punk girl lying at her feet.

The moaning noise continued, and it seemed to me that it was coming from the open mouth of this mysterious stranger. The noise got louder, and more rhythmical. It began to pulse like an African War Drum or an electronic oscillator. I don't know what happened next. It would be easy to say that this strange unearthly girl began to make love to "Scab" but this would be simplistic. They didn't even touch, but somehow in a strange and indescribable way they became one.

I suddenly felt paralysed and could see someone standing over me. It was the same girl, and as far as I could see, not only was she still standing over "Scab", but she was standing, completely naked, over everyone else in our party. Somehow she was everywhere and nowhere, something and everything and in at least eight places at once.

I looked up at her and felt a slight twinge of recognition. Could this be the same girl that Jim and I had spied upon eight years before? One thing was certain: the sound, which was getting painfully loud in my ears, was coming from her. It was her song but although, like her, it was beautiful in a strange way, it was a terrible song that no human being was every meant to hear.

Then she entered me. Without touching me she entered my body and my soul and took me to a level of sexual ecstasy that was quite beyond my comprehension. As we became one under the pale death-coloured moon, her song built up to a disgusting crescendo like a thousand rabid dogs howling and screaming at each other.

I passed out. When I woke up I was lying in a pool of my own vomit, and although the familiar scenery of Abbotsham Cliffs were back to normal I knew that I would never be the same again. I looked around at my companions of the night before. Everyone was dazed. One of the girls had covered "Scab" up with her overcoat and was trying to rouse her. The whole place smelt of death and decay, and at that moment I decided that I would never take psychedelic drugs again. And I never have.

On the way back to our cars we passed the stretch of pasture where, only the evening before, the two elderly sheep had been grazing. They were still there, but they were both dead. Although none of us investigated any closer, one appeared to have been ripped completely to pieces and the other had its throat torn out.

The only thing that any of the rest of us had in common was that we were friends of Danny's, so when I stopped taking psychedelic drugs, I stopped seeing the others. "Scab" works in an office in Exeter; and one day, whilst I was waiting for my psychotherapy appointment at Wonford House Psychiatric Hospital in Exeter during the early spring of 1998, I saw one of the other members of our jolly band. Now twenty years older, he had the sunken eyes and sallow skin of someone whose liver is beginning to fail after decades of substance abuse. Our eyes met for a moment. We recognised each other, but after all this time there was really nothing to say so we passed each other in silence.

As for Danny it was another eight months before I saw him again, but that is another story.

Could the girl have been a succubus - a female sexual daemon that preys on men? What was the hideous crouching predator Jim and I thought we had seen that summer's day in 1972? Could it and the girl have been the same thing? Could it all have been a bizarre and disturbing set of coincidences? I don't know what happened to us that night. I don't even know if *anything* happened except for a bunch of vulnerable young druggies playing psychedelic games under the tutelage of a very powerful and manipulative young man. I don't know whether the experience that I remember so vividly actually happened, or whether it was merely a drug-fuelled fantasy, which combined two voyeuristic episodes from my young life into an arcane synergy.

The last word on the North Devon werewolves came many years later - from a telephone-call to BBC Radio Devon in Exeter following on one of my weekly *Weird About the West* radio shows that ran between 1996 and 1998. It was from a young man called Chris (who asked not to be identified further), who had been visiting the Valley of the Rocks near Lynton the previous Sunday, when he saw what he described as a strange creature like "a man on all fours but covered in black shaggy hair," rushing across a field about a hundred yards away from him. There were sheep in the field but they appeared to ignore the "creature," which made no noise, and soon vanished from sight. It was only afterwards that Chris realised that the "creature" had been moving several feet *above* the surface of the ground.

I remain convinced that there is a very real mystery to solve in Abbotsham, and although my paths have strayed away from the sinister, dank woods at the top of the rugged cliffs that overlook the Bristol Channel, I have a sneaking suspicion that before my career as a monster hunter is over, I shall return there and solve the mystery once and for all.

CHAPTER THREE

OUTSIDE THE ASYLUM

In the spring of 1982 I left Bideford and moved, loc,k stock and barrel, to South Devon. After just over a year a working as a nursing assistant at a small unit for mentally handicapped people in North Devon, it seemed a good career move to become a qualified nurse. I did my training at one of the last of the Victorian asylums - an imposing Gothic edifice named the Royal Western Counties Hospital. It was situated at Starcross - a tiny village between Exeter and Dawlish, whose only claim to fame was that it had a loony bin situated in the middle of it. For such a tiny village, it surprisingly boasted four pubs. As the nursing profession - at the time at least - was not known for its abstemious lifestyle, it is not perhaps surprising, that each of the four pubs was largely populated with off-duty nurses, ex nurses, wannabe nurses, and *bona fide* nurses who were preparing to go on duty, found that alcohol was the only way to make a bloody awful job bearable. I soon became one of these.

Within months of commencing my training, I knew that I had made a mistake. Whereas, on a whole, I had enjoyed working with the patients at the Kingsley Hospital in Bideford, I soon found that the rampant paranoia which infested the nursing profession - especially in a hospital which was in the process of being closed down as Mrs. Thatcher enforced her doctrine of 'Care in the Community' on a community that didn't care - was just too weird for me to deal with. However, I had been brought up in the best traditions of the Empire - of a stiff upper lip, devotion to duty and *noblesse oblige*. I felt - stupidly as it turned out - that I had no option but to complete my training. It was the only honourable thing to do - or so I thought.

I was billeted at a glorious Edwardian house called 'Staplake'. It had once, obviously, been a desirable residence for one of the local gentry. However, in recent years it had become sadly down-at-heel, and had - at 20 or 30 years before - been bought by Exeter Health Authority as a nurses' home. It boasted a medium-sized garden with beautiful trees, and glance it to flower beds, and the house itself - that had something in the region of 15 bedrooms, some gorgeous baroque architecture, and the most impressive main staircase that I have ever seen (outside of a stately home), that was irresistibly reminiscent of one of the houses are described by Agatha Christie. If it had only had posessed a library, you would have been certain that there would have been a body in it.

It had two ghosts. Again, I will resist the temptation to rewrite history and pretend that I ever encountered one of them. I didn't. However, those of the younger and more impressionable female residents did - including my friend Sharon, and her best friend Alison; the girl who was later to become my wife. I have to admit that I can't remember the exact details of the ghosts. I have a sneaking suspicion that they were probably just as much the result of overactive imaginations fuelled with too much alcohol, as they were genuine paranormal phenomena.

Apart from the hospital, the village was dominated by two artifacts. The remains of Isambard Kingdom Brunel's spectacularly unsuccessful atmospheric railway, and the estates that surrounded Powderham Castle on the outskirts of the village. Powderham Castle was the home of the Earl of Devon, and had a rich and bloody history. It was surrounded by glorious forests, a deer park and acres of historic countryside. Over the next few years I was to have a number of quite peculiar adventures whilst trespassing happily in these woods.

The hospital itself - a sprawling Victorian edifice which has sadly, been pulled down - was also haunted. The older nurses, and nursing officers, took great delight in telling horror stories to each successive generation of young students and one of the horror stories - which apparently *was* true - concerned an unruly patient who had, allegedly, been put into an isolation ward - or side room - because of his disruptive and potentially harmful behaviour. He had been tranquillised, so that he would sleep it off. In complete contravention of the rules, a second patient was incarcerated in the side room with him. The result was deeply and nastily tragic. According to hospital folklore, while one of the patients was asleep, naked and huddled up on a mattress in the corner of the room, the other patient investigated his supine body. The sleeping patient had a prolapse of the rectum. The other patient found this fascinating, and pulled at it. The sleeping patient was so deeply drugged that he didn't wake up, and when staff came in the next morning they found that one of their patient was dead - disemboweled through the anus by the other who had pulled out all of his intestines, colon, and part of his stomach through the anal passage in a spirit of investigation. What became of surviving patient, or indeed whether - as one would suppose - the staff members responsible were prosecuted for gross negligence, no one seems to know.

Another story, which I am sure was told me in good faith, and which even now I do not know whether to believe, apparently took place during the Second World War. There had - apparently - been a number of occasions when captured German aircrew and pilots who had been shot down over South Devon or the English Channel were kept, temporarily, in a remote wing of Starcross hospital until they could be transferred to the prisoner-of-war camp high above Starcross on Haldon Hills. On one occasion - or so the story goes - the Home Guard had been searching for a fugitive German airman in the woods surrounding Powderham Castle about half-a-mile away from the hospital. They had ventured into the deepest parts of the wood in search of their quarry. Suddenly, the small band of elderly men and boys too young to join the Army saw, what they believed, was the fugitive airmen running through the woods in front of them. The leader shouted at him to stop, but to no avail. The old man who told me the story was actually one of the Home Guards, and he told me that one of the party had been a teacher in Germany before the war and could speak the language. "*Anhalten! Oder wir schiessen!*" he shouted, but the fugitive ignored him. In 1942, the war was not going well - at least as far as the British were concerned - and Home Guard units, especially in rural areas, were desperately under-equipped. Most of the patrol were only armed with pitchforks, although one had a dilapidated shotgun and the captain - who led the unit - had his old First World War service revolver. If it had been a normal patrol there would only have been about half-a-dozen of them, but large parts of Exeter had been levelled by successive waves of German bombers in what was known as the Baedekker raids and the opportunity for a population of a tiny village like Starcross to actually face the enemy on equal terms was an irresistible lure. According to my informant, the Home Guard patrol had been augmented by a gang of villagers baying for blood and desperate for revenge.

The captain was an educated man, and had no intention of using force to capture the fugitive unless it was absolutely necessary. The man with a shotgun - a local farmer who had lost two of his sons in the desperate weeks leading up to Dunkirk - had no such compunction. He was also drunk. Shouting, "I'll get you bastard!" He raised his weapon and fired. The dark figure ahead of them let out a grunt of agony and fell to the ground.

The captain was furious. He immediately put the drunken farmer under arrest and confiscated his shotgun. The party then ran on towards what they thought was an injured German airman, but they found, to their horror, that it was nothing of the sort. Instead of a proud member of the Luftwaffe, they found a naked man in his early twenties covered in hair and plastered in mud.

Even 40 years after the event, it was obvious that my informant had been badly shaken by this experience. He was an elderly retired nursing officer in his early seventies. Spared military service because of his profession, he had eagerly embraced the Home Guard as his opportunity to fight "The Hun", and it was equally obvious that that these years had been the happiest of his life. The rest of his professional career had been spent at the hospital, and he intimated that he had found the increasing struggle with a moribund bureaucracy exponentially tedious, and the when he was offered early retirement he was quite happy to spend the rest of his days fishing, and propping up of the corner of the bar in the pub which had been named after Brunel's spectacularly unsuccessful foray into setting up a mass transit railway system.

Apparently compulsory told me, the badly injured wild-man was taken to Starcross hospital in the middle of the night, and all efforts were made to make him comfortable. Then, in the early hours of the morning, apparently an unmarked black van had arrived, and two men in uniform, and another wearing a long white coat had manhandled the mysterious victim on to a stretcher, loaded him into the back of the van and taken him to an unknown destination. My informant never heard anything about the case again. However, he hinted that the authorities had warned everybody involved not to say anything - and in the prevailing culture of careless talk costing lives, they had all concurred. I was, apparently, the first person that he had ever talked to about the incident, and that was only because he had recently found out that 60 years of smoking had taken their toll and that he was doomed to die of lung cancer within the next 18 months.

I sat back on the barstool, and gulped at my pint. This was possibly the most bizarre thing that I had ever heard - in a life that had already seen several bizarre and inexplicable incidents. I had heard of Bigfoot - indeed, I had even been on a hunt for it whilst living in Canada in my late teens, but I had never heard of such things in the United Kingdom. Could it be? Surely not.

But my informant seemed genuine enough. He sat in the corner of the bar puffing away on a cigarette and wheezing gently like a dilapidated steam engine. His face had the unmistakable translucent aura of somebody struck down by incurable cancer, and he sat telling me of these extraordinary events in a matter-of-fact tone, as if he was recounting the previous weekend's football results. Did he, remember the exact location? If so, would he be prepared to take me there? I asked these questions diffidently, and to my delight he agreed.

There was no time at the present, he told me, and finishing our beers, we went outside and walked towards the castle grounds. If you're traveling towards Exeter from Dawlish, go through Starcross village and when you pass the *Atmospheric Railway* public house, go on past the large car park on the right-hand side of the road, but instead of following the main road round to the left towards Exeter, take the right-hand fork which is signposted to Powderham. Carry on down this little road for about half a mile. On the left-hand side you will see an expanse of deer park bordered by a wide ditch full of brackish water that acts as a moat. Just before you come to a railway bridge, the moat peters out, and although it may not be there now, back in 1982, there was a convenient gap in the fence. This was apparently well known to the poaching community in the village, and formed their main entry point to the woods where Lord Courtenay and his family raised their pheasants. We wriggled through the gap in the fence to find ourselves blissfully trespassing in the forbidden grounds of the castle.

Realising that even on such a brightly moonlit night it would be impossible to venture any further into the thick and uninviting woodland, we turned round and retraced our steps back to Starcross village. I was on duty for the next three days, but I made arrangements to meet my companion in the pub the following weekend. Sunday came around, and I rushed down to the *Atmospheric Railway* to fulfill our tryst. Sure enough, my friend of a few evenings previously was there, puffing away on a cigarette and drinking his customary pint of light and bitter. However, something had changed. I tried to broach the subject of the mysterious wild-man, but he was unwilling to talk about it. "I should not have said anything the other night," he muttered, "but I'm an old man and I wanted to share it with you."

Whether it was the intimation of his imminent demise, or whether it was just a memory of the promise of that he had made back in the 1940s, I don't know but in stark contrast to his verbosity of our previous meeting, on this occasion he was adamant that he didn't want to talk about it. So I bought him a beer, challenged him to a game of cribbage and spent the evening doing the sort of things that blokes normally do in a pub. The whole affair fascinated me. Over the next months I cautiously broached the subject of ape-men in Powderham woods with a number of the elderly men who drank in the pub, or who hung out in the hospital social club. None of them knew anything - or if they did they weren't saying.

By this time I was becoming cordially miserable as a nurse. It was obvious that my mindset was completely at variance with that of the old men who ran the hospital. I was still a confirmed punk rocker. In my off-duty times I habitually wore a leather jacket emblazoned with the logo of a well-known anarchist punk band, a T-shirt bearing the image of Mrs. Thatcher on the day of her election as prime minister in 1979 when she had accidentally reversed the V for victory sign she had been intending to flash to the cameras, and a pair of jeans emblazoned with a motto proclaiming that "we are all prostitutes."

With hindsight, this was probably not the best way to impress the elderly bastions of respectability that ran the National Health Service. However, I believed then - and a certain extent I believe now, although I am far more pragmatic about it these days - that what I did in my private life should have had no bearing on my professional status.

With the benefit of hindsight I can also see that my practice of allowing the patients to call me by my first name, and the fact that whenever I could I would take them out on visits the to the local pub, or occasionally to rock concerts, was one that would raise hackles amongst those in charge. I also drank too much, and played guitar in a local rock band, and the unmistakable odour of marijuana could, on occasion, be discerned coming out of my room in the nurses' home. Looking back, I am surprised that I lasted as long in the health service as I actually did. It was a vicious cycle. As I got more and more miserable at work, my behaviour - and my social life - became more bizarre. As I recounted in the previous chapter, the seeds of the mental health problems that were to plague me in later life - and which, eventually, with a delicious irony, were to free me to follow my lifetime goals - were, I believe, sown during my sojourn with Danny on Abbotsham Cliffs, but I believe that those seeds were cultivated and encouraged to sprout and grow by my early years as a student nurse. I am sure that I did nothing to advance my case for acceptance by the hospital authorities by systematically approaching every person who had been at the hospital during the war years, and asking them whether they knew anything about the mysterious advent of an ape-man. Many years before I actually had a piece of paper from the government confirming the fact, the powers-that-be had already dismissed me as a bloody lunatic.

As a burgeoning monster hunter I was perturbed by the whole affair. Despite my peculiar experiences on Abbotsham Cliffs, and my ever-increasing library of books on the occult, I was yet to make the paradigm shift between believing that all mystery animals were creatures of flesh-and-blood, and the realisation that some most definitely are nothing of the kind.

It may seem strange, but the concept of what I was later to dub zooform phenomena had not even occurred to me at this stage. As far as I was concerned, things were flesh-and-blood, or there were ghosts or they didn't exist. According to my burgeoning monster-hunting library, there were unknown species of higher primate awaiting discovery in many parts of the world. I believed then - and I believe now - that the Yeti is nothing more than a species of unknown great ape. I was also convinced that smaller mystery primates reported from many parts of Asia, and Africa, were equally valid. I was not prepared to discount the possibility that there was a creature similar to the Yeti living in the wilds of North America. But a wild man in Britain? It made no logical sense.

The months passed, and the old man who had told me of the events in Powderham woods during 1942 was admitted to the cancer ward at the Royal Devon and Exeter hospital in Exeter. I visited him on a few occasions - the last, a couple of days before he died. I smuggled him in a bottle of Guinness, and sat at the end of his bed as he drank it with relish. However, in view of his condition - and because I truthfully didn't think that I could get anything else out of him, I refrained from asking him any more about an incident, which he obviously regretted having shared with me. I attended his funeral. I was one of the few people there. When his lonely black coffin trundled behind the curtain at Exeter crematorium I was convinced that the truth that this mystery would go up in smoke along with his elderly, cancer-riddled corpse.

Christmas came and went. In the early weeks of 1983 I found myself going through the voluminous filing cabinets that held over a century's worth of patient records. This was part of my training, and although I was supposed to be looking into the distribution of different syndromes of mental and physical handicap from which the patients at Starcross hospital suffered, much to my surprise I found what I strongly suspect to be the solution to my 40-year-old mystery. In amongst some of the older files I found a number that referred to members of a very wealthy and noble local family. These were *not* the Earls of Devon by the way, but because the family is *still* very wealthy and very powerful, I do not feel comfortable with revealing their identity.

It appeared that there was strong vein of mental illness, and possibly more significantly, metabolic disorders running through this family. I discovered the details of some terrible human tragedies reaching back over a century. It turned out that an old lady, known affectionately to all the staff as 'Winnie', who at the time I knew her, must have been in her early nineties, was in fact a member of this noble family who had committed the unpardonable sin of becoming pregnant at the age of 13 following her liaison with one of the stable boys. This had happened way back before the First World War, and although history didn't relate what had happened to her boyfriend, she had been forcibly given an abortion and incarcerated for the rest of her life in Starcross hospital. It turned out, that before the Mental Health Act of 1959 there were three criteria under which a person could be admitted to hospital without any real recourse of appeal. The categories were 'idiots' (nowadays known as people with moderate learning difficulties), 'imbeciles' (nowadays known as people with severe learning difficulties), and moral defectives. As the criteria for becoming a moral defective could be anything from being a homosexual, an unmarried mother, sexually promiscuous, behaving badly at school, or even having been caught shoplifting, in these more enlightened times most of the people that I know - including myself and most of the Faculty of the Centre for Fortean Zoology - would, in times past, have been in danger of a lifetime's incarceration. I looked at Winnie with new respect from then on, and whenever I had the chance I would give her a packet of cigarettes or some chocolate.

The files also contained details of a number of her relatives. Several of them suffered from congenital generalized hypertrichosis: commonly known as Wolf-man syndrome. In extreme cases, this disease not only causes bizarre behaviour and radical mood swings, but the body of the victim is excessively hairy. Although several people from Winnie's family had been diagnosed as suffering from this syndrome there were no hospital records proving that they had been resident at the hospital after the First World War. What I did find out, however, was that the bloodline definitely had not died out. The family was still very important in the Devon area. They were notable benefactors to local charities, and at one time, at least, members of the family had been on the governing board of Starcross hospital itself. As the condition is an inherited one, it seemed quite probable that the strain of congenital generalized hypertrichosis had not died out in the early years of the 20th century, but that a more enlightened generation of the family had decided to treat these poor unfortunates at home rather than subject them to the rigours of institutional life. Maybe this was the truth behind the story of the Powderham ape-man.

I thought that it was quite likely that the unruly rabble that had accompanied the Home Guard on that fateful night in 1942 had actually shot a member of or the local ruling family in the mistaken belief that he was a German airman. This would explain everything. It will explain why the whole affair been shrouded in secrecy - in those days, the part of the landowner and the patrician establishment was far greater than it is today. There is still a stigma surrounding mental illness, mental handicap, and disability. This poor idiot covered in hair was still a member of the family who, after all, still paid the wages of most of the members of the posse that had hunted him down. Especially at a time when the nation was facing the deadly peril of the Nazi hordes, the powers-that-be would not have wanted the populace at large to be aware that one of their own was an unstable, dangerous, lunatic who had escaped from his carers and was wandering, naked and belligerent, across the countryside.

My nursing career continued to go slowly downhill. My intake of alcohol and drugs was beginning to reach crisis point. I was taking more and more time off sick. It seems ridiculous to me that at no time did the occupational health department recognise that I had a severe problem. They were content to label me a lazy malcontent, and do their best to get rid of me. In the spring, I was hauled up before the senior tutor and given a stern warning that if my behaviour and attitude did not improve them-my nursing career would be at an end. That night I went back to my room, drank a bottle of Jack Daniels, swallowed the best part of a bottle of tranquillisers and wrote my suicide note. This was not a cry for help. I just wanted to die.

I would have achieved my aim had the bloke in the next room not knocked on my door wanting to borrow something trivial, and forced me to be sick. He walked me around and around the corridors of the nurse's home until I regained full consciousness. He told the senior tutor what had happened and I spent the next week in bed. Extraordinarily, my - very nearly successful - suicide attempt didn't alert the authorities to the fact that I was dangerously mentally ill. They merely docked my wages of three days' pay and left me to get on with it.

The day I went back to work was one of the most difficult of my life. I was hallucinating wildly, and I really had no conception off where I was or what I was doing. That evening I drove back to the nurses' home, determined to have a hot bath and a good night's sleep. But it was not to be. There, sitting on the steps of Staplake House was Danny Miles - as flamboyant and as irritating as ever. I knew that whatever was going to happen next, I was probably going to regret it.

Much to my surprise, for once, Danny's agenda was not to lead me into some improbable adventure, after a life-threatening binge on alcohol and drugs. He had actually come to me for help. He was homeless, and had nowhere to stay. Completely against the rules of the Royal Western Counties hospitals, I invited him in and told him that he could stay with me for as long as he liked. It is, I believe, a testament to those members of the Staplake community who were my friends, and that an equal testament to the stupidity of those who weren't, that Danny lived - rent free - at the nurses' home for most of the next six months. Indeed, he wasn't the only one. Well aware that my days as a nurse were likely to be numbered, I had resumed my parallel career as a rock 'n' roll entrepreneur. At various times I managed the affairs of several local punk bands, and at various times Staplake acted as both a rehearsal room and a *pied-a-terre* for a motley collection of inept musicians with spiky haircuts. Those were good days. Much to my surprise, the shifting population of my houseguests fitted in quite well with the bona-fide residents of the nurses' home. There were never any complaints - at least that I heard of - and we all lived together in slightly bohemian squalor.

One weekend my old friend David Braund came to visit. We had been close friends since we were both 11 and I had moved all the way from Hong Kong to the house next door to him in Woolsery. By this time, David - a talented musician - was a student at the Royal College of Music in London, but we kept in touch, and I went to visit him - and Lorraine and Kaye - every time that I returned back to my home village to visit my parents. David was one of the most talented people I have ever met. A virtuoso piano player, he had a glittering future mapped out ahead of him. I drove from Starcross to Dawlish to meet him off the train, and on our journey back to the nurses' home I confided my troubles to him. He was always understanding of my mental health problems, and sympathised with me. He urged me to quit the career that I had chosen for myself that was, he was certain, the root cause of many of my problems. As he pointed out, working with mentally handicapped people was an extremely high stress occupation, and, furthermore, one which most people couldn't handle. The fact that I couldn't handle it either was no disgrace.

As I manoeuvred my battered blue Toyota sports car on to the gravel driveway outside Staplake House, I explain to him about my motley collection of houseguests. By that stage there were about half a dozen of them. Danny had been joined by two punk musicians called Spike and Alfie, an Iranian drug dealer with the soubriquet of "Persian Sam", and my old friend Ian - whom I had known since we were at Public School together, and who drifted from one dodgy sales job to another whilst doing his best to carve himself out a career as a jazz musician.

I ushered David in to the Gothic mansion, and introduced him to my bizarre, extended family. Not at all to my surprise, he fitted in perfectly. That night, David, Danny and I went out to the pub where we chatted about this and that in a desultory manner. Then Danny dropped a bombshell into the conversation. "How far away is Buckfastleigh?" he asked. "Not far," I replied, swallowing a mouthful of lager. "Why?"

"I am sure that you know about the Black Dog legends," he said, "but did you know that people are still seeing them?"

The phantom black dogs of the West Country were the first mystery animals of the area that I ever learned about. In the autumn of 1974 I had a serious bout of whooping cough, which much to my delight kept me off school for well over a month. During my enforced bout of idleness I embarked on two new pastimes that were destined to become integral parts of my life over the coming few decades - politics and writing, and I continued my monster hunting researches.

It was the time of the second General Election of the year. More by luck than judgment, Conservative Prime Minister Ted Heath had managed to hold onto the reigns of power after an election held earlier in the year. However, that autumn, the Labour Party finally managed to wrest control of Her Majesty's Government away from Heath, and a new era was upon the country. In the events nothing really changed. As Pete Townshend had written a few years earlier: "Meet the new boss, the same as the old boss," but the events on the hustings were a fascinating diversion for a fifteen year old boy who was semi bedridden with a debilitating disease; and I was imbued with a fascination for politics that has stayed with me ever since. I soon realized, however, that no matter who you vote for, the Government gets in, and nothing really changes.

However, another long-standing effect that my enforced bout of absence from school had on me took place because of my regular visits to our family Doctor. Woolsery has changed almost beyond recognition in the last few decades but when I lived there it was still a magickal place for a young naturalist to grow up. Every spring the fields and hedgerows were carpeted with wild flowers; the streams contained such strange and wonderful creatures as the brook lamprey; and each summer, the deep sunken lanes, imbued with the hallucinogenic smell of honeysuckle were home to various species of bats and the unearthly ghost moths (*Hepialus humili*) which fluttered like spectres just out of reach as one wandered home at night. It was a magickal place to grow up, and together with my earlier childhood in Hong Kong, it is one of the parts of my life that I hold with extreme reverence.

However, it was during my absence from school that autumn that I discovered that the ancient sunken lanes were not just the home for a rich and beautiful array of wildlife, but they were also home for monsters. Our family Doctor had his surgery in a nearby village called Bradworthy, and because of my particularly virulent strain of whooping-cough I had to visit him on at least a weekly basis.

It was during one of these regular visits, when my father would drive me to see the middle aged doctor that I first heard about the Yeth hounds. There had been several generations of Doctors from the same family working and living in the same village, and one evening as we drove home from the surgery my father told me how the father of the present incumbent (who was still alive and probably in his late seventies or early eighties at that time) had encountered a ghostly pack of wild hounds on a number of occasions.

On one occasion, he told me, the old Doctor had opened the back door to his house and heard the sound of a charging pack of wild dogs rushing up the stairs past him. Needless to say, he didn't see anything. I was fascinated and over the next few years I began to collect black dog legends from all over the county.

I soon found out that the Bradworthy case was far from being unique. In the 1920s, Mrs. Barbara Carbonell, travelled around mid Devonshire researching these apparitions. Following in her footsteps, I discovered that these 'creatures' (but of course they are nothing of the sort) are one of the most widespread animal archetypes in the world and commonly take the shape of a large black dog, the size of a calf, sometimes distinguished by one large eye in the centre of their foreheads, and on a bad day have dripping fire from their mouths. They are usually thought to be the harbinger of death, although occasionally they have appeared simply to accompany people on dark, lonely roads. They are found all over the world, but are more widespread in the Celtic lands.

Mrs. Carbonell became interested in stories of the Black Dog and found that many legends and sightings were clustered around a particular stretch of road that ran from Torrington to Copplestone, a distance of some twenty miles. Beginning at Copplestone, Mrs Carbonell was told by several local people that the Black Dog had often been seen near the Cross, actually a squared granite pillar some fourteen feet high, inscribed with Celtic symbols and known to date from before the sixth century. It is in the centre of a junction where three roads meet, and for many years has been both a centre for occult activity and UFO sightings. From Copplestone the road is accompanied by an ancient lane which runs into the crossroads at the hill-top village of Down St Mary, where there is an ancient Saxon church.

Several people living in the village told Mrs Carbonnel, "…how the Black Dog ran up the old lane on dark nights, past the smithy and between the church and the school. The dog was said to knock down the corner of the school, which juts out into the road, the noise of falling masonry being heard, but no damage was ever seen."

But surprisingly, I had never heard of the most notorious Black Dog legend of them all.

At that time I had become mildly obsessed with the notorious blues singer Robert Johnson who died in mysterious circumstances seventy odd years ago, after having recorded only a handful of classic songs, including one called *Hellhound on My Trail*. The mythology that has built up around him claims that he sold his soul to The Devil in return for a gift of musical genius that has guaranteed him a degree of immortality. The song tells of the young singer being followed by an immense, spectral black dog … a hellhound on his trail.

According to what Danny told us in the pub that night, and which I subsequently confirmed from a thorough perusal of the documents in the Devonshire Association's folklore collection, in the case of Richard Cable, Shakespeare's maxim is certainly true. From the accounts that have survived, he was a creature of pure evil, and it is an evil which has lived down three centuries and, according to those who believe in such things, still exists to the present day. Richard Cable was the Lord of the Manor at Buckfastleigh in the seventeenth Century.

"We know very little about his life, or indeed about the manner of his death, but his horrific exploits have become legendary," said Danny. David and I gazed at him in awe, not realising that he was quoting almost verbatim from the published works of the Devon folklorist Theo Brown who wrote:

"… We know practically nothing about him except that he rebuilt part of his house (the date 1656 is carved over the door), and enjoyed a terrible reputation as a persecutor of village maidens. Having captured one, he would keep her under lock and key across the valley at Hawson (….) he had an unenviable reputation as a violent and powerful squire, and when he came to die in 1677 his end was unpleasant. "

According to Danny, the precise details of his death remain obscure. "One version says that as he lay dying Whisht hounds gathered around the house howling horribly…" He told us.

The Wisht hounds, also known in Devonshire as the Yeth or Seth (pronounced *zet*) hounds are a common archetype in Celtic folklore. The word Seth may be a corruption of the word 'Heath' because of the moor lands on which the phantoms are seen, or is more likely a corruption of the name Set or Satan, because these terrifying, ghostly black dogs, with red glowing eyes are also known as "The Devil's Hunting Pack." The Devil has been a regular visitor to Devon and plays a major part (albeit tangentially) in this story.

After Cable's death his body was placed in a granite coffin within a peculiar pagoda shaped tomb in Buckfastleigh churchyard. A huge granite slab was placed on top of the coffin so that his ghost would not walk; and a thick oaken door and an iron grille blocked the entrances. Oak, being popularly considered at the time to have been the wood which made the cross on which Christ was crucified, and iron being two substances through which a ghost or vampire cannot pass. Even so, it was popularly believed by children in the vicinity that if they walked around the tomb, mouthing certain incantations, and then inserting their finger in the keyhole of the door, then they could feel Cable's ghost "nibbling" at the end of their fingers.

The black dogs were seen intermittently and often coincided with mysterious and sinister attacks on livestock.

Some attacks were almost Vampiric in nature and the sightings and unpleasant occurrences continue to the present day. One witness, Mrs Moore, who lived in a house built in the grounds of Cable's old haunt of Hawson Court saw three black dogs, appear 'floating' in her bedroom one night in the summer of 1981: "They were totally black, medium sized hunting dogs with pointed noses. They were not quite in line and overlapped one another - but appeared identical. I saw all three heads, but the rest of the middle one was indistinct..."

Apparently, during one of his furtive visits to Exeter, Danny had wandered into the West Country Studies Library, where he decided to while away a rainy afternoon by reading the latest volume of the Transactions of the Devonshire Association. There he found Mrs. Moore's account, which is quoted above, and as a result he became interested in the whole phenomenon. Unlike me, he had never heard of the black dog legends before, and the whole thing had fascinated him. He told us, eagerly, how the life of Richard Cable had quite probably been a pivotal influence on Arthur Conan Doyle's legendary novel, *The Hound of the Baskervilles*. Written in 1902, it is as fresh now, over a century later. It starts, as do so many of the stories, in the flat at 221b Baker Street when Holmes and his sidekick John Watson MD are visited by a Dr. Mortimer who presents them with the legend of a spectral hound which is said to haunt the members of the Baskerville family, and the mysterious death of a Sir Charles Baskerville that seems to confirm the legend. Mortimer says that his heir, Sir Henry Baskerville will be coming from America to take over the family estate, and asks Holmes if he believes it is safe for him to go to Baskerville Hall. Holmes says Sir Henry should go, but sends Watson with him because he (Holmes) has a case to solve in London.

At Baskerville Hall, in Devonshire, Watson writes to Holmes on anything that might be of relevance, and sends descriptions of the Barrymores (Sir Henry's servants), and the mysterious Stapleton, who lived by the great bog known as Grimpen Mire. Watson relays to Holmes the events of each day, but one day he discovers that Holmes had secretly come to Devonshire and was living in a hut of an old Neolithic settlement.

Holmes goes to Baskerville Hall with Watson and while looking at family portraits realises that Stapleton was in fact one of the Baskerville family. Holmes sets a trap for Stapleton, and Holmes and Watson end up killing Stapleton's immense hound, painted in phosphorescent paint to make it glow, as it chases Sir Henry across the moor. However, Stapleton himself was never found; Homes guessed that he sunk into the muck of the Grimpen Mire as he tried to escape.

The most glorious thing about the novel is that some of it is actually true, and so as well as whiling away the long winter evenings by sitting around your fire *en famille* reading this book, which is possibly the epitome of Edwardian Macabre, you can make plans about how, when the winds of winter have finally blown themselves out, you will be able to visit these dastardly locations for yourself.

We owe *The Hound of the Baskervilles* to Arthur Conan Doyle's good friend Fletcher "Bobbles" Robinson, who invited Conan-Doyle to visit him at his house on the moor. During his visit Fletch told Conan-Doyle of the old legends surrounding Squire Richard Cable - certainly the original for the villainous Hugo Baskerville.

By this time, both David and I were as enthusiastic as Danny and we made plans to visit the churchyard the next day. I put my beer back down on the table, lowered my glasses, and glared at Danny. "No drugs, no funny business, and no weird magical rituals. Right?"

Danny looked a little shamefaced, and we had to explain the events of the autumn of 1981 to an astonished David. He took it in his stride; he had been a friend of mine for a decade by that time, and he knew something of the extraordinary life that I had tended to lead, and of those occasions that I did stray away from the straight and narrow. David laughed. "I don't take drugs, and I certainly don't believe in magic," he said finishing his beer. We stayed in the pub until closing time and then walked unsteadily home.

The next day was one of those days that could have come straight out of the pages of one of the Enid Blyton books that I am so fond of making reference to in this memoir. It was a glorious early summer day, the sun was shining, the birds were singing, God was in his heaven and all was right with the world. We drove to Exeter, took the A30, and were soon driving up the twisting, winding hill which leads from the town of Buckfastleigh to the tiny church high up on the hill above.

Those of you who have read this book thus far, will no doubt be expecting a tale of Gothic strangeness. You are, no doubt, expecting me to describe how we spent the night in the Church, and came within a hair's breadth of encountering either Cable, his satanic master, or at the very least a bevy of sinister hounds - black as night, with glowing red eyes. Well, we didn't.

We parked the car by the lych gate, and the three of us strolled into the churchyard. We must have looked a strange sight. My punk coiffure was beginning to grow out, and I was well on my way to adopting the shoulder-length hair which I have worn intermittently ever since. I was still wearing my punk rocker clothes, however, and the combination of me dressed like a plumper Sid Vicious, Danny, wearing his extraordinary 'new romantic' get-up which made Boy George look like John Major, and David - looking for all the world like an off-duty longshoreman in roll-necked pullover, body warmers and Wellington boots - must have made heads turn. It certainly would have done if there had been any one there. But the place was deserted.

We examined Cable's tomb with interest. I have to say that I didn't pick up even the slightest inkling that the place was haunted, or the abode of the evil spirits mentioned by Theo Brown and others. It was just a gentle, rather beautiful, and utterly deserted country churchyard. We went into the church, and there we saw the only other human being that we were going to encounter during our entire stay in the village. There was a very old lady arranging flowers on the high altar. David went up and introduced himself to her. He told her that he was a regular church organist, and asked for permission to play on the organ. She smiled pleasantly and David, happiest as always when he could express himself through music, went, sat down at the organ and began to play. Watching David play was always like witnessing somebody going through a religious transformation. Like one of the Master Musicians of Jajouka in the High Atlas, or possibly a Sufi mystic, when he was making music he became a transcendent being of light - not really part of this world any more. The old lady sat down on in one of the pews to listen. Danny and I tiptoed outside.

If, in the previous chapter, I gave the impression that Danny was merely a manipulative drug addict who liked playing mind games with people then I am sorry. He was - and presumably still is - all of those things, but he was something far more. In the same way that David became transformed by his music, under certain circumstances Danny would become a far more spiritual - almost ethereal creature, and I often had a sneaking suspicion that he wasn't entirely human. He was one of those people whom - in previous centuries - would have been called a changeling. The reason that he behaved so badly towards the rest of the human race was that he didn't understand them. He was as alienated from mainstream society as I was, but whereas this alienation threatened to destroy me, it was what made Danny special. I lay on the grass by the side of Cable's tomb listening to the sound of a Bach fugue billowing out through the open door of the Church and watching Danny as he skipped, danced, and almost flew round the churchyard rejoicing in a beautiful summer's day and the sound of the music. When I look back over my life, that afternoon in Buckfastleigh churchyard is one of my happiest memories.

It was many years before I returned to Buckfastleigh Old Church. Events had taken a sinister turn in the early nineties, when both the church and Cable's tomb itself were attacked by Satanists (or a local nutter - depending on which version of events you choose to believe). The church is now a burned out shell and for the first time in three hundred years, the door of the tomb is now open - wrenched off its hinges. The vandals attempted to take the slab off the sarcophagus itself - but thankfully were unsuccessful. Many local occultists believe that Cable's spirit is now free, roaming the countryside again as he did three hundred and fifty years ago, and that he has been responsible for at least one, rather gruesome, murder.

In May 1995 I visited Cable's tomb together with a TV crew to make a documentary about Celtic Black Dogs.

The *zeitgeist* of the area had changed dramatically. Not only was the church itself gutted by fire; there was occult graffiti everywhere and a makeshift altar splattered with pentagrams drawn in red paint had been erected where the church organ used to be. It broke my heart to see a place where I had been so happy so desecrated. However, it was my first paying gig as a television presenter and I was determined to do my best. Only one incident of note happened. As part of the TV show, we decided to try and recreate the local belief that if you run of 13 times widdershins around the tomb its occupant will rise up to greet you. The guitarist in my band had been kind enough to lend us his five-year-old daughter. She was one of the most beautiful children I had ever met, although she was in extremely bad mood that day and was behaving very badly. However, like most actresses, the tantrums vanished as soon as she was in front of a camera and she behaved perfectly for the film crew. Wearing a pretty party dress, she ran innocently around the tomb several times. As she had been told she diffidently approached the great oak door and stuck her finger in. The door promptly fell in and hit my then manager on the head. There was a burst of profanity and a cloud of cigarette smoke, and a dishevelled looking alternative type emerged from the ancient tomb to a hail of derision from both myself and the film crew.

Within days of the programme being broadcast I was receiving mysterious telephone calls from people claiming that I was 'tampering' with forces that I didn't understand. Who these people were I don't know, but they seemed unwilling to accept my argument that I was only making a light-hearted TV show about local folklore and that I wasn't tampering with anything. However, all that was about to change.

Until my visit there I was unaware that the church and the tomb had been desecrated, and I was horrified at suggestions that I had unwittingly been a catalyst in the events that were to follow. I received reports of vampiric attacks on local livestock. Such things are hardly new in the West Country. Theo Brown had described such things forty years ago in her classic, *Tales from a Dartmoor Village*, and I had, more recently, been involved in investigating similar events in other parts of the West Country. I am a believer in 'clusters' of Fortean events, and it certainly began to seem as if Buckfastleigh Old Church was the epicentre of such a cluster.

Late one night I received another telephone call. It was from an old and valued friend of mine, and he very politely suggested that I should pay him a visit. This I did on the following afternoon. He introduced me to three earnest young women who claimed that they were witches who were preparing to carry out a cleansing ritual in the vicinity of the Church. The three weird sisters insisted that, if something were not done, a tragedy would ensue. At the risk of sounding blasé about such things, I meet people like this all the time. My files are crammed with reports of people who predict natural disasters, wars and famine, and 90% of the time they are wrong. I listened politely and accepted their offer to watch part of the ritual at sunrise the next morning. I was even given permission to photograph the aftermath of the ritual, which I duly did.

The three witches separated and took up position in what was, essentially, an equilateral triangle with the churchyard in the centre and one woman on each corner. I couldn't be in three places at once, and was not allowed to witness much of the actual ceremony. Those parts that I was allowed to witness were very moving indeed. I had always imagined that the experience of photographing beautiful naked women would be an erotic one, but on this occasion - although it was not the only time in a long and chequered career that I have ever done it - it wasn't.

It was a very spiritual and beautiful experience, and although I was sceptical about their claims and the efficacy of their actions, I drove home that morning feeling that in a little way I had been part of something very special.

A few months later I was sitting up in bed reading the regional news on the Teletext and I was stunned to read that a stable girl at Hawson Manor had been battered to death.

A local man was arrested and charged with the murder of Jessie Hurlstone, a pretty girl in her late twenties. At his trial a few weeks ago it was revealed that he had been obsessed with Jessie to such an extent that when she started a relationship with someone else he was driven to batter her head to a pulp with an iron hook. The prosecution even referred to him as being "like a man possessed". I have wondered many times over the last few weeks whether they were not speaking the literal truth! He was found guilty and sentenced to life imprisonment. Since the trial and the subsequent publicity some local occultists are convinced that there is a definite link between the murder, the attacks on local livestock, the black dog sightings and the desecration of the church and Cable's tomb.

Amongst people who have knowledge of such things there was a growing feeling of tension and foreboding. I have no idea whether the ritual that I was privileged to photograph that morning had any effect for good or for ill. As Jessie Hurlstone was murdered soon after, it seems that the incantations of the three women either had no effect whatsoever or at the very least were not strong enough to combat the power of a man who, like Robert Johnson two and a half centuries later, was popularly believed by his contemporaries to have sold his soul to The Devil. Like Robert Johnson, Richard Cable has taken his place in folklore, but whereas the worst that can be said of Johnson's legacy is that he directly inspired several generations of not-very-good blues bands in pubs, it seems eminently possible that Richard Cable's legacy is something far more sinister. I have proved on a number of occasions that I am singularly inept at foretelling the future and therefore I have absolutely no idea what is going to happen next. I believe, however, that people in the Buckfastleigh area, and especially those who have an interest in what is broadly known as the paranormal, should be on their guard.

I make no apologies for for this narrative hopping about a bit in time. Because of the arcane, and esoteric nature of what I do, it seemed more appropriate to try and organise this book and a thematic manner than a chronological one. So, with your indulgence, we rejoin my life during the autumn of 1983 - a few months after our visit to Buckfastleigh. Danny was still living with me - part of the time at least - and although I still knew in my heart of hearts that I was never going to succeed to any great degree as a nurse, I still felt that I was doing more good than I was doing harm. I was still drinking too much, and one night when one of my hippy friends came up to me in the pub, remonstrating with me and telling me that my body was a temple, my reply was "yours might be, dear boy, but mine is a fuckin' chemical treatment works!"

About this time, I discovered a pub in the nearby village of Kenton. It was called the Dolphin Inn, and it was a hang out for a motley collection of social malcontents who all had more brains than sense, and whose major thing in common was that they never had any money. I introduced Danny to this crowd and he took to it like a fish to water. One night we were sitting around in the lounge bar bemoaning the fact we had no money to speak of and no women whatsoever, when another old friend of mine walked in. He was clearly upset about something because he ignored us totally, strode right up to the bar and ordered a double whisky. This, from someone who usually only drank cider, was bizarre behaviour indeed.

The new arrival was a chap called Mike Davis. Several years before, when I had been doing my best to become the Brian Epstein of the South Devon music scene, I had been driving along the road between Starcross and Exeter, when I saw a disheveled looking man with dreadlocks, some impressively brightly coloured trousers and a Bob Marley T-shirt. He was hitchhiking along the road and he was carrying a guitar. As:

a)   It was pissing down with rain
b)   I was searching for new talent for my "stable" of artists
c)   I was bored and I wanted someone to talk to

I pulled over, picked him up and gave him a lift into Exeter. We have been friends ever since. Over the years I have worked with a number of musicians and songwriters ranging from the obscure to the very famous. I can truthfully say - with my hand on my heart - that he is the most talented songwriter I have ever met. Completely unschooled, he writes and sings with a bewitching honesty that is unmatched by anyone - except perhaps the young Lou Reed. At the time he was living with his first wife just outside Kenton, and had a quiet, domesticated existence that I - tiring of my dissolute bachelor existence - envied beyond words. He was not a great drinker, and therefore despite the fact that he lived in the same village, it was very unusual to see him in the pub of an evening. He is also one of the most unflappable people that I have ever met, and so to find him gulping down whisky, and in a complete tizzy was a great surprise.

I approached him at the bar. "Is everything OK, mate?" I asked with concern.

He stood in silence gulping down whisky, and then turned to face me. "You're not going to believe this, Jon, but I've just seen a fucking great giant rabbit!"

Giant rabbits are quite an important part of the zooiconography of cryptozoology. In *On the Track of Unknown Animals,* Bernard Heuvelmans describes sightings of such things in Australia, and suggests that could possibly refer to encounters with an animal called *Diprotodon* - a giant relative of the wombats which was supposed to have become extinct about 10,000 years ago at the end of the Pleistocene epoch. He goes on to tell the story of Dr Ludwig Leichhardt (1813-1848) - a German explorer and scientist who came to Australia in 1842 to study its rocks and wildlife. Leichhardt explored parts of Queensland and Northern Territory. While attempting to travel from Moreton Bay (Brisbane) to Perth, his party disappeared. Many search parties went out to try and find traces of the party. Some of these found bones, but they were not able to prove that it was any of Leichhardt's party.

According to Heuvelmans, Leichhardt became obsessed with the accounts of miners and backwoodsmen who had reported seeing giant rabbits/diprotodons and his last, fateful expedition was essentially an expedition in search of these mysterious giant wombats. Heuvelmans spins a convincing and romantic yarn, and it was one of the parts of his seminal book that impressed me most and inspired me to dream about following in the footsteps of Leichhardt and go in search of Diprotodon. There is only one problem with Heuvelmans's supposition.

There isn't a word of truth in it.

At the end of the 1970s when I was still living intermittently at home, I entered into a long correspondence with a woman who worked at the Zoology library of the British Museum (Natural History). I was due to inherit a small legacy on my 21st birthday and I intended to invest the majority of it in an expedition to somewhere of cryptozoological interest, and my first thoughts were to go to Australia - a country I have only visited once back in the summer of 1968. I asked my friend at the library for copies of some of Leichhardt's documents appertaining to his quest for Diprotodon. She searched through the available material and found nothing! During the preparation of this book I did the same thing, and apart from finding that Leichhardt did indeed donate some Diprotodon fossils to the British Museum in 1844, there is no evidence at all to support Heuvelmans' claims. Sadly, I learned at a very early age that even the Father of Cryptozoology can be pictured as having feet of clay. However, his claims that giant rabbits seen in the remote outback of the deserts of Western Australia may well be surviving Diprotodons, are interesting ones, and it would be a rash fellow indeed who would say that they are completely without foundation. However, although surviving remnants of the Pleistocene megafauna may well exist in the Australian outback, it is inconceivable that the same creatures could be responsible for sightings of similar creatures in the woods around Kenton.

I sat Mike down, bought him another drink, and asked him to tell me his story in his own words. It was a simple enough story. He had been trespassing in Powderham Woods looking for chestnuts. At the name of Powderham Woods my ears pricked up. I well remembered my moonlight visit to the centre of the woods in search of the place where the wild man had been shot four decades previously. I questioned Mike and it turned out that - serendipitously - the place where he had been going to pick chestnuts was almost exactly the same location where the wild man had allegedly been shot all those years before. Although by this time in my life I had discovered the books of John Keel and I was becoming aware of the indisputable fact that waves of anomalous phenomena do tend to happen in the same specific places, and that - logically - there must be some linking or causative factor at work, I dismissed any thoughts that there might be a link between the wild man and these giant rabbits. After all, I had solved the mystery of the wild man to my own satisfaction, and the idea of a giant rabbit in Powderham woods just seemed completely absurd.

However, I had known Mike for years and he was a good natured, sober, honest and generally trustable geezer, so I asked him to continue. There wasn't much more to the story in fact. Mike had been hunting for chestnuts when he was startled to see what looked like a rabbit, was shaped like a rabbit, and even hopped like a rabbit - it just happened to have been about three feet tall! I sat back slightly dazed. Mike was, as I have said, one of the most reliable witnesses that I have ever had the honour to interview, and he had just told me a spiel of utterly bizarre nonsense. It just didn't make sense.

Just then something very strange happened. One of the ever-shifting members of the local hippie population who seemed to spend their entire lives propping up the bar in the *Dolphin Inn*, stepped forward. "Err, I couldn't help hearing what you said there, man", he muttered into his rather straggly and Hobbit-like beard. "I've seen giant rabbits in those woods as well." We gestured to the bloke to come and join us, or took a long swallow of beer, and sat back ready for the latest installation of these extraordinary revelations.

Apparently he (and I'm afraid, that I've forgotten his name after all these years), had been tending his crop of home-grown marijuana plants in the midst of one of the pieces of woodland that Lord Courtenay's gamekeepers use to rear pheasant chicks. As all good horticulturists will do (especially when your crop is eminently smokeable) he had been sampling his produce when into the clearing in front of him hopped what he described as a 'Giant Rabbit'! We all burst out laughing. I have to admit, that despite my own and peculiar experiences over the years, and even despite the fact that my own history of drug abuse had had little or no influence on the things that I had seen, I immediately assumed that this particular outsized lagomorph was merely a hallucination brought on by over-exposure to the dreaded weed and was about to expel the matter from his mind when another hirsute gentleman at the other end of the bar piped up that he had experienced a similar thing. When a third member of the gathering - this time an eminently respectable local businessman, whom I knew personally - then admitted in a sheepish voice that he too had seen a giant rabbit and that he had never touched marijuana in his life, then I realised that despite my early misgivings this was a very real - and presumably a very tangible phenomenon.

Therefore, for the second time in my life, I exited a pub just before closing time, and in the company of a motley band or drunks, hippies, and the aforesaid respectable businessman, I made my way towards Lord Courtenay's woodland in search of a mysterious creature. Danny was prancing along, singing a peculiar little song to himself under his breath. Mike, looking slightly bemused by the whole affair brought up the rear. In stark contrast to my earlier visit to these woods a year or so before, there was no feeling of foreboding. This was a slightly drunken Sunday-school picnic rather than a serious journey into the heart of darkness. Somehow, I felt, that even if this ridiculously surrealchemical animal was real, it was considerably less threatening than a putative hairy and ferocious wild-man would have been. Also, on this occasion, I was not trampling through uncharted territory in the company of an old man who was dying of cancer. I was going to a place that I had been before in the company of a band of friends and acquaintances.

These days, I receive regular emails from school children around the world asking for advice about how to become a professional cryptozoologist. They often ask for hints about how to carry out a specific investigation. I am happy to answer these letters because I believe that one of my greatest roles as one of the foremost cryptozoologists in the world is to educate and guide the new generation who will, hopefully, follow in my footsteps. For some reason, I have never used my hunt for the giant rabbit of Powderham as an object lesson - even though one of the cardinal rules of any wannabe monster hunter should be - "Never go in search of a giant rabbit when you are accompanied by half-a-dozen hippies all of whom who are half-cut". One of the watchwords of the cryptozoologist, and indeed any field zoologist or naturalist, has to be stealth. In an ideal situation the intrepid investigator will tiptoe into the target area, preferably wearing camouflage, and making as little noise as possible. What one should never do is to blunder into an area where you have reason to believe that there is an unknown animal lurking, accompanied by a party of high-spirited drunks who insist on singing "Do Wah Diddy" with obscene words at the top of their voices.

"There she was just a walking down the street", sang one of my companions in a tuneless, but enthusiastic manner.

"Bum Fuck Bastard Bugger Wank Bugger Wank", chorused the rest drunkenly. I shuddered to myself, and thanked the gods of crypto-investigative theory that not only was it a damn good thing that this was a completely pointless exercise and that there was no way that you ever going to see a giant rabbit in these woods, or indeed anywhere else, but also that the elder statesmen of cryptozoology such as Bernard Heuvelmans or Loren Coleman were nowhere near us, and therefore were not going to be in a position to witness this fiasco.

Then it happened. We were deep in the middle of the woods, and were within a couple of hundred yards of the place that I had visited so many months previously in search of the wild-man. The woods were still dank and unpleasant, and they stank of fox urine. I was doing my best to work out how I was going to turn this party around and get back to the pub for a lock-in, whilst still retaining some semblance of dignity, when a giant rabbit hopped out of the bushes and stood in front of me.

I stopped dead. My motley band of companions did likewise. For a good two minutes, we stared at a giant rabbit, and the giant rabbit stared back at us. Then the figurative penny dropped. It wasn't a rabbit - I thanked my lucky stars for that, because the idea of having to go down into the annals of Cryptozoological history as the man who emulated Jimmy Stewart in the film *Harvey* by discovering a giant rabbit when he was pissed, did not appeal to me. But the creature standing before us was very real. It was a wallaby.

After a few more minutes, the Mysterious Marsupial obviously realised that the pastime of standing in the middle of a Devonshire wood gazing myopically at a bunch of rowdy drunks, had only limited entertainment appeal, and so it hopped off to go about its own wallaby-oriented business. My companions and I stared at each other in stunned silence for a few minutes. "I told you that had seen a giant rabbit", said Mike smugly, and I turned to answer him when the night air was rent by a desperate weeping, wailing and gnashing of teeth. "That fucking rabbit has eaten all my bloody dope plants", wailed the hippie with the Hobbit-like beard, and the entire party burst out laughing. We returned to the Dolphin Inn, where the accommodating landlord was so pleased to hear that a quest had been successful that he arranged a late night - and highly illegal - drinking session for us all. During the course of the evening I introduced Danny to another friend of mine, an elderly, and highly eccentric hippy called Basil. The rest - at least if you have read my book *The Blackdown Mystery* - is history.

From a Cryptozoological point of view, however, the matter was far from over. Wallabies - like most marsupials - are residents of Australia. I was well aware, and that there were isolated populations in the UK. Probably the best-known is one in the Derbyshire Peak District which started when several specimens escaped from captivity from the grounds of Roaches House in 1939. In his book *Naturalised Animals of the British Isles* Christopher Lever noted another, smaller colony in Sussex and in recent years other colonies of escaped wallabies have appeared to thrive in different parts of the country.

However, I had never heard of such a thing in Devon. So I did some digging.

The case of the Giant Rabbits of Kenton had a bizarre, though surprisingly straightforward, answer.

It transpired that for forty years or more, a Mrs. Butler, a lady living near Holcombe (just outside Dawlish) had kept wallabies as pets on her farm. During the great storm of 1986 some of her fencing had blown down and an unspecified number of wallabies had escaped. Some of them were recaptured. One was hit by a car on Haldon Hill. One was seen at a bus stop at Teignmouth, which caused great consternation to the customers of Western National. At least one, however, had made its way about eight miles due east of its former home and was living a carefree existence in Lord Courtney's woodland where it could nibble the leaves of marijuana plants and frighten the occasional hippy and generally live a happy marsupial-oriented life-style. Case closed (but it was good while it lasted).

The hunt for the giant rabbit in Powderham woods saw, in many ways, an end to one period of my life. Danny went off to live with Basil, and I began a tumultuous relationship with the girl who lived upstairs from me at the Nurses' Home. Her name was Alison Huntingford, and before very long we were engaged. She made me promise not to take drugs anymore, and because - for one of the first times in many years - I was happy, I cut down on my drinking as well. I still didn't enjoy my career, but with the prospect of married life - and a mortgage - before me, I resolved to knuckle down and get on with it.

We got married in April 1985, honeymooned in France, and a few weeks later moved in to a house in Exwick, where I have lived ever since. Even my cryptozoological researches took somewhat of a back seat. It became a hobby rather than a way of life. On the plus side, not only was I relatively settled, but I was now the proud owner of a house of my own, which meant that I could proceed with my life's ambition of filling every nook and cranny available to me with books and filing cabinets to contain my ever-increasing collection of cryptozoological source material.

I applied myself diligently to my new wife and to my studies and, six months after my marriage I qualified as a nurse. I tried very hard to eschew my wild ways and embrace a world of suburban respectability. But, as events were to prove, I wasn't very good at being respectable.

CHAPTER FOUR

MY STRUGGLE

As the long hot summer of 1985 imperceptibly changed into the season of mists and mellow fruitfulness, and as the damp grey autumn became my first winter in the City, I did my best to adjust to my new life. However, it wasn't long before by realized that it was going to be a long, hard haul. There were problems in our marriage from the beginning, and I still cordially disliked my job. However, I had new-found responsibilities - a wife and a mortgage - and so the option of leaving the NHS never really crossed my mind.

A few months after I married - during the end of my period as a student nurse I became seriously ill with an abscess on my jaw. I spent two or three weeks off sick, and two important things happened. I was in unimaginable pain, and I was prescribed a noxious compound called papaveretum, which consisted of a mixture of heroin and morphine. Even this did not completely relieved my agony, but it did teach me that the fruit of the poppy was not only a palliative for physical pain, but that it also worked in a remarkably effective manner against the emotional pain which I was feeling more and more as each day passed. I don't want to give the impression that I became a junkie overnight. I didn't. Indeed, by accepted terms of reference I have never been a junkie. However, starting then, I occasionally took refuge in chemical bliss when the world around me got too much to bear. As the years passed, and my unfulfilling career - and difficult marriage - trundled on, these episodes became increasingly frequent.

The second thing that happened to me during this period of illness was that I began one of the most important relationships of my life. Against her better judgment, Alison gave in to my pleadings and agreed that I could get a dog. In those days I was particularly lonely. For some reason, the NHS - at least in the Exeter Health Authority - operated a working shift of two and a half days consisting of twelve and a half hours, followed by two and a half days off, and working every other weekend. Despite my pleas that we were newlyweds and that it was causing us a considerable amount of unhappiness, the powers-that-be insisted on making Alison and me work opposite shifts. This meant, that essentially, that although we had only been married a few months, we hardly ever saw each other. During the important parts of our marriage - the time when most couples are bonding with each other - we were essentially strangers. We only ever saw each other for a few hours in the evenings, by which time the person who had been at home all day was stir-crazy, and the person who'd been at work was tired, and irritable and just wanted to go to bed. Alison had always said - with some justification - that one should not keep a dog in a small house without a garden. However, I maintained that as one or other of us were going to be at home pretty well all the time that it wouldn't make any difference. And she eventually gave in.

During the days when I was off sick and existed in a haze of opiates, we scoured the newspapers, and the adverts in the windows of the pet shops for puppies. Eventually, we found one. We drove to a rather disheveled housing estate on the outskirts of Dawlish, knocked on the door of the house described in the advert and were greeted by a hail of barking and scrabbling. A harassed looking man in late middle-age answered the door. He was accompanied by a horde of twelve puppies who were rushing about his feet, tripping each other up, and all doing their best to make more noise than the others.

The harassed man explained that Toby's mother Gladys - a pedigree Black Labrador bitch - had been in his family for years, and had never evinced any interest in the opposite sex. For this reason, and also because of some unspecified medical complications he had never had her spayed. Much to everybody's surprise (including, one suspects, Gladys's), at the venerable age of eight she had escaped from the house and succumbed to the charms of a dishevelled and rather disreputable male dog of uncertain antecedents which was kept by a seedy looking bloke about four doors up. The twelve puppies - who by this time were doing their best to eat my right foot - were the result.

I would like to be able to say that Toby's eyes met mine, it and that an immediate bond was forged between us. However, it wouldn't be true. We chose him almost by default. Of the litter of twelve there were only three left that had not already been adopted. Two were bitches, and having heard the cautionary tale of Toby's mother, and both of us having had experience of bitches in heat, howling and scratching at the paintwork, and doing their best to escape in order to fulfill the sexual desires with any available canid, Alison and I had already decided that we wanted a male dog. Handing over a fiver in payment for the only boy puppy left, we drove back to Exeter, with Toby - at that time even smaller than one of my shoes - curled up asleep on my lap.

That night, we committed what many people consider to have been a cardinal sin in dog ownership. We made up a doggie-bed in the kitchen and retired up to our room. Toby howled, cried and whined. The book that we had bought on the subject of dog ownership had warned us that this would happen, and had advised us to steel our hearts and ignore the pitiful vocalisations of the frightened young puppy. I couldn't do this. Toby's cries were breaking my heart, so in the middle of the night I walked down the stairs to the kitchen, picked him up and took him up to our bedroom. That night he slept in bed with us - a position he was to occupy for the next 15 years.

Soon after I qualified I went to work as a staff nurse at a hospital in one of the nearby towns. This had been originally built as a workhouse in the closing days of the 19th century and had been the place where generations of social inadequates had lived and died. It eventually became a hospital for the mentally handicapped - and for full much the same role. By the time I started work there it was scheduled for closure, as part of Margaret Thatcher's care-in-the-community programme. Closing down the old asylums seemed like a good idea - but there was one problem with care in the community. The Community didn't care, and the powers-that-be were too busy spending the money that they would gain from the sale of so many prime real-estate plots which had once upon a time been occupied by huge, red-brick and grey-stone asylums which had provided a safe haven - and indeed a home - for generations of people who were incapable of living in the outside world, to think about spending some of that money on educating the public at large to expect - nay, to welcome - the ex-inmates into small enclaves in suburbia. Mental illness - and to an even greater extent mental subnormality - are two of the last taboos in a society where abortion, divorce, homosexuality, and the break-up of the nuclear family have not only become accepted, but have become the subjects for third-rate television situation comedies. Even now, nearly 20 years after the events that I am describing, society has not yet evolved to a state where a series called *Maurice the Mongol* has taken over from *Friends* as the prime time Friday evening entertainment. Looking back, it seems inconceivable that the aforementioned powers-that-be had actually believed that Mr and Mrs Joe Average would feel comfortable living next door to people that only a few decades before had been designated as idiots, imbeciles and lunatics and who had - for centuries - been locked away where they could not offend the sensibilities of their peers. One is left with the sad conclusion that neither the politicians nor the nurse managers actually gave a damn about the sensibilities of either the mentally ill, the mentally handicapped, or the ordinary people in the street.

Most of the go-getters amongst the nursing staff had already secured themselves decent jobs working in the newly-founded community teams, and with a very few exceptions most of the staff who were left were the discontented, the alcoholic, the unmotivated, and the plain bored. It was a very tight-knit community - most of the staff were related to each other, or had known each other socially since childhood. The advent of an idealistic young hippy, especially one who was already exhibiting the early signs of manic depression, was treated with distrust and suspicion. I was made unwelcome from my first day - and it went steadily downhill from then on.

However, outside my failing marriage and the living hell that was my career, my cryptozoological investigations continued apace.

During the spring and summer of 1986 there were a number of attacks on domestic livestock - especially guinea pigs and rabbits in the St. Thomas area of Exeter. This is the next suburb to the one where I live, and as I have always kept small animals as pets myself, I was particularly disturbed by the incidents - especially as the locations moved slowly nearer my own house in Exwick. With unnerving originality the local newspaper referred to these incidents as being the work of "The Beast of St Thomas".

The exact number of incidents is unclear, especially as at least some of the killings were proved to be the work of a vicious schoolboy, and yet others were said to be the responsibility of two dogs - a terrier and an Alsatian seen wandering unsupervised around a local housing estate.

Local officials blamed the killings on mink, and even badgers, but on at least one occasion it appears that something rather less tangible was responsible.

One night in October 1986 I was sitting on the back step of my house, looking up the thirty feet or so of steep slope which the Council Tax assessors still insist is a garden. My so-called 'garden' backs on to the slightly less derisible gardens of the houses in a street parallel to the estate where I live and just up the hill. Suddenly I heard a scream. When agents Mulder and Scully *et al* are sitting in their gardens minding their own business and suddenly hear a scream they reach for their hand-guns and their mobile telephones and suddenly adopt the personae of suave FBI agents. I, being both English and ever so slightly drunk, came over all middle-class and reticent and pretended to ignore the whole thing. Then I heard another scream and the sound of a woman crying so hard that she appeared almost incoherent with grief.

I shouted into the darkness to find out what was wrong and to offer my assistance. Much to my surprise she shouted back and accused me of owning an enormous grey Alsatian that had just run down her garden towards my property and which had killed over a dozen of her pet guinea pigs. At that time my dog Toby, (who had always been rather fond of small cuddly creatures, and to my knowledge at least never killed anything larger than a spider) was only about eighteen months old and was asleep in an untidy heap in the middle of my kitchen. I tried to reassure the woman of this, but she was so upset, she was beyond reason, and so I retreated into my house for more whisky, and it was only the next morning that I realised that if she had seen a 'grey Alsatian' run down the slope into my garden, it should have run straight past me, and I had seen nothing of the kind.

By dint of a little detective work I found out which householder owned the garden in which the event took place, and the following weekend, feeling a certain amount of trepidation, I knocked on the door. The woman answered and upon being introduced to Toby (who was gambolling around her ankles, and engaged in a fierce battle to the death with one of her shoelaces) both absolved me of blame and invited me into her garden. By this time she had disposed of the carcasses, but according to her description, although they had been covered with 'saliva' they had not been mutilated and there was no blood visible.

I examined the hutches that had once housed the unfortunate beasts. The front doors appeared to have been wrenched off in a manner that suggested a far greater degree of manual dexterity than that one would have associated with even the most intelligent dog. Yet, according to her account, the grey 'dog' had been seen by her in front of the ruined hutches with a dead guinea pig in its mouth. The ground was quite damp, yet there were no paw marks of any kind.

I would like to say that in the best traditions of Gothic horror, Toby refused to go near the scene of the 'crime' but in fact he appeared unconcerned, and mildly blotted his copybook by cocking his leg against the hutch and having a nonchalant pee.

Neither the police nor I ever solved the mystery of "The Beast of St Thomas" and the killings stopped soon after. However it is perhaps worth noting that Burrator Drive, where my particular incident took place, was the location in 1997 of the particularly brutal killing of a young girl. Fourteen-year-old Kate Bushell had her throat cut by person or persons unknown

- and at the time of writing, the case is still unsolved.

Although my investigation into the "Beast of St. Thomas" was essentially fruitless, it did inspire me to return to my cryptozoological investigations. Sadly, the stresses of the rest of my life were beginning to to show in my marriage. From the beginning a relationship was stormy one. With hindsight it is easy to see that we were incompatible socially, intellectually, professionally, sexually - and indeed in pretty well every way - but we loved each other and were determined to make it work.

Over the years I did my best to interest Alison in cryptozoology, and although she was never passionate about the subject, she and I collaborated happily on several investigations. One of the first was a request for the singing mouse of Devonport.

I first discovered the story in the Westcountry Studies Library. This library is a boon for all researchers living in the Exeter area, and I have used it again and again. As well as an unparalleled collection of books, journals and documents on the subject of the four counties of the West Country it also contains a complete collection of the two local newspapers going back well into the 19th century. At the time, I was researching a book, that I later decided not to write, about the mystery animals of Devon and Cornwall, and was on a ceaseless trawl through newspaper archives in search of zoological anomalies.

An item in the 43rd report of the Scientific Memoranda section of the *Transactions of the Devonshire Association* caught my eye. The headline read *"Singing Mouse", and* it quoted an item from the *Western Morning News* of 2 February 1937, which referred to:

"Mickey, the singing mouse caught by Mrs A. Eddey of Trafalgar-place, Stoke, Devonport.

Prof. Crews, of Edinburgh, wishes to investigate the vocal mouse in the interests of science, but Mrs Eddey's primary wish is that it should broadcast. . . "

This was an opening paragraph worthy of anyone's attention. A singing mouse whose owner had showbusiness aspirations was a beast out of the pages of one of the *Dr. Dolittle* books. Mrs Eddey herself seemed almost prosaically matter-of-fact about the whole affair:

"It is true I have a lovely little singing mouse which I caught on the morning of January 10th. It sings like a canary. It is an ordinary house mouse, very small, and its little body seems to vibrate with music. It first came to my bedroom at 12. 2 [sic] A.M. on New Year's morning and it has sometimes sung the whole night. Even when trapped it did not stop chirping to me. I am sorry I can tell you nothing more, only that it is quite tame. . "

The headline in the *Western Morning News* read *"Mouse that has won fame",* which seems eminently appropriate for such a peculiar story. George Doe, the Recorder of Scientific Memoranda for the Devonshire Association, reported that 'Mickey' was again in the news, when the *Western Morning News* of 12 March 1937 reported that Mrs Eddey's ambitions for her pet had been fulfilled:

"Apparently pleased with the success of his broadcast audition on Wednesday, Mickey, the Devonport singing mouse, kept his owner awake all night with his celebration tunes.

If all goes well, Mickey will soon be issuing a tuneful challenge across the ether to Minnie, his American rival. On Wednesday, Miss Mildred Bontwood, of the National Broadcasting Company, of America, travelled to Plymouth especially to see Mickey, having previously wired his owner Mrs A. Eddey, of Trafalgar-place, that she was bent on seeing him.

Mickey was put into his cage and taken around to the Plymouth Station of the British Broadcasting Corporation, and as a result of the audition Mrs Eddey has a contract to take the mouse to London and it is expected that Mickey will broadcast from there to the United States. "

By the time I had finished reading this extraordinary series of articles I was almost in tears of laughter and was in imminent danger of being asked to leave the library. It all seemed too surreal, even for inclusion in a universe which experience has taught me and my colleagues is often totally absurd. The fact that the whole report had been compiled 54 years before by someone whose surname is commonly used by American policeman as a designation for unidentified corpses made the whole affair seem even more bizarre.

I decided that before proceeding with the affair the sources should be checked. I had the *easy* job. I checked the relevant issues of the *Western Morning News* and found that Mr Doe had indeed quoted the original press reports correctly. The BBC still had a copy of the recording, but unfortunately the documentation that went with it had gone astray. Alison, however, had the unenviable job of trying to find out something about Mrs Eddey.

Even if she had been a relatively young woman at the time, by 1991 Mrs Eddey would have been at least in her seventies. The odds were that she was dead. Trafalgar Place in Stoke didn't exist any more, and even if she were still alive, tracking her down seemed as if it was going to be an impossible task.

We were right. It was!

In 1991 there were 26 telephone numbers under the name of 'Eddey' in the Plymouth telephone book with Devonport addresses. Alison telephoned them all. Unfortunately none of them had heard of either Mrs Eddey or her talented rodent. Some people were helpful and polite, others abusive; none had any information that was actually any use in our quest.

There were several hundred people with the same surname living in other parts of Devon so we did what any sensible Fortean researchers would have done under the same circumstances. We gave up!

Instead of continuing the search for Mrs Eddey or one of her close relatives, we went back to searching the newspapers for more stories about this remarkable rodent, and we were not disappointed.

Back in 1937 the plot had thickened, as by April, 'Mickey' had another British rival.

The headline in *The Times* on 22 April 1937 was:

"BBC Tests the Singing Mouse - (like a nightingale)"

The story read:

"Another singing mouse has been found - this time in Wales. It will be brought to the microphone on May 8th for a national broadcast, which will be relayed to the United States. The mouse, 'Chrissie', owned by Mr Gale of West Cross, Mumbles, Swansea, was given a test at the Swansea studio of the BBC and an official told a press representative that she sang 'like a nightingale'. For the test the mouse was held up to the microphone in a bottle.

The National Broadcasting Corporation of America has challenged any country to produce a singing mouse to beat the singing mice of Illinois. Mr Gale discovered the singing ability of his mouse last Christmas. Soon afterwards 'Chrissie' was missing. She was found hiding inside the piano. Before this it was claimed that the only singing mouse in Britain was that owned by a Devonport woman, which has also been tested for broadcasting. "

The Illinois mice had made their media debut the year before on a Detroit radio station when on 15th December they broadcast a recording of "Minnie the Singing Mouse" to mixed responses from the audience. *"Some people thought that she sang like a robin, others compared her to a tone-deaf canary. The trouble with Minnie was getting her started, but once she opened her mouth she wouldn't stop. "*

Three days later, according to Young, another Illinois mouse, named 'Mickey' and billed as her 'co-star', made his debut with a less than impressive performance. He, apparently, got his feet wet while drinking water from a fruit jar, and refused to sing. After half a minute's silence an announcer told listeners that Mickey usually began a recital with a soft whirring trill rising into a crescendo, followed by a two-note jump, tapering to a diminuendo. No-one believed him.

Writing in a book called *Secrets of the Natural World,* my friend and colleague, the British cryptozoologist Dr Karl P. N. Shuker, also described 'Minnie' and her career, and told how *".... in May 1937, a transatlantic radio contest for singing mice was staged, featuring rodent songsters from as far apart as London, Illinois and Toronto. "*

The first English entry was a duet between Mickey from Devonport and Chrissie, a Welsh mouse. They piped quite brightly, but no-one could tell them apart. America's Minnie (from Illinois) ran round and round and refused to open her mouth. Mickey (also from Illinois) performed like a trooper, his top notes were described as being comparable with the greatest Italian tenors of the day.

Next came Johnny of Toronto, billed as the Toronto Tornado. He never had a chance; tens of thousands of radio listeners heard cries of 'Miaow! Miaow!', followed by a solemn announcement that the Tornado's career had ended.

It was back to London for another 'Mickey', but listeners mistook him for a leaky tap in the radio studio. At the end of the contest the sponsors (Canadian, American and British Broadcasting Corporations) announced the winners would take part in an international mouse opera broadcast live. Over half a century later we are still waiting for the grand results of the competition. Both NBC and the BBC have ignored my requests for the winners' names to be publicised, and to our knowledge the mouse 'grand opera' so eagerly awaited by Dr Dolittle and his friends has never been staged.

Young treated the whole affair in such a light-hearted matter, that, although there is enough corroboration to confirm that the event actually took place, the true details are obscure. We have succeeded in part of our original aim, however. 'Mickey' the singing mouse of Devonport definitely existed. He was not an unlikely hoax dreamed up by George M. Doe. There is even a picture of him, but there do not seem to be any records of his life after May 1937. Like so many semi-legendary historical characters, little is known of him apart from his brief flirtation with fame for five months in 1937. Mice don't as a rule live very long, and so we can reasonably suppose that he has passed over to pastures new.

The same can be said about the other mice in the story. Essentially the main part of our research was over. We were, however, still intrigued. Why had so many singing mice turned up between December 1936 and May 1937? What made them sing? Was there a historical precedent? Were there singing mice around today? If so, where could we get one?

I have to admit that my motivation at this point was not merely the furthering of the sum total of human knowledge. I have always had a strong and irrational dislike of Walt Disney. In the early 1980s there was an inept American punk rock ensemble called *Bomb Disneyland* and although the music was terrible I bought all their records because, unusually amongst the practitioners of American punk rock, here was a sentiment with which I could sympathise. I was particularly incensed at what Disney Studios had done to great classics of English literature like *The Jungle Book* and *Peter Pan* and it would have amused me greatly to have proved that the whole Disney Empire had been based on an idea stolen from as peculiar rodent living in a suburb of Plymouth.

So, fuelled by a heady mix of righteous indignation and a surreal sense of humour, and ignoring the protestations of my wife, I continued my researches. I discovered a number of letters to *The Times* discussing singing mice which were published during the 1930s and over a few months I amassed what I believe to be the largest archive of material on the subject to exist in the world.

It seemed that the phenomenon of 'singing' mice is quite a well-known one. As with so many things the phenomenon captured the interest of a number of Victorian writers and naturalists who discussed the matter at length. It seems that, despite our initial surprise in the Westcountry Studies Library, singing mice were a well-known phenomenon amongst out forefathers, and that it is only the effete researchers of Forteana and zoology at the end of the 20th century who had not heard of them. It was a little comforting to find out that with three exceptions, Dr Karl Shuker and my friends Clinton Keeling, the veteran British Zoologist and maverick zoological researcher Richard Muirhead (and they know all sorts of ridiculous things), no-one we would talk to during the rest of our investigations had heard of them either!

The 'craze' for singing mice during 1936 and 1937 led to much information becoming available. In *The Times* of 22 April 1937 it was stated that a singing mouse had been found in Wales, and that it was to broadcast on May 8th. A letter in the same issue informed the British populace that according to Red Indian mythology, *'Mish-a-boh-quas'* the singing mouse always comes to tell of war. It may sing at other times but not to the same extent. The author of this letter cited "Ernest Thompson Seton's wonderful book *'Rolf in the Woods'*."

This was just too much for me to deal with. What had originally been a mildly amusing piece of research into an obscure item of Devonshire zoology now seemed to have analogues all over the world. A good friend and colleague of mine is a bloke called Tom Anderson. He lives in Scotland and it is a mark of the peculiar nature of the technological society in which we live that we have become firm friends by letter, email and telephone conversation without ever having actually met face to face.

Besides being a highly amusing raconteur of tall tales and a collector of strange Scottish stories, Tom is an expert on matters appertaining to the Native American peoples, did some research for us, but was unable to unearth any solid facts. He wrote to me:

"Despite strenuous efforts and consulting about thirty books on folk customs, anthropology and totemic realisation and ceremonial, I can find no reference to singing mice. Their name sounds Algonquian, which limits them geographically but it doesn't appear anywhere, even as a sub-clan of a linguistic family such as kiowan, Siouan, Athabascan, etc.

"Mice are an unusual tribal choice, either as totems, guardians or emblems. Not having the power of the Thunderbird to control the elements for the northern tribes, or the storytelling significance of the Coyote or Grandmother Spider further south, it's difficult to imagine its purpose. The nomadic tribes used medicine bundles for personal protection and luck, as you probably know. Feathers, lucky stones, weasel skins, claws, etc., symbolic of speed, running and other desirable traits.

"Custer's nemesis, the Oglala, Crazy Horse (Masunka Witco), whose war paint consisted of painting his face blue with white spots, symbolising hail, and wearing a sacred stone behind one ear and a hawk's body in his hair, was the rare combination of a mystic and a war leader."

Tom continued describing Crazy Horse for some paragraphs before returning to the main subject:

".... mice are representative of nothing I'm aware of in Indian culture. Nor can I find evidence of them as design subjects for the Pueblo cultures on pottery, etc. Deer, yes. Mice, no!"

He concluded:

"I suspect it could be a 'retro myth'. A possibility, maybe even likely, but basically unfounded. It wouldn't be the first as Amerindians are 'hip' right now because of their 'green' lifestyle. I won't bore you with the shortcomings of this theory."

To confuse things further, Arkady Fielder wrote a book called *The River of Singing Fish,* referring to a type of sheat fish in the Ucauali River, which apparently produces a noise like bells clanging. But no mice. Richard Muirhead, a bloke I had actually been at school with back in Hong Kong nearly three decades before, eventually managed to track down the passage in the aforementioned book by Seton:

"A few nights later. As they sat by their fire in the cabin, a curious squeaking was heard behind the logs. They had often heard it before, but never as much now. Skookum turned his head on one side, set his ears at forward cock"

At this point, we feel, the reader should be reassured that 'Skookum' is the name of the dog owned by the eponymous hero, Rolf, during his sojourn in the woods. The narrative continues:

"Presently, from a hole 'twixt logs and chimney, there appeared a small, white-breasted mouse. Its nose and ears shivered a little, its black eyes danced in the firelight. It climbed to a higher log, scratched its ribs, then rising on its hind legs, uttered one or two squeaks like they had heard so often, but soon they became louder and continuous:

'Peo, peo, peo, peo, peo, peo, peo, oo,
Tree, tree, tree, tree, trrr,
Turr, turr, turr, tur, tur,
Wee, wee, wee, we'

"The little creature was sitting up high on its hind legs, its belly muscles were working, its mouth was gaping as it poured out its music. For fully half a minute this went on, when Skookum made a dash; but the mouse was quick, and it flashed into the safety of its cranny.

"Rolf gazed at Quonab inquiringly.

" 'That is Mish-a-boh-quas, the singing mouse. He always comes to tell of war. In a little while there will be fighting.' "

There are times, when I look at my life as if from an outsider's point of view, that I think that everyone I know is either massively eccentric or barking mad. Some are both. For Richard Muirhead was so excited by his discovery of the original 1915 reference to the Native American singing mice as a portent of war, that he decided that merely posting me a photocopy of his discovery, or even telephoning me, would be a wholly inadequate way to communicate this momentous discovery to me.

Nothing so tame! Despite the fact that the weather was appalling and it was a Bank Holiday weekend he decided to trace (I believe by a mixture of hitch-hiking and railway train), all the way from where he lived at the time in Salisbury to my home in Exeter in order to tell me of his fantastic find in person. Unfortunately he forgot to warn me of the fact. Alison and I were upstairs watching television when he arrived and didn't hear his repeated knockings. Apparently he was standing on my doorstep for several hours singing the Red Indian mouse song *a-la* Ernest Thompson Seton before giving up and hitch-hiking back to Salisbury, still without having given me the original documents!

Rolf in the Woods is a dreadful book. From the photocopied excerpts eventually sent to us by Richard Muirhead, we are exceedingly glad that we didn't have to read more of it than was absolutely necessary. It is also a work of fiction, although the author claimed to have based it on his own experiences. It also appears, although we cannot confirm this, to be the original source for both *The Times,* and the Young references.

We have not been able to find any other pre-1937 references to this legend. In the absence of any further supportive evidence we are forced to conclude that Tom Anderson may well be right and that the story of *Mish-aboh-quas* may well be nothing more than a relatively modern 'retro myth' based on an incident in a (not very good) novel.

Whether or not the Native Americans did have this legend, we can establish that native North American mice do sometimes exhibit this 'musical' ability. So far all the mice which we have discussed which exhibited this 'musical' ability appear to be common house mice *(Mus musculus),* originally a Middle Eastern species which is commensal with man, has spread to every corner of the globe. Writing in 1871, however, William Hiskey noted:

"The cage had a revolving cylinder or wheel, such as tame squirrels have. In this it would run for many minutes at a time, singing with its utmost strength. This revolving cage, although ample as regards room, was not over three and a half inches long, and two and a half inches wide. "

It could be argued, perhaps, that the sound of a mouse 'singing with its utmost strength', was in fact the sound of a desperately unwell animal wheezing and gasping for breath whilst rushing around in its wheel. I feel, however, that this hypothesis is unlikely, if only because of the unlikeliness of an animal suffering from such a severe and debilitating condition voluntarily taking exercise to this extent. And any way, Lockwood was a fine naturalist, and it would seem eminently unlikely that a man of his observational powers would have been unable to recognise diseased squeakings when he heard them. As we explored the surprisingly large body of source material about singing mice, it became more and more apparent that whilst it seems entirely likely, nay probable, that many of these 'singing' mice were, indeed, suffering from a debilitating respiratory tract infection, others, probably including 'Hespie', were exhibiting behaviour symptomatic of something else entirely. When an animal is ill, it is usually self-evident, especially to a competent naturalist, and Lockwood, in particular, spent some considerable time testing the 'respiratory infection' hypothesis, before rejecting it out of hand.

The final irony is that if indeed 'singing mice' are suffering from various respiratory tract infections, then the ancient Wiltshire folk legends of the advent of a singing mouse foretelling sickness could be nothing more than literal truth. The story of the 'Black Death', a global pandemic spread by lice living on the (then) ubiquitous black rat, is well known. If there is/was a disease of the respiratory tract which affected both mice and humans (and we should here remember that one of the best rationalisations for vivisection experiments on mice is that they are biologically relatively similar to our own species), then the advent of a diseased mouse could well have been the forerunner of an outbreak of disease amongst the human beings of the neighbourhood.

Unfortunately, it turned out that my main objective in this quest was fruitless and it was not possible to prove that Walt Disney made his fortune from an 'empire' based around the bastardised images of two rodents with debilitating upper respiratory tract infections, but the sheer peculiarity of our quest fascinated me and inspired me to go on stranger and more peculiar investigations into the soft white underbelly of the natural sciences.

In the summer of 1987 I managed to secure myself a job away from the main hospital in a group-home, which had been set up to house one-time patients from the main hospital. I saw this, at the time, as a glorious opportunity to do what I actually wanted to do - care for people with learning difficulties outside of the institutionalised regimen of a crumbling Victorian asylum. I was greatly looking forward to the move, but sadly I had forgotten one thing. My new workplace was going to be staffed by the same people who had worked at the old one - and most of them either despised, disliked, or were scared of me. I soon found that the opportunities for my actually achieving anything worthwhile were going to be just as limited here as they had been throughout my nursing career.

In those days nurses were not paid very much. From the earliest days of our marriage, Alison and I had financial problems. To be quite honest, our lives were so bloody miserable that we tried to overcompensate by spending far more money than we could possibly afford. The 1980s were a particularly horrible time in British history, and as the decade progressed and the doctrine of Thatcherism had imbued society - at all levels - with a disgusting selfish ambience whereby greed was good, and things were more important than feelings. We were surrounded by advertisements for credit cards, store cards, and apparently affordable consumer goods - that no household could be without. To my everlasting shame I have to admit that both my wife and I were suckered by this and were soon deep in debt. We realised that we would have to do something. At the time, cryptozoology was - for me at least - still only a hobby. It never occurred to me in a million years that I would ever be able to support myself - and you have to remember at the time that I not only had a wife, but I was still convinced that despite our physical incompatibilities that I would eventually father a large tribe of hungry sprogs - by investigating such bizarre zoological side roads as the singing mouse of Devonport. No, I had to look elsewhere amongst my interests and talents for a possible new career (or at least a way of making a few quid to augment the pittance paid us by society to look after those of its members that it found socially embarrassing).

From the age of 12, I had been a big fan of rock music. From the day I picked up my first guitar two years later, I knew that if I couldn't be a monster hunter for the rest of my life then I wanted to be a pop singer. I formed my first band during the autumn of 1975, and have been writing, recording, and playing music ever since. I made my first record - called *The Mistake* - in the spring of 1982 and it was almost universally ignored. None of my many records sold in any quantity at all, and even when - in the early to mid-1990s - I finally established a fan following, I was to find that my peculiar musings which sounded alternately like Syd Barrett, or the *Buzzcocks* were never to propel me further than the most obscure cult status. However, this book is not my life story - it is the story of my life as a cryptozoologist, which is not necessarily the same thing, and those who want more than a cursory look at my musical career (or indeed many of the other things that I have done over the years), will not find it here.

Between 1987 and 1996 I made half-a-dozen more records, and played several hundred concerts with successive line ups of my band: *Jon Downes and the Amphibians from Outer Space*. However, even in the earlier days of my musical career it was pretty obvious that unless I was going to be very lucky I was highly unlikely ever to make any money out of my songs. I would have to look elsewhere for an income.

I was just as interested in listening to music as I was playing it. I had (and still have) an enormous record collection, and my library of books on contemporary music was nearly as large as my library of books on cryptozoology. I had gone beyond record collecting, and had begun an enormous collection of bootleg recordings. I had live shows, demos, unreleased recordings, sound checks and general studio inanity by all my favourite artistes. One day, Alison and I had a brainwave. Why not become bootleg dealers? We could make a reasonable amount of money selling these - admittedly highly illegal - cassette tapes at record fairs all over the country. Furthermore, we could manufacture them at home, and I could surreptitiously duplicate the covers at work. So we did it. And it was a great success.

For the first - and only - time in my career as a nurse I was popular amongst my co-workers. Who else employed by Exeter Health Authority could get hold of live recordings of the nursing staff's favourite pop music?

As I was able to provide such goodies at a knock-down price. I was even in the enviable position of being able to take unauthorised days off - with the connivance of my line-manager who would do anything for obscure country and western records - in order to visit record fairs around the country. Over the next few months, Alison and I travelled the length and breadth of southern England. Sometimes we were accompanied by my friend Richard Dawe - a shifty, unkempt, and eminently lovable bloke a few years younger than me, whom I had met wandering down Exeter's Fore Street with a handful of Frank Zappa LPs under his arm. Wherever in the country we went, I always made sure that I bought a book on the local folklore - especially when it appertained to animals - to bring back to Exeter and add to my burgeoning collection of books on the broad subject of cryptozoology. Occasionally on our travels I even managed to do a bit of investigation.

One of the best record fairs was held in a church hall in Salisbury. This was a part of the country of which I have always been very fond. My earliest memories of the UK were of Hampshire and Wiltshire. On each of our rare visits to England from Hong Kong we have stayed with, or at least visited my maternal grandparents at their home in the little village of Grately. It was my grandfather - when I was five - took me to Salisbury Museum where he told me stories of his youth working for the eccentric naturalist Lord Rothschild at his estate near Tring in Hertfordshire. Rothschild had - among other eccentricities - adopted the habit of driving round the Hertfordshire lanes in a carriage pulled a pair of zebras. In the years before the First World War, my grandfather - a scion of the famous Rawlins family of fair folk and showmen - looked after these zebras. When I finally visited Tring museum a century after Rothschild had founded it I saw the world-famous collection of sunbirds and hummingbirds that my grandfather had described to me so many years before. Once again, I could almost smell the aura of pipe smoke, which always seemed to surround the old man. I could hear his distinctive voice in whatever the aural version is of the mind's eye, and for a few, brief moments I was five years old again. On the wall of the main room of the museum was a picture of its founder, standing alongside his trademark form of transport. Leading one of the zebras by a halter was a small-boy of about 11. I like to think that it was my grandfather who had been born in 1888, and thus was about the right age.

As well as telling me about Lord Rothschild, my grandfather also showed me a case of most peculiar birds. They were a family of great bustards - enormous game birds the size of a turkey which had once lived on Salisbury Plain, but which had been hunted to extinction by the early 20th century. Grandad told me how a charitable trust had been formed to try and reintroduce these magnificent birds to the area. Sadly, this remarkable project had been a singular failure (although as we go to press, a new project is trying to do exactly the same thing). However, at the time when I visited the museum first during the cold winter of 1963, the original project had looked as if it was going to be able to succeed, and I remember putting my pocket money, eagerly, into a collecting box for the project, and daydreaming happily about the day when these glorious fowl would once again flying over the chalky downs and grassy hummocks of Salisbury Plain. Over 20 years later I am fairly sure that my childhood dream came true.

On this particular occasion, during the early summer of 1997, Alison was working so Richard and I drove to Salisbury without her. We had a particularly successful fair and were driving back along the A303 past Stonehenge with nearly 200 quid nestling in my denim jacket pocket. In 1987, 200 quid was quite a lot of money and we were feeling quite pleased with ourselves. I was mentally spending our profits when Richard suddenly grabbed my arm and shouted "What the fuck was that??" He was pointing at the sky in front of us where a huge bird could be seen flapping along in an ungainly manner. To this day I am convinced that it was a great bustard. But how did it get there? The only successful breeding project had finally petered out many years before, and the birds had been sent off to a zoo. Suddenly, the thrill of the chase - something which I had not experienced since that night, years before, when I had chased giant rabbits through Powderham woods - returned, and the miserable nurse who moonlighted as a low-budget purveyor of bootleg tapes vanished in a figurative puff of smoke to be replaced by an intrepid monster hunter whom I was beginning to be afraid had vanished forever. Conveniently ignoring the fact that I had promised to get back to Exeter in time to collect my wife from work, I explained to Richard how exciting this sighting could turn out to be, and we determined to try and follow the bird to wherever it was going.

This was not such a daft endeavour as it might sound. The bird was very large, and was flying very slowly. Just to the west of Stonehenge there is a small coppice. Suddenly the great bird flew off towards the right hand side off the road and flew over the little wood. Just beyond the wood there is a little roundabout. Doing my best to emulate one of the heroes of Starsky and Hutch, I threw the little car up at the right hand exit and careered up the bumpy road in pursuit of the giant bird. We drove for miles, aghast at the stamina of the great fowl, which fluttered in an ungraceful and unlovely manner but never seemed either to tire or to make any attempt at a landing. By this time we were so engrossed in our chase that we didn't realise how far we had strayed from our original route. Salisbury Plain is criss-crossed with trackways, which lead for miles across the chalky terrain. Many of them are reasonably easy to drive along, and so when it was no longer possible to follow our quarry along the orthodox roads, we left the road and drove as fast as we could along one of the chalk track ways. I have always thought that Salisbury Plain is one of the most beautiful parts of Britain. Brown hares ran across the path in front of us as we careered along. The little chalk track was fringed by foxgloves and yellow toadflax. Wild orchids grew along the verge, and every few miles, wherever there was a slight hillock, it was surmounted by a small green wig of tatty undergrowth from which, occasionally, a fallow deer could be seen furtively peeking out from between the bushes.

Still the great bird flew on. Still we drove on after it, quite oblivious of the red flag which designated an army firing range. It was only when we drove round a particularly steep bend in the track and found ourselves confronted by two armoured cars and a bevy of men wearing battledress and brandishing machine-guns that I realised quite how much trouble we were in

."Oh shit", I said.

With regret I stopped the car and watched our quarry flap a way out of sight. As the soldiers glared at us I got out of the car to apologise. A fierce looking military policeman came up to us and demanded to know who the hell we were and what the hell we were doing. As I started to try and explain about the great bustard, I realised how unlikely it sounded. The military policeman demanded to look in the boot of the car. As I opened it I remembered that not only did it contain nearly 1,000 illegal cassette tapes, but it was also that temporary home for two plastic machine guns - from a fancy dress party that we had attended a few weeks before - and a human skull wrapped in a plastic bin bag. I had found the skull in a pile of remnants from the days when the hospital had been used for teaching purposes. It had no doubt once belonged to a pauper who had died intestate in the old poorhouse and who, having no goods or chattels to repossess, had ended up having his or her very body taken over by an uncaring state. A century after the long-forgotten pauper had died, his or her skull had found itself in a skip awaiting removal to the incinerator. After checking with that the powers-that-be, I had taken possession of the skull, meaning to keep it as a *memento morii,* put it into the boot of my car, and promptly forgot about it. I gasped, and half-a-dozen soldiers raised their weapons and pointed them at Richard and me. I continued to bluster on about great bustards, until the grim looking military policeman threatened to arrest us if I didn't shut up. There was an IRA terror alert in operation. For the first, but not for the last time in my life I found myself facing the very real possibility of being arrested under the Prevention of Terrorism Act.

Britain is probably the only country in the world where I could have got away with anything as stupid as this. Anywhere else in the world, I would have certainly been arrested, charged, tried for treason and probably ended up in a secure mental hospital somewhere far beyond the reach of Amnesty International, and where I would probably have spent the rest of my days. Furthermore, I would have been the only person there who wasn't sane. As it was, even during the days of Thatcher's notorious 'ring of steel' protecting the capital from Hibernian terrorists, and at the height of the Cold War, British justice and common sense prevailed, and after confiscating the plastic machine guns, and giving us the worst dressing-down I have ever received, they accepted my story about the great bustard and let us go.

Sadly, the identity of the great bird that we had been following, (and which had nearly got us shot), remains a mystery. However, over the last decade and a half I have been collecting material about the great bustard project. Because, even now, people still occasionally see these birds, it is tempting to theorise that the ill-fated project was more successful than those in charge of it had thought. Because so much of Salisbury Plain is set aside for use by the military, if there are indeed small numbers of these magnificent fowl still living there, it is the British Army who has provided a mechanism for their survival. It would be sad if a by-product of the downscaling of the British military in the wake of the end of the Cold War was the final, ignominious extinction of these beautiful and exotic creatures.

Richard and I drove back to Exeter, chastened though excited by our adventure. We decided not to tell either Alison, or Sarah - Richard's girlfriend - what had happened. We thought, with some justification, that a lecture from a military police sergeant would be as nothing compared to the wrath of our respective womenfolk when they found out how stupid we had been.

It was during another record fair that I was introduced to the concept of the small press fanzine. I picked up a copy or something called *Missing Link* which purported to be dedicated to David Bowie.

However, it wasn't the subject matter of this slim, typewritten, and badly photocopied publication that blew me away. It was the entire concept. Like so many others of my generation I had read punk fanzines in the late 1970s, but I had no idea that an entire culture of independent, small press publications had evolved. I fell hook, line and sinker in love with the concept, and determined to start my own fanzine as quickly as possible. However, the idea of starting a foray into the world of the small press was all very well, but I needed a subject to write about. That night, my wife and I sat up in bed discussing the matter. Alison had a bright idea. At the time she was a fan of a slightly tedious Irish singer called Chris de Burgh. Why not start a magazine dedicated to this short bloke with ridiculously bushy eyebrows? I couldn't think of a better idea, and so, that night, Spanish Train Publications - named after de Burgh's most famous song, which also gave its name to our magazine - was born.

We were very proud of our first issue. We drove all the way to Brighton so that we could attend a concert and give a copy of our debut edition to the man himself. After the show, a little group of fans waited in the cold November evening and in the middle stood Alison and I - feeling and looking a little embarrassed. When the diminutive singer - whose eyebrows looked even more ridiculous from close up - shambled out, we thrust a copy of issue one into his hand and waited for him to shower us with praise and invite us on to his tour bus or for rock'n'roll excesses such as the ones we had read about in all our Rolling Stones biographies. However, nothing of the sort happened. He took the magazine, smiled in a rather embarrassed manner and disappeared without saying anything. Sadly, we were both so overwhelmed by being in the presence of a celebrity rock star that we didn't pay attention either to his stupid eyebrows or the fact that he was actually an arrogant little prick. We just got back in our car and drove back to Exeter flushed with happiness at having mixed - albeit briefly - with the rich and famous.

As we were driving through the dark roads that lead towards the New Forest, at about two in the morning I was startled to see what looked like an enormous cat stalking silently along the hedgerow. I only saw it for a few brief seconds but for the first time I *knew* that there were, indeed, exotic big cats species roaming the British countryside.

I had been interested in the phenomenon of British mystery cats for some years. During my brief and undistinguished career at public school I had, as already recounted, been unable to escape from the public school malaise of compulsory sports, and school spirit. From an early age, I had decided that the 'healthy mind in a healthy body' thing was complete bullshit, and had done my best to rebel against the prevailing culture which celebrated it to the same extent as it had a century before when the various massacres of the First World War had their dress rehearsal on the playing fields of Eton and Harrow. And then Somme. My *alma mater* was a shabby, grey stone building called West Buckland which perched on the edge of the great moor just like - as Dylan said about someone's brand new leopardskin pillbox hat - "a mattress balances on a bottle of wine". I hated every minute of it there, and I particularly hated the headmaster's insistence that everybody joined in the school's endemic sport of cross-country running.

All the way through the spring term each year, there was a rigorous season of these events - ranging from small ones a mile or so in length, which took about an hour, to the *piece de résistance* - the "Exmoor" - which from memory (and I cannot be bothered to find out), was something like 14 miles in length and took a whole day. I thought at that time, that this was just another example of the pointless brutalism of the public school system. Many years later I found, to my amusement, that renowned science fiction author Brian Aldiss had attended the same school as me, decades before, and furthermore had used it as the template for one of his books which had portrayed it as a hotbed of brutality and homosexuality. I did my best to avoid all these athletic anachronisms but, to no avail. I may have been a hip young 17-year-old doing his best to immerse himself into the prevailing culture of nihilistic rock music, but I was still a public schoolboy subject to the same rules and by-laws as everyone else who attended this out of date and scholastically dodgy establishment. So, with the worst possible grace, I attended each of these events. On each occasion, I would team up with my particular band of cronies - slackers to a man - and amble along smoking cigarettes, and talking about girls.

One of my fellow dullards was the scion of a local farming family who had obviously decided that the best way to approach the fine art of social-climbing was to name their son Ashley and send him to the local public school. Presumably this was for reasons of snobbery and social advancement, and not for any more altruistic reasons, because Ashley was as stupid as he was ugly, and showed no interest in anything except for fox hunting, football and masturbation. Not entirely to my surprise, at the height of Thatcherism, I read that he had stood for Parliament as a Tory MP. He narrowly avoided being elected after details of his scandalous and somewhat esoteric sexual exploits were plastered across the front pages of all the Labour Party newspapers.

But I digress.

Back in the cold wet spring of 1977, Ashley, I and the rest of the ranks of the walking wounded, were ambling along, in the wake of these aforementioned cross-country runs. Someone had bought a bottle of cider, and was passing it around for us to drink as we smoked and chatted. Somehow the conversation got on to fox hunting. Even as a child, I found bloodsports abhorrent, and I wasn't really paying attention to the conversation. However, my ears pricked up when the appalling Ashley mentioned that, at the previous weekend, whilst chasing one some poor unfortunate fox across one of the less prepossessing parts of the family estate, the MFH had spotted what looked like an enormous black panther careering out of one of the covers and tearing off into the middle-distance.

This was my first encounter with what, several years later, would become famous all over the world, as the Beast of Exmoor. At that time, my investigations went no further than listening - with a wide-eyed disbelief - to the testimony of my unlovely companion. However, three or four years later, I was in a much better position to be able to carry out some reasonably concerted investigations into the mystery cats of the countryside between South Molton and Barnstaple. As described in chapter two, I was, at the time, working as a nursing auxiliary at Kingsley Hospital in Bideford and moonlighting as a promoter, and manager of musical ensembles in the punk rock idiom. I spent much of my time in Barnstaple, usually in a pub called the *Royal Norfolk*, which was - I guess - to the Barnstaple scene what the Cavern was to Merseybeat. However, there was one great difference. Merseybeat had the *Beatles, Gerry and the Pacemakers*, and the *Searchers*. We had *At the Wheel* and the *Cult Maniax*. The *Beatles* went on to write songs like *Sergeant Pepper's Lonely Hearts Club Band, Hey Jude* and *Let it Be* which summed up the very *zeitgeist* of an entire generation across the world. *The Cult Maniax* had a song called *Black Horse* which they wrote after they had been banned from their favourite pub by the landlord who was of German descent. John Lennon has often been described as being the greatest English poet of his generation but he never came up with any lines as poetically apt as:

"The landlord is a Nazi, his wife's a fuckin' Jew, don't you ever go in the door or they'll be banning you".

As I sit writing these lines I am on an InterCity train travelling between Exeter and Newcastle. I am dictating this deathless prose onto my laptop using voice recognition software. Sitting opposite me is my friend and colleague Richard Freeman. I won't introduce him to you just yet, because at the present rate of writing he won't arrive in my life until about chapter eight, but he is vaguely listening to this narrative as I dictate it, and making stupid comments where he feels it appropriate. Usually these stupid comments take the form of bad puns or half-assed homosexual innuendo, and usually I ignore them. However, my mention of the *Cult Maniax* grabbed his attention and he wanted to know:

a. Was the landlord a Nazi?
b. Was his wife a 'fuckin' Jew'?
c. If so, why did he marry her?
d. Didn't anybody ever sue the band for this unquestionable libel?

The answers are:

a. No, although he was a German.
b. Not to my knowledge but it rhymed better, and certainly had a damn sight better punk credentials than Richard's suggestion of "and his wife was one too"
c. See above answer.
d. Well, yes they did actually. The single resulted in a libel action at - I believe - the Old Bailey, following which the record was withdrawn, and the record company, which was owned by two mates of mine called Lynton and 'Bunker', went into abeyance.

I used to hang out at the pub because I managed the other band I mentioned earlier - *At the Wheel*. They were a surreal bunch of nutcases who fused then-contemporary musical stylings with confusing childlike lyrics mostly describing the daily doings of characters in an imaginary world of their own creation. I was a huge fan. Sadly, I was the only one. Their one album *Five Billion Calories* sold approximately three copies and practically bankrupted me, as I was the only person stupid enough to invest large amounts of money in recording a six-piece experimental punk rock band that nobody in the world - apart from me - actually liked. Every lunchtime when I was not at work, I would be found sitting in the corner of the saloon bar of the Royal Norfolk, desperately trying to persuade somebody to give me some money so that I could finish recording the album. No one ever did - and by the time I could afford to finish the record the band had split up.

However, I became part of the social scene at the *Royal Norfolk*, and together with my then girlfriend Samantha, (who was only 15, and who was five or six years later to inspire my most famous - and probably most scurrilous - song), became well known within the musical community in the town. Over the year or so Samantha and I drank there, we became friendly with most of the local musicians, and artistic oddballs including Harry Williamson - either the son or grandson (I forget which), of the author of *Tarka the Otter*, who was at that time a performer with jazz-rock weirdoes *Gong*, and Brian Davidson, one time drummer with Keith Emerson's band *The Nice*.

One of the strangest people that I met was a bloke called Derry who lived in a small hut in the middle of the woods on one of the steep valleys on the edge of Exmoor six or seven miles from Barnstaple. He wrote - what I thought at the time - were extraordinary songs, but which - with the benefit of hindsight - were probably just stoned drivel. However, fuelled by the legendary exploits of such outsider artistes as Syd Barrett and Julian Cope, I was determined to have a go at making a record with him, and so when he invited Samantha and me to visit him in his tawdry little shanty, I jumped at the chance. Samantha - who was, admittedly not too bright, although she was a complete slut, which was fine by me - looked askance at the idea. She liked hanging around at the *Royal Norfolk* because she had ambitions to be a rock chick and was determined to dump me as soon as she had the chance to jump on one of the roadies from *Motorhead*, and was not at all impressed with the idea of sleeping in a grubby, rough, wooden shack with no electricity, her on-off boyfriend with a penchent for alfresco lovemaking, and a smelly, hirsute and not very talented singer-songwriter with a silly name.

The following Saturday we drove out of Barnstaple, and with some difficulty I managed to locate the nearest bit of road to the hillside where Derry had set up his home.

Samantha complained for the entire duration of the journey. The truth is that we didn't actually like each other very much, but she was determined to get a rock-star boyfriend and, although I wasn't actually a rock-star, I had made a record, played the guitar, and had even written a song for her called *Beautiful Mutant Monkey*. As far as I was concerned; I just wanted a slutty girlfriend with big breasts and no morals. She was perfect.

Reading the above paragraph I suddenly became aware that I have intimated culpability for a very serious offence. However, I would like to point out that I was only just 20 years old at the time - and I was a very naive and innocent young man. Samantha wasn't quite my first girlfriend, but she was certainly the first one that I had ever managed to get undressed. Samantha, however, was 15 going on 40 and combined the sexual sensibilities of Cynthia Plastercaster with the commercial morals of an entire tribe of Levantine usurers. Anyway, we never actually completely consummated our relationship until she was of age. However, I have done my best in this narrative to be honest about the various people whose paths have crossed mine during my three and a half decades as a toiler within the Cryptozoological vineyard. When, as in the case of Samantha, the truth of the matter actually does not show me in the best light, then so be it. I would be the last person to claim to be perfect. Far from it. However, I would prefer any revelations to come from my pen - or in this case computer - than from anyone else, and I have reached that certain age when revelations of a misspent youth tend to be a matter of pride, rather than regret.

We parked the car, locked it, and slowly climbed up the steep, heavily wooded hillside. Eventually we reached the hut where Derry lived. Not entirely to my surprise there was nobody there although the hut was unlocked. We pushed the door open and peered in. Imagine, if you will, if a family of alcoholic badgers with a penchant for football hooliganism had lived together in a pile of cardboard boxes on a diet of tinned pasta and pickled onions. Then multiply your mental image tenfold. Then pour yourself a stiff drink.

Over the years I have visited some of the most squalid places to live that one could possibly imagine. I have even lived in them myself, but this was by far the worst dwelling place that I have ever seen a human being inhabit. It was filthy dirty and full of rubbish. In the corner were a pile of pelts which had been removed from road killed animals and outside various decomposing skulls from these animals were perched on poles and left to rot.

I was feeling somewhat amorous by this time, but unfortunately even the ever-horny Samantha did not feel like making love on top of a pile of half-cured fox skins. I managed to inveigle her into the woods, and we were semi-dressed by the time that Derry - stoned out of what was left of his tiny mind - wandered back up the hill towards the hut, and we rearranged our clothing hurriedly. He had, of course, forgotten that we were coming, and furthermore had left his guitar at some squat in Barnstaple, so although I had gone to the expense of hiring an expensive 4-track Revox tape recorder with which to record his songs, he was in no condition to record anything, and being without a guitar, would not have been able to play them anywhere. So, we spent the rest of the afternoon sitting in the little clearing in the woods, trying - half-heartedly - to seduce Samantha, and chatting about this and that.

Samantha was in no mood to be seduced and went off into a sulk, while Derry and I chatted inconsequential nonsense and puffed away on suspiciously long cigarettes. I asked him why he had decorated the clearing in the forest with animal skulls on poles, and he told me that it was to appease the spirits of the wood.

"Eh?" I asked, wondering what on earth he was talking about. I pointed out that the spirits of the wood would - if, in fact they actually existed - be the guardians of animal life, and would therefore not be particularly impressed - or indeed appeased - by the sight of over a dozen semi-squashed dead animals impaled on sticks outside a malodorous shanty. However, he was unimpressed by my argument. He had seen the avatar of the earth spirits, he told me, and apparently she had taken on the guise of a giant black panther.

Then, at last, I started to pay attention to what my seriously deluded and annoyingly insane companion was saying. At this time the predations of the "Beast of Exmoor" were only just beginning to make the papers and only the cognoscenti - like me - had every heard of the possibility that alien cat species had begun to colonise the British countryside.

Then, slowly at first, but gathering momentum in the way that a snowball will get bigger and bigger as you roll it slowly downhill, an idea began to take shape deep in my subconscious. I had always angrily regretted never following up Ashley's original report. It had been one if the worst failings of the overly repressive regime at my school. The powers-that-be bore no truck with such modern ideas as schools having a major role in the development of the personality of a growing child. A brief perusal of the 'Friends Reunited' website will reveal that during the year I attended West Buckland School, it had continued to do what it had successfully done for centuries - churning out middle-level civil servants and army officers well trained in the esoteric arts of doing what they were told and not thinking for themselves. Even if I had approached the governing body of the school for permission to go off in search of a mystery big cat, they would have been certain to refuse. However, now - four years later - I was young, free, independent, I could drive a car, and I had access to an entire army of spikey haired youths wearing stylish, anarchist t-shirts.

Grabbing Samantha unceremoniously by the arm, I pre-empted my future career as a journalist by making my excuses and leaving. We drove back to Barnstaple as quickly as we could. We went into the *Royal Norfolk,* and looked around for all the spiky haired young oiks that I knew. After about half an hour we went on to another pub - the *Three Tuns* in Boutport Street - which was another hip hang out. By the time we had finished I had about fifteen young helpers ready for the fray. I made arrangements to meet them all in the *Three Tuns* the following day and then drove back to my little flat in Northam to sleep. By this time Samantha was getting so fed up that I made the value judgement that I have made so many times since - when its a matter of women versus monsters the monsters win every time - dropped her home, and watched slightly regretfully as she pouted and flounced back to her Mum's house.

The next day I was back in Barnstaple. I had worked out a rough plan of attack. I decided to divide my troops into three groups and comb the woods where Derry lived using a series of human chains. It was the first time that I had ever planned a major group investigation of a mystery animal - although I have done it on many occasions since - and I was both excited and nervous. I hadn't bothered to telephone Samantha to ask if she wanted to come along. She had made it perfectly obvious that while she was prepared to get down and dirty with a rock musician, she wouldn't even pass the time of day - let alone take off her clothes for - an itinerant investigator of mystery animals. Making a mental note that I would have to write another song for her, I put her out of my mind, and decided to get on with the matter at hand.

It all went swimmingly - that is, up to the time when I strode into the *Three Tuns* to muster my troops. Then it became an absolute bloody disaster!

The place was crawling with punk rockers of all shapes and sizes. There were at least sixty of them, and even the most cursory of glances at the spiky haired throng made me realise that something was badly wrong. Firstly, I had only invited about twenty of my cohorts, and I had no idea where the other forty had come from.

Secondly, there was a very ugly mood in the air. Feelings were obviously running high and there were a couple of minor scuffles in the further flung corners of the room.

And, thirdly, as soon as I made my entrance, a bunch of my particular cohorts cheered and one particularly fearsome looking bloke who looked ridiculously like Vivian from *The Young Ones* threw a bottle at my head.

Suddenly, all hell broke lose and I found myself in the middle of a very vicious and nasty bar fight. Following advice that my father had given me as a teenager, I dove for cover and tried to hide beneath a nearby table, but the weight problems that were to plague me in later life had already started to take their toll, and as I was wriggling corpulently beneath the table someone hit me over the head with a bar stool and everything went black.

I woke up in a police cell with three of my mates, and the worst headache that I have ever had in my life. Slowly, I began to piece together what had happened. Essentially, it turned out that as the word of our forthcoming investigation had leaked out, the rumour mill had been working at full tilt and the word started spreading that not only were my friends and I going off in search of a mysterious big cat, but that we were armed and were planning to shoot it! Despite the fact that this was completely untrue, another gang of punk rockers - who were vehement animal rights supporters - took exception to what they perceived as a gross exercise in animal cruelty and decided to stop us. Add to this a third bunch who were just in the mood for a damn good ruck and you had all the makings of a riot! And a riot was just what happened.

The early eighties were times of civil unrest in the UK, and many people needed no excuse whatsoever to become street fighting men. Apparently, after I had been knocked out, the fight spread into the street and a large number of arrests ensued. Eventually I was questioned, reprimanded and released without charge. It was, however, over twenty years before I ever ventured into the *Three Tuns* again, and even then I kept a wary eye over my shoulder in case of trouble.

Over the years I took part in a number of other big cat hunts, but never found a jot of evidence, and - in one of those amazing pieces of serendipity that always seem to plague fortean investigators, the first time that I actually saw one of the damn things was completely by accident. However, although there was no way that we could try and follow up our sighting and - indeed - this is the first time that I have ever made the details public, but following that night on the way back from Brighton my attitude towards the British Big Cat situation changed. I no longer needed to prove that they were there. My efforts were now dedicated to trying to work out their position within the British ecosystem, which is a far more complex and difficult task.

Over the next few years we produced over a dozen issues of the Chris de Burgh magazine. Not a mean feat at all, especially considering that we had no contact with the man himself - apart from a brief message left on our answerphone one day - and also, although my wife was nominally the editor, I actually did the editing and had little or no interest in the subject of the magazine. I felt that he was a purveyor of dull, suburban and eminently bourgeois pap of little or no artistic merit. However, I didn't tell that to my wife - who was still a besotted fan. I contented myself by sneaking the odd bits of subversion in through the back door. Amusingly enough, nobody really noticed. I spoofed the then current furore surrounding Peter Wright's *Spycatcher* in a piece called *Chriswatcher* about obsessive fans who used to turn up uninvited at his home in Ireland. I wrote an impressive piece of nonsense claiming that de Burgh had played bass for the Sex Pistols during their brief sojourn on A&M records. I doctored a press picture of him to give the Duchess of York's favourite pop singer a spiky haircut, a safety pin in the ear, and a swastika T-shirt. This practical joke caused great offence amongst the readership, and marked the beginning of the end. My final atrocity - in the eyes of de Burgh's management company at least - was when I get hold of a photo session from 1975, which featured the man himself in the company of a well-endowed young lady with her tits out. Such youthful indiscretions had no place in the politically correct career of the bloke who wrote *Lady in Red*, and when I not only reprinted the pictures (but did so under the headline *The last temptation of Chris*) I was very much *persona non grata*.

It was obviously time for a career move.

CHAPTER FIVE

UNKNOWN PLEASURES

In the autumn of 1987 my life was rocked by a series of tragedies and I commenced my long, tortuous and inexorable slide into madness. Late one evening, my father telephoned me to tell me that David Braund - my best friend from childhood, and my companion on many adventures including the bizarre trip to Buckfastleigh Old Church with Danny, had died. It was the first time that I had been confronted with the death of a friend of my own age. What made it worse was that I was a bearer at his funeral and I was one of the six men who lowered the casket containing his young body into the unforgiving ground of Woolsery churchyard. For years afterwards my dreams were haunted by the vision of the mortal remains of my best friend slowly decomposing away six feet under the ground. I became obsessed with the Roman Catholic doctrine of incorruptible bodies and read the articles in Peter Brookesmith's *The Unexplained* on the theories that under certain circumstances decaying human flesh is converted into a waxy substance called adipocere. These concepts filled both my dreams and my waking hours until I was forced to ask my Doctor for tranquilisers that would help me through the dying day.

Then, one evening, when I was sitting at home with Alison, in a haze of benzodiazepines, drinking whisky and waiting for the pain to end, there was a telephone call from one of the girls at work. She was crying and bordering on hysteria. She told me - through the sobbing - that one of my patients (a severely subnormal Irish lass called Eileen O'Donnell) - had collapsed and was lying still on the floor. I rushed down to the car, oblivious of the fact that I was dangerously over the legal limit of alcohol and drugs in my body, shouted to my wife to telephone my line manager and the ambulance service and drove as fast as I could down the little winding country lanes to the outskirts of the small town where I worked.

It was the worst journey of my life. Not only was I horribly drunk - after all I had spent the evening with my wife and some friends - and I had been preparing for bed when the fateful telephone call came, but it was a dark and stormy night reminiscent of something out of a Gothic horror film. The gale was so strong, that as I drunkenly threw the car round of the hairpin bends of the tiny back roads, entire branches were being blown off the trees, and on two occasions ancient trees were blown down - and I had to swerve alarmingly to avoid them. I am not usually a fast driver, and I hope alone never have to drive like that again. I don't think that I went under 90 miles an hour at any point in the journey, and to be quite honest how I wasn't killed I don't know. I shuddered to a halt in the road outside the group home, kicked the door open and ran up the stairs two at a time.

Eileen was lying on the floor of her bedroom. She was motionless and her skin - and lips - were bright blue. I had heard of corpses being blue before, but I had never seen one. I can confirm that yes, under certain circumstances; a recently dead human being *can* appear a vivid blue. However, I believed that it was my duty as a nurse, to try and preserve life, and so I did my utmost best to resuscitate her. I ripped open her blouse and applied CPR to the exposed chest. I lowered my mouth to hers, and started to attempt to breathe air into her lungs as I tried to get her heart started again. Her poor, battered body spasmed involuntarily and the muscle spasms forced about half a pint of mixed phlegm, blood and vomit into my mouth. There was no time for me to feel disgusted, so I spat the revolting the mixture out to the carpet and terror on with CPR and mouth-to-mouth resuscitation. It was to no avail. When the ambulance crew arrived 10 minutes later they pronounced her dead and I threw up in the corner of the room.

What happened next, is one of the most shameful episodes of my life. It turned out, during the official investigation that the two nurses on duty had taken the patients to the pub earlier that evening and had brought back a few small bottles of beer. There is no evidence whatsoever that anybody involved was drunk. Indeed, Eileen's autopsy showed no sign of alcohol in her blood or stomach contents. However, there was a prevailing culture within the NHS at the time, that when something happened - *especially* something terrible - that someone had to be made into a scapegoat. The two girls who had been drinking on duty were immediately suspended. They protested, with some justification, that they were only doing what all the senior members of staff - including me and my immediate superiors - did nearly every evening on duty. I was in a position where I could have saved my colleagues' careers, but was too scared of losing mine.

I was not only party to this disgraceful cover up, but I was actively responsible for orchestrating it. Because of me, two completely innocent young girls were in severe trouble. I was frightened to death that the details of my drunken drive from Exeter on the night of Eileen's death would be made public and that I would end up by losing my driving license, my job and eventually my house. Some of my immediate superiors were in the habit of drinking heavily on duty and several were engaged in drunken extra-marital affairs with other members of staff. At least one staff member regularly stole the patient's medication, and there were rumours that some staff members were guilty of embezzlement and even sexual abuse of the patients. When the two - totally innocent - young girls were accused of drinking on duty, and therefore contributing to Eileen's death because of their negligence, the first thing that they did was to intimate that they would lift the lid on the cauldron of corruption and depravity of which they were aware.

I was instrumental in assuring that none of this knowledge ever came public, and although - to my credit - I managed to do some behind the scenes horse trading to assure that the two girls didn't actually lose their jobs and that the police were not involved more than was absolutely necessary, I made certain that the true extent of the corruption of which everyone was aware was never made public.

However, the horror of what I had done, and the sheer enormity of David's and Kathy's deaths hit me hard. The memory of Eileen's poor battered corpse vomiting an unholy mixture of fluids into my mouth, and the memory of her poor, dead, blue breasts, bruised and battered where I had tried to perform artificial resuscitation haunted me for years. I was slowly losing whatever grip I had ever had on reality when the next blows struck.

Innocently, I had imagined that the powers-that-be would have been grateful for my Machiavellian machinations in preserving their careers and pensions, but nothing of the sort. Within weeks I was facing a disciplinary panel myself, in what I can see now, with the benefit of fifteen years hindsight, was the first battle in a long and concerted war of attrition aimed at getting me out of the NHS.

Even though we no longer worked in the main hospital, we still had to work twelve and a half hour shifts, and because we were in what was essentially a converted suburban house, there were no rest facilities for the staff. Twelve and a half hours is a long time to be working. Most of the staff lived in the vicinity and went home for their breaks. However, I lived some ten miles away and had nowhere to go. By that time, mainly because of my burgeoning psychiatric problems I had developed an eating disorder, and as I overate when I was unhappy, as my life became more and more miserable my weight ballooned. I was doing my best to lose weight, and so I didn't join the other staff members to eat a mid-day meal. I used to go into the patient's sitting room to sleep. One day, I was taking my midday nap, when a senior member of staff made an unscheduled visit to the unit. I was accused of professional misconduct by being asleep on duty, and was sent before an industrial tribunal.

My protestations that I was only sleeping through my lunch-break, that I had nowhere else to go, and that being the only qualified member of staff on duty I was unable to leave the building, were ignored and I was punished. Over the next weeks and months a parade of similarly trumped up charges followed, and I was disciplined on a number of occasions. My life, and my mental health were spiraling out of control. I had lost whatever authority I ever had over the staff members over which I was supposed to be in charge. They refused to follow my instructions, mocked my life, my clothes, my beliefs, my accent and my lifestyle. I was bullied by my superiors *and* most of my staff, and my life was rapidly becoming unbearable. My marriage was also rapidly falling apart, and I was desperately miserable all the time. I took solace in binge eating and drinking ridiculous amounts of whisky, and my weight ballooned out of all recognition and the rest of my health declined rapidly. I was hallucinating most of the time - both audially and visually - and, although I did not realize it at the time, I was rapidly falling into a bottomless pit of psychotic despair.

Ironically, however, while my personal and private life was rapidly getting out of control, my extra curricular activities were becoming ever more successful. I started a second magazine called ISMO (after a gloriously anarchic children's novel by Sir John Verney). It covered the new-hippy movement, and its manifesto was taken from John Sinclair, the *White Panther Party* and *The MC5;* Dope, Rock and Roll, and fucking in the streets. Over the first couple of years of its existence we met, interviewed, and made friends with a number of minor (and even some, major), celebrities including members of *Fairport Convention, Pop Will Eat Itself, The Shamen, Hawkwind, Gong* and other luminaries of the festival/hippy scene.

Following the success of the nascent magazine, Alison and I started promoting gigs in local venues. The first was at the Exeter Arts Centre where we promoted a show by *Nik Turner's Allstars*. Turner had been a pivotal member of the seminal space rock band *Hawkwind*, and went down in history as the only man ever to have been arrested for carrying heroin in his saxophone whilst dressed as a frog! I have to admit that at this stage of our promoting career, we had only the vaguest idea of what we were supposed to be doing. The band stayed at our house after the gig, because we couldn't afford a hotel room. Alison and I designed the posters, fly-posted the area, sold the tickets, manned the door, looked after the band and provided security - all by ourselves.

It was whilst performing the duties of a security officer that I checked all the possible entrances to the gig. I was quite surprised how many people were trying to get in for nothing. I was essentially very naïve and with a firm grounding in middle-class morals and at that time I would never have considered gatecrashing a concert. Many people did, however, and I spent much of the gig trying to extract money from people whom I had apprehended climbing in through the fire escape.

About half way through the gig, I had to pay a visit to the gents' in order to answer a call of nature. Whilst washing my hands I was surprised to hear a crunching noise coming from the toilet windows behind me. I turned around and was astonished to see a painfully thin male torso and a pair of bedenimmed legs flailing wildly as someone had obviously got stuck as he was climbing through the toilet window. I started to laugh. "Its not funny you stupid bugger" growled the man, still half in and half out of the un-ideal aperture. Forgetting, for the moment at least, that this was a miscreant actively engaged in trying to defraud my wife and me of a fiver's worth of ticket money, I helped him through. Bizarrely, the window was not broken. As soon as he reached ground level, he turned and smiled at me. He was a scruffy looking bloke with a patchy beard, collar length dark hair, a weatherbeaten face and wild, piercing, rather shifty eyes. His name was Graham Inglis and we have been firm friends ever since. Fifteen years later and he still hasn't paid me for the concert ticket.

During this period I also continued my cryptozoological studies. I frequented the Westcountry Studies Library as often as I could, and one day, whilst perusing some nineteenth century volumes of the *Transactions of the Devonshire Association* I made, what I believed - and indeed still believe - was a significant discovery.

I have always been interested in small carnivorous mammals. As a child in Hong Kong one occasionally came across a road killed civet cat or ferret badger. On my return to the UK, I always kept an eye open for weasels and stoats. I knew from my reading, that in recent historical times there had been other species of small carnivore living in the wilder parts of the southwestern peninsula of the United Kingdom. These creatures - the polecat, the pine marten and the wildcat - were now found only in the wilder parts of Scotland and Wales.

I wondered when these rare and beautiful carnivores had become extinct in the rest of England, and I also wondered what had happened to them. This particular afternoon I had been in search of information to help me solve these two problems so I was perusing the earliest mammal reports for the county of Devonshire that I could get hold of. It was then that I made a momentous discovery. Much to my great joy I discovered that not only were all three of these species well known residents of the region until the end of the nineteenth century, but that mammal recorders in Devon, Cornwall, Dorset and Somerset noted *two* species of marten living in the region. As well as the pine marten *(Martes martes),* a second animal, The Marten Cat, Beech Marten or Stone Marten *(Martes foina)*, was also a well-known denizen of the heavily forested areas of the southwest. Indeed, in some areas it was better known, and appeared to be even more common than the pine marten.

In Dorset historians noted that these creatures had been so common at one point during the eighteenth and nineteenth centuries that they had been the focus of a lucrative fur trade, and its attendant small industries. Perhaps the most exciting aspect of my discovery, however, was an account of a road-killed beech marten, which had been found by the side of the road between Exeter and Exmouth in the late 1970s.

The idea that all the books that had been written on the subject of British mammals - at least for the last century - were wrong was a tremendously exciting one. Although, I had been studying mystery animals since my earliest childhood, I was the first to admit that although I had had some exciting adventures and had amassed some useful data, I hadn't actually set the zoological world on fire with any of my discoveries were. However, if this was true - and there was an entirely new species of British mammal, and furthermore it had been my discovery, then all sorts of exciting vistas were now open to me. I decided, however, that before I went public with my new discovery I would have to do some more research into the status of the British small carnivores - especially those living in the Westcountry.

It was then that the true extent of my discovery became obvious. It turned out practically everything that had been written on the subject of the smaller carnivores of the westcountry was fundamentally flawed - if not downright wrong. Two well-known mammologists - Langley and Yalden - had written a paper listing the extinction dates for the three species in which I was interested. In each of the four counties of the westcountry I managed to prove that the dates they had given were complete wrong. The most interesting anomalies were those concerning the wildcat population, and those concerning the pine martens. It seemed that everywhere I looked and I could find more evidence.

I discovered that in the years immediately prior to the First World War, a lady called Hope Bourne had written about an entire population of strange wildcats in North Devon. I also discovered that eyewitnesses - for many years - had been reporting what they described as giant Siamese cats near Newton Abbot in mid-Devon. I discovered that until the mid 1970s when there had still been a few remaining bombsites in Exeter itself, a tribe of enormous tabby cats had lived for many years amongst the ragwort and the ruins.

My investigations into the pine marten situation were even more exciting. I discovered that despite claims that the species had been hunted to extinction by the end of the 19th century, there were decent reports of pine martens in various parts of rural Devon up until the 1970s and 1980s. Alison and I made friends with the staff at the Royal Albert Memorial Museum in Exeter, and they allowed us access to their mammal reports. We followed up the most recent, and discovered that there was a lot of good evidence for there being at least two well-established populations of Martens living wild in the Devon woodlands.

Just as I was beginning to work out how I could make my discoveries public, I found a fly in the ointment. I discovered the work of H. G. Hurrell - a famous Devonshire naturalist. When I read his books I found out that he had an obsession with pine martens. He loved the creatures. He kept them as pets for many years. He wrote books about them - for both adults and children, and although his surviving daughter irately denied it to me - I was told by some pretty impressive sources that he had carried out to an unofficial reintroduction programme on Forestry Commission land for many years between the 1950s and the 1970s. When I put this claim to his daughter, she was furious and I don't really understand why. If these claims had been true, her father had done nothing illegal - it was many years before the Wildlife and Countryside Act, which forbids the intentional release of alien species into the British countryside. Even if it that Act *had* been in force at the time it is questionable whether Hurrell's actions would have been illegal. The pine marten is after all a British animal that had been unquestionably living in the area in question within the previous century or so. What could the problem have been?

On and off, the riddle of the smaller mystery carnivores of the westcountry took up most of my attention for several years. Alison and I travelled all over the area gathering information. We found - much to our surprise - that the Hurrell family had donated nearly all the mounted specimens of pine martens that could be found in westcountry museums. According to Hurrell's own writings, his pine martens had originally come from Germany. Eventually, however, we encountered claims that the animals kept by Hurrell - and presumably this included those which would have been used in any introduction programme were actually American martens *(Martes americana)* - a closely related but distinct species. If this were true - and not having access to Hurrell's original papers, or (at that time at least) a laboratory which could carry out DNA analysis, (and I want to stress that this is all hearsay) then this might well explain why Hurrell's relatives were so unfriendly towards me when they heard about my researches.

Eventually, I tracked down the last two surviving museum specimens of *bona-fide* westcountry pine martens. One was - apparently - part of a large, static display, in the eaves of the museum at Combe Martin in North Devon. We approached the curators and asked for permission to examine it, but were told that it would be impossible at that time.

We asked for an explanation, but none was forthcoming. A few years later, I would probably have pushed it. As my career as a cryptozoologist advanced, I found that my new-found fame opened doors which had been closed only a few years before. As I progressed through the self-exploration of psychotherapy I found myself getting more assertive, and less able to take rejection lying down. However, in the days of which I write - back in the late 1980s - my position as Britain's foremost cryptozoologist was so far beyond the bounds of even *my* imagination, that I was quite happy to take no for an answer.

It was, however, a great pity that those in power at Combe Martin museum had not allowed us to examine their specimen. Because, unusually amongst the exhibits at small, parochial collections, this particular specimen had a peerless provenance. Hidden among the treasure-trove of documents in the Westcountry Studies Library was a catalogue of exhibits at the Combe Martin museum during the first decade of the 20th century. It included this specific pine marten - and furthermore gave details of the local nobleman who had shot be put it on the edge of Exmoor before donating it to the museum. The accounts of the demise of this unfortunate creature tied in perfectly, not only with the other reports from the latter days of the 19th century which placed a thriving population of the species in the heavily wooded valleys on the north side of Exmoor - both on the Devon and the Somerset side of the border - but also with a small, but ever-growing, number of accounts that I was beginning to receive of what appeared to be modern encounters with the same creature in exactly the same place. Renowned Devon naturalist Trevor Beer, telephoned me to tell me of his contemporary encounter with what he believed were these animals, and he was not the only one.

However, because we were unable to get any co-operation from the Hurrell family, we were not able to find out where - if indeed any such experiment had taken claims - Hurrell had released his animals. Were these animals that Trevor - and others - were telling me about on Exmoor descendants of the original populations or were they descendants of animals released by Hurrell?

The matter was confused further when we heard of another spate of sightings further south - near Ilsington on the eastern edge of Dartmoor. Were told about these sightings first of all from accounts in the mammal register at the Royal Albert Memorial Museum in Exeter. Much to our great joy we found several accounts of sightings of what appeared to be pine martens in these woods all the way through the 1970s and 1980s. We telephoned these witnesses and were impressed by the level of corroboration that they gave each other. Although none of them were actually naturalists, they gave perfect descriptions of these beautiful and rare animals, and one couple - on the night we telephoned them, the wife had just gone into labour, and they were waiting for the ambulance - told us how and they had heard strange noises as if an animal was crashing about in the trees above them on several occasions whilst they were walking their dog through the dense woodlands near their home.

Despite the imminency of his wife giving birth the proud father-to-be gave a creditable imitation of the sound that he had heard so many times. It was unquestionably that of a pine marten chasing its chosen prey - squirrels - through the leafy canopy of a dense broadleafed wood. Our telephone conversation was truncated by the arrival of the ambulance, so Alison and I sat back to work out what to do next.

Matters were complicated a few days later when we discovered the existence of another colony of these creatures in the woods of south Teignbridge near the small village of Combeinteignhead, and the same day we were sent a photocopy of the document that had dealt the taxonomic death sentence to the British beech marten. It was a paper by Edward Alston which had been published in the 1890s and which had suggested that all the British martens were, indeed, one species rather than two. Despite the fact that this treatise conveniently ignored the fact that country folk all over the British Isles had considered the animals to be of two separate species as they were across Europe, that they had two different names in Devon dialect, and that they were even treated separately by the laws of the time which had considered them both to be vermin but had offered different bounties for the two species, the textbooks were rewritten and the beech marten ceased to exist as a native British mammal.

But had it?

We knew that there had been at least one beech marten living wild in Devonshire at the end of the 1970s. Could there have been more? Indeed, could Alston's paper have been complete nonsense all along? All the evidence was pointing in this direction. What we had to do now was to find an unimpeachable specimen of a British beech marten. There the matter stopped.

We eventually tracked down the only other surviving West Country pine marten specimen. It was a very moth-eaten animal which, for many years, had been stored in a back room at Truro museum. Despite its condition, it was a very humbling experience to hold it in my hands. Here was a rare and beautiful animal, which had been hunted to extinction by my own species. Looking back I really don't know what I had hoped to achieve by locating an original mounted specimen. The emotional rush that I got from handling the creature meant a lot to me. However, it added little to the sum total of our knowledge about the precise status of the westcountry marten population. I suppose that I had been hoping that the Truro animal would turn out to be a beech marten. But it wasn't. Its pelt was very faded until it was of little no interest as a museum specimen, but it is still certifiably a pine marten. It had the diagnostic cream coloured bib on its throat and there was - sadly - nothing else that it could have been. We were just about to embark on the next stage of our investigation (detailed, belatedly, in my 1996 book *Smaller Mystery Carnivores of the Westcountry*) when events in my non-cryptozoological life took an unfortunate turn for the worse, and my studies into the Westcountry mustelidae were forced onto the back burner.

While my hobby of cryptozoology continued apace, and my extra curricular activities within the fringes of the music business were beginning to make me both a burgeoning reputation and - at last - a small but regular income, my life as a nurse was rapidly becoming untenable.

When I first read Peter Wright's unreadably bad book *Spycatcher* in the late 1980s I was immediately struck by the truth of the whole affair. The author had only written his dreadful book in order to get his own back on the people that he considered had conned him out of the pension to which he believes that he was entitled. Having read many people's autobiographies over the years I have come to the conclusion that many people decide to write books for much the same reason - to get revenge for some real or imagined slight. During my long and chequered career I have had a lot of people do things for me and to me that I did not deserve. Many of them have been good things - boosts to my career, for example, which were certainly not justified if the crypto-investigative community had been a pure meritocracy. An equal number of things that have happened to me have been bad things which I at least believe that I never deserved. However, I am not writing this book in order to get revenge on anyone. I am not even writing this book because I expect anyone to read it. I hope that they do - I am an author and selling books is how I make my living. However I am writing this book for me - mostly because a strange elderly man with piercing blue eyes told me to on the night of my fortieth birthday. Therefore when I describe the unpleasant parts of my life, and the times when I was bullied, victimised and even emotionally tortured it is purely so I can explain how these events moulded my life, my work and my theories, and not because I am trying to gain some petty revenge. Life is far too short for that.

Within months of Eileen O'Donnell's death I had a new boss. The old one had retired and been replaced by an unconvincing transsexual with a prominent Adam's apple and a big nose. I had always disliked her even when I had been a student, and it appeared that the feeling was reciprocated. At the time I felt that there was a concerted effort on the part of my immediate superiors to get rid of me. That may not have been true, but looking back a decade and a half later it is hard to see what else they could have done to destroy my life had such a programme been underway.

Under the new regime my life got even worse. My new boss actively encouraged staff members to disobey my orders, and complain about me to those in authority. It got to the stage that nothing I could do was right. On one occasion I was disciplined for "unnecessary use of the telephone", after having telephoned the Weymouth Sea Life Centre in order to arrange a discount for a party of my patients. On another occasion I was disciplined for "unnecessary waste of patient's money", after another member of staff had - while I was on duty - purchased butter rather than margarine. I didn't even have solace at home. Not only were my staff encouraged to telephone me while I was off duty in order to complain about things that I had or had not done at work, but it turned out that my transsexual boss was close friends with my next-door neighbours - something which I most assuredly was not - and she took it upon herself not only to visit my neighbours on a regular basis but to discuss my shortcomings with them in a loud voice. Even when I was lying on my bed in the evening waiting for my wife to come back from work, I could hear them performing an ongoing character assassination of me.

If I was downstairs in my sitting room, then my neighbours knew that I was in because of the light in my window, and would make any excuse to knock on my front door and complain that my music was too loud, that my dog was barking, that one of my cats had dug up their petunias or any one of a hundred other pointless, niggling complaints. Whenever they paid me one of these they nocturnal visits they would make a point of mentioning - in passing - that that they had heard about my latest professional problems, from my boss. I had absolutely nowhere to run or hide. I couldn't even turn to my wife for comfort. Our marital difficulties were exacerbated by the fact that we still hardly ever saw each other, our sex life was practically non-existent, and we were always broke.

I turned to the bottle and for several years I drank a bottle or so of whisky each evening. Matters came to a head in the early summer of 1989. It is probably a good thing that I have very few memories of that time. The precise details of my massive breakdown, which paved the way for my exit from the Exeter Health Authority, remain locked deep within my brain and I have no intention of trying to revisit them. It is probably a good thing that although I have lost five or six weeks of my life forever, the next bit that I can remember - the enchanted high summer of 1989 - remains one of the happiest times of my life.

Back in 1974 when I had been a spotty and callow youth with a fixation about cryptozoology and a taste for somewhat pretentious rock music, my best friend - apart from David Braund - was a young man called Tim. We actually had very little in common, but shared a similar sense of humour and filled our school exercise books with sub-Monty Python ramblings which we thought were works of genius and which nobody else in the entire universe found the slightest bit funny. Two or three times a term I used to spend a weekend with his family, and on one of these weekends, my life was changed forever.

We were watching Top Of the Pops and suddenly - with no warning - an extraordinary sight filled the screen. It was a young man called Steve Harley who was the singer with an ensemble called *Cockney Rebel*. I can still remember this extraordinary performance as if it were yesterday. Harley, wearing a velvet suit and a bowler hat (which I was too young to realise had been purloined lock, stock, and barrel from either *Cabaret*, or possibly *A Clockwork Orange*, and most possibly both), crouched in the corner of the stage like an epileptic Caliban. His vocals were so stylised as to be almost unrecognisable as the English language, but when eventually I did decipher them I realised that this man wrote the most bewitching prose as well as composing the most subversive pop music that I had ever heard. For the first time since I had discovered the books of Gerald Durrell as a small boy I had found myself a role model.

Years later, in 1989, bruised and battered from the nervous breakdown that I still cannot fully remember, in the guise of music journalists, Alison and I went to see Steve - with the latest incarnation of Cockney Rebel - at the Bierkeller in Bristol. Although the hit singles had dried up many years before, and it had been a decade since he last released an album, he was absolutely fantastic! His band made an elegantly brutal noise over which Steve, pranced, preened and cavorted. It was like he had never been gone. Just as I had been at the age of 15 I was entranced. Alison's and my tenure running the Chris de Burgh magazine had pretty well run its course, and one of us - I can't remember which - nervously suggested that we approach Steve's management about running the official fan club. This we did, the very next day - coincidentally, the day before my descent into complete and utter madness.

The saying that when one door closes, another one opens has always been a truism in my life. Most of the early summer of 1989 is a complete blank to me. I can remember odd, disjointed images, terrifying dreams that seemed to go on forever, I can remember screaming and slashing at my arms with household cutlery, and I remember my darling wife holding me close to her and trying, vainly, to comfort me. Most of the time, however, I was drugged into a near comatose state. Then, one morning, I woke up. Outside, the sun was shining and the birds singing. Alison came running into our bedroom. "You are never going to believe it", she gabbled, so excited that she could hardly get the words out. "That was Steve Harley on the phone. We've got the job".

For the next five years, Alison and I worked for Steve. Over the years we progressed from just running the fan club, to flogging merchandise and various other jobs until we were an integral part of the touring party. For a while, Steve and I even became friends.

In the mid-20th century a psychologist called Abraham Maslow identified what he called his "Hierarchy of human needs". It was shaped like a pyramid. At the very apex was what he called Self-Actualisation, or Social Role Valorisation. According to Maslow, human beings needed to achieve this in order to achieve happiness. His definition of this point was the place where a human being was fulfilling a social role in which he or she felt happy. For the first time in my life I had achieved Social Role Valorisation. I had been an unhappy and disaffected schoolboy, and my adult life had not been much better. I loathed my career, and only stuck at it out of an old fashioned belief that I had to support my wife. Although I loved

Alison more than mere words can possibly express, our marriage was not a happy one, and until the summer of 1989 my life was pretty awful. Suddenly everything changed. I was working for one of my heroes. I was making enough money to augment my meagre sick pay from the NHS, and I was getting the chance to travel all over the country, seeing places that I had previously only read about, and - for one of the first times in my life - I was truly happy.

I was also given an unprecedented opportunity to continue my cryptozoological studies. Our almost continual travels around the country gave me the chance to see many of the places that were of Cryptozoological interest in the UK. Alison and I explored them all avidly. Gigs in Hastings, and Worthing, for example, allowed us to explore St. Leonard's Forest in Sussex where - according to contemporary writings - a fearsome dragon had lived as recently as the year of Shakespeare's death. We spent several days travelling round this dank and mysterious stretch of woodland. It had a dark and foreboding atmosphere, and whilst we didn't see a dragon we found its figurative fingerprints everywhere we went. There were several pubs named after the great beast, and we found Dragon Lane, Dragon Street and even a Dragon Tea House in one of the local villages.

For the first time we visited the places in the Home Counties where the eponymous Surrey Puma had kick-started the mass-market British alien big cat phenomenon back in the early 1960s. Like so many other people, I had always believed, that the Home Counties - if only because of their proximity to the metropolis - were an extremely unlikely location for a mystery predator to lurk. When I finally reached the forested valleys near Godalming, which had been made famous in the children's books of Monica Edwards, I realised how wrong I had been. Within a stone's throw of London there were miles upon miles of veritable wilderness. Alison and I parked the van in the middle of The Devil's Punchbowl - just around the corner from the farm that Monica Edwards had immortalised. Earlier that day I had visited a second-hand bookshop in Guildford, where I had bought a couple of books about life at Punchbowl Farm. Reading them for the first time since my childhood I suddenly realised that the clues had been there for me all along. Monica Edwards not only described the lush, thick, wooded valleys of the Surrey countryside to perfection, but also included mystery animals in at least two of her books. *Fire in the Punch Bowl* included a description of a relict population of pine martens, extremely similar to the ones that Alison and I had been hunting on the eastern slopes of Dartmoor. Another of her books even featured the Surrey Puma - although according to the story it was a solitary female animal that had escaped from a travelling circus and then had a cub.

We spent the night - the first of many - sleeping in the back of our van in the middle of the enchanted woods. At about four in the morning I looked out of the back window and saw a pair of young badgers frolicking in the moonlight. The night was deadly still. In the middle-distance the eerie sound of a vixen calling to the spirits of the midnight woods split the air. Tiny horseshoe bats coursed up and down the Forest Path - deadly hunters only a few inches long engaged in a ferocious quest for the night flying insects which surrounded the fragrant honeysuckle bushes in a miasma of living mist.

We also visited two of England's ancient forests - Sherwood Forest, where the spirit of Robin Hood and that of the ancient English forest-daemon; the wodewose (or Robin of the Wood), had met Robin Goodfellow and together coalesced into a glorious spirit of high strangeness which has allowed this ancient preserve of Kings to survive into the modern age with its integrity just about intact. And Epping Forest, a place with a rich Cryptozoological history of its own. A place where - according to unimpeachable sources - as recently as the beginning of the 20th century wolves ran free hundreds of years after they had vanished from the rest of these islands. Of course, the story behind these latter-day lupines has a matter-of-fact explanation. It seems that at the beginning of the 20th century the local foxhunt had pretty well driven the fox population to extinction. In order to secure a future for their sport, the local MFH had introduced an entire shipment of what he believed were young foxes from the Black Forest in Germany. Apparently some of the shipment turned out to be young wolves. A slightly less plausible explanation involved the foolhardy behaviour of a man who had spent many years as a trapper in the wilds of Canada. So the story goes, on his return to England he brought one or more timber wolves with him, and for reasons, which remain obscure, he released them into the Forest. Whatever their provenance, it does seem as if the story of the Epping Forest wolves is substantially true, because one was shot - I believe - in 1903, and its mortal remains exhibited for some years in Epping town hall.

Ironically, although we visited Epping on many occasions during our career with Steve, and indeed, I had visited the town in a my younger days when, before my marriage, I was briefly involved with CRASS - the notorious anarchist punk band who lived in a commune just outside Epping - I have never actually gone to the town hall to check whether the stuffed wolf is still in residence. It is just one other thing that has been relegated to the mental " I've really got to do it, when I get round to it some time" filing tray in the deepest recesses of my psyche.

Probably the most important part of the summer - at least as far as my Cryptozoological investigations were concerned -

was the fact that for the first time in my life I had some spare money in my pocket. The first thing that we would do, on entering a new town, (after ascertaining where the evening's performance was going to be), was to make a beeline for the second hand bookshops, and the charity shops, and the second hand record shops. Initially, I was looking for new Cryptozoological and fortean titles for my collection. I also looked for rare, and unusual records by Steve Harley or any artistes connected either to him, or to any of the members of his current touring band. Then, suddenly, one day somewhere along the South Coast the penny dropped. I had access to an almost limitless supply of rare collector's items. All I had to do was to get Steve to autograph some of the more unusual records that we found and - hey presto - I had possession of a reasonably valuable artefact.

Some of Steve's rarer records were worth a fair amount of money anyway. A copy of his 1974 single *Big Big Deal*, was, for example, at that time at least, worth something in the region of 15 quid. A promotional copy was worth double that. Get Steve to autograph a promotional copy and you had something worth a small fortune. It would have been very easy for me and Alison to make a lot of money from selling these records to the gullible public. However, we felt that, as Steve had been so kind to us, that it would have been completely immoral to have done so. However, once the word went around the fan club membership that I would accept any books, videos, or magazines on the subject of unknown animals and those areas of forteana in which I was interested, the proverbial floodgates opened. I soon had several hundred people around the country - and later gone round the continent - scouring second hand bookshops for me and before long the foyers in rock venues around the country began to resemble one of the less salubrious car-boot sales in a particularly scuzzy neighbourhood as Alison and I - and our ever-growing band of helpers - not only enrolled people into the fan club and sold both our books and magazines and the official merchandise, but carried out a thriving - and unofficial - swapmeet whereby rare records were exchanged for enormous numbers of books which - together with my already not inconsiderable collection - became the nucleus of what is now the library off at the Centre for Fortean Zoology.

It was a magical summer. Even when we were not on tour we travelled. We went from rock festival to rock festival, from sacred site to sacred site, from concert to concert. Everywhere we went we sold our home made magazines. Whenever possible we took Toby with us. By now what he was a full-grown black-and-white dog. Although I had attempted to train him, it had been to no avail. He was completely unschooled, and sadly - and I admit that this was completely our fault - ridiculously neurotic (probably because of the bizarre way in which he had been brought up). However, he loved us - particularly me - fiercely, and the feeling was reciprocated a hundred percent.

During this enchanted summer, Toby and I forged a partnership that would last for the rest of his life. It was him and me *contra mundum*, without question and without exception and I can truthfully say that I have never been so close to another living creature in my life - and I never expect to be again.

Several years before, when I was still a student nurse I had been bullied by my peers into shaving off my beard, and adopting a short-back-and-sides haircut. During this enchanted summer I grew my beard back, and allowed my hair to grow. Alison and I - for a few short months - became the sort of hippy flower children that I have to admit that I now find mildly revolting. We believed in peace, love, and understanding. Alison adopted a wardrobe of shapeless tie-dyed odds and sods from charity shops, while I wore beads and called everybody 'man'. I followed the advice of Frank Zappa in *Who needs the Peace Corps* (blithely ignoring the fact that it was a cynical satire about people like the one I had become) and had "a psychedelic gleam in my eye at all times and smoked an awful lot of dope".

However, the sun, the open air, the travelling, and most of all the general good vibes were having a beneficial effect upon me. My poor, battered, emotions, and my shell-shocked psyche were beginning to repair themselves. At the end of the summer I was in far better shape than I had been at the beginning. Alison and I were happier than we had ever been, and for the first time it looked as if both my marriage - and indeed my life in general - were at last beginning to work effectively. As the enchanted summer rolled on towards the season of mists and mellow fruitfulness, and my mental and physical health improved I decided that the time had come to return to work. I contacted both my GP and the Occupational Health Department and they both agreed that I could return to work, if - and only if - I did so in a lower stress environment, working relatively shorter days, and with a minimum amount of travelling.

I contacted my employers, and communicated the two sets of doctor's rulings to them. Within days I received a telephone call. Yes, I could return to work. I was to start the following Monday - working 12 and a half-hour shifts, three-quarters of the time on night duty, in Axminster (some 35 miles away).

It was then that I made a very bad mistake. Rather than refusing, and returning to the Occupational Health Department and insisting that they negotiate an easier working regimen for me, I reverted to form. I had been brought up in the outpost of the British Empire, where an Englishman was noted for his devotion to duty and his stiff upper lip. As an English gentleman, I believed that I had no option but to accept the posting to Axminster. So, to Axminster I went.

I had thought that my previous hospital had been bad. It *was* badly run, ill maintained and staffed, and administered by an inefficient hegemony of poorly motivated idiots, most of whom had either known each other since childhood, were related to each other, were married to each other, were having sex with each other, or some combination of the above. However, compared to St Mary's Hospital, Axminster, it was the greatest institution in the world.

I would be the first to accept that during its glory days it might have been a much better place. I pride myself on a scientific approach to life, and it would be grossly unscientific for me to claim that after I left - somehow - it had not improved beyond measure. However, during the six-months that I worked there - from the autumn of 1989 to the spring of 1990 it was a complete and utter disgrace. Furthermore, I cannot prove this, but I am convinced that from the moment I was sent there the idea was to get rid of me. If my relationships with my staff had been bad at my previous posting, they were worse here! I was nominally in charge of one of the shifts on a residential ward. In my first week, I decided to call a staff meeting to introduce myself to the other people working on my ward. I sent a memo to all members of staff inviting them to attend. I thought that it might be a nice idea - especially as it was my first ward meeting - to provide refreshments, so I went into town, and bought - with my own money - some cream cakes and biscuits. When I returned to the ward after my lunch, ready to chair the meeting, I found my cakes and biscuits in the waste bin, together with all the invitations to the meeting. All except one that is. This had been a pinned to the ward noticeboard. On it had been drawn an obscene caricature of me, and the caption "we are not going to pay any attention to what this fat twat says are we?"

I realised then that I was not just fighting a losing battle - but that I had lost. It was then that I stopped fighting. From then on, half the staff would not even speak to me. The others were nice enough, but those that mattered made it obvious that I was not welcome and that, whatever I did, I would not be tolerated for very long.

Over the next few days, the campaign of civil disobedience against me continued. Whenever I asked any of my so-called "staff" to do anything they would ignore the instruction, entirely. On several occasions, I was hauled over the coals by my superiors because of tasks that I had instructed my underlings to do, which had not been done. On one occasion, I made an official complaint about the staff member in question to the senior nurse on duty. My complaint was, of course ignored, and I was told that "I had a lot to learn about management technique". This was probably true, but didn't make my life any easier. I had to get up at five in the morning in order to shower, dress, and drive to work. It was after 8.30 in the evening before I got home. On several occasions, the staff who were supposed to be working the night shift didn't bother to turn up until, gone 8 o'clock, and I was even later home. I was permanently exhausted, and an emotional wreck. I went to my superior officer and asked for lighter duties. A week later I was placed on permanent night duty - as the only qualified member of staff in the whole hospital.

The hospital at night was a very strange place. Whereas once upon a time there had been upwards of half a dozen wards, by the time I was - in effect - acting night nursing officer, only two wards were left. Over the previous four or five years, the Gadarene rush to empty the asylums and fulfill Margaret Thatcher's policy of "care in the community" had denuded all the hospitals in the region of the most able patients. Whereas once these hospitals had been asylums in a very real sense of the word - places where those who were not able to live within the fabric of an ever more complicated and ever more technologically reliant society were able to live up - more or less happily - under the supervision of trained nursing staff, all the able patients, and indeed all the able staff, have long gone to the newly set up group homes within the community itself. All that were left were those that nobody wanted.

The same - on the whole - applied to the staff. With hindsight, it seems surprising that there were not more people like me. However, again with hindsight that the other mildly-hippyesque idealists and social malcontents who had been unwise enough to join up to the National Health Service during its declining years has not been burdened with the ethos of empire as I had. I was probably the only person working in the entire hospital system of that time who actually believed in an old-fashioned belief in the concept of "Duty" with a capital D. To me, at that time, it was unthinkable that I would leave my job voluntarily when I had a wife to support and a mortgage to keep going. The fact that said job was rapidly driving me insane had nothing to do with it. I also believed that I had a vocation to look after the mentally handicapped, and a moral duty to continue to do so.

Although it was obvious that as far as the powers-that-be were concerned, I had been placed in this hospital because I was -

in their eyes - a useless malcontent that they didn't know what to do with, and that the tortuous employment laws still wouldn't allow them to sack, my fellow malcontents and I had very little in common. They were the alcoholics, the serial womanisers, the bone idle, and the people who had serious chips on one or both shoulders because of their sexual orientation or their ethnic origins. Most of them were pretty awful people, and furthermore they were people that any sane system would have sacked years before.

Luckily for me, the permanent night duty staff, were - on the whole - much nicer people. They were ordinary, down to earth, country folk who on the whole had worked at the hospital for years and years, and who were bewildered at being the unwilling witnesses of its slow and ignominious decline. They also - quite surprisingly in view of the way that I had been treated by nurses great and small over the previous few years - were kind and welcoming to the grossly overweight, hirsute, staff nurse who had been foisted upon them as a result of internecine hospital politics far beyond their ken. Much to my surprise, I settled into night duty quite easily. There was actually very little to do. The few remaining patients were either in a persistent semi-vegetative state, or were so sedated as result of persistent - and often quite disgusting - behavioural disorders that they slept through the night. Apart from supervising the other members of staff on duty, my job, dole out medication at eight in the evening and 6.30 in the morning, to change the nappies and incontinence pads of those patients liable to befoul themselves during the night, and regularly make sure that all my charges were still alive.

These meagre duties gave me plenty of free time. As nurse in charge, it befell me to make regular sorties around the hospital to make sure that everything was in order. It was a particularly unattractive building. Unlike the sprawling Gothic edifices at Starcross and Exminster, this was a squat grey-blue building which looked like it had been designed as a cross between a low budget 1920s seaside hotel and an enormous municipal public lavatory. It was scheduled for demolition as soon as the final patients had either died or been rehoused, and so the minimum of maintenance had been carried out on it over the previous few years. What had once been attractive - indeed elegant - formal gardens featuring rhododendron bushes and pampas grass, were now a heavily overgrown and down-at-heel wasteland, smelling of cat piss, stinging nettles and decay. Once upon a time the grounds would have been attended by the more able residents who proudly referred to each other as "high grades", and looked down with distain upon the less able "low grades", who languished in ignominy in the corners of the wards. Those days, however, were long gone, and the few basket cases who were left were not only such that the "low grades" of old would have found them beneath their contempt, but were almost uniformly wheelchair-bound and thus confined to the main building.

One of the few exceptions was a vicious young man called Stevie. Stevie was in his early twenties and gave the lie to the claims that those unlucky enough to be born with de Lange Syndrome never survive into adulthood. He had practically no power of speech. The only words that he could say - at least on a regular basis - were "fuck off" and "Stevie wants a bumming". Both phrases were muttered malevolently, almost beneath his breath as he stamped around the building and the dilapidated grounds brandishing a pointed stick with the severed head of a doll impaled on the tip. He spent all his waking hours marching around the gardens looking for stones to turn over so that he could find live snails and woodlice to eat. Any attempt by a member of staff - or indeed anybody else - to initiate a conversation or to interact with him in any way were returned in one of three ways. He would either bite you, start screaming, or unzip his trousers, pull out his penis and proceed to piss all over you.

Another mobile patient was Derek. Having spent most of his life living with his elderly mother - who was now in her late eighties - he was tremendously spoiled and whenever he came into the hospital (which was about once a month for a week or so in order to give his poor mother some respite), he would swagger around the place like a perverted analogue of Little Lord Fauntleroy, alternately punching and biting staff whenever he didn't get exactly his own way. Most of the rest of the time he spent sulking. He was also sexually attracted to pianos. Having spent many happy hours reading the entire Kinsey Reports on human sexuality, and also having read most of Havelock-Ellis's tortuous but undeniably fine explorations of human sexual behaviour, I have never encountered anyone like Derek. The only times that he was happy was when he was masturbating over a piano keyboard. Being the grooviest of hippies at the time, and believing that people should be able to do their own thing, I saw nothing really wrong in that and suggested that as one could purchase a second-hand piano for next to nothing, and that as there was plenty of spare room at the hospital it would be easy for us to provide an empty room with a piano and a box of kleenex which could act as a love chamber for Derek's tortuous fantasies, and spare the rest of us an enormous amount of annoyance and frustration. However, like all my other ideas, this one was roundly ignored and Derek was punished every time he was found in the chapel (which is where the only piano in the building was situated), squatting over the object of his desire and pulling his pudding.

Mickey was another of our patients. He suffered from an obscure endocrinal disorder which meant that not only was he in complete agony all of the time, and meant that apart from the time when he was in a fitful and drugged sleep he was continually screaming. He was also doubly incontinent and so those put in charge of him had 18 hours a day of screams, and the most offensive pungent urine and diarrhoea but I have ever had the misfortune to encounter.

However, night duty was far more restful. At least three times during the course of my twelve and a half hour shift I would make the rounds of the hospital, and wander - reasonably happily - around the hospital grounds, secured in the knowledge that I was not just having a reasonably pleasant, but that I was in fact doing my duty. The hospital at night was as quiet as a grave. Except for occasionally encountering Stevie, pointed stick and doll's head in hand, marching around the dilapidated grounds like a one-man battalion of stormtroopers, I saw no other human beings. What I did see - in profusion - was feral cats.

As the hospital continued its slow journey towards decommissioning, more and more of the outbuildings, and even entire wings of the main building itself fell into disrepair and as the humans moved out, the cats moved in. It was the first time that I had been granted access to a colony of feral cats over any length of time. It was interesting to see how animals - that only a few generations before - had been beloved household pets had acquired a complex social pack structure. I had always assumed that feral cats - like their domesticated siblings - were essentially solitary animals. However, when living in a large extended family group, one could discern the beginnings of quite a complex social structure. The obvious boss was an enormous tabby tom that I christened Lazarus after the hero of Robert Heinlein's novel *Time enough for Love*. He had a harem of three or four females, and a motley collection of kittens and half-grown young. It was interesting to see how even three quarter grown male cats would act a subserviently in his presence, proffering their hind quarters to him in a posture of sexual submissiveness, and generally acting in a very subdued manner. On a couple of occasions I saw one of these junior males away from Lazarus, and then their demeanour would be completely different. They would act like any other Tom cat, and march up and down the dilapidated pseudo art-deco battlements of the disused mental hospital as if they owned the place.

The hospital was also haunted. On the second floor there were two or three wards that had been closed off as the decommissioning process snowballed. One of these was directly above the ward in which I was based during my sojourn as senior nurse on night duty. Despite the fact that the last patient had left several years before, and that nobody apart from me had access to it, one could hear running footsteps echoing along the bare wooden floorboards nearly every night. The labyrinthine passageways of the main hospital were also the home for - what appeared to me at least to be - a number of spectres. In order to get from the ward where I was stationed to the only other operative ward remaining in the hospital one had to walk along a long, straight, corridor over a hundred yards in length. Off the sides of this corridor were passageways and doorways leading to what had once been the physiotherapy department, the occupational therapy department, and what were still the kitchens. I had to walk along this passageway at least eight times a night, and on nearly every occasion I would see flickering shadows disappearing into the night as if a mysterious two-dimensional figure made of mist were running away from me. Less often I would see mysterious glowing lights as if candles were reflected in the long windows from rooms which no longer existed, and on one occasion I saw a glowing orb of whitish blue light suspended in mid-air about 30 feet in front of me. Cackling laughter, and the cries of babies could be heard - or rather sensed - coming from the empty wards.

Only too aware of my history of mental health problems, and beginning to be seriously worried that my brief flirtation with psychedelic drugs nearly a decade before had seriously unhinged my mind, I gingerly asked some of my companions on night duty whether they too had experienced odd sights and sounds around the hospital at night. To my great relief, they had. They explained to me that in the early days of the 20th century, the hospital had been a poor house and they believed that the sounds of babies that we had all heard where no baby had been for at least 50 years were some arcane reflection of the hospital's past. An elderly woman called Pam - who although completely unqualified, had assumed the mantle of den mother to all the other staff on night duty, and who had taken me completely under her wing, told me that on several occasions she had seen the ghostly figures of women wearing early twentieth-century nurses' uniforms stalking up and down the corridors. Coming to the conclusion that if I didn't bother the ghosts, they wouldn't bother me, I ceased to pay them any attention. After a few more nights I even forgot that they were there.

One of the great advantages of being on night duty was that I had plenty of time to read. I have always been a fast and voracious reader, and as already described I had acquired an enormous number of books on cryptozoology and esoteric Fortean subjects during Alison's and my journeys around the UK with Steve Harley the previous summer. Now I had the chance to read them. Over the winter of 1989/90 I became extremely knowledgeable on a wide range of esoteric subjects and slowly began to formulate some theories of my own.

For the first time I became aware of theories that ghosts are not necessarily the spirits of the dead, and I began to look upon the ghostly apparitions around the hospital in a new light. For the first time I read Karl Shuker's *Mystery Cats of the World* and I began to wonder whether such animals as the Kellas Cat, the Onza and the King Cheetah were not ancient species which had managed to avoid being discovered by Western civilisation, but were in fact emergent species in the process of evolving from well-known root-species such as the Scottish wildcat, the puma and the cheetah. Maybe, I began to wonder, in a few thousand years, Lazarus and his kin would have evolved far enough to be deserving of full specific status. I realized - in one of the most important bursts of insight that I have ever gained - that not only were some a mystery animals are not anything of the sort and not even animate in the true sense of the word - but that they were still governed by apparent laws of which mainstream science were completely unaware.

Driving back to Exeter the next morning, I coined the term Zooform Phenomena to cover these "things" (as Ivan T Sanderson would undoubtedly have called them), although it was several years before I was to share these insights with anyone, even my long-suffering wife.

In March 1990 after an entire winter spent watching the feral cats, ignoring the ghosts, stopping Derek from masturbating over the chapel piano, and allowing my mind to wander untrammeled throughout the highways and byways of quasi-fortean literature, the events which were to precipitate my final exit from the NHS took place. As part of the inexorable road toward privatisation, and more and more nurses from private agencies were being used. In my experience at least they were uniformly useless. They were churlish, inexperienced and lazy. On this occasion I had been subjected to a particularly horrible night. Because of staff absenteeism there were only two of us on duty to manage the entire hospital, which was at the time undergoing a nasty stomach bug, and nearly all the patients had been suffering from continual diarrhoea. Many of them at also developed projectile vomiting. After twelve and a half-hours of this I was looking forward to getting home. Half past seven came and went with no sign of the staff nurse who was due in to relieve me. None of the senior staff who were meant to be on call answered their telephones, and there was only an answering machine at the agency who had supplied the woman who was supposed to be relieving me.

At 9 o'clock I tried phoning them again, but there was no answer. At quarter to 10, she finally turned up. By this time I had been on duty for 15 hours, and had been awake for nearly 24. I had had no break in that time. However, I did my best to be polite. The woman stormed in, and refused to take over until she had "had a cup of coffee and chilled out for a bit". I cracked. I told her in no uncertain terms that she was an unprofessional and stupid bitch. I told her that in my opinion scum like her were playing into the hands of the people who wanted to end the National Health Service. She threatened to report me to my superiors. I told her to report me to anyone she fucking well liked, threw the keys down onto the table and stormed out.

Two days later I was suspended from duty pending an investigation. It was only then that I realised quite how determined the higher echelons of the Exeter Health Authority had been to get rid of me. I was presented with a very thick dossier detailing my crimes. I was accused of gross professional misconduct, mostly because of my attitude towards the woman from the agency, but also because I had made a mistake on one of my time sheets and claimed the princely sum of £23.70 more than I had been entitled to. This was an honest mistake caused by the fact that because of the enormous amount of travelling that I had to do each day, and the rigours of my appalling job I was exhausted most of the time. The other crimes of which I had been accused were trivial enough. Mostly minor infringements of pointless paperwork, or the occasional use of bad language. A mildly amusing aspect of the whole affair was that the secretary who typed the letter had misspelled the word "professional". It seemed a fitting epitaph to my nursing career.

I went to see my trades union representative. He was fat, balding and stank of stale cigarette smoke. I asked him what I should do and pointed out that at least 60% of the charges against me were groundless, and that I had a pretty good defence for the rest. I also told him of the disgusting conditions in which I had been forced to work, and - more seriously - a whole generation of mentally handicapped people had been forced to live. It was - I pointed out - a veritable scandal. But it was to no avail. My trade union representative was as much of a part of the decaying cesspit which was the National Health Service at the end of the 1980s as anyone else that I had been forced to deal with. This bloke wasn't the slightest bit interested in protecting workers' rights or in righting injustices. He was only interested in preserving the status quo. "It looks like you're fucked, my son", he said in a disinterested manner. But almost as an afterthought he advised me to go and see the Occupational Health Department.

Dr McIntoch was a fine man of the old school. I had known him for over a decade, and had grown to respect him deeply.

For some reason he had not been around during my illness of the previous summer, and I am convinced that if he had been then events would have taken a completely different course. He sat me down and talked to me long and hard about my predicament and about my deteriorating mental health. For the first time I became aware that there was actually something seriously wrong with me. Dr McIntoch looked at my sick certificates from the previous year. "Anxiety and Depression my arse", he said with a grunt "You should be given retirement on health grounds, laddie". He shuffled off into the other office leaving me alone with a pile of copies of *Country Life.* Twenty minutes later he came back. "From now on, you are off sick, sonny. There'll be no more of this disciplinary bullshit." He patted me on the back and ushered me out of his office.

I was on the sick list for nearly a year until my retirement finally took place in February 1991. During that year I spent most of the time on the road with Steve Harley - one of the happiest times of my life, and one that I eventually immortalised in my book *Road Dreams*. During the summer of 1990 my household was expanded. A teenage girl called Lisa Peach came to stay. Initially she came to record some songs on my home studio. Then she stayed to look after the house and the animals during our increasingly frequent periods on the road. Imperceptibly - and I don't really know how it happened - she shifted from being a friend to being a member of the family. One night, after she had been living with us for a month or so, she started calling me and Alison Ma and Pa. I suddenly realised that I had a daughter, and although our relationship has been rocky at times, a decade and a half later I still consider her to be my daughter and love her as much as if she were my own flesh and blood.

The process of retiring on the grounds of ill health was a long, slow, and painfully tortuous one. For nearly a year I had to go before a series of tribunals, medical boards, doctors, psychologists and psychiatrists, but eventually the end was in sight. I was told that, after one final interview with a consultant psychiatrist I would be granted a cash settlement, and a monthly pension for the rest of my life.

The final meeting was oddly uneventful. Alison drove me up the long, tree lined drive that led to Wonford House Psychiatric Hospital and gripped my hand reassuringly as we walked down the empty corridors to the Consultants Room. It was a blustery day in early February and the winds threw a sprinkling of mushy sleet over the conifers outside the window. I had been to so many of these psychiatrist's appointments that I no longer paid any attention to what was going on. I didn't consider myself to be mad - the things that were described as being examples of my mental disorder were familiar to me. They had been my constant companions since boyhood. I had seldom been happy, and had come to believe that happiness was an unattainable state, which, like the mystery animals that I had dedicated so much of my life to pursuing occasionally passed by and allowed one a precious glimpse of what might have been before disappearing off to pastures new leaving one far behind, breathless and too disillusioned to pursue it.

I knew that my hallucinations, and the voices that I heard in my head were not real. But they were as much a part of me as my overweight body or the scars on my knees from the operations I had undergone as a child. They were part of my personal normality and I couldn't imagine life without them. As the old, grey doctor droned on I looked out of the window of his office, entranced as a pair of squirrels - sensing that spring was finally soon to arrive - chased each other up and down the branches of one of the trees blissfully unaware of the human tragedies unfolding behind the cold grey walls of the asylum.

Suddenly I came back to the present with a jerk. "In my opinion, my boy", said the kindly old Doctor, "you are very seriously ill. Although this should be confirmed with a proper diagnosis I believe that you have a chronic bipolar condition..."

I shrugged. I had no idea of what he meant, and after nearly a year of groveling before a series of medical tribunals, in order to secure an income whereby I could fulfill my obligations to my wife, my newly acquired daughter and to the mortgage lenders, I had reached a state of utter numbness. I no longer existed as a human being, I was just a pile of papers bound together in a faded manilla folder...

"Uh huh," I said, unhelpfully.

The elderly doctor looked at me with a sad look on his face, and continued. "You might have heard of it as Manic Depression"...

I still must have looked blank and disinterested

"Do you like pop music?" he asked. It was such a radical change of subject that, I answered him immediately. "Er yeah".

"Have you heard of Jimi Hendrix?"

I nodded.

"Well, he wrote a song about it. "

Half remembered words, and a searing guitar riff came into the back of my mind.

```
"Manic Depression's touching my soul,
I know what I want,
but I just don't know how to go about getting it.

Feeling, sweet feeling
drops from my finger, fingers
Manic Depression's captured my soul."
```

"It is a very serious disease", the Doctor continued. "But you can be treated for it, and whilst it can't be cured, we can help deal with the symptoms."

Tears started to roll down my cheeks. Despite myself, I began to cry. For the first time in my life I knew that none of the things that had happened to me were my fault. I wasn't bad. I wasn't mad. It wasn't the drugs. It was just that I was suffering from a serious disease, and furthermore it was a disease with hip rock and roll credibility.

```
"Music sweet music,
I wish I could caress, caress, caress.
Manic Depression's a frustrating mess.
Well, I think I'll go turn myself off an' go on down.

Really ain't no use me hanging around.
Oh, I gotta see you."
```

sang James Marshall Hendrix inside my head, as I continued to cry inconsolably. The pain and terror of the past few years had finally caught up with me, and finally I could let it all out. The stiff upper lip had disappeared and I could finally allow myself to feel what I had always known, but never allowed myself to accept.

The Doctor continued:

"Apart from music, what else are you interested in?" he asked.

Sobbing, I told him that since childhood I had been interested in the study of unknown animals. He nodded sagely.

"One of Heuvelmans's disciples are you?" he asked.

I was astonished. Here was an old man in his late sixties. Not only was he *au fait* with Jimi Hendrix, but he had read *On the Track of Unknown Animals* as well. This man was a God!

"You are behaving as if this news is a death sentence", he said. "Don't be so damned silly. It is nothing of the sort."

I wiped away my tears and looked at him quizzically. *The Jimi Hendix Experience* was still thrashing away furiously inside my brain.

"This isn't the end, this is the beginning", he said. "You can do what you want to do now".

He smiled, took a rubber stamp, and stamped the form in front of him. I was now officially insane, but I was also now officially free.

"Good luck with the cryptozoology" he said to me as he shook my hand and I left the hospital a free man.

That night I got drunker than I had got in many years. I went on a memorable pub-crawl round half a dozen pubs in the middle of Exeter with a small posse of my most disreputable cronies. There was one thing left that I knew that I had to do, and I needed to be very drunk in order to summon up the courage to do it.

At about one in the morning I staggered down Exeter's Southernhay. I was clutching a spray can and a marker pen. In those days - luckily for me - there were none of the surveillance cameras that are prevalent everywhere now, and which would doubtless have turned my last, stupid gesture against the Exeter Health Authority into an open and shut case of criminal damage.

There was no-one about as I approached the main doors of the Exeter Health Authority building at Dean Clark House. I got out my spray can and prepared to make my final art statement. For a moment I couldn't think of what to write, but then the inspiration came. I remembered the words that my hero Heuvelmans had used to open his groundbreaking first book. I sprayed an anarchy sign - the capital A in a circle on the front door of the Health Authority building, and underneath in unsteady capitals I wrote (using the marker pen), "The Great Days of Zoology are not done!"

"I'm going to be a fucking Monster Hunter!" I screamed at the unforgiving winter sky above me. "And there is nothing you stupid bastards can do to stop me!"

Unsurprisingly, no-one answered, and so I staggered off home to sleep. The next day I woke with the worst hangover that I have ever had in my life, and realised that my new life had begun. It was up to me what I was going to do with it.

CHAPTER SIX

STRANGELY STRANGE BUT ODDLY NORMAL

Once I had made my decision to become a professional monster hunter, I then had to work out exactly what it was that I was going to do. It was all well and good announcing my intentions to all and sundry, but the thorny problem of how, exactly I was going to make a living remained. I decided that as my early forays into self publishing had gone reasonably well, and as - at that time - I was the publisher of two reasonably successful fanzines and had already written one book (on bootleg recordings by *The Beatles*) that had sold reasonably well, then I should try and write a book about the mystery animals of the area in which I lived.

After all, I had already discovered to my surprise that there were quite a few zoological mysteries to be solved in the Westcountry. I had already investigated the mystery surrounding Westcountry martens and other small carnivores, and as recounted in earlier chapters, I had chased quite a few other strange creatures in the area. So, once again I began to frequent the Westcountry Studies Library and spent days poring through their archives in search of new zoological worlds to conquer.

The richness and the variety of the stories that I began to unearth dazzled me. Amongst the first of these weird vignettes of natural history that I found was the story of the golden frogs of Bovey Tracey.

According to an old Devon folk story, once upon a time a poor woodsman lived with his family on the outskirts of the village of Bovey Tracey on the south side of Dartmoor. Their child was suffering from an unspecified illness and was not likely to live much longer, One night in the middle of a severe thunderstorm there was a knock on the door and a mysterious lady entered demanding shelter and food.

Despite their many misfortunes the woodsman and his family welcomed the mysterious lady, gave her milk and food (which they could ill afford) and a seat by the fire. She then blessed the ailing infant who was miraculously cured, and before vanishing (up a road called to this day Mary Street) she said that so that her benefactors would know this was not a dream, not only would the child be forever cured but that the next day the family would discover a new spring full of crystal clear water and bright golden frogs which were said to have populated the area for many years.

If so, what were they? The concept of brightly coloured amphibians inhabiting the English countryside is not as unusual as one might suppose. Several small pink frogs were found in Gloucestershire in the early 1990s and others have been recorded over the years from Sussex and The Cotswolds.

But Golden Frogs?

In February 1994 local and national newspapers were full of the story of Jaffa, a three-year-old frog discovered in a garden in Truro. Jaffa was, as his name implies, bright orange. The Westcountry TV News carried a story about him, which said that he, and a similarly coloured mate had been released in a secret location. Mark Nicholson of the Cornwall Trust for Nature Conservation revealed that far from being an isolated occurrence these oddly coloured amphibians are popping up all over the place. Ranging in colour from bright orange, through yellow to pale cream, these creatures have been reported from all over the Westcountry and even from elsewhere in the UK although they appear to be much rarer.

They turn up each year, and in the early spring of 2000 we found one hopping around in the mud by the dustbins outside our front door! It was a fully-grown female of a bright mustard colour and almost immediately laid copious amounts of spawn, which unfortunately proved to be infertile. We kept her for several months until she escaped into the wilderness behind our conservatory where we keep some of our animal collection during the summer months. We hope that the coming years will supply us with more specimens that will help us determine what exactly these creatures are.

Although I am as aware as everyone about the damage that man is doing to the planet on which we live, there is a distressing tendency in these politically correct days to blame all anomalies of nature on the ubiquitous 'global warming' or some other plague of the modern age. Whilst not wishing for a moment to deny that these threats exist and a very serious towards the future of all living creatures on the planet, it is, I think, counter productive to blame everything on man's stupidity. Various commentators including Internet news groups have suggested that these brightly coloured batrachians are the result of a damaged environment. Whilst not denying that the environment is certainly damaged, we have proved that these animals have been around for at least five hundred years and we are determined to find out what they actually are!

For the present however, it is fairly clear that the charming medieval legend of the Golden Frogs of Bovey Tracey might not he so far fetched after all.

As my investigations continued, my fame - such as it was - spread, and I began to make contact with fortean researchers all over the region.

Joan Amos was an elderly lady and veteran UFO researcher who for many years lived on the edge of Dartmoor. At twenty past six on a cold morning in April, 1978, she was in a ward of her local hospital with four other patients, waiting for their morning cup of tea. The sun was already up, the sky was blue, and the window gave a good view up over the moors. She little knew that something was about to occur that would change her life . . .

A halo of bright light appeared, hovering over the small market town of Tavistock, on the southwestern fringes of the moor. Joan and the other patients looked at it in surprise, and many years later Joan recalled to me her excitement as she saw a gun-metal grey, saucer-shaped craft in the middle of the halo of light. It stayed in the same position, at a low altitude, for six minutes, before banking and disappearing from sight beyond the hills. "I was rooted to the spot and couldn't believe what I had seen," she recollected.

That event set her on an investigative course that resulted in her becoming widely known and respected as a collator and investigator of UFO reports and theories. When I met her, she was a veteran in her field who had read and collected every piece of information that she could find on the subject.

Joan's investigations of UFO incidents soon led her to the seemingly-connected field of animal attacks. Always fascinated by mysteries she began to keep a scrapbook of reports of sightings of big cats, and, in conversation with Mr Dave Nicholls (a UFO researcher friend of hers in Camborne, Cornwall) heard of a large yellow cat that he had seen drinking in the river. He told Joan that he had reported it to Di Francis, a naturalist who was then writing her book *Cat Country*. Joan wrote to her and started to send her copies of her reports.

When *Cat Country* was finally published Joan read it avidly. She subsequently read Francis' *The Beast of Exmoor* and was interested in the author's concerns about a government cover-up on the subject of roaming big cats and the hunt for them. The author refers to film and photographs which had been sent away for processing which had come out blank, although test shots on the same reel had come out perfectly. Francis noted that this had happened in various parts of the country. (The phenomenon involving unsuccessful developing of photographs of a fortean or possibly-supernatural nature is a well-known one within crypto-investigative circles.)

"For some time", Joan told me, "I've had good reason for believing that there is a connection between the big cats and sightings of UFOs. "

She continued, "The first case which I had investigated personally that led me to these conclusions was in March 1982 when a C. B. radio user was on Dartmoor one night, talking to a lady in Cornwall. Seeing a light behind him and thinking that it was a car, he turned - and what he saw frightened him so much that he ran back to his vehicle.

"About forty feet in the air was a flying object shaped like an egg with the bottom cut off, shining a huge beam of light onto a pony which was rearing up and whinnying with fright. The bell-shaped craft appeared to have a fin on one side and underneath was a ring of small lights, which appeared to be turning around. The craft was completely silent. "

Within days of this incident, a strange cat turned up at a farm about a mile away. According to the farmer, Mr Knowles, it was a very weird animal, which also had a strange effect upon the farm dog.It was a faithful sheep dog, which went everywhere with its master, but on this occasion it, hid under the table and refused to come out. It was reportedly the first time that it had ever behaved like this. The farmer showed Joan where the beast had leapt over a wall.

He described the creature as "having a snout like a pig, wet and quivering and moving from side to side".When his powerful torch had shone into its eyes, there was no reflection at all. The head was like a colt and the face was long, with pointed ears turning forward. It had a large body with a drooping stomach and a tail like that of a greyhound curved between its legs. Upon telling his elderly father of the phenomenon, the old man replied,   "It's witchcraft - it's witchcraft!"

This report intrigued Joan, and she decided to hunt through back copies of *Flying Saucer Review* for similar cases. She found a number of interesting cases.

*   Volume 25 #2 contained an account of a Canadian schoolgirl's abduction aboard a transparent UFO. She said that she was able to pass her hands through everything aboard, except for a large domestic cat. When she asked why there was a cat aboard the UFO she was told that they were 'growing it' and then it would be returned.

*   In Volume 26 #1 (Spring 1980), Charles Bowen wrote an article hypothesising that mystery animals were involved closely with UFOs. He states, "We should be prepared to accept that UFOs and alien animals are inextricably linked. "

In the same article, he described how an Alsatian dog cringed frightened in the corner when a 'puma' with a foul smell made nocturnal visits to the farm where he lived. These visits were usually preceded by strange lights, from an indefinable source, playing upon the roofs of the farm buildings.

*   Volume 15 #5 there is a description of an animal very similar to that described to Joan by Mr Knowles, the Dartmoor farmer:

It had a brown head, large black eyes, and a nose extraordinarily like that of a pug. Its left ear was pricked, but the other one hung down like it was torn. . Its ribs were a bright pale chestnut turning to a sort of dirty ginger-brown and its hindquarters were darker still.

As well as searching her archives, Joan Amos also began collating contemporary reports of big cats and UFOs. She concluded that the South West seems to be especially prolific for sightings of both large cats and UFOs.   Animals have been reported which appear to be black leopards, pumas - and even a family of lynx.   Having started asking around, she found that, for instance, her hairdresser had seen a large cat on Dartmoor, and that her travelling fishmonger had a customer who places a regular order for nine pounds of fish, which he uses to feed the lynxes, which are a regular visitor to his garden.

Tales of animal teleportation are not uncommon.   Joan Amos heard of a cow that was apparently teleported from one field to another, and there were burn marks on its sides. She tried to get more details on this case but the farmer refused to discuss the matter.   One possible non-UFO explanation is that this was a failed cattle-rustling attempt.   However, stories of UFO encounters do often involve sightings of animals.

Domestic cats are the focus of many stories that conceivably involve teleportation or could be explained by their having fallen victim to attack by big cats.

Tales of young cats being discovered in inexplicable locations are numerous; one story is of a half-grown kitten that was missing from home. It was eventually found stranded on a deserted beach three miles away. It was very distressed and was in an almost inaccessible place, from which it was rescued by some fishermen who have no idea how it could have got there.

According to Joan, a village in Cornwall lost thirty domestic cats in the early months of 1993. According to a lady from a local animal welfare charity the police were notified, but six months later, there was still no trace of the missing animals. Joan spoke to one of the residents, who described how, late one night, she went out of her cottage and heard 'the blood-curdling scream of a big cat'. More recently, around a hundred black cats were reported missing from the Clevedon area, near Weston-Super-Mare in Avon.

Joan Amos suggested that the occupants of UFOs are abducting domestic cats and treating them with growth hormones, prior to releasing them back onto the moors. However, as most zoologists will affirm, big cats would be prepared to prey on their smaller domestic 'cousins' as a food source. Where UFOs fit into the picture, and what the real explanation of these mystery disappearances and attacks are, we just do not know at present. But as Loren Coleman has so rightly said, there does seem to be a link of some kind between these seemingly disparate phenomena and the mystery cats all over the world do seem to be spookily elusive.

Joan was instrumental in my investigation of what was one of the weirdest, and probably the most sinister investigations that I have ever taken was done retrospectively and involved what I facetiously dubbed "The unidentified flying wallaby slasher of Newquay.

It seems (although the accounts do not all tally exactly, from what I have been told, by one ex-employee of the zoo, who has asked me to respect her anonymity) that the events of the early summer of 1978 started when, one morning, staff at the zoo found a dead, mutilated Muscovy duck.

I first heard about the matter, sixteen years after the event in the early spring of 1992, when I was engaged in research into the Alien Big Cat sightings in Devon and Cornwall.

One afternoon, I was engaged in an interview with a sergeant from Middlemoor Police Station in Exeter. I will not name him, as I have not received permission to do so; and I am quite aware that certain senior officers in the Devon and Cornwall Police Force do not approve of their officers talking to paranormal researchers. It would be easy to build into this some paranoiac conspiracy theory about how the powers-that-be are trying to suppress information about these events; but the truth is, I fear, far more prosaic. I have been told, on good authority, that the police, especially in the West Country, equate an interest in the paranormal with drugs and the excesses of a hippy lifestyle. Indeed, they have a fair amount of justification in so doing: many so-called researchers that I have met over the years turn out to be stoned wannabe anarchists, with wild staring eyes, dreadlocks and a thin dog on a string. Equally, just as many researchers turn out to be genuine, intelligent people with an interest in what lies beyond the next turn of the road; but, in many cases, the attitude of the police is understandable.

However, at the time, I had hair which reached far below my shoulders and I drove a pink hi-topped Transit van with what I thought at the time were highly fetching and monumentally groovy hippy symbols drawn in dayglo paint on the sides, and at the time would probably have shocked the unfortunate police officer into silence, if we had actually met in the flesh. However, luckily we didn't, and my relatively cultured telephone tones won him over.

I had spent something over forty minutes talking to this particular officer, when he stunned me by asking whether I had heard of the wallaby slashings in Newquay. I hadn't; so he told me what he could. In 1976 and 1977, there was a series of inexplicable attacks on livestock at Newquay Zoo. Mystery big cats had been seen in Devon and Cornwall at that time, and it was thought by many that the events were somehow connected. ' He couldn't remember any more details, but suggested that I should telephone the one man who knew more about the killings than anybody else: Mr Marshall, the Head Zookeeper at the time.

I tracked down Mr Marshall, by dint of a number of telephone calls, some barefaced cheek and a lot of luck. I eventually found him in a small house on the outskirts of Newquay. He was long retired and in failing health; and, since the death of his wife, he had been living with his daughter. The day that Alison finally tracked him down, I was in bed, recouperating from a bad dose of flu. I had managed to connect a tape recorder to my telephone by dint of some sub Heath Robinson mechanics and so was able to record the conversation.

It was one of the most eerie experiences of my life. Still light-headed from the flu, I lay back in bed fascinated by the terrible story that I was hearing:

We had a spate of beheadings. The suggestion at the time was; because there was no blood or gore or anything at all anywhere in the zoo, and the head had been removed; we thought that it was the same as the rustlers do in Australia. They lay sacking on the ground and kill the sheep, and then they wrap it up so there is nothing left.

We lost - I think it was - two wallabies, some black swans and some geese. All beheaded. Now this, apparently, was happening all over the world at this time. It was happening in America, Japan and China, as well as here; and they tried to link it up with sightings of UFOs.

Only a year before, I would have pooh-poohed the very idea of UFOs being linked to any zoological mystery, but then I discovered the books of John Keel, and *Phenomena* by Bob Rickard and John Michel, and I had come to know a new Keelian universe full of delightful possibilities and macabre twists.

This universe eminently suited my new mindset. Since leaving the National Health Service I had begun to re-evaluate the universe as a whole. The idea that mysterious animal mutilations could have taken place in conjunction with other paranormal occurrences on my own figurative doorstep made perfect sense to the new me. So I shifted around in my big double bed to make myself comfortable and listened to what the old zookeeper had to say.

There was no blood left in the animals at all, and I had the area UFO compositor - or whatever he called himself - come down, and the suggestion was that it was beings from outer space who came down and needed the blood - or whatever else it was that they drew out of those animals - to survive. It never developed any further than that. I believe that they got a radiation count in the wallaby paddock at that time. And also the pads off the wallabies' paws, or feet - whichever you want to call them -were white.

I asked Mr Marshall whether they had ever found the culprits.

No, but the same thing was happening all over the world. I can tell you that. I've got to be honest about it. As far as I am concerned, I would suggest - and I did say this at the time - Cornwall has got black magic. It's got witchcraft and witch covens; and, if anything, I think this was what or who did it. The strange thing was that there was no blood anywhere. That was a strange thing. There was the thing with the Geiger counter, but I think that could have happened anywhere. You're bound to get a certain amount of radiation; and possibly, it being an area of tin mines and whatever, it is an area of granite mixed with other substances. Nothing else materialised whatsoever. It happened on several occasions, and I've got a feeling that there was another one since I left the zoo...

Mr Marshall's voice became a little strained then. He hinted that he had more to tell me, but didn't like to say too much on the phone. I let the matter drop, intending to bring the matter up again when we met face to face.

We ended our conversation by discussing the then current set of Alien Big Cat sightings on Dartmoor and Exmoor. Mr Marshall asked whether he could accompany me to the next set of sheep kills. I eagerly agreed: at that time I knew no professional zoologists, and I was only too happy to have a pro on the team. We parted cheerfully, with Mr Marshall again hinting that he had more to tell me about the Wallaby killings. Two days later, he was dead.

A few weeks later, I was approached by Rosemary Rhodes of Ninestones Farm on Bodmin Moor. She asked me to come and visit to investigate the spate of sheep killings and sightings of mysterious creatures on her farm, that over the next few years became known as "The Beast of Bodmin". I was only the second researcher on site; and, true to my promise, I wanted to take Mr Marshall along with me.

I telephoned his daughter cheerfully. She answered the phone in a voice thick with grief, and told me that only days after talking to me about the mysterious killings in Newquay, her father had been taken suddenly ill and died. She knew nothing more and didn't want to talk to me. Even as I write this, many years later, a shiver goes down my spine as I remember Mr Marshall's hints that he hadn't told me the full story.

Alison and I visited Newquay Zoo incognito.. We had camped in a lay-by just outside the town the night before, and it was a glorious mid-summer morning. We were the first punters in through the gate. It was obvious that the zoo had seen better days. It had just been taken over by yet another change of management who were desperately trying to give it a face-lift; but at the time we visited, it was desperately in need of a lick of paint, and looked sad and forlorn.

It was, however, surrounded by high chain-link fencing and all the paths and many of the enclosures were covered in raked sand and gravel paths. It was as Mr Marshall and other ex employees had described. If, as it seemed was the practice, the paths had been raked each night as the zoo employees left work, then it was difficult to see how anybody, or anything, could have climbed over the fence, visited the enclosures, killed sizeable creatures without a struggle, and left them decapitated and exsanguinated with no footprints or traces of blood on the ground. Twenty years on, it remains a disturbing and unpleasant mystery.

I discussed the mystery with Joan. She had not only heard of the case, but somehow - and I never discussed how - had managed to get hold of the official documents appertaining to the case. On our next visit to her tiny cottage she presented me with a mysterious bundle of papers containing the official police reports on the Newquay Zoo killings as well as the autopsy report from the local vet and a pile of typewritten papers from the un-named UFO investigator who had, I believe, been the only person (apart from me) to ever fully investigate the mystery.

The police report was by far the most suspicious of the three documents. It had been photocopied so many times that it was almost indecipherable in parts, and large sections have been censored so the information is unreadable. I am making no claims as to whether it is genuine or not. I had several "official" documents in my' possession, which, in my opinion, at least are palpable fakes.

They have usually come from the UFO fraternity. They are also photocopied to a state of near illegibility, and they have large sections of them that have been censored. Unlike this document, however, they usually purport to be Ministry of Defence memoranda regarding crashed UFOs, and they usually have an aura about them which suggests that they were originally manufactured by an hormonally-challenged teenager with an overactive imagination, sitting in his bedroom with a home computer.

This document, while I cannot guarantee its authenticity, has a certain stamp of professionalism about it, which makes me think that it is probably genuine. I have described them all in detail in my book *The Owlman and Others* that also contains other parts of my investigation into the subject. I have lived with these documents now for over a decade but when I read the account of the killings themselves they still send shivers down my spine.

Over the past months a number of incidents have occurred at the Newquay Zoological Gardens at Trenance Gardens, Newquay. These incidents were thought at first to be unconnected and possibly due to the incursion of a marauding animal, but as will be seen this has now been discounted.

On the 3rd June 1978, a wallaby was discovered to have been beheaded in it's (sic) paddock. This was found by staff when first opening up the premises in the early morning. The head of the animal was not found but the point of severance was unusually clean cut.

On the 17th August 1978, a black swan was found to have been beheaded also. The head and neck were missing, but the body of the swan was unruffled, showing no sign of a struggle. No blood was to be found at the scene. Later the neck was discovered in undergrowth on the premises, but the head was never found. The point of severance was again very clean.

Between these dates, a Chinese goose, which is a fairly large species of goose, was removed from its enclosure and it's (sic) carcass, minus head, was discovered stuffed between a loose wooden fencing panel on the outer security' fence. This was jammed tightly in a very confined space. At this spot the security fence was completely intact.

On Saturday 25th September 1978 a young wallaby was found to have been removed from its enclosure. It had been taken about fifty yards over several other fences to a paddock with the lower part of it's (sic) carcass remained.

The upper part of the body was missing and there was no trace of blood at the scene. Marks in the grass showed signs of someone or something having flattened the grass and several particles of meat were visible. An examination of the remaining carcass in the presence of the Zoo 's Consultant Veterinary Surgeon, W. Clifton Green of Edgecumbe Gardens, Newquay, and his Assistants, brought the unanimous verdict that the carcass had been dissected by a human being rather than an animal as the skin around the wound was clean cut, and there were no teeth or claw marks visible on the carcass. The backbone had been deeply severed between the vertebra and some of the internal organs were missing.

The estimated value of the stock lost to date is approximately £600. Initially, the above incidents were not regarded too seriously and were thought to have been due to a marauding animal but closer examination of the facts of the incidents made the possibility' very' remote. The lack of wounding or marking elsewhere on the carcasses have ruled out this possibility, and the behaviour in the most recent incident with a young wallaby, which weighed approximately four feet in height into a paddock approximately 50 yards, again makes the involvement of any known animals most unlikely.

The quest for the truth behind these remarkable documents took up much of my time for the best part of a year. I telephoned everybody that I could that was even remotely connected with the case, and - without realising it - became involved in trying to investigate other cases of animal mutilation which had occurred at around about the same time. One of these had taken place in 1977 in the Cherry Brook valley - the place where I had rescued Katie from quicksand a few years earlier. I went to visit the Valley in 1991 - nearly 20 years after my ill-fated schoolboy Expedition, the only result of which had been my first kiss. On this occasion I was accompanied by my wife, my dog Toby, my *quondam* daughter Lisa, and her pet sheep Bobby.

Over the years, various members of my family have become involved in the pursuit of genealogy, and have pursued my family tree with varying degrees of success. I don't know whether it is true, but various of these aspiring family historians have alleged to me at various times that one of my ancestors - on the distaff side of the family - was the last bloke in England to be hung for sheep stealing. It is probably not true, but I like to think that I have an outlaw heritage. It would, perhaps, explain how and why I committed the same crime as my (probably mythical) desperado ancestor in early 1992.

It is, I believe, one of the failings of the current Mental Health Services that unlike any other service industry there is little or no customer after-sales service. In February 1991 I was made redundant on the grounds of my deteriorating mental health. I was given 5000 quid, a pension for life, a pat on the head, and left to get on with it. In any sane system, my case would have been passed to a psychiatric social worker, and I would have been at least offered counselling, therapy or some degree of supervision. But this was the Exeter Health Authority. This was Britain in the early 1990s, just about to go to war with Iraq - but not to finish the job; and eventually to commit the most appalling act of betrayal imaginable on the Iraqi people. This was the Britain governed by the impossibly boring son of a circus performer, desperately doing its best to recover from 11 years of the Iron Lady. I was left to run riot. It was quite peculiar, really. On some levels I functioned perfectly. I tried my best to be a good father to Lisa, my cryptozoological researches were a model of efficiency as was Alison's and my administration of the Steve Harley fan club, but otherwise my life was completely out of control. I was extraordinarily paranoid and was convinced that there were government files on me. My undoubted persecution at the hands of the idiots who ran Exeter Health Authority, and the peasants who worked for it, had managed to convince me that my brief involvement with some notorious anarchist punk musicians a decade or so before, and my inflammatory comments and diatribes in the underground press had made me a marked man. At one stage, I was so mad that I had even got hold of a couple of totally illegal shotguns that I kept under my marital bed.

It was at this stage of my life - probably the nadir of my existence - that my darling daughter went out to walk the dog one night, and returned with a sheep. Although you would not believe it now, as it is a faceless and rather vulgar jungle of utterly identical houses constructed so that low and middle-income families can live beyond their means, and produce more and more consumers for a market forces led society, but back in the early 1990s, the valley in which I live was a kid green and relatively pleasant place to live with a little stream, a coppice or two, and plenty of verdant fields. On this particular night, whilst walking Toby through one of the aforesaid fields, Lisa had heard a plaintive bleating. There was obviously an animal of there in distress. She tied Toby to a lamp post, and went to investigate. She found a tiny lamb, no more than a few days old, tangled up in some barbed wire in the middle of the stream. She managed to disentangle it, and as it was more dead than alive she brought it home. Not expecting it to live the night, she put it in a warm box with a blanket in her bedroom and hoped for the best.

Much to everyone's surprise - one suspects even the lamb's - the next morning Lisa was woken by the pitter-patter of tiny hooves, as a junior member of the sheep family climbed on to her bed and head-butted her awake demanding breakfast. Lisa, joyously, came rushing into Alison's and my bedroom brandishing Bobby (as he had been christened, after Senor Zimmerman; the one time voice of a generation), who promptly pissed all over the bed. I had only recently begun my infatuation with Robert Heinlein's novel *Stranger in a Strange Land* and I identified greatly (and must confess still do) with Jubal Harshaw - one of the main characters. As I saw it, the Gods had sent us a new member of the family. Especially as we were all vegetarian at the time, it would be immoral to return Bobby to his rightful owner and a certain death. So we stole him. And for several months if you knocked on my front door, it would precipitate a helter-skelter of animals - two dogs, six or seven cats, a couple of ferrets, and a sheep running downstairs in a flurry of leg, fur, joyous barks and clattering hooves to meet you.

So it was that my little extended family included a sheep when I revisited Cherry Brook valley for the first time since my adventures as a horny teenager. It was a bright spring day, and the world looked far more attractive than it had during my previous visit. The gorse was just beginning to flower, and the bright yellow blooms had already begun to imbue the warm air with the scent that I - and as far as I know nobody else - have always thought smelt just like coconut. As Alison, Lisa and I strolled along the dog and the sheep rushed ahead of us, Toby chasing after (mostly imaginary) rabbits whilst the sheep that had been named after the one-time voice of a generation frisked about in the way that the lambs in books by Enid Blyton are always supposed to do. The first butterflies of spring were fluttering about and Bobby - who was obviously completely unaware of the fact that as an aspiring sheep he was supposed be a herbivore - would leap off the ground in a peculiar vertical movement more reminiscent of a spring driven toy than of anything familiar from the animal kingdom - and, all four trotters clacking together excitedly, he would snap at a luckless fritillary, and if successful, eat it with every evidence of satisfaction.

The party trundled on contentedly, occasionally frightening ground-dwelling birds which would fly up to the blue sky above us with frightened squawks. It was one of those days in England, which Roy Harper sang so happily about, and which Alfred Bestall - the originator of the Rupert Bear annuals - had immortalised for generations of children and adults. We walked over the rise of a small hill, and everything changed.

There, in front of us was a dead pony. I am not squeamish. I have seen many dead creatures, but there was something particularly ghoulish and grotesque about this one. Its stomach had been slit open and its glistening intestines - a murky, though shiny mixture of reds, blues and greys - were spread out all over the landscape for many yards around as if they were some grotesque art installation in one of the more fashionable and unpleasant *avant-garde* art galleries. Its throat had been cut, and its very life blood had stained the white and pale tan pelt a rich scarlet fading to a pale pink as it ebbed away and flowed into the all forgiving earth beneath it.

My mouth began to fill with the clear fluid known as water-brash as the bile rose from my stomach and I fought back the impulse to be sick. There was something quite horrific about the scene. Adding to the horror were an extraordinarily large number of animal bones and skulls - mostly those of sheep, but with a couple of ponies as well - that were scattered about the place. Anyone who's ever walked on Dartmoor will be no stranger to bones - they are a relatively common sight - but not in the numbers which we found that day. There was nothing to show how these creatures had died. The dead pony, and indeed many of the bones showed signs of secondary predation by creatures such as foxes or badgers - or even other sheep (as Bobby showed every sign of wanting to investigate the edibility of the disgusting mess before us).

The spell had been broken, and we walked back to our van in silence. I had no way of proving it but I was convinced in my own mind at least that this was the location of a notorious killing of a number of Dartmoor ponies during the summer of 1977.

The dead ponies were found on 11th April 1977 by Alan Hicks, a shopkeeper from Tavistock, who had been walking on Dartmoor with his children. They came across fifteen carcasses in a small gully at Cherry Brook. On 13th July that year the *Western Morning News* reported:

Fears that the mystery deaths of fifteen ponies near a Dartmoor beauty spot were caused by visitors from space were being probed by a 'Torbay team yesterday. Armed with a Geiger counter, metal detectors and face masks, four men are investigating what leading animal authorities admit seems a "totally abnormal happening," and are hoping their equipment will throw a new light on the three month old mystery While other investigators have looked for signs of malnutrition, disease or poisoning or even gunshot wounds the four men are seeking proof that extra-terrestrials were responsible for the deaths.

The same newspaper story quoted Mrs Joanna Vinson, the Secretary of the Livestock Protection Society, as saying:

1 still suspect that something dramatic happened - something very strange indeed. No one can give any logical explanation. One theory is that the ponies died of redworm but that does not explain the broken necks and legs.

A particularly bizarre aspect of the case was that, according to some reports, the animals had almost completely decomposed within forty-eight hours. Even the local Chief Inspector of the RSPCA accepted that this was a mystery. The *Western Morning News* on the following day suggested some other hypothesis. Miss Lilian Martin, a member of the Livestock Preservation Society, suggested that the ponies had been grazing in the deserted valley when a sudden rainstorm flooded the valley:

My theory is that the ponies were in a very enclosed valley. There was a waterfall at the head of the valley, and they may have been caught in a sudden burst of water and knocked against the boulder.

The same newspaper report said that the UFO research team from Torbay had "come across no evidence to confirm or deny any of the theories put forward. "

A few weeks later an unnamed representative from the Dartmoor Pony Society claimed that the ponies had died in various parts of the moor and had been dumped there by a farmer who was unwilling to bear the cost of paying for their burial. ~ Mrs Vinson replied scathingly:

"One wonders if the people who say this sort of thing can possibly have been to the valley and seen the distribution of the ponies or of the terrain."

Two other theories were promulgated in the weeks that followed. A botanist from Exeter suggested that the animals had been poisoned by eating a plant called the bog asphodel. This theory does not explain the broken bones and seems unlikely.

The second theory came from Mrs Ruth Murray of the Animal Defence League. She claims that the animals were stampeded by a local farmer engaged in a feud with a neighbour, who deliberately drove the animals into the gully so they would be killed, as a deliberate act of malice. The Centre for Fortean Zoology began to investigate the affair in the summer of 1991, fourteen years after the event. We spoke to Mrs Vinson, who was rather reticent and referred us to Mrs Murray. We telephoned Mrs Murray, who was unwilling to speak to us at the time. She did, however, tell our researcher to phone back a week later when she had more time.

This we did, to be greeted with an extraordinary tirade from her. She shouted at our researcher, accusing her of "pestering" her day and night, and of "not taking no for an answer. " As we had only spoken to her once, and were only phoning back then because she had asked us to, it seemed rather peculiar.

Her claim that we "had pestered her day and night" was irresistibly reminiscent of certain events chronicled by veteran UFO researcher John Keel in his book *The Mothman Prophecies :*

I kept a careful log of the crank calls I received and eventually catalogued the various tactics of the mysterious pranksters. Some of these tactics are so elaborate they could not the work of a solitary nut harassing UFO believers in his spare time. Rather it all appears to be the work of either paranormal forces, or a large and well-financed operation by large and well-financed organisation with motives that evade me.

I can certainly vouch for the enormous numbers of "crank" telephone calls that one habitually receives, and which seem to intensify remarkably, when one is engaged on research into the more "sensitive" areas of Forteana. I would not be at all surprised to find out that Ruth Murray had received a spate of these quasi-Fortean annoyances soon after she had spoken to us, blamed them on us; and, not surprisingly, had become very angry about the whole affair.

Four years after, another one of our researchers, using a different name, telephoned her, and this time she was reasonably happy to talk to him. She still claimed that an unnamed farmer had stampeded animals maliciously, and that she was sick and tired of "nuts" claiming there was a paranormal element to what was, after all, merely a straightforward, if rather nasty, story.

I have never been entirely convinced by any of these explanations. To me they are all too glib, and none of them give a satisfactory explanation for all of the facts of the case. If there is - indeed - any truth behind the story of the hairy hands, which had entranced me as far back as 1973, then I believe that somehow it is linked not only with the macabre events of 1977, but with the carnage that I witnessed in 1992.

However, I had to put aside my investigations into the animal mutilations on Dartmoor, and at Newquay Zoo, because we had a living to earn, and there were two new Steve Harley tours looming on the horizon. By this stage, we had got the whole business of touring down to a fine art. The afternoon before the tour began, we would drive up to Harlow in Essex to meet the other couple with whom we generally toured and with whom we ran the fan club. I always liked - and rather fancied - Kim, a pretty blonde a few years younger than me, but was always wary of her husband Paul, who was one of the rough, tough, Essex men that the Conservative Party began to appeal to at roughly the time that they ceased to appeal to me. After a brief rest, and a meal, we would drive to the location of the first gig, and if necessary camp out overnight to be ready and willing for the events of the next day.

This tour was in two halves - at least as far as we were concerned. There was a brief rampage around the Midlands and the post industrial north, after which the band would travel around Europe for five weeks, before we rejoined them for a handful of Scottish and English dates later in the spring. I cannot truthfully say that I remember much about this early part of the tour. Given half a chance, I had always been a heavy drinker, and when surrounded by people with the same vice, I would always indulge. Paul was even more of a drinker than me, and when the two of us were put together - and especially when you add in several hundred rabid Steve Harley fans, all off the leash from their respective families, and clamouring to buy us drinks - then scenes of a Hunter S. Thompsonesque nature were bound to ensue.

I vaguely remember riding around the car park of a particularly seedy venue in Manchester on the bonnet of a Land Rover belonging to the management of the venue. Paul was perched on a similar vehicle, and we were both brandishing half-empty bottles of whisky. The vehicles were being driven at high speed by two blokes we didn't even know, and the object of the exercise was so we could get close enough to each other to be able to pass a spliff from one of us to the other. We were surrounded by cheering fans and members of the band doing their best to egg us on to even greater heights of excess. In the distance could be heard occasional bursts of gunfire - for this was the time that 'Madchester' was at least partly ruled by armed gangs and psychopaths. I can't remember what Alison or Kim thought of our behaviour at the time. I assume that they disapproved, but neither Paul nor I cared. We were having the time of our lives, and as far as we were concerned part of the touring experience involved us behaving like animals.

On another occasion, I remember driving up the M4 from London to Bristol, so drunk that I couldn't walk. Refreshing myself from yet another bottle of whisky, I was in the fast lane when I decided that I didn't really want to drive any more. Despite the fact that we were well over the speed limit, I stood up and swapped places with Paul who was in the passenger seat of the van, without even bothering to slow down. We then continued our merry way, still drinking, still smoking pot, and still continuing with our game of the moment which was racing with the lorry which was carrying most of the band's equipment, and whenever we managed to overtake it (and *vice-versa*), the bloke in the passenger seat would drop his trousers and wave his bottom out of the window at the other vehicle.

Only one event on this leg of the tour had any significance. We were at a small venue in the Home Counties. Although, on most of the tours we played a London gig, this was mostly for prestige. The logistics of putting on a concert in the metropolis were such that it was very difficult to make money out of them, and so for every London show there were half a dozen at places like Hayes, Brentwood, Blackheath or the like. It was at one of these shows, in a leisure centre with no redeeming features that I can remember, that I met a young man called Spike. His appearance was highly unusual for a Steve Harley concert, because - at that time of which I write - the vast majority of people in the audience were perfectly normal folk approaching middle age. This had always surprised me. When I had been at school, the normal people - those who had grown-up to become the sort of people who went to Steve Harley concerts had listened to bland, boring, suburban music by people like *Status Quo*, or Elton John. The people who had bought Harley's records back in the innocent days of 1974, had been the ones who were headed for art school; the ones who read - or at least pretended to read - Kafka; the ones who smoked dope and the ones who looked dangerous. In 1974 I desperately wanted to be one of these people, and a decade and a half later, it was for them that I had started the fan club. The trouble was that wherever these people were in 1992, they weren't coming to Steve Harley concerts.

Spike strode straight out of a time-warp. He could well have been one of the sixth-form boys that had hung around the art room talking about existentialism, and whom I had idolised as an adolescent. He was dressed completely in black. He had shoulder length blonde hair, he was painfully thin and with his only adornment being a wolf tooth on a silver chain around his neck, he looked elegantly wasted and absolutely Fabulous. He had a brown paper bag containing about half a dozen books under his arm. He came straight up to me at my seat behind the stall and said:

"Hey, are you the bloke who swaps rare Cockney Rebel records for books about monsters?"

I nodded my assent, and as business was spectacularly slow that day I gestured to him to come and join me in my lonely vigil behind the stall. As was usually the case, Alison and Kim went in to watch the show and Paul was wandering around looking nefarious. This left Spike and me alone, talking about John Keel, Ivan T Sanderson and Aleistair Crowley. Over the previous winter I had read as much as I could about Crowley and his time as the Laird of Boleskine on the shores of Loch Ness. I had come to realise that although there was no doubt in my mind that that there were, indeed, mysterious and new species of animal waiting to be discovered, that some monster accounts - especially those more singular ones at Loch Ness - could not be explained by using a purely zoological model. I became convinced that in many cases there was strong paranormal - and magical - element too many of these mysteries. I became fascinated by accounts in Aleistair Crowley's biographies of his attempts to conjure up demons. According to one account - repeated over and over again - his house in Brighton had become infested with semi-corporeal, beast like entities. And became convinced that at least some of the manifestations at Loch Ness were a similar sort of thing.

It turned out that Spike believed much the same as me. However, he had taken it several stages further. He described himself as a chaos magician - a term which was new to me. He told me how - together with his friends - he had carried out experiments to raise demonic entities. He hinted how far some of these had been far more successful than even he had wished, and - most excitingly of all - had been involved in a series of rituals to invoke the Babylonian snake goddess Tiamat on the shores of Loch Ness. He claimed that as a result of his magical incantations, he had seen a head and neck of the Loch Ness monster looming at him out of the misty lake.

I have never been so excited in my life. Could he - I cajoled - possibly tell me the words of the incantation. He frowned at me. Such information - he told me portentously - was only available to those who had achieved an immense degree of magical attainment. "Ours", he said, " is a high and lonely destiny". It was then that I realised that Spike might have been a magician of renown, but that he was also a dreadful poser!

The quote was taken verbatim from *The Magician's Nephew* by C.S Lewis - a long time favourite of mine, and furthermore a book which I know almost off by heart. I have no problem with people quoting from their favourite authors - I do it a lot, as anyone who has read this book so far will testify. However, to pass off a throwaway line from the villain of a well-known children's book as one's own is somewhat beyond the pale. It was at that point - I believe - that I realised that that the wolf tooth, the black clothing, and all the other trappings of the urban wizard were equally ephemeral, and that it was quite possible that he was no more a chaos magician than I was. However, he had some interesting books to swap, and he was a congenial enough companion for the evening.

A few days later, the tour ended, and Alison and I travelled back to Exeter. In the five or six weeks hiatus before the second leg of the tour, I had some serious thinking to do. One of the forthcoming concerts was in Aberdeen, and I had already managed to persuade the others that following the show we could make a slight detour of a couple of hundred miles and visit Loch Ness. If there was any possibility that the stuff that Spike had told me was indeed true, and that by the simple recital of - what I had always thought of as - mystical mumbo-jumbo, I could actually make my chances of seeing the monster for myself any greater, then there was no way on a earth that I wasn't going to do it. There was however, one enormous problem. My wife.

Whilst Alison had always been surprisingly indulgent towards my peculiar whims, there were two things that she would never allow me to do. She was deadly scared of snakes, and always refused to allow me to have one as a pet. She was also very wary of anything that she considered to be even approaching black magic. I knew that there was no way - once she had waded through some of the papers which I had obtained from Spike, which dealt with such subjects as raising demons - that she would ever allow me to even attempt to summon up the Loch Ness monster for myself. However, equally, there was no way that I was going to pass up this opportunity.

I am quite proud of the fact that in all the years we were together, this is one of the only times that I knowingly misled my wife. If I had to be unfaithful to her - and I supposed that what I was planning was a kind of infidelity - at least she was being cuckolded by the Loch Ness monster. I had another problem. Whereas I was quite prepared to believe that much of what Spike had told me was clouded by a miasma of juvenile affectation, I could also believe that the bare bones of what he had to say were true. And - no matter how much I tried to fool myself - I found it nigh-on impossible to believe that someone who had never even thought of practising magic before (that is if you ignore my juvenile fantasising, and my ill starred involvement with Danny Miles a decade or so previously), could successfully carry out what appeared to be a highly complex series of rituals. Luckily, I had an acquaintance to whom I could turn for help.

I have always prided myself on having a wide range of peculiar acquaintances - all of whom have an even wider range of peculiar skills. I attribute this to my early grounding in the popular pulp fiction of the years between the two world wars. As, I believe I have mentioned, my mother fuelled my early desire for reading material by introducing me to books featuring heroes like Bulldog Drummond, Simon Templar - known universally as the Saint - Allan Quartermain, and the like. One of my favourite of these books was by Leslie Charteris and was entitled *Boodle* - it was a series of short stories about the aforementioned Simon Templar. In it the eponymous hero attributed his success in life, to his wide selection of peculiar friends and acquaintances. I think, that after 45 years on this planet - at the time of writing - I can attribute my success, such as it has been, to much the same thing.

During my years as a rock and roll bootleg dealer, and later as a rock music journalist, I amassed quite a network of contacts - both legitimate and otherwise - within the music industry. It was surprising how many of these contacts turned out to be quite useful during my much more successful career as a Fortean. During the summer of 1987, for example, a swarthy young man with an Italian surname was rumoured to be hawking a videotape purporting to be of Elvis Presley's autopsy around the seamier side of the record-collecting fraternity. When, in 1994 the first rumours began to surface that a man called Ray Santilli was doing his best to sell supposed videotape of an alien autopsy, I for one, was not particularly surprised.

Another of my acquaintances was obsessed with Led Zeppelin, and had an ever-growing collection of records, bootlegs, and memorabilia - especially that appertaining to their guitarist Jimmy Page. At the end of the 1980s I met John Paul Jones - the erstwhile bass player, who was filling in as a bass balalaika player for a Polish folk group fronted by a guy with the amazing name of Basil Bunelik (pronounced bunny lick). He was kind enough to grant me an exclusive interview, which I printed in ISMO. A few weeks later, I bought some Led Zeppelin videotapes from a small ad in the back of *Record Collector* magazine. After a few weeks I became quite friendly with the vendor - a weird little guy called Colin Pottinger, who was never referred to - by himself or anyone else - except by his surname. Although we had never met in the flesh, we had long, tortuous telephone conversations that lasted well into the night. He had a peculiar squeaky voice that made him sound a little like a cartoon rabbit, and what he didn't know about Jimmy Page - and indeed, the rest of the band - wasn't really worth knowing.

It is a well-known - and rather disturbing - facet of fandom that the most obsessive fans often tend to succumb to the same failings that had proved to be the downfall of their idol. Pottinger was no exception. Like his hero he had developed a fairly serious heroin habit, and had also emulated Jimmy Page by taking a deep interest in the occult in general, and the life and works of Aleistair Crowley in particular. In the early 1970s, Jimmy Page purchased Crowley's old abode of Boleskine House on the shores of Loch Ness. He used it to house his massive collection of Aleistair Crowley memorabilia and it was popularly believed that he used the house to carry out recreations of some of Crowley's more notorious experiments.

Pottinger too, had become obsessed with the dark arts in general and with Aleistair Crowley in particular. I had discovered this early in our friendship, as I discovered that every question I asked him, and that every conversation that we had, sooner or later - and usually sooner - ended up on the subject of magic. To be quite honest it ended up getting quite tedious. Although he was one of London's leading bootleg dealers and purveyors of knocked off rock music memorabilia he couldn't talk about anything else. For example, on one occasion, I was trying to locate a recording of the legendary "nine man jam" - an occasion in 1969 when the four members of Led Zeppelin had been joined onstage by Keith Moon, Rod Stewart, Jeff Beck and two members of Jethro Tull for an impromptu version of a number of rock and roll classics. As soon as I asked him about this, I could hear Pottinger grinning like a Cheshire Cat on the other end of the telephone line. He immediately launched into an incomprehensible tirade about how all the aforementioned musicians were members of a magical order which had been founded by Eliphas Levi hundreds of years before, and how somehow the chaotic performance of a number of old Elvis Presley songs by an impromptu supergroup had actually been a magical ritual in order to summon up a number of demons whose names I thankfully forget.

It was obvious even to the most gullible of listeners that Pottinger was barking mad. However, he was the only link that I had to anything even resembling practitioners of the dark arts, and so at the first possible opportunity after Alison's and my return home, I telephoned him. In those days, Lisa lived in the spare room and Alison was still - and nominally at least -

working for Exeter Health Authority. One evening when she was at work, I telephoned Pottinger. The ensuing conversation was a success beyond my wildest dreams. It turned out and not only was Pottinger completely *au fait* with the ritual that Spike had told me about, in which devotees of Crowley had claimed to have successfully raised the Loch Ness monster after performing a homage to the Babylonian snake goddess, but - wonder of wonders - he actually claimed to possess a tape-recording of the ritual being performed. Even more wonderful, for a consideration, he was prepared to let me have a copy of the tape.

Now, as I have already explained, Alison was - fairly justifiably - adamant that she would never get involved in anything that even slightly smacked of the dark arts. She was always equally adamant that she wouldn't let me get involved in anything like that either. We had been married for seven years by this stage, and I was fairly sure that she would consider a ritual written by Aleistair Crowley with the stated intention of invoking a Babylonian snake demon to ever-so-slightly smack of black magic. However, there was no way on earth that I was going to pass up the chance of seeing the Loch Ness Monster if there was even a possibility that this magical ritual - which I still secretly thought was mystical mumbo-jumbo - might succeed. According to Pottinger, there was a pretty good chance that I didn't even have to perform the ritual myself. He told me, that the magical vibes from the tape recording would be strong enough on their own.

As I write this, over a decade later, I not only have the benefit of hindsight, but also have the benefit of a decade of studying a wide range of subjects - *including* ritual magic. With the benefit of my present knowledge of arcane lore, I think that it is highly unlikely that my plans would have worked, but back in 1992 I was a magical innocent and I was determined to go ahead. For the first - and as far as I can remember the only - time in my marriage I carried out a complex and predetermined scheme to outwit my wife. For some reason - Pottinger always seemed to make everything far more complicated than I felt that it need to be - he was adamant that I had to come and collect the tape from him myself and in person. The tape was - or so he said - far too valuable a magical artefact to be entrusted to Her Majesty's postal services. And therefore, there was no alternative but for me go to London to collect it.

Alison and I had a very close relationship. In all the years that we were together we hardly ever went anywhere socially without the other. We enjoyed each other's company, and - as happens in so many dysfunctional relationships - we had become interdependent to a frightening degree. We had only just returned home from one trek around the country, and I was sure that I would not be able to persuade her to come to London with me, even if she had been able to get the time off work, which was doubtful. Even if she had come to London with me - she disliked Pottinger, even though neither of us had met him in the flesh - and I couldn't think of any way that even if I had managed to persuade her to go, that I would have managed to slip the leash for long enough to visit Pottinger, obtain the tape, and receive fairly detailed instructions about what to do with it.

I had to work out an excuse to get to London by myself.

Looking back at my life in general at this time and not purely at this one episode, I can see quite how ill I was. These days, I *really* resent the years that I sacrificed at the altar of hippiedom. If, upon being made redundant from the NHS, I had concentrated my efforts upon getting treatment my condition, and also upon getting hold of the state benefits to which I was undoubtedly entitled, then my mental-health would never have deteriorated to the level that it did, and I would have avoided five or six years of abject penury. Alison and I would not have been forced into some of the money-making measures that we took (and which I have no intention of revealing in this book), and we would very probably still be married. However, if I had done all this, as will be seen in a few chapters time, the Centre for Fortean Zoology would almost certainly not have become the success that it is today.

The fact remained, that back in 1992 I was extremely unwell. My mood was swinging erratically between pits of black depression, during which I was unable to leave my bedroom except to perform the most basic bodily functions, and during which the slightest stress would trigger the most horrific outbursts of temper, and my manic phases during which I would rush around excitedly like a puppy with a squeaky toy, spending money like mad and getting wildly excited about the most impractical schemes. In between I was pretty normal, but - at that time at least - I could spiral out of control into a manic or depressive state with very little notice. It is not surprising, therefore, that when I first broached the idea of going to London - ostensibly to see *Pink Floyd* play at the London Arena - Alison was not wildly enthusiastic. Eventually, she gave in, on the condition that I took two of my more responsible friends with me, and the game was afoot. However, it has to be said that at that stage of my life even my most responsible friends were wildly eccentric, alcoholic party animals. My mate Ian Wright - who had been at school with me, and who had been one of the ever-shifting contingent of my friends who had squatted at the Nurses' Home at Starcross - was driving. At that time, he was in the terminal stages of a career as an estate agent, and I believe that the events of the Saturday morning when two longhaired, drunk, idiots barged into his office brandishing a case of beer and demanding that he drive them up to London to see a rock concert, was one of the final nails in his professional coffin.

The morning after the *Pink Floyd* show, my pals and I woke up with terrific hangovers. As one can imagine, they were not particularly impressed with the idea of us having to travel all the way across London from the squat in Croydon where we had spent the night, to Holloway, in order to meet some dodgy friend of mine just so that I could get hold of a tape recording of a magical invocation to a Babylonian snake goddess. However, my powers of persuasion were second to none, and after I stressed the fact that Pottinger was bound to have a flat full of rare and interesting rock'n'roll memorabilia, they reluctantly agreed.

The journey across London was a nightmare. Our hangovers had developed from a state of dehydration and mild discomfort to a feeling akin to the German situationist rock band *Einsterzende Neubaten* performing a sound check with jackhammers inside each of our cerebral cortexes. In these days of mobile phones and instant communication it seems difficult to recall that only a decade or so ago, travellers in a strange place were dependent on telephone boxes in order to keep in contact with each other. Then, as now, public telephones were often vandalised, and with hindsight it seems extraordinary that anybody travelling to meet somebody with grossly inadequate instructions was ever able to succeed in their quest.

Hoping against hope that nobody would stop and breathalyse us we drove in an unsteady fashion across the metropolis. Eventually - about two hours later than we should have been - we found Holloway and looked in vain for a telephone box. As there was not a single one to be seen for miles, and the general consensus of opinion was that a dose of the hair of the dog that had bitten us so effectively the night before was in order, we made a beeline for the nearest pub.

Leaving my colleagues to order a round of drinks, I made my way to the telephone box in the corner of the bar to phone Pottinger. I was slightly surprised to find that the telephone box was painted bright pink, and had been lined with the most peculiar decor of polka-dots and shocking pink fake fur. However, I was far too hungover to care. When Pottinger answered the phone the first thing that he did was to ask where we were. When I told him the name of the pub in question he immediately burst into gales of uncontrollable laughter. Even by Pottinger's standards this was a remarkably eccentric thing to do, and after we had come such a way to meet him it was more than mildly annoying. He refused to tell me why he was laughing, but suggested that he meet us about 20 minutes later in another hostelry just down the road. Still laughing, he assured me that this new pub would be far more to our liking. When I returned to my companions I discovered why Pottinger had found the news of our location so wildly amusing.

It was not just a gay pub; it was an S&M gay bar full of the most unconvincing drag queens that it has ever been my misfortune to see. Add to that the fact that we were certainly the only straight people in the place, and that the horribly made up person behind the bar who looked like a cross between Big Daddy and Diana Dors obviously was making eyes at Ian, and that the whole place was decorated with items of sado-masochistic dungeon equipment, and glossy posters of muscular men wearing leather shorts, we were soon feeling horribly out of place. We drank our beers, and ignoring the wolf whistles from some of the more macho members of the clientele, we stumbled out into the uneven sunlight of Holloway High Street.

It didn't take long for us to find the pub that Pottinger had decided was a suitable pace for a motley bunch of hungover weirdoes to conduct the business that had - although my colleagues didn't actually know it - brought us all to London. It was a fairly nondescript looking boozer with a name like the Red Lion, or something of that ilk. It looked like any other - slightly run-down - hostelry in one of the less salubrious areas of the metropolis. I had been in hundreds of pubs like it over the years, and I expect that I will drink in hundreds of others during the course of what remains of my lifetime. The three of us entered the swinging glass door of the saloon bar. We looked around us suspiciously making sure that there were no signs that this too was a hotbed of homosexuality. We breathed a collective sigh of relief, as we saw that the pub not only looked, resolutely heterosexual, but that it also looked reassuringly normal, if a little down-at-heel. We ambled up to the bar and ordered a round of drinks, and then returned to a seat in the corner where we could relax and wait for Pottinger to arrive.

In the corner of the large room was a small stage illuminated by spotlights. And there was a rather ramshackle looking PA system and a couple of microphone stands. In the centre of the stage was a small blackboard, which proudly announced that the entertainment that the management had laid on for this Sunday lunchtime was a duo called 'Sandy and Barbarella'.

There is nothing more annoying in this world than a trio of hippies who believe that their rarefied tastes in music somehow makes them superior to the hoi polloi who happily enjoy the karaoke stylings of a female duo with an unimaginative name - for this is what, by a process of deduction, we had decided was in store for us. There is little more annoying on a Sunday morning when you have a hangover and you are waiting to see a weirdo about chaos magic, than a exceptionally talentless pair of slightly tarty young ladies who wandered onstage, a few minutes later, and started to sing a medley of Tammy Wynette songs in a listless and uninterested manner. My companions and I sneered snobbishly at each other secure in the moral high-ground of three people who, the night before, had expended a small fortune on going to see each a group of middle-aged rock musicians performing exactly the same show as they had on several hundred other evenings around the world - a show which though technically perfect, was soulless, and differed not one iota from the show we had seen them perform at Wembley three years previously. The three of us soon lost interest and were deeply enmeshed in a conversation about various obscure records that we had in our respective collections that we didn't even notice when Sandy - a buxom blonde who looked like she should be petitioning her agent to get her a walk-on part in *EastEnders* - started taking her clothes off.

Sandy was half-naked before one of us noticed her, and quickly jabbed the other two in the ribs with his elbow to alert us to the spectacle that had been put on for our edification. I had been going to pubs since the age of fifteen, and back in my student days I was quite aware that many hostelries provide bar snacks for free on the Sabbath. I spent many happy Sunday lunchtimes during my younger days, quaffing pints and scoffing the roast potatoes that mine host had put on the bar so - as I saw it - so that the impecunious student nurses were not forced to spend their meagre pennies on food rather than on alcohol.

Over the years I have seen a lot of pub entertainers. Indeed, during my long and varied career, I have - on occasion - been a pub entertainer myself. On the whole, I have always found that the standard of pub entertainment inflicted upon the general public during a Sunday lunchtime is even more futile, fatuous, and downright boring than that which is on offer in the evenings. It usually consists of a solo artist or a duo, performing dreary cover versions of Country Music classics, and the worst that the Top 20 has had to offer over the preceding three decades. It has never before - at least in my experience - consisted of a pair of faux lesbian strippers.

I had, actually, seen a stripper before. On my 21st birthday I inherited a small sum of money from a dead aunt. I invested most of it in a trip back to the place where I had spent my boyhood - Hong Kong. Even in the nine years that had elapsed between my family returning to England, and my visit as a young adult, the place had changed immeasurably. I spent a happy week exploring the countryside that I had known as a child, but each evening - when I was not hunting for moths attracted to the light at the top of the tower at the top of the Peak Tram I sat confused and unhappy in the hotel bar. Already beginning to feel the pain of the mental illness that would eventually overwhelm my life, I had returned to the land of my childhood in a vain - and ultimately fruitless - attempt to try and recapture what I perceived as a relatively carefree childhood. Thus, I was completely unprepared for a Hong Kong after dark - a world of prostitutes, drugs, vice and sins of the flesh.

One night, I met a bloke in the bar. He was about 10 years older than me, and a junior cog in the complex machine of colonial government, which had once been overseeing my father. We got talking, and he offered to show me some of the best that the nightlife of Hong Kong could offer. If the truth were known, I would have been much happier staying in the bar, drinking whisky and Coke, reading Herklots, and wondering what had happened to my childhood. However, I was now a man, and as - I believe - St. Paul is supposed to have said, it was time for me to put away childish things. So I allowed my new acquaintance to take me to a strip club. It was somewhat of an archaic establishment, and I sat bored, as an equally disinterested Chinese woman wearing a sequinned G-string, gyrated around and made the tassels on her nipples contra-rotate. Apart from wondering - vaguely - how she had managed to affix the aforesaid tassels onto the aforesaid nipples, the whole affair had left me cold. I had found it about as erotic as rice pudding, and it put me off going to such establishments ever again. I was certainly completely unprepared for the display that was going on only a few yards in front of us on the small stage in a corner of the London pub.

By this stage Sandy was completely naked, and her colleague was not far behind. Soon they were rubbing baby oil onto each other, pretending to masturbate, and feigning lesbian sex. The three of us were transfixed by a mixture of sexual arousal and abject embarrassment. We had been completely unprepared for a display like this and we didn't really know how to behave. Neither, it seemed, did the rest of the audience. Half of them were shouting lewd comments and suggestions, and the other half - which to my amazement included some highly respectable and prudish looking middle-aged women - were complete ignoring the whole thing. It wasn't the sort of situation that you might have envisaged where the respectable members of the audience were doing their best to pretend that such a display of lasciviousness was not going on - they were simply paying no attention as if the two nubiles, indulging in fake girl on girl action in front of them, were really a tedious TV programme in which they had no interest.

My companions and I were hypnotised by the display the front of us. Not knowing quite what to do, we stared at the two girls, entranced like a cobra in front of a mongoose. Suddenly the spell was broken as somebody tapped on the shoulder, and a familiar voice - sounding even more like a cartoon rabbit than he did on the telephone - shattered our sexual reverie.

"Ullo lads", said Pottinger, " I thought you would prefer this gaff to the pub full of poofters up the road."

I will be the first to admit that it takes something really extraordinary to distract me from watching two pretty young girls pretending to have sex with each other. But, my goodness, Pottinger was certainly extraordinary. He not only sounded like a cartoon rabbit, but he looked like a has-been children's entertainer who had spent the last fifteen years or so living rough on a municipal rubbish tip. His skin was peculiarly powdery, pale and transluscent. His eyes were bloodshot, and his teeth were non-existent. On his head he wore what looked very much like a badly knitted tea-cosy which some well-meaning old lady had made especially for a charity bazaar, and which had been thrown out because nobody in their right minds would have wanted it. His clothes were a uniform shade of a peculiar mustard yellow, and were filthy dirty.

It turned out that he had not brought the tape of the Aleistair Crowley invocation with him, so we finished our drinks, and followed him up the road a couple of hundred yards to his flat.

If Pottinger himself had been an extraordinary sight, his abode was a revelation. It only had a bedroom, a living room, a kitchen, and a bathroom, but every available square inch of space was taken up with items of rock'n'roll memorabilia. There were broken guitars, cassettes, reel-to-reel tapes, and items of studio equipment everywhere. There were concert posters, promotional photographs, and backstage passes. Our host claimed that he had got all of this stuff - a veritable Aladdin's cave for the discerning record collector - by searching through skips outside record-company offices and recording studios. Knowing - as I do - how the music business works, I am pretty sure that his claim was true. Knowing - as I do - how the rock music memorabilia market works, I would hazard a guess that the contents of this shabby Council flat, inhabited by a toothless madman who looked like an alcoholic tramp, was probably worth - then - well over half a million quid.

We spent about an hour at Pottinger's flat. I took possession of the cassette that I had travelled so far to obtain, and at about three o'clock the three of us trooped back to Ian's car and commenced the long drive back to Exeter.

Along with the cassette tape that Pottinger had given me was a small bundle of grubby photocopies which contained fairly detailed instructions about what I was to do when I finally got to the Great Glen. I smuggled them, and the tape, into the house and secreted them in a place where I was fairly sure that Alison would not bother to look. There were now only a few more days left for us to prepare for all the tour, and, as always, life was particularly hectic.

By this stage, we had have been working for Steve Harley, for nearly three years. This was something like our eighth tour with him, and by this stage we had got it down to a fine art. Even when you're only flogging T-shirts and magazine, there's still an enormous amount of planning to go into a road trip which could last anything up to a couple of months. This particular jaunt was only going to last for a couple of weeks, but leaving aside my hidden agenda, the precarious finances of my household dictated that we would have to bring at least 300 quid home with us if we were going to survive over the next few months. We had to pack an enormous amount of stock as well as our clothes and sleeping things, and the burgeoning supply of second-hand records, which we were determined to swap for more and more books to add to my ever-growing Fortean library. Finally, that day of the tour dawned. We kissed Lisa goodbye, patted the dog on the head, and headed off in our battered and rather ancient Ford Transit van up the A30 in search of adventure.

I look back at this particular tour as being probably the peak of the time that I spent on the road with Steve Harley. His performances on this tour were transcendent - possibly the finest rock music that I have ever heard. He had a particularly fine band that spring, and the set lists effortlessly mixed old and new songs together to produce two-and-a-half-hours of peerless entertainment. At this time, Steve and I were friends. I had managed to break through the barrier which separated fan from friend, and in the long hours before sound checks, and when the technical people and the backline crew were doing their own inimitable thing, Steve and I would often talk. He told me about the early days of his career - when as a young reporter on a Colchester newspaper he dreamed of forming a rock band, which would be a glorious mixture of the

Beatles, Marc Bolan, Bob Dylan and his own peculiar vision. He told me how once, tripping on acid, he had seen an old tramp in the park, and how he when their eyes met had been inspired to write one of my favourite of his songs - *Tumbling Down*. We often talked about our own tastes in music - particularly Smokey Robinson and Bob Dylan, and on one unforgettable occasion he strummed at an acoustic guitar and we sang *You Really Got a Hold on me* rather badly - but in some semblance of harmony - together. He also told me how - in the days before *Cockney Rebel* had got their first record contract - they had recorded some demos, mostly of their own songs but also Bob Dylan's glorious *Absolutely Sweet Marie*.

It was a song that could have been made for Harley's nasal, estuarine drawl, and all tour I had been badgering him to try his hand at singing it again. Harley always refused, but our long and rambling conversations would continue. He had always been my biggest influence as a musician and as a songwriter, but it was on this particular three weeks sojourn in the provinces, that he taught me everything that I know today at about the way that the media works. He was in a unique position - he had been both a journalist, and the target of journalists. He had been the hunter *and* the hunted, and he had become an expert at beating the media at their own game. Although he had been my favourite pop singer since I was 14 years old, it was only on this tour that he became my mentor - joining Gerald Durrell as somebody who upon whom I had modelled my life. Looking back over the last 10 years, one can see both Harley's and Durrell's figurative fingerprints writ large upon the way that I have run the CFZ, and indeed my life. Neither man was a saint. In both their cases their feet of clay are sometimes spectacular, and I see know that I have inherited some of their bad points as well as some of their skills. But if it were not for these two men I would not be where I am - or who I am - today.

I lost my old tour diary notebooks years ago, so am unable to recount exactly where this tour took us. I remember playing Bolton, I remember playing at least two shows in the north-east, and I know that at the end of the tour there was an extraordinary performance in Glasgow. I suppose we must have played of the cases, but after a gap of more than a decade, I'm afraid that the nuances of individual gigs are now lost in the mists of time. For me, after all, the highlights of that tour was always going to be the show in Aberdeen, because this was the show after which we were going to drive to Loch Ness.

I remember Aberdeen as been a particularly strange place. It was completely made of great, grey, blocks of granite. It was quite a stately town, but as Paul drove us down the main street, all I could see out of the window where these huge buildings like mildewed cathedral walls towering above us on either side. One thing, which I found most peculiar, was the fact that although it was a Friday night - and as everywhere on Friday night - gangs of young men roamed to the streets looking for beer, girls, and trouble not necessarily in that order - in Aberdeen they did so wearing immaculate pin-striped suits. It was almost as if a convention of five or six thousand juvenile delinquent bank clerks had picked this particular night to go on the razzle.

We were late arriving at the venue and we assumed that the soundcheck would have been over hours before, and be was surprised to see the distinctive for figure of Steve Harley pacing up and down outside the backstage entrance with an impatient frown on his face. As we pulled up he flashed just a mischievous grin and disappeared. We unpacked the van and went inside to set up a stall. We had only been there a few minutes, when Roy - the impossibly thin, and very elegant sound man - strode menacingly out into the foyer to find us. With a stern frown on his face he told us that Steve wanted it to speak to us urgently and immediately. My heart dropped. The look of panic and consternation on the faces of my wife, and our two companions told me that they were thinking exactly the same as me. What the hell had we done? Our sins were not a very serious ones, but we had never actually asked permission to use concerts as a venue to swap second-hand records for books on cryptozoology, and nobody had ever sanctioned my completely unofficial flexible guest-list policy which had allowed various friends, cronies, and associates of ours to get into the shows for nothing. Maybe this was it and maybe the game had run its course. The four of us walked into the auditorium convinced that we were about to be sacked. However, as soon as we set foot into the cavernous room, the stage lights flashed on, there was a shout of "one-two-three four" from Steve - centre-stage - and the band leapt into a frenetic tune that seemed oddly familiar. Then Steve started to sing:

Well, your railroad gate, you know I just can't jump it
Sometimes it gets so hard, you see
I'm just sitting here beating on my trumpet,
with all these promises you left for me.

Steve Harley was singing *Absolutely Sweet Marie* just for us.

It was a magical moment. To paraphrase P.G Wodehouse, the sight of me dancing is enough to make one re-evaluate the concept of man as the pinnacle of God's creation, but dance I did. It was probably the only time in my adult life when music are managed to inspire me to uncontrollable terpsichorean excess. All four of us danced, but I was like a man possessed...

Well, I waited for you when I was half sick
Yes, I waited for you when you hated me
Well, I waited for you inside of the frozen traffic
When you knew I had some other place to be
Now where are you tonight, sweet Marie?

It is very difficult to describe this magical moment. On one level it was merely Steve doing something nice for a bunch people who had been working for him, and following him on tour for several years. However on another level - for me at least - it was something far more magickal. At the risk of sounding like an old hippy the experience itself was so affirming that it gave me the inner strength which I knew that I needed in order to carry out my - entirely covert - tasks which lay ahead.

Well, anybody can be just like me, obviously
But then, now again, not too many can be like you, fortunately.

Back in those days I still believed that somehow rock music had healing vibes that were going to save the world. Looking back from a far more rational, less drug-addled, and far more cynical viewpoint, I am more than a little embarrassed to admit this. However, as far as is possible, I'm making this memoir an honest one, and I am sure that, to some readers, a belief in the healing power of music is no more bizarre than some of the ideas about surrealchemy and ritual magick that I was to pick up from Tony Shiels only a few years later.

We continued to dance. Steve continued to sing and it was as if he was somehow channelling the spirit of something far greater than all of us. We were all dancing, but I was whirling like a dervish - it was as if I was a man possessed. As I span round and round, images of the deep, dark, water of Loch Ness filled my inner eye. Steve Harley, his band, and my three companions may well have been in a purpose-built local council leisure centre in Aberdeen, but I was somewhere far stranger.

Well, six white horses that you did promise
Were fin'ly delivered down to the penitentiary
But to live outside the law, you must be honest
I know you always say that you agree
But where are you tonight, sweet Marie

Bob Dylan's arcane wordplay was a perfect counterpoint to the visions I was seeing as I danced. As Steve spat out the lyrics in a gloriously vitriolic estuarine howl, I was chanting the words of Aleistair Crowley's invocation. As the band thundered to a climax and I spun around and around like a gyroscope on methedrine, I could see the dark waters before me parting and the great head and neck of an antediluvian creature looming up before me with its eyes ablaze and its mouth open.

Then...........

Suddenly it was all over. Steve grinned at us and Roy ushered us out into the foyer where we continued setting up our stall for the evening.

I have to admit, that I remember absolutely nothing about the evening's gig, and although I vaguely remember the four of us cadging somewhere to sleep for the night from two girls - complete strangers - that we had met at the show, my thoughts and my emotions were elsewhere. The next morning we said our goodbyes and drove North-East towards Inverness.

It was my first time in northern Scotland and I was overwhelmed by the bleak majesty of the landscape. Somehow I had always imagined that it would be similar to my beloved Dartmoor, but it wasn't. It is the only place within the United Kingdom that I have ever experienced that feeling of sheer space, which I have found in Canada, and in deserts around the world. During the journey back to England from Hong Kong in 1971 we made a stop-off in East Africa, and visited Tsavo game reserve in Kenya. It was - to date at least - the only time that I have seen the big, herding, animals of the African savanna. It was also my first visit to Africa since my infancy in Nigeria. I was only 11 years old, but I remember it like it was yesterday. My most enduring memory of the day on the game reserve was not the giant elephants, the graceful and feminine giraffes or even the lioness that did her best to keep as much of a distance between her and our Land Rover as possible. The image that has stuck in my mind most is that of my father - still a relatively young man of 46 - taking me by the hand and leading me to the top of a small hillock just inside the park entrance. With his hand pointed outstretched towards the horizon he said to me words which I will never forget:

"You know what that is, Son?"

I shook my head. My father's voice was solemn as if he was in a great cathedral.

"That's Africa. Miles of fucking Africa."

I looked up at him and I could see a tear beginning to form in the corner of his eye. This was the land that he loved - that he had sweated for and nearly died for - a land where he would always feel that he belonged, but where - because of the changing political map - he would never be anything but a tourist again.

I have experienced that feeling of immense space again, since, but never with such an almost sexual intensity. I have felt it in the middle of the Mexican desert. I have felt it when I stood on the top of a ridge in Colorado on my 40th birthday as I looked out over miles of the countryside which previously I had only seen in cowboy films. But, the nearest that I have ever come to the orgasmic intensity of my father teaching me to grok Africa, was on a glorious spring day as we drove over the Scottish Highlands on the way to Loch Ness.

The main difference between the Highland moors and Dartmoor was the absence of the tors. On Dartmoor every hilltop is surmounted with the fossilised remains of the cores of ancient volcanoes. Although I had never realised it, they not only dominate the Dartmoor landscape, but their sheer size makes the hills and dales of Mid Devon gloriously claustrophobic and almost Lilliputian in their intensity. Without them for far larger hills and mountain sides of northern Scotland seemed almost gentle undulations, although they were obviously no such thing. The landscape was carpeted in purple heather. Again, something with which I was familiar from Dartmoor. But again it looked completely different. I had never realised that there were so many shades of purple. I don't know whether the hillsides were carpeted with a myriad of different types of the plant or whether it was just the subtle interplay of sunlight on the varying textures of leaf and flower, but it was easy to get hypnotised just by staring at the ever-shifting patterns of purple, white, and grey upon the ancient hillsides.

At the bottom of one valley Paul slammed his foot onto the brake and we shuddered to a halt just in time to let a magnificent stag with his three wives dutifully following him charge across the road only a few feet in front of us. About half-an-hour later we stopped to watch a small family group of black grouse - the only endemic British tetrapod - going about their business by the side of the road. The cock was magnificent - his jet-black plumage, magnificent white tail feathers and red cap made him look like a senior officer of an ancient dragoon regiment, resplendent in his full-dress uniform. The rest of his family - drab and subservient - stood around admiringly. I felt very guilty for all the times that I have eaten these magnificent game birds.

Eventually by mid-afternoon we reached Loch Ness. We drove right around the Loch, keeping our eyes firmly on the cold black water below us, convinced that we would see the elusive monster. As we drove past the gates of Boleskine House I felt a chill run down my spine. I realised that we were within figurative spitting distance of one of the most notorious sites (from the point of view of both a fortean and a Led Zeppelin fan) in the British Isles. I made the others stop the car and I got out to investigate. There were obviously people around, so I didn't dare to investigate too closely but I gazed in awe at the stone eagles on the pillars of the gate and looked longingly at the driveway, but I decided that as Jimmy Page was a notoriously reclusive bloke with a reputation for giving unwanted visitors short shrift, that I had better not investigate further.

We found somewhere that looked perfect for us to camp. It was a little side path leading off the main road and on the north side of the lake. There was room for us to park the van and for Paul and Kim to pitch their tent. What was best of all was that if you followed the path down only about 100 yards, by dint of climbing over a five bar gate, you could reach the lake itself. We had no problem with committing the act of trespass, but decided that discretion was the best part of valour and that it would be better for Paul and Kim to camp on the common ground out side the gate rather than to set up camp by the water itself. I couldn't help but grin to myself about this decision - it was tailor-made to leave the coast clear for me to carry out my secret mission uninterrupted.

That night we sat in a pub in Drumnadrochit and got talking to a rather shifty looking bloke called Charlie. Much to our surprise, it turned out that Charlie wasn't, like us, a *sassenach* on a monster hunting expedition but he was originally from Harlow - the home of Paul and Kim - and had moved up to Loch Ness several years before with his family, and was an employee of the local water company. He hated it up there and longed for his native fleshpots of the South East, but, he said, he could never return. He was trapped up there for the rest of his life.

As you do, we got talking about the monster, and I expressed the opinion that some sightings, especially those which had taken place on land, could have been of otters. Although most specimens of the European Otter are only a few feet long specimens measuring up to six feet in length have been shot, and in Ireland there are legends of a creature called the *Dobhar Chu* or master otter which is supposed to grow even bigger.

"Don't talk to me about bleeding otters" said my new friend, with far more venom than I could ever have imagined the subject warranting. "It was bleeding otters that stopped me making my bleeding fortune…"

Well, an opening conversational gambit like that could not be ignored and I had to know more, so I bought Charlie a pint of Tennants 80 Shillings and a malt whisky chaser and sat back to enjoy his story.

It all began when one of Charlie's colleagues had been visiting a garden centre which sold koi carp as a sideline. He was immediately entranced not just by the ancient beauty of these gorgeous and majestic fish but for the fact that some of them were going for prices of up to a grand. He told Charlie about it. "'ere, I want a bit of that" he thought elegantly, and the two of them began to hatch a cunning plan.

They were both water board employees and the huge water tanks of which they were joint custodians, would, they thought make fine rearing vats for koi carp. Wouldn't it be a wizard wheeze to buy lots of small fish at a couple of quid and rear them in these giant, secluded stone vats where nobody else ever went, and then flog them for a grand apiece?

However, a quick visit to the library soon disillusioned them of this idea. As soon as they realised the length of time it would take for a two quid koi to turn into one worth a grand they gave up on it, but they soon came up with a bigger, better and far more nefarious scheme. Charlie had a brother-in-law called Big Colin who lived in one of the less salubrious suburbs of Harlow New Town. Big Colin was usually described by his associates as being a "Diamond Geezer" but from what I could gather from talking to his brother-in-law he was a rather unpleasant thug and petty criminal whose stock in trade were "dodgy motahs" and "bent MOTs" but who was not averse to the odd bit of petty thievery on the side.

Whereas garden centres that sell koi carp are few and far between in the Scottish Highlands, they are two a penny in Essex and between them Charlie and Big Colin started to plan a commando style raid on one of the more secluded Essex Garden Centres. The idea was to steal about thirty thousand pounds worth of koi carp, and rush them in Big Colin's van up to Inverness where they could be released into the water board ponds where they could be kept in seclusion until they were fenced on with forged paperwork to unsuspecting customers. Big Paul, Charlie and Charlie's un-named "mate" looked likely to net a cool ten grand each out of the operation.

The raid went ahead like clockwork. It had been planned with military precision and was carried out in a fashion that would have made the SAS proud. Charlie and Big Colin then drove hell for leather up the M1 towards Scotland. By the time that they reached the secluded water treatment works in the hills above Loch Ness it was the following morning and they were exhausted. However they still had one task to do. Taking the big plastic containers that they had brought especially for their precious cargo they carefully carried each one to the side of the great stone basin, where they took the lid off and tipped the enormous fish into the water.

After the whole of their ill-gotten gains had been liberated, Charlie and Big Colin sat back, lit cigarettes and surveyed their swimming swag with a feeling of a job well done. However theirs were not the only eyes watching the great red and gold fish.

"So what happened?" I asked. "Did you get away with it? Did your employers find out?"

Charlie grimaced at me "They didn't get a bleeding chance. There were thirty five fish in that storage tank and within a week they were all gone."

I looked at him quizzically and would have raised one eyebrow if it wasn't for the fact that although it looks incredibly cool I have never been able to do it.

"It was the bleeding otters" he said "They ate the bleeding lot. Thirty bleeding grand's worth of the bleeders"…

I started to laugh uncontrollably. Although I was sorry that the noble fish had met such an ignominious end the whole affair had an irresistibly comic side to it. I was laughing so hard that I almost missed what Charlie had to say next….

"… and that's why I'm stuck here in the bleeding north of Scotland, because Big Colin says if I ever come back to Harlow without his ten grand, ee'll bleeding have my kneecaps".

Realising that a platitude about crime not paying would not really be appropriate at this stage, I bought Charlie another beer and went out into the gathering Inverness dusk. However, before we left we told him where we were camped and invited him to join us for a picnic lunch the next day.

Early the next morning - just after dawn - I wriggled out of the sleeping bag which I was sharing with my wife, dressed while sitting on the tailgate of the van, grabbed the portable tape recorder (known, at the time, by the unlovely and somewhat racist sobriquet of a ghetto-blaster), and my briefcase, and tiptoed down the winding lane towards Loch Ness. I slipped past the tent where Paul and Kim were sleeping and was soon at the side of the water.

This was the moment that I had been anticipating for so many months. I had planned, schemed, and actually worked quite hard to bring this plan to fruition. Now was the point of no return and I was both excited and very scared indeed.

I am a fairly bashful person, and am quite shy about my body. However, I desperately wanted to see the Loch Ness monster, and there was not much that I wasn't prepared to do in order to fulfil this ambition. According to the lengthy notes that Pottinger had given me, all the celebrants in an invocation to Tiamat had to be naked. Furthermore, an offering of "The Male Essence", had to be made in supplication. Although I had prepared myself for this moment a hundred times, the reality of standing naked by the shores of Loch Ness and dispelling my "essence" into the dark waters was somewhat daunting. I had brought a bottle of wine with me to steady my nerves and although it was only just after six in the morning I took a hearty swig, and sat down on a convenient rock to have a cigarette and to prepare myself for what - at the very least - was going to be a singular experience.

As I drank and smoked, I looked out over the still, dark, water. There were wisps of ethereal mist swirling like ghosts a few inches above the water itself. Apart from them, however, everything was completely silent and completely still. I braced myself. If I wasn't going to do this thing now I was never going to do it. I flicked my cigarette butt into the lake, put down my bottle of wine and got undressed.

According to the photocopied grimoires I had been given, the "offering", had to be made at a specific point in the ritual. So - naked as a frog - I pressed the play button on the ghetto-blaster, and stood - as if spreadeagled - on the very shore of the lake. The music began, and I began to chant along with the voices on the tape. I had done my best to learn the ritual off by heart, and so it began.

Together we chanted, and I could feel a weird energy pulsing through my body. It was as if I was electrified. The chanting continued and I began to feel as if I was becoming at one with the land around me. Suddenly, the fact that I was a grossly overweight man badly in need of a haircut, standing, naked on the shores of a Scottish lake made perfect sense. Even the climax - if you will excuse the pun - of the ritual no longer seemed grotesque and embarrassing, and I began to prepare myself for the act of supplication which - by this time I truly believed - would bring the snake goddess Tiamat Herself, to the surface of the lake to greet me.

The chanting became more intense and as the ritual approached its apotheosis I began to prepare for my pivotal role when, suddenly, the spell was broken.

"Foooking Hell" ejaculated Charlie (our friend from the night before), who had wandered over to find our campsite and invite us to breakfast.

I turned round with a start, and knocked both the ghetto-blaster and my half-empty bottle of wine into the lake. Charlie and I stared at each other in shock for a few seconds. I grabbed at my clothes, but it was too late. Charlie muttered something that sounded like "Fookin' Pervert", and disappeared up the path as fast as his feet could carry and we never saw him again. By this stage, even if I hadn't managed to break the ghetto-blaster, I had lost my nerve. The magick had gone, and Loch Ness returned to normal. I got dressed, carefully burned my photocopied grimoires, and went back to bed.

The rest of our sojourn in Scotland was uneventful, and two days later we rejoined the tour in Glasgow, for the final three shows. There was, however one more incident of note that happened before we returned to Exeter. At the final gig - in Manchester - we ran into one of the more bizarre people who had decided to spend his life following Steve Harley around the country. He was an ever-so-slightly camp Irish lad called Gerard. Over the course of the evening I told him about my adventures as a monster hunter, and my dear wish to be able to become a cryptozoologist on a full-time basis. I also told him of the problems that I had been encountering whenever I tried to deal with officialdom. He suggested that as there were so many self-styled independent researchers, and that as so many of them were barking mad, it might not be a bad idea if Alison and I were to found an organisation to deal with cryptozoology - in the UK at least - in a sensible and professional manner. What a bloody good idea, I said, and a few days later when the tour was over, Alison and I discussed the matter with our good friends Dave and Jayne Simons from Derby with whom we were spending a few days post-tour R&R.

The rest is history. Dave was far more computer aware than we were, and he soon managed to design us our first logo, and a few years later our first website. However, it was Gerard who not only came up with the initial idea of our founding an organisation dedicated to research into mystery animals but named it.

After Steve Harley parted company with Alison and me a few years later I lost touch with Gerard. However, years later in 1999 I was back in Manchester. I was doing a TV show hosted by Terry Christian (best known for fronting the seminal "yoof" show *The Word*), and following the filming I was ensconced in the bar at Granada Studios with Terry, a couple of ex-members of *Oasis* and a number of other minor celebrities. The subject of conversation somehow turned to Steve Harley, and it transpired that the various Manchester musos and I had several acquaintances in common. One of them was Gerard.

It appeared that the intervening years had not been kind to him. Even when I knew him he had been a heavy drinker, but apparently, he had gone from bad to worse and by the end of the decade was an alcoholic mess. He had also developed some mental health problems, which resulted in some peculiar, and sometimes outright bizarre behaviour.

Apparently, he had been arrested, for wandering into the local leisure centre - drunk as a skunk, and with a half-empty bottle of Scotch in his hand - in order to watch the local under 14's team of synchronised swimmers. While watching, he got drunker and drunker, and was arrested after shouting sexually explicit comments to the little girls in the pool. As a result he spent many months in a local lunatic asylum, and also acquired a rather unfortunate new nickname.

You may ask why I am telling you this. It is, I feel, time to set the record straight. Although - as I have stated in public on many occasions - the Centre for Fortean Zoology *was* founded by Alison and me at the house of my friend Dave Symons, the world's greatest Cryptozoological research organisation would never have come into being if it had not been for a drunken conversation in the bar of the Manchester International II with a bloke called Gerry the Nonce!

CHAPTER SEVEN

KIP OF THE SERENES

When we returned to Exeter, the full enormity of what I had agreed to do, hit me like a house brick between the eyes. Although, when it had first been mooted, the original idea of the CFZ was, essentially, to provide me with some sort of spurious credibility which I lacked being an independent researcher, the more that I thought about it, the more I was becoming convinced that the concept of a truly global, non-partisan and community orientated organisation to study mystery animals across the world was at a good idea. But was it a workable one? The only appearance that Alison or I had ever had in organising anything like this was in organising the fan club for a singer who - despite my admiration of his talent - was, commercially at least, not as hot a property as he had been two decades before.

For once in my life, I was determined that I was going to do the thing properly. All through my life - to date - I had rushed into things full-tilt in a half-assed manner, and I was beginning to realise that my established *modus operandi* was not a particularly successful one. I decided that if I was going to do this then I had to have a manifesto of how I intended to proceed, and this was a thing that could not be taken lightly.

Looking back, I can see that I was right. It took nearly two years from my own initial inception of the Centre for Fortean Zoology to there being more than a handful of members. For the first 12 months there were only three of us, and it wasn't until the launch of our magazine in April 1994 that membership increased to any significant degree.

With the zeal which is felt by any young man who truly believes that he is embarking on a journey to do something important - and furthermore a journey which would (if done properly), take him the rest of his life, I began to look around at the cryptozoological community with new eyes. And I was not impressed at what I saw.

There was already an organisation which - allegedly at least - was claiming to do it what I want to. So I joined it. And I wasn't impressed. Although undeniably impressive from an academic point of view, I felt that they were badly missing the point. I believed - and still do believe - that one of the most important functions of an organisation like the CFZ is to foster a sense of community. And I was appalled to find that what was at the time the leading organisation for the cryptozoological community worldwide was - in my opinion at least - doing exactly the opposite. In an attempt to claw back the trappings of academic respectability they adopted the mantle of a scholarly scientific journal. All very well and good - so far as it went. However, when such a journal is published without the moral and social safety-net of an established academic institution such as a university, the practice of devoting a large chunk of each of your journals to rebuttals and negative comments about one's colleagues, can only - in my opinion at least - be divisive. This particular learned journal was full of statements like "so and so made a ridiculous assertion in such-and-such a dissertation", and it became clear after I had read several of them that far from being a good-natured forum for debate, these people were turning their own community against itself. The deeper I dug, the more that I realised that most of the more vocal and higher profile members of the cryptozoological community hated each other's guts, and that it was largely a fault of the organisation to which they all belonged.

I was determined that when I finally got the CFZ on the go, one of its main stated policies and purposes was to foster a sense of community and to build bridges rather than set one group off against another for no apparent reason. This was where the experience that I had gained working for years on the fringes of the music business became invaluable. I had soon discovered that the whole subject of mystery animals was one in which many people just were not interested.

Generations of hack writers specializing in cut and paste paperbacks with titles like *The world's most mysterious mysteries*, and *Bigfoot, Roswell, and spontaneous Human Combustion - the truth*, had fouled the pitch just as badly as had the anally retentive academics. They had managed to imbue the whole subject of mystery animals with a grotesque, sub-Erik von Daniken miasma which immediately dissuaded many of the people whom - I was convinced - should really be members of the global cryptozoological research community, and that those people who were actually in said community were becoming increasingly marginalised. However, I believed that with my experience working with fringe communities within the music business, and even - to a certain extent - with integrating long-term hospital residents into a care-in-the-community scenario, I believed that I could do a damn sight better than the people in whose tender care the cryptozoological community was - at that time - languishing.

Another thing that I realised, was, that although both the journal and the newsletters of the only organisation which was at the time dedicated to the subject of cryptozoology, appeared on the surface to be academically beyond reproach, much of what they printed was dull, uninformative and of little or no interest to the man in the street. Like so many other quasi-academic organisations, these people were so determined to take themselves seriously that they had built themselves a whole industrial estate of ivory towers, which contained such a rarefied atmosphere that mere mortals soon found themselves suffocating from sheer disinterest.

Again, I felt that I could do better. I already had over seven years experience in publishing small press magazines aimed at popularising subjects which were themselves somewhat marginalised. I had become quite a master of spin - several years before I had heard the term. With Chris de Burgh, for example, I had managed - for several years - to make an increasingly inane, mainstream, and dull performer seemed interesting for the sake of those people who had been following him since he was a worthy young singer-songwriter in the early seventies. With ISMO, I had established a magazine that had actually become the voicepiece of a whole community of people who followed music that had not been popular in the mainstream for many years. ISMO unwittingly foresaw the advent of magazines like *Mojo*, which reintroduced a middle-aged audience to popular music. As I read the newsletters and journals which purported to be published for the Cryptozoological community, I discovered that they were on the whole so tedious, that I was convinced that I could do better. I had a vision of a series of publications that were both informative, literate and - the most important - interesting. I had discovered, with the magazines that I'd published over the years, that a modicum of humour never did anyone any harm, and over the months I began to draw up a blueprint for how I wanted my cryptozoological research organisation to progress. However, even with my capacity for self-delusion, I was unable to pretend that the Centre for Fortean Zoology was (as 1982 became 1983, at least), anything more than a slew of pipe dreams, a rusty old filing cabinet full of photocopies and a membership of three.

And I had no idea how I was actually going to get the CFZ up and running. So, although I continued with my daydreams, I spent more time actually getting on with my researches.

In the early summer of 1993 I finally visited Bodmin Moor for the first time. We had been in contact with one of the farmers in the area for some time, but due to a mixture of problems - some financial and some logistical - we had been unable to take her up on her offer of allowing us to come down for a visit to investigate the predations of what was beginning to be known as the "Beast of Bodmin" for ourselves. We had just finished a long and gruelling tour with Steve Harley. For the first time I hadn't enjoyed it. Paul and I had been at each other's throats continually. Looking back, I can see that this was largely the result of me being forced into a situation when I had to be in very close proximity with a number of other people when - unbeknownst to anyone - I was in the middle one of the depressive faces of my bipolar illness. I had found the tour an excruciating ordeal and was only too happy to get back home again.

Alison and I drove down to Bodmin Moor in relatively high spirits. We were looking forward to our visit to the farm. For the first time it looked as if we were going to be treated as real professionals - true leaders of the cryptozoological community. The fact was - sadly - that at the time we were no more than well-meaning amateurs and that (despite my hopes to the contrary), being able to write letters on a piece of paper which proclaimed me as being the director of the Centre for Fortean Zoology meant diddley-squat when the truth of the matter is that I was an eccentric, fat, and more than slightly mad bloke with shoulder-length hair driving around the country and a strawberry pink transit van driven by his long-suffering and only mildly interested wife. I know that when we drove up the long drive to the farmhouse we were expecting to be hailed as visiting heroes. It has to said that even today, when the CFZ is far better organised and can live up to its claim of being the biggest and best cryptozoological research organisation in the world, we have very seldom been greeted with the plaudits and acclaim that I had been unconsciously expecting on Bodmin Moor in the summer of 1993. It goes without saying that we didn't get it.

The farm itself was a fairly undistinguished and ordinary-looking place. The owner came rushing out to greet us as she heard our rattly old van come clattering up the driveway. She did a double-take and looked at us in horror. Who were these two weirdoes? We looked like the remnants of the so-called peace convoy which had been known travelling around England for nearly eight years by this time spreading the word of peace and love and leaving a wake of mayhem behind them. Where were the two scientists she had been expecting?

She made us welcome - albeit with a slightly wary glint in her eye - and ushered us into her house to introduce us to the rest of her extended family. It says a lot - I am ashamed to admit - for our appearance at the time it that we hadn't been in the house for more than 10 minutes before one of the permanent residents at a farm took me aside and quietly whispered in my ear that she wanted to buy some dope and did I have any on me?

We spent several hours listening to our hostess's long-drawn-out story about the predations upon her flock of sheep by a panther or panthers unknown. What soon became evident was that she had an agenda on her. However, it would not be for some years before we were to find out what that agenda actually was. It also soon became obvious that none if the inhabitants of the farm were in the slightest bit interested in our theories, or us for that matter. We were there purely as light entertainment. The cabaret, if you like - to be paraded before the lady of the house's family and friends as the visiting monster-hunters. The fact that we appeared to be out-to-lunch hippies only added to the novelty factor.

Then - in the early evening, as we were all sitting around the big wooden table in the kitchen, and Alison and I were beginning to feel more and more uncomfortable with the situation, we heard the most peculiar wheezing noise. It sounded like an asthmatic barrel organ being played by a company of elderly budgerigars. It was our hostess's husband.

As most people know, I have a weight problem. It is the result of an eating disorder, which in turn is a result of my bipolar illness. I have spent much of my adult life in a struggle against this problem, and several times a year I embark on a stringent diet under the supervision of my doctor and the community dietician. It is generally believed that weight problems such as mine are the results of a deep-rooted unhappiness - I know that mine is. Our hostess's husband - a professor emeritus at some university or other but I can't remember which - must have been the unhappiest man in the world. He was enormous. To give some idea of scale, if you take for the difference between one of the skinnier Kate Moss style supermodels and me - and then pretend that I was the supermodel and that he was me, then that might give you some kind of idea. I am fat and as a result of my obesity I have developed arthritis and various other musculo-skeletal disorders. As a result will sometimes walk with a stick. However, I hope and pray that I shall never become a figure of a man like this poor chap. He is dead now - unsurprisingly - which is a pity, because during the only evening when I met him it was obvious that he was a remarkable and highly intelligent man. He and I spent the evening in a bizarrely freewheeling conversation that took in the theories of Fred Hoyle, the evolution of birds, the current political climate, and the novels of Robert Heinlein - all by way of a few forays into quantum physics. I have seldom enjoyed an evening's conversation more. As he and I talked, Alison, our hostess and the various other people who made up her extended household - from memory, mostly single females of a certain age - talked about whatever they talked about. It began to appear as if there were two distinct conversational and respected intellectual) sub-groups in this somewhat dysfunctional family. There was the professor, and there was everybody else. I - by dint of being a male and being relatively intelligent - had been made an honorary member of the first sub-group.

I have always been of the opinion that intelligence tests are a very flaky concept. In 1905 the French psychologist Alfred Binet first started work on a test to measure what he called intelligence quotient - mental age x chronological age x 100. About 10 years later a he teamed up with scientists from Stanford University and produced the first universally recognised test for IQ. I personally believe that the Stanford Binet IQ tests have caused more trouble in the world than anything since the invention of gunpowder. Generations of children and adults have found themselves pigeon-holed according to their so-called IQ. Binet decided - arbitrarily as far as I can tell - that a score of 100 was the norm for society. It may well have been the norm for the people in Paris that he was originally experimenting on but as by his own admission he had been sponsored by the French government in order to find a means of easily identifying those children too dull to go to a normal school, that figure is already meaningless. The average IQ is - I believe - actually something in the region of 112. Anything above 150 is deemed to be genius level.

In my experience the higher above 150 somebody's IQ is, the less socially adaptive they are. The people I have met who have frighteningly high IQs tend to be - in one way or another seriously flawed individuals as regards anything that does not require pure intellectual thought. I have an IQ of 174 (which puts me in the top 0.02% of the human race), and although there are several aspects of life at which I excel, many ordinary everyday things are quite beyond me. I have a friend with a similar IQ who has similar problems. The professor I met that evening down on Bodmin Moor over a decade ago was so far above me in intelligence that I had to work very hard to work out what the hell he was talking about half the time. It is only now - with the benefit of hindsight - that I can begin to understand the social structure of this peculiar and somewhat dysfunctional family. It is obvious to me now that the only way that the good professor could function within society was to surround himself with a gaggle of hangers-on who cushioned him from the slings and arrows of outrageous fortune and allowed him to get on with doing whatever esoteric business it was that he was engaged in. This is not a criticism. I have done much the same thing but to a lesser degree. I need people around me to help me with the things in everyday life that I am incapable of doing. But I know how to operate a launderette. I know how to negotiate a supermarket. And I can wire a plug. I have a sneaking suspicion that the late lamented Professor could probably do none of these things and so he needed a veritable tribe of people around him purely in order to carry out a normal existence.

Some of the peripheral members of his household were highly peculiar. There were two middle-aged spinster ladies who lived in a semi derelict caravan at the other end of the farmyard. One of them looked a little bit like Felicity Kendal gone to seed. She was very feminine in a giggly girlie sort of manner which is just about bearable in a 15 year-old and which is utterly contemptible in a woman approaching 50. Her "companion" - and the inverted commas are mine because I have no idea of the precise nature of their relationship - was a swarthy looking woman about 10 years younger. She had short-cropped hair, far more tattoos than is becoming, and wore shapeless baggy clothing apparently constructed from Hessian sacks. She had been the one who had tried to buy cannabis from me within minutes of our arrival. Her name was Hetty and she also seemed to have a peculiar relationship with our hostess. However, whenever she spoke to her, the girlie companion would start displaying all the signs of jealousy and would puff herself up like a horned toad and - exuding clouds of a cloying sweet perfume - face-up to our hostess as if preparing to start a fight with her. There were a number of teenagers - two boys and at least three girls. Whose children they were I never did find out, but I imagine that they had at least two different sets of parents because one of the boys and one of the girls seemed intent on investigating each other's tonsils throughout the evening. After about four hours of this I was getting very weary indeed. The professor had been drinking solidly throughout the evening. He was a very peculiar drinker. He had a large bottle of port by his place at table and he drank all of that without offering anyone else a drink or indeed even seeming to notice that he was the only one drinking. As he got drunker his flights of esoteric fancy became wilder until by about 10 o'clock I can truthfully say that I haven't a clue what he was talking about. I could only understand about one word in five.

As the Professor got drunker and more incomprehensible his womenfolk continued playing out their peculiar social rituals and I began to feel quite sorry for Alison. In turn each of the little warring factions would try to lure her on to their "team" (as it were). When Alison - doing her best to exhibit well-bred middle-class reserve - did her best to remain on an equal footing with all the people there, each faction in turn began to make snipey remarks at her. By this stage the young lovers on the sofa in the corner had become so engrossed in each other's bodies that it seemed imminently likely that their mutual explorations would descend into full-blown coition before too much longer. By 11.30 I couldn't handle any more, and realising that we were unlikely to get any more information about the Beast of Bodmin out of this rum crew, we made our excuses and went to bed.

The next day we rose in time for breakfast, and our hostess and her companions greeted us as if nothing had happened. After breakfast, she drove us in a rickety old landrover around the areas of the farm where - according to her at least - the mysterious big cat, which still had not yet been christened "The Beast of Bodmin", had been seen. It was only then, that I realise that our entire expedition to this peculiar farm had been a waste of time. From the age of 11 when I first came back to England to the age of 18 when I left my country home in search of bright lights and a rock-and-roll lifestyle I had spent much of my time on farms. My father, following his return to the UK had set up a small business consultancy company working within the agricultural sector and was close friends with several of his clients. The knock-on effect of this was that I had been given the freedom of several local farms to wander where I chose, and I spent much of my adolescence wandering around the hedgerows and sunken lanes of various farms in the vicinity of the village. It may have been 15 years later, but this tiny, slightly down-at-heel smallholding on the edges of Bodmin Moor seemed familiar to me. As our hostess hurled the rattly old landrover around the corners of the ramshackle dirt tracks at a breakneck speed I realised - with a jolt - something that I should have realised the evening before. Our hostess was not only barking mad, but she had no empathy whatsoever with the countryside. Indeed, she was so miserable living with their genius husband and their coterie of eccentric hangers-on that she would do anything to be in the centre of attention.

We juddered to a halt. Our hostess leapt out of the driver's seat of the landrover and pointed proudly at spot about five-and-a-half feet up the trunk of a rather unpleasant looking oak tree. "There you are! Conclusive proof" she spluttered self-importantly. Alison and I gazed hopefully at the trunk of the tree. "What more proof do you need?" who asked triumphantly. We continued to look at the trunk of the tree and continued to see nothing even approaching any sort of evidence. Finally, Alison summoned up the courage to ask our hostess what on earth she was talking about. Our hostess looked stunned, angry, and hurt all at once. Angrily, she strode towards the tree, determination oozing out of every pore of her being. Her voice rose to a crescendo and she was almost shouting at us over one shoulder about "all us City experts were war being the same and refusing to listen to the testimony of good old countryfolk", as she ran towards the tree. Alison and I look at each other in appalled embarrassment. Our hostess was reaching a fever pitch of apoplectic rage as she tripped over a tree root and stumbled head-first into a pile of rather sludgy rotting leaves. It was all that I could do to stop myself bursting into hysterical laughter. As I ran towards her, lying prone in front of me I could see Alison stuffing her handkerchief into her mouth, with tears rolling down her cheeks. I helped our hostess to her feet, and asked a very politely to point out the nature of this 'conclusive proof'. We agreed, that yes we were indeed poor ignorant city folk who didn't understand the ways of the country, and that we would be grateful for any crumbs of bucolic wisdom to other hostess would be gracious enough to impart to us. She looked at me in triumph. Beams of pride and pleasure lit up her slightly porcine features, and she drew her breath portentously. Looking up at the dilapidated Oak Tree she opened her mouth and said "I shouldn't have expected you city folk to be able to notice something like this - but does something wrong with this tree. It has obviously..............."

She then spluttered, almost as if in the throes of an epileptiform seizure. "Damnation and Fuck" she roared. "It's the wrong fucking tree!!!"

That was it. We couldn't hold back the gathering tide of mirth any longer, and as our hostess continued to swear at the tree, Alison and I surrendered to paroxysms of laughter. Eventually, our hostess regained her composure long enough to take us to the *right* tree and somewhat shamefacedly, she pointed out what she claimed was a regular scratching post for the mysterious big cat. Sure enough, there on the trunk of another massive oak tree were some deep scratches about eight inches long, and three-quarters of an inch apart. I was, however, significantly underwhelmed. I thought then and I think now that although the scratches were undeniably impressive, there was no reason to suppose that they had been done by a cat. They could equally well have been done by a Stanley knife, and bearing in mind the coterie of oddballs that made up our hostess's household, I, for one was not prepared to risk my (then insignificant) reputation by endorsing them.

Then our hostess dropped her big bombshell. She had lured us down to Cornwall with the promise of conclusive evidence to support the hypothesis that her farm was the home to a variety of different Mystery Cats of all shapes, colours and sizes. Where, I asked was the rest of this conclusive evidence? She gazed at me dumbly. This was it. What more did I want? And furthermore, she blustered, now she had shown me the aforesaid conclusive proof, she wanted me to immediately call a press conference to announce to the world, not only that she, our hostess, had conclusive proof of strange and mysterious creatures living breeding on her land, but that she wanted the army to come in with helicopters and heat-seeking missiles to destroy them.

"You must be joking!" I said. But she wasn't. I tried to explain that at that time I had very few contacts with the national newspapers, and that I was certainly not prepared to jeopardise them by making unsubstantiatable claims which would certainly meet with nothing but a hail of derisive laughter. Furthermore, I said, I had no evidence whatsoever to support any attempt at a cull with or without heat-seeking missiles. By then I had come to realise that the presence of big cats in the British ecosystem was a good thing rather than a bad thing. The British environment was a completely artificial one and had been for centuries. We had wiped out all of our large carnivores many years before. The wolf had vanished during the 18th century, the Brown Bear and the European lynx many centuries before that. I believed that the accidental introduction of a new and highly successful species of higher carnivore to the top of the British food chain could only be a good thing and would only lead to our enormously crippled ecosystem beginning to repair itself. Our hostess was not having any of this. By this time she had the bit well and truly between her teeth and she was not gonna let go.

We parted company about 15 minutes later on less than cordial terms. As Alison and I drove our pink Transit van down the winding path that led to the main road, and eventually to the A30 and Exeter we could see our erstwhile hostess and various members of her household standing, stock-still, in the farmyard glaring at us. Negotiating the potholes on the dilapidated track, we were only able to drive at about 20 miles an hour. Suddenly, there on the road in front of us we saw a flash of something muddy and brown running across our line of vision. Alison threw her foot onto the brake pedal and we shuddered to a halt. There was a bang on the side of the van, and I gingerly lowered the window and put my head out to investigate. It was Hettie. "C'mon man, I really wanna buy some gear badly................"

I finally managed to convince her that I had no marijuana and that even if I did I was not gonna sell her any, and the two of us resumed journey to Exeter.

In many ways this was the happiest time of our marriage. The trials and tribulations of our earliest years together were over. OK, we both knew that we were fundamentally incompatible, and that we were never going to have the sex life or the social life to which we both individually aspired. We came from radically different backgrounds. My father had been a senior Colonial Service officer with an equivalent rank to a Brigadier. Alison's father worked in a timber yard. But we were hippies. We believed that all you needed was love, and although we had no money we had plenty of love. During these years Alison and I were not just in love with each other, we are friends and we were companions. The idea of either of us embarking on a new project without the help, succour, and support of the other was unthinkable. We had been through so many adventures together, that the idea that he would not be together for the rest of our lives was unthinkable.

I have to admit, with hindsight of a over a decade, at that time I was becoming very frustrated with my cryptozoological research. I had been doing it as a hobby for nearly 25 years, and whilst it was all very well forming something called the Centre for Fortean Zoology, I had no idea how I was going to turn my vision into reality. So, when during the summer of 1993 one of my acquaintances - a lady called Jan Williams who lived in Congleton in Cheshire - announced that she was going to start up her own cryptozoological organisation, I was happy to put my own plans for the CFZ on hold and throw myself into working for S.C.A.N - The Society for Cryptozoogy and the Anomalies of Nature.

The arrival of this new organisation could not have come at a better time for me, because although I was quite happy to continue my researches, pressure of other commitments was getting in the way of my plans for starting up the ultimate Cryptozoological research organisation of my own. I had another tour to do with Steve Harley, and after years of talking about it and recording lo-fi album length audio cassettes I wanted to have a proper go at making it in the music business.

The tour with Steve turned out to be somewhat of a damp squib. It was beset by problems from the beginning, and nobody was particularly surprised when - about half way through - a whole clutch of dates from the end the tour suddenly got cancelled. To make things worse, Paul and I were hardly on speaking terms by this time. The old saw about familiarity breeding contempt had proved to be true. Whereas at first, Paul had been content to leave me in charge of running the fan club, the magazine and everything else we did, and - as a fan - was happy just to be a minor labourer in the Steve Harley vineyard, after several years of touring with us he wanted more. As is so often the way with people who strive for a higher position than that which is their lot in life, he didn't mind how he did it. The upshot of it all was that somehow he managed to inveigle himself into a higher position of power than us within Steve's management company, and soon after the final tour Alison and I were dismissed.

I was angry, upset, and hurt and wrote an exceptionally vitriolic letter to Steve. With hindsight, I realise that this was unwise - and unnecessary hurtful - thing to do, and the result was that I was not to see him again for over seven years.

However, in many ways, my estrangement from Steve Harley was a good thing. It certainly allowed me to throw myself into other projects. The first and foremost of these was to form a touring band of my own, and making - for the first time in my life - a professionally recorded album. As first stated elsewhere in this memoir, this is not the story of my life. This is the story of my life as a cryptozoologist, and I only bring in other aspects of my life story in when they are of direct relevance. I'll not, therefore, even attempt to describe all the adventures, and the amusing trials and tribulations that Alison and I went through as I tried it to make my conceptual band - *Jon Downes and the Amphibians from Outer Space* - a real living, breathing, entity. Looking back, I really shouldn't have bothered. I was too old and too fat to be a pop-star, and the fact that we were based in Exeter really precluded us from ever making the jump from being pub musicians to properly hitting the big time. We were in the wrong place at the wrong time. If we had been around 10 years earlier, we might have managed to ride to the wave of nu-hippiedom, which made stars out of such bands as *Ozric Tentacles*. If we had been around 10 years later, the explosion in information technology would have allowed us to make high-quality, low-cost digital recordings, and disseminate them across the Internet. However, in 1993, a seven-piece band with a silly name and a policy of resolutely refusing to do any but the most ironic of cover versions in the course of a two and a half hour set, was pretty well doomed to obscurity. I think that it says a lot for us that we survived for three years, made two records and played over 80 concerts.

For several years, our home away from home was a basement flat in Queens Terrace, Exeter. This was where Graham lived. You may remember that I first met him as he was climbing in through the window of the gent's toilet in Exeter Arts Centre. I was promoting a concert by *Nik Turner's Allstars*, and he had been trying to get in for nothing. Surprisingly, given such an inauspicious start to our relationship, we became firm friends. He was interested in my musical ambitions and volunteered, not only to become the band's unpaid roadie, but also to allow us to rehearse in his enormous and frighteningly untidy basement flat. I've never seen anywhere quite like Graham's basement at Queen's Terrace. It was dank, dark and slightly sinister. There were books and empty beer cans everywhere, mostly perched on pieces of home-made furniture that looked as they had been constructed by somebody who was very drunk out of bits of flotsam and jetsam that had been salvaged from local skips. As I got to know Graham better, I realised that my initial impressions were not too far from the truth. However, Graham was (and is), an eminently capable man who could turn his hand to just about anything, and so, as the band moved in to become welcome guests in his subterranean home, Graham and I became even closer friends.

By the mid 1994 we had settled on a reasonably stable line-up. Me on guitar and vocals, Dave Penna on drums, Marcus Sims on bass, Natalie Board and my daughter Lisa on backing vocals, Peter Popert on guitar, and a slightly annoying young man called Nigel Smith on keyboards. On the whole I got on very well with the band. Many of us are still friends 10 years later, but right from the beginning I found Nigel annoying. I am fat because I have an eating disorder. I have an eating disorder because of deep-rooted emotional problems which years of therapy have never yet managed to cure. Unlike some people who are as fat as I am, I do not hide away from the public eye. I have been a TV presenter, a lecturer, and a rock singer - all in the glow of the spotlight. However, I find it irksome and embarrassing when somebody makes an issue out of my weight. Nigel used to annoy me continually by calling me "big fella", prodding me roguishly in my belly, and snapping my braces. However he was a passable keyboard player, and Alison liked him, so rather than rock the boat I said nothing. After about six months in the band, Nigel left suddenly to join in one of those homogenous musical ensembles that are available for weddings and bar mitzvahs. He announced that he was leaving within days of a substantial series of concerts, which had taken Alison and myself months of work to put together. I was furious and threatened him with severe repercussions. Much to my surprise, although it had been her work that had largely been ruined, Alison took his part in the argument. Nigel left, was replaced by an infinitely more talented keyboard player called James, and I promptly forgot all about him. This was not necessarily the most sensible thing that I could have done.

Back in the world of cryptozoology, my new-found position as a member of the rank and file of SCAN was not going too well either. I have never found out why - and after this length of time it is none of my business - but all was not well between Jan Williams and Trevor Beer (the co-founder of the organisation). After only four issues of their newsletter she announced that they were going to close. Then, I had a wonderful idea. I telephoned Jan and suggested that she joined me in making my vision of the Centre for Fortean Zoology into a reality. I told her of my background in small press publishing and suggested that we start a magazine dedicated to cryptozoology. I even had a name for it - *Animals & Men* (the name of a song on the first album by *Adam and the Ants*). I suggested to her that if we were to take over the membership list of SCAN (after having let all the members have the chance of their money back if they wanted it), then we would not be in the awkward position of starting up a new publication without the benefit of having any readers for it. To my great joy, Jan agreed, and in April 1994 - a year after I had originally founded the CFZ in the backstage bar of the Manchester International II following a drunken conversation with a bloke called Gerry the Nonce, a first issue of the new magazine was posted out to the 40 or 50 people who had decided not to demand a refund from Jan and Trevor. The first, faltering steps towards a proper Centre for Fortean Zoology had just been made.

Three months after issue one came out Alison and I were in London. We had written enough material for the second issue but we did not have anywhere near enough money to pay for it to be printed. For reasons with which I shall not bore you, Alison and I were perilously short of money and were facing the threat of imminent bankruptcy. I had been an avid reader of the magazine *Fortean Times* since about 1986, and was overjoyed to here that they were planning their first ever convention. The two-day event - named the Unconvention - was being held in London, and we had to go. However tickets were prohibitively expensive (at least to us), and although we wanted to attend we just couldn't afford it. We parked up the van in the car park at Leatherhead station and took the train into central London. We had no idea whatsoever about what we were going to do when we got there. We realised that we had just about enough money for one ticket, and so we decided that I should go in, and somehow see if I could sneak Alison in through a fire door. The Gods of cryptozoology must have been smiling upon us that day. We took our places in the queue and waited. Suddenly there was a bang on my shoulder, and I turned to see the unmistakable face of one of our closest companions from several Steve Harley tours standing there grinning at me. He had parted company with the Harley organisation about a year before us and was now - or so it transpired - working as part of the security team for the company who promoted the Unconvention.

"What the fuck are you two idiots doing queuing up for this?" he said cheerfully as he hustled us to the head of the queue and pinned VIP badges onto our lapels. I told him that the vagaries of fate had meant that we were no longer working in the music business, but were instead trying to make a mark as monster-hunters. He laughed, wished us well, and disappeared into the crowd. We made our way, gingerly towards the bar. As we had found on countless occasions before, the mere fact that we were wearing little pieces of plastic announcing to the world in general that we were very important people, made all the difference and despite the fact that we were there entirely under false pretences, we suddenly felt full of confidence and ready for the events that lay in store for us.

Standing at the bar, Alison and I found ourselves next to an extraordinary Irishman. I've never met anyone like him up before or since. "I want a fokkin' Guinness and I want it now", he bellowed, and a dozen acolytes from all over the room hastened to his side, eager for the chance to buy him a drink. It took several minutes for me to realise who it was. It was Tony "Doc" Shiels, surrealchemist, and magician, sometimes referred to as the 'Wizard of the Western World'. I whispered as much to Alison, who turned to me with a withering glance and told me that she had realised this fact all along. Tony, overhearing our conversation turned to me and boomed, "Yes, of course I'm Doc Shiels. Who the fokk else would I be?" - and a friendship was formed, which, although it has been through its rocky moments, has lasted ever since.

Alison went exploring, whilst Tony and I sat down to the serious business of getting drunk. About half-an-hour into our mutual self-congratulation session, a middle-aged man in a brown suit approached us. He saw that I was wearing a VIP badge and that Tony was wearing a badge proclaiming him to be one of the speakers. He introduced himself as a features writer for one of the more anally retentive of the Sunday newspapers. He offered to buy us a drink, and gingerly asked who we were and could he have an interview with us? Tony bellowed at him: "Of course you can buy us a drink, you Saxon bollocks. And if you buy us a drink you can ask us anything you bloody well like. Who are we ye ask? I'm the Wizard of the Western World and this fat bastard is the greatest fokkin' cryptozoologist in the fokkin' world!"

I had arrived. As soon as the interview was over, we were surrounded by people wanting to talk to me about cryptozoology. One of them was a man called Dr Karl Shuker - then the leading cryptozoologist in Britain. We had spoken on the telephone but never met in person. However one of the fortean luminaries present took a photograph of us together and with the apparent endorsement of both Shuker and Shiels, I sold 200 copies of *Animals & Men* that day and signed up 30 new members. Alison and I had started the day practically bankrupt and we finished it with nearly 500 quid in our pockets and a completely unwarranted reputation for being a major player in the cryptozoological community. The following weekend the interview with Tony and me appeared in the Sunday paper. It described my work in glowing terms, none of which I even faintly deserved, and didn't even allude to the fact that Tony and I were so spectacularly drunk when we did the interview that to this day I have no idea what I said.

We returned to Exeter in a bullish mood. It was beginning to look as if the Centre for Fortean Zoology could actually be a success. Emboldened by my new found relationship with Tony Shiels I decided that the time was right to reopen investigations into one of the most grotesque, though fascinating, creatures in the British fortean zoological bestiary - the Owlman of Mawnan.

Back in April 1976, Tony Shiels had written a letter:

A very weird thing happened over the Easter weekend. A holiday-maker from Preston, Lancs., told me about something his two young daughters had seen ... a big, feathered bird-man hovering over the church tower at Mawnan (a village near the mouth of the Helford River). The girls (June 12, and Vicky, daughters of Mr Don Melling), were so scared that the family cut their holiday short and went back three days early. This really is a fantastic thing, and I am sure the man wasn't just making it up because he'd been told I was on a monster hunt. I couldn't get the kids to talk about it (in fact, their father wouldn't even let me try), but he gave me a sketch of the thing drawn by June.

There have been no reports, so far as I know, of anybody else seeing the Bird-Man ... even if it turned out to be just a fancy dress hang-glider, you'd think someone else would have spotted him ... but Mawnan is not a place for hang-gliding! I really don't know what to think ... its as if a whole load of weirdness has been let loose in the Falmouth area since last autumn!

Although if you read any of the books on general mystery animals such as *Alien Animals* by Janet and Colin Bord, or indeed any of the contemporary copies of *Fortean Times* the claim that Cornwall had been particularly weird at the time is often made, it is not until you visit the Cornish Studies Library in the back streets of Redruth, sit yourself down at one of their microfiche machines, and physically examine twelve months or more's issues of *The Falmouth Packet*, *The West Briton* and *The Western Morning News* that you can see quite how strange the time actually was. For a period between the late autumn of 1975 and the early spring of 1977 it seems that Southern Cornwall was seized by a period of collective madness.

Much of this is chronicled in some depth in my book *The Owlman and Others* but even there I think that I failed to give a true picture of quite how strange the area had become.

There were dramatic extremes in the weather - droughts and floods - heatwaves and frozen wastes. The local animal life went crazy; one unfortunate woman was imprisoned in her house by hordes of attacking birds which literally beat themselves to death against the walls of her house, which was dripping red with their blood. Another woman was similarly imprisoned by a mob of feral cats, dog attacks trebled, swimmers were attacked by dolphins (who also saved other swimmers from drowning), and there were reports that cattle belonging to local farmers had developed the power of teleportation. Most interesting to the fortean were the burgeoning numbers of UFO sightings and the reports of three entirely different sets of mystery animal in the region; Morgawr (the Cornish Sea Serpent), the Cornish mystery big cats and the Owlman of Mawnan.

The first reports of these 'creatures' in print were in an obscure booklet entitled *Morgawr-the monster of Falmouth Bay* by Anthony Mawnan-Peller. He gave a brief description of the events of Easter Saturday:

During the Easter weekend, the two young daughters of a holidaymaker ... Mr. Don Melling, from Preston, Lancashire ... saw a 'huge great thing with feathers, like a big man with flapping wings', hovering over the church tower at Mawnan. The girls ... Vicky, 9, and June, 12 ... were so frightened that the family holiday was cut short by three days."

It has been stated on many occasions that Anthony Mawnan-Peller didn't exist and that he was nothing but a pseudonym for Tony Shiels who was manipulating the whole affair in order to capitalise as much as he could. This is quite simply not true. Anthony Mawnan-Peller *is* a pseudonym, but not of Tony Shiels. Tony drew the illustrations but the author was a local journalist who wanted to remain anonymous purely because he was 'moonlighting' on the Morgawr project and didn't want his boss to find out. Again and again within the field of forteana we find what seem to be gloriously peculiar examples of fortean chicanery, and they usually turn out to have equally mundane explanations.

Although not widely read outside Cornwall, this booklet was available extensively throughout the county and was read by many people including two young girls of fourteen, Sally Chapman and Barbara Perry, who in early July 1976 were camping in the woods by Mawnan Old Church when they, too, saw the Owlman.

They met Tony on Grebe Beach, below Mawnan Old Church the day after their sighting. Sally, who was from Plymouth, had been staying with her friend Barbara, (who would only admit that she lived 'quite near the river'). Sally approached Tony and said: "Are you Doc Shiels? We've seen the bird monster"

Sally described what they had seen: "It was like a big owl with pointed ears, as big as a man. The eyes were red and glowing. At first, I thought that it was someone dressed up, playing a joke, trying to scare us. I laughed at it, we both did, then it went up in the air and we both screamed. When it went up you could see its feet were like pincers"

Her friend added some details of her own: "It's true. It was horrible, a nasty owl-face with big ears and big red eyes. It was covered in grey feathers. The claws on its feet were black. It just flew up and disappeared in the trees".

Although as Tony admitted at the time - it is possible that the two young ladies were trying to hoax him, he is convinced that they were genuine.

He separated the two girls and had each of them draw a picture of what she had seen. The two pictures are dissimilar enough to rebuff suggestions of collusion but have enough points in common, both with each other, and with the other accounts of the 'creature' to be considered as a significant piece of evidence.

Both girls made brief additional notes underneath their pictures. Sally's read: "I saw this monster bird last night. It stood like a man and then it flew up through the trees. It is as big as a man. Its eyes are red and shine brightly".

And Barbara wrote: "Birdman monster. Seen on third of July, quite late at night but not quite dark. Red Eyes. Black Mouth. It was very big with great big wings and black claws. Feathers grey"

The two girls agreed on most points with their pictures although Sally thought Barbara had "done the wings wrong". At the same time as Sally and Barbara were talking to 'Doc' on Grebe Beach, two other girls also saw what Tony refers to as 'his Owliness':

It has red slanting eyes and a very large mouth. The feathers are silvery grey and so are his body and legs, the feet are like a big, black, crab's claws. We were frightened at the time. It was so strange, like something out of a horror film. After the thing went up, there were crackling sounds in the tree-tops for ages. Our mother thinks we made it all up just because we read about these things, but that is not true. We really saw the bird-man, though it could have been someone playing a trick in a very good costume and make up. But how could it rise up like that? If we imagined it, then we both imagined it at the same time.

Two years later, a young lady called 'Miss Opie' saw 'A monster, like a devil, flying up through the trees near old Mawnan Church'. A few days later Tony Shiels wrote to Janet and Colin Bord of the Fortean Picture Library: "The owlman is certainly back in business, it seems. I poked around his area, around Old Mawnan Church, a couple of days ago, and the atmosphere was positively crackling with 'odd presences', if you know what I mean.

As soon as anything really exciting happens, I'll let you know. It would be terrific if I really could get a picture of our feathered friend, but, he only seems to pop up for young girls … and I ain't one!"

The Owlman, as it was now generally known, (it appears that Tony coined the name in late 1976), was seen again on the 2nd August by three young, unnamed French girls. The landlady of the boarding house in which they had been staying told Tony that the three girls had been frightened by something "very big, like a big, furry bird with a gaping mouth and round eyes" This was all that the landlady could tell him, so Tony left a message for the girls to contact him, but as always seems to be the case he never heard anything further.

Many commentators on the case have questioned Tony's role in the affair. Mark Chorvinsky of *Strange Magazine* even claimed that, because so many of the sightings were connected with him, Tony had made the whole thing up.

Such people do not understand the reticence of the Cornish people. They do not like to talk to outsiders, and I am convinced that if it had not been for Tony's presence in the area as a trusted 'local' the affair would never have been made public. The case of the French girls for example:

Tony wrote to me in 1995 explaining how he had become involved: "The French girls were students (at Camborne Tech - now known as Cornwall College), lodging in Redruth. I think they were on some sort of 'summer school' course. Their landlady 'phoned me about this sighting. Remember, at the time, I was getting quite a lot of media coverage. People reported weird shit to me"… Two years later the creature re-appeared when, "an enormous, bird-like creature" was seen flying "over the Helford River and into the trees near Grebe Beach".

At Hallowe'en 1986 Tony was at the centre of a media storm when the Bishop of Truro, and the local newspapers accused him of having committed unspeakable acts of blasphemy inside Mawnan Old Church whilst attempting to invoke the Owlman. The affair was somewhat of a 'five minute wonder' in the press and the actual sequence of events remains obscure. Ten years or so later Tony told me: "I did a few bits and pieces inside the Church … There was a lot of misreporting that I was throwing out challenges to God, and saying I'd smack him in the gob. I don't think God has a gob, and I wouldn't do that anyway to the deity. He'd give me a harder smack back wouldn't he?" Eventually - more by luck than by judgement - I pieced together the true story.

He had indeed visited the church with a local radio team, but the "huge crowd of people" turned out to be ONE rather shy bloke called 'Dave'. He told me that there was no blasphemy, no swearing, no naked witches and no cigars, and that the wizard had entered the church, muttered a few things under his breath in a foreign language and then left again. It turns out that the radio team had approached my friend and asked him what he had planned to do to celebrate Hallowe'en. He said: "Buy me a drink and I'll show yeh."

This the radio people did, only to find that like many wizards, my friend has a legendary capacity for the stuff. Finding at the end of the evening that they had nothing to show for their severely depleted expense accounts, I have a sneaking suspicion that someone decided that it would be a good idea to concoct a bizarre tale of blasphemy and psychic mayhem.

Unfortunately Dave Shenton, the only other witness to the events of All Hallow's Eve 1986 died whilst we were putting the finishing touches to this volume. He was a nice guy, as well as being a pivotal part of one of the more bizarre bits of forteana to take place during the closing years of the 20th Century and he will be sadly missed.

In 1989 a young man called 'Gavin' and his girlfriend 'Sally' (not their real names), encountered the Mawnan Owlman. This was perhaps the most important sighting to date from a cryptoinvestigative point of view, because it is the only sighting that cannot in any way be linked to Tony 'Doc' Shiels.

I first became aware of this particular case, due to a peculiar set of circumstances that took place in early 1995 as the CFZ consolidated itself as being Britain's leading Cryptozoological research organisation. For about the error had been aware of another magazine - *The Crypto Chronicle* - which was published by young man called Craig Harris who lived in Worcester. Alison and I soon became a mildly friendly with Craig and his wife and visited him on a number of occasions. However, after we had known them for about six months it was obvious that all was not well. It is not for me to comment on the state of somebody else's marriage - but it seemed to me at that Craig was in a position that he had to make a decision as to whether to carry on his part-time career as a cryptozoologist and fortean book dealer, or whether he was going to concentrate full-time on his family commitments. He chose the latter option and offered Alison and me the opportunity to take over his entire subscriber list and to buy his not inconsiderable archives.

By this time we had published four issues of *Animals & Men* and had nearly a hundred subscribers. Deciding that the only way was up, we found ourselves in Worcester one Sunday morning writing out a cheque for several hundred pounds and loading about a dozen voluminous cardboard boxes overflowing with paper into the back of our van. Now we had 150 members and an invaluable archive of letters, research notes, photocopies, and press cuttings. Amongst the letters were a number from a young man in the south of England, which colluded to an incident which had happened about six years previously when he and his then girlfriend had been on holiday in Cornwall.

To this day I count my discovery of these letters as one of the greatest thrills in a lifetime of cryptozoology. Alison was driving hell-for-leather down the M5, as I sat on my haunches in the back of the van reading through Craig's voluminous archives. When I found the first direct evidence of Owlman that was not linked to Tony Shiels I let out such a yelp of excitement that Alison nearly crashed the van causing a multiple pile-up. As soon as we got home and had unpacked the van I rang him. Thus started another relationship that has - despite rocky moments - lasted to the present day.

I have interviewed 'Gavin' on a number of occasions and am convinced of his veracity. This is his story in his own words:

We had a torch and I was shining its beam across trunks about fifteen feet off the ground. I am fairly sure that the animal was standing in a large conifer tree and the illustration we made after the sighting (but not till we got home actually) does depict the animal in a conifer tree, but I'm not that sure now.

Here is the actual sighting as written down in my diary:

"Every couple of hours we would walk along the fringe of the wood. This was the third time that evening and it was beginning to get dark. From a distance trees looked black but closer up the branches and trunks could be seen. We saw the animal at about 9. 30 P. M. It was standing on a thick branch with its wings sort of held up at the arms. I'd say that it was about five feet tall (but please read on). The legs had high ankles and the feet were large and black with two huge 'toes' on the visible side. The creature was grey with brown and the eyes definitely glowed. On seeing us its head jerked down and forwards, its wings lifted and it just jumped backwards. As it did its legs folded up. We ran away.

"We had a pretty good idea what it looked like. We didn't know what to do about it, and essentially vowed never to tell anyone. I last saw Sally about two years ago and talked about it then. She was as unkeen to share the information then as she was earlier, and I promised I wouldn't tell anyone about her involvement, but I could 'do what I liked' with my interpretation. I respect this and have never disclosed any information about her".

I couldn't wait to tell Tony Shiels about this. After all, this was proof that all the accusations against him had been wrong. However, he seemed neither surprised nor particularly pleased. "I don't know why all you fokkin' forteans make such a fuss about this. It's all just stuff. It's the way that the world is."

But he gave me his blessing to write a book on the case, and so the most famous quest in my career to date commenced. It was a quest that was eventually nearly to destroy me.

CHAPTER EIGHT

TO WIT TO WOO

As the months passed I became more and more obsessed with the monsters of Cornwall. Alison and I spent a large portion of the next to a year visiting Tony Shiels and his various compadres in Falmouth. Tony is unlike anyone else I have ever met. Alison once said that meeting him for the first time was like being struck by a whirlwind. Tony was born in 1938; and, over the next fifty-seven years, a would-be painter, conjurer, gunslinger, musician, playwright and busker. He is also a self-admitted wizard. He has never claimed magical powers of his own; but, then again, he has never claimed not to have them either. My own feelings are that Tony is a very similar character to Reg the time traveller in Douglas Adams's *Dirk Gently's Holistic Detective Agency.* Reg discovered the secrets of time travel by accident because he could never be bothered to learn how to programme his video recorder, and who could never figure out alternative ways he could see episodes of TV shows he would otherwise have missed.

I think that Tony developed his very real magical skills because he could never figure out how to hide the hard-boiled egg up his sleeve like a proper conjuror He is shorter than I (as are most people - but, then, I am six-and-a-half feet tall), and has piercing, powerful eyes which twinkle when he is amused, and cut like a laser beam when he is annoyed; short-cropped, grey hair; and an enormous, bushy beard which bristles magnificently in all directions. He comes over like a cross between a genial Mephistopheles and Captain Birdseye with a cosh in his pocket. He drinks Guinness and smokes small cigars. For nearly a decade now I have been proud to count him as a dear, if somewhat unpredictable, friend.

The good doctor, whom an Irish Newspaper dubbed "The Wizard of the Western World" at the height of his infamy during the late 1970s was, as we shall see, pivotally involved in the Morgawr story, although as we will also see, the accounts of a giant sea monster off the Cornish coast date back for hundreds of years.

In late March 1976 Tony and a colleague called a press conference in a Falmouth pub called *The Chain Locker*. According to the local newspaper report of the time:

The great Falmouth monster hunt got underway this week, with the arrival in the town from America of a 36 year old Professor of Metaphysics, Michael McCormick, who plans to devote the summer to his search. The professor called a press conference in the Chain Locker on Falmouth's waterfront on Monday, when he was accompanied by his 'psychic advisor', 'Doc' Shiels of Ponsanooth. He had with him a number of strange relics from previous monster hunts, including the skeleton of an imp. This was about eighteen inches long, with a miniature human shaped skull out of which horns protruded. It also had clawed feet and wings, and did not smell too wholesome.

He also produced a small, clawed foot, wrapped in a red cloth, which promptly caused oscillations on the sound recording equipment brought along by television engineers. Prof. McCormick said he had recently been lecturing at the University of New Mexico on the basic need for monsters from a Jungian point of view. He said he had come all the way from Alberquerque, New Mexico, as a result of reports in the 'Packet', about sightings of the Falmouth monster.

'It has cost a wad of money', he said, 'I shall spend the next two months in a determined focussing effort using "Doc's" remarkable mental processes to produce the beast'. He said that he thought the monster was probably migratory, and thought it could vary its size at will.

The professor, who is also a fire-eater and juggler, is causing some problems for his partner. Said Mr. Shiels, 'The whole place is throbbing from the things Mike has brought over. I shall have to do something to stop the headaches'.

According to students of the ancient and now practically extinct Cornish language, the word 'Morgawr' means 'Sea Giant', and was used to describe an enormous marine monster which has always been said to live in the waters of Falmouth Bay. According to an 1876 newspaper report:

Port Scatho. The sea-serpent was caught alive in Gerran's Bay. Two of our fishermen were afloat overhauling their crab pots about 400-500 yards from the shore when they discovered a serpent coiled around their floating cork. Upon their approach it lifted its head and showed signs of defiance upon which they struck it forcibly with an oar which so far disabled it as to allow them to proceed with their work after which they observed the serpent floating around near their boat. They pursued it, bringing it ashore yet alive for exhibition soon after which it was killed on the rocks and most inconsiderately cast into the sea.

Author and Zoologist Michael Bright is amusingly sceptical about this incident. In 1989 he commented "How anybody can continue with their work after an encounter with a strange sea creature beats me. And the report does not say what happened to the creature after it had been 'cast again into the sea'. " and I have to say that I cannot help but agree with him. From the description, the creature was probably an enormous eel of some description.

However, not all the historical accounts of Morgawr appear to refer to giant eels. Fifty years after the unfortunate anguilliform was so summarily slaughtered in Gerran's Bay a Mr. Reece and a Mr. Gilbert, trawling three miles south of Falmouth netted an amazing creature. It was twenty feet long, with an eight-foot tail, a 'beaked' head, scaly legs, and a broad back covered with 'matted brown hair'. Marine Biologists of the day were unable to identify the beast.

Again, unfortunately for those who would like to claim that all of the historical accounts of unidentified sea creatures off the Cornish coast refer to species presently unknown to science, it is fairly easy to identify this beastie as well. As long ago as 1968 Professor Bernard Heuvelmans noted that:

It seems to be quite normal for basking sharks to take on a plesiosaur's shape when they decompose. This is because of the peculiar structure of their gill-slits which ate extremely long and go almost right round the neck. A live basking shark is virtually decapitated. As soon as its tissues decompose and become soft, the whole gill apparatus easily falls away taking the jaws with it, so that nothing remains in front of the pectoral fins but the tiny skull and the spinal column clad in its muscles and thus looking like a thin neck. At the other end of the body, the lower fluke of the tail soon goes with nothing to support it, since the spine extends only into the upper one. The body then seems to have a long thin tail.

The final monstrosity of these pseudo-plesiosaurs is that they seem to be hairy. In the selachians the fibres of the surface muscles break up into whiskers when the skin rots or is eaten away. These fish then seem to have coarse stiff fur, varying from dirty white to reddish in colour, as the body decomposes or dries out on the shore. if parts of the dorsal fin remain these hairs can even look like a mane. Thus there is no need to be as bold or simple as a mediaeval artist to produce a creature with a fish's skeleton, the general shape of a reptile and with mammal's hair.

Unfortunately the newspaper reports of the time are unclear whether the creature found by Reece and Gilbert was alive or dead. However, if, as seems likely, the creature was dead when they hauled it in, one need look no further for an explanation of its provenance than Heuvelmans's masterful description. Furthermore, providing even more bad luck for those who are truly in search of an antediluvian monster Heuvelmans went on to describe another strange carcass which was washed up on Prah Sands in southern Cornwall in 1933 and states that he believes that this animal too was a decomposed Basking Shark.

However some Cornish monster sightings are far less easy to explain. In 1949 author Harold Wilkins was in the Cornish fishing village of Looe when they saw:

Two remarkable Saurians, 19 - 20 feet long, with bottle-green heads, one behind the other, their middle parts under the water of the tidal creek of East Looe, Cornwall, apparently chasing a shoal of fish up the creek. What was amazing were their dorsal parts: rigid, serrated and like the old Chinese pictures of dragons. Gulls swooped down towards the one in the rear. These monsters - and two of us saw them - resembled the plesiosaurus of Mesozoic times.

It seems that there really were some strange creatures in the briny depths of Falmouth Bay because one sunny evening in September 1975, Morgawr was spotted off Pendennis Point. Mrs Scott, of Falmouth, and her friend Mr. Riley, saw a hideous, hump-backed creature, with 'stumpy-horns', and bristles down the back of its long neck. The huge animal dived for a few seconds, then resurfaced with a conger eel in its jaws. Mrs. Scott told local journalists at the time that she would never forget 'the face on that thing', as long as she lives. Shortly after the Scott/Riley sighting, Morgawr was encountered by several mackerel fishermen, and blamed by the superstitious fishermen for bad luck, bad weather and bad catches.

In February 1976 the *Falmouth Packet* newspaper published two photographs of Morgawr, taken in February by a lady who called herself 'Mary F'. They showed a long necked, hump backed creature, at least eighteen feet long, swimming in the water off Trefusis Point, near Flushing. A letter accompanied the photographs:

The enclosed photos were taken by me about three weeks ago from Trefusis. They show one of the large sea creatures mentioned in your paper recently. I'm glad to know that other people have seen the giant brownish sea serpent. The pictures are not very clear because of the sun shining right into the camera and the haze on the water. Also I took them very quickly indeed. The animal was only up for a few seconds. I would say it was about fifteen to eighteen feet long. I mean the part showing above the water. It looked like an elephant waving its trunk, but the trunk was a long neck with a small head on the end, like a snake's head. It had humps on the back which moved in a funny way.

The colour was black or very dark brown and the skin seemed to be like a sea-lion s.
My brother developed the film. I didn't want to take it to the chemist. Perhaps you can make them clearer. As a matter of fact the animal frightened me. I would not like to see it any closer. I do not like the way it moved when swimming.

You can put these pictures in the paper if you like. I don't want payment, and I don't want any name in the paper about this. I just think you should tell people about this animal. What is it?

Yours sincerely
Mary F.

These photographs are, with the possible exception of the 1967 Roger Patterson/Bob Gimlin Bigfoot film, the most contentious images in contemporary forteana. They polarised the fortean establishment with many people staking their reputations on the veracity or otherwise of these two rather dubious images. One of the people who came out most strongly on the side of those who believed it was a hoax was veteran American fortean Mark Chorvinsky. He devoted an entire issue of his excellent *Strange Magazine* to debunking them, and to exposing Tony "Doc" Shiels as the perpetrator of the hoax.

In order to substantiate the claim he relied strongly upon evidence given by several of Tony's friends *including* the aforementioned Mike McCormick and some appallingly crude photographs published by Tony in a 1976 book in which he explained various techniques for producing a 'Psychic Superstar' by media manipulation. These techniques included the hoaxing of monster photographs.

The photographs were credited to 'G. B. Gordon', and Mark Chorvinsky announced with a flourish that they were actually fakes by none other than Tony himself! Of course they were. Tony has never denied this. They were never meant as anything apart from slightly amusing illustrations for a book, which was itself, an amusing spoof on a bestseller by Uri Geller.

In my 1997 book *The Owlman and Others* I described how in my opinion Mark Chorvinsky had developed somewhat of an *idée fixe* about Tony Shiels and his propensity for playing the psychic prankster. I maintained then, as I do now, that Mark is a fine researcher and someone for whom I have nothing but praise. Unfortunately I believe that the whole affair of *Strange Magazine #8* was and is Tony Shiels's greatest ever hoax!

In recent years, and certainly since the early 1990s Tony has been keen to be seen as an artist rather than as a fortean and he has done his best to play down his monster-raising past. He has featured in a number of high profile art exhibitions and his surrealist paintings, drawings and sculptures are at last beginning to achieve the fame, and the prices that he has deserved for so many years.

He has been a painter for nearly half a century now, and he has told me on a number of occasions how he is tired of only being known to the general public as a genial eccentric who "messes about with sea serpents".

I believe that when Mark Chorvinsky first approached Tony and his compadres for information about the genesis of the Mary F photographs and other monster pictures allegedly associated with Tony over the years, the shamrock shaman saw his chance to redress the balance.

Chorvinsky interviewed a number of people on the subject, and various people from his past, like McCormick, Roy Standish - an ex-editor of the *Falmouth Packet* - and Alistair Boyd, the researcher who finally uncovered the truth about the infamous "Surgeons Photo, " which for well over half a century was seen as the most convincing piece of evidence of the Loch Ness Monster.

They painted a convincing picture. Roy Standish said that even at the time, that he had been convinced that Doc was responsible for the Mary F photographs, and several people alleged that Doc had sent them prints which were slight variants on the Mary F photographs several weeks before the images we have come to know appeared for the first time in the *Falmouth Packet.*

This was probably true. Tony even admits as much. He claims, (and knowing the way the Fortean underground works I tend to believe him), that several different versions of the photographs had been circulating around the Falmouth area before they were actually published.

This makes sense, and although by implication the story given to the *Falmouth Packet* with the photographs is probably untrue, there is no real reason to suppose that Tony is responsible for the photographs.

The main problem with viewing the Mary F photographs as a piece of art by the great surrealist painter Tony Shiels is that they are actually not terribly good, which is something that no one could say about his other pieces of work. They are spectacularly unconvincing pictures which I have no difficulty in believing were made by using a plate of glass and some modelling clay. I just have a sneaking suspicion that if Tony had produced them, they would have been done much better.

I said as much in *The Owlman and Others,* but I stressed that although I was, and still am convinced that poor old Mark Chorvinsky was well and truly bamboozled by Tony Shiels, that there is no shame in being bamboozled by such a master of the art as the good doctor. He has pulled the wool over my eyes on various occasions and I believe that the only reason that I managed to come to such diametrically different conclusions in my research than Mark did in his was that I had access to far more of the original source material, and that I was lucky enough to spend an inordinate amount of time drinking Guinness around Cornwall's pubs with the man himself.

Here, I should perhaps include a note on Cornish pubs for the aspiring fortean investigator. If you visit one of the more traditional hostelries and order a pint, you can drink about two thirds of it, and then ask for a "Cornish Half". They will then top it up for the price of only half a pint. Not all pubs in the county do this, but by asking for one you immediately establish yourself as someone 'in the know' which may prompt the more taciturn of the locals to be more voluble on the subject of sea serpents and owlmen!

There is no doubt that the Mary F photographs are fakes. The only serious doubt is over the matter of who took them. Forteana is a very strange business by its very nature, and Tony Shiels told me on a number of occasions that there really isn't any such thing as a coincidence. Therefore, I was saddened, though not particularly surprised when, as I was putting the finishing touches to this chapter in late January 2001, I received a letter from Tony telling me that the person that I had always suspected has been the real hoaxer of the Mary F photographs had recently died. His name was John Gordon, and during my long and tortuous researches into the truth about what happened during the long, hot summer of 1976, at least three people hinted strongly that John had been the real perpetrator of the Mary F hoax.

I hinted as much in *The Owlman and Others* but as my informants had been speaking strictly off the record, and also because at that time John was still alive, I was not really in a position to reveal the fact. Now he is dead it seems a reasonable premise to do so.

The important thing is that Tony did not fake the pictures himself. They are fairly unimportant as fortean artefacts, unlike his later pictures of Irish lake monsters and even Nessie herself. I believe that to cast doubt on Tony's veracity *vis a vis* the Mary F photographs is dangerous to forteana as a whole because it then brings the results of Shiels's very real contribution to contemporary forteana into jeopardy.

Despite the highly dubious provenance of the Mary F. photographs, there was still a reasonably good body of evidence to support the hypothesis that there was indeed some strange creature at large in the waters of Falmouth Bay. Even more astounding was the evidence suggesting that somehow, it was indeed linked with some kind of magickal energy and that Tony "Doc" Shiels was capable of summoning the beast under certain circumstances.

In December 1976 Tony Shiels was on the shoreline below Mawnan Old Church with David Clarke from *Cornish Life* magazine, who was doing a photo shoot on him. He wanted photographs of Tony invoking Morgawr to illustrate a feature he was planning. Tony duly obliged, and David Clarke was taking photographs when:

"I saw a small dot moving towards us, which I presumed to be a seal. It came across the river to within 60-70 feet. It started to zig-zag backwards and forwards, and I could see movement in the water well behind the head, which suggested that it was a great deal longer than a seal. '"

Clarke's dog started to bark at the animal, and it sank from view. He was immediately suspicious of Tony, and accused him of setting up the illusion as some kind of trick. This is something that Tony has always strenuously denied.

The interesting thing is that while Tony's pictures, which were taken on an inferior camera without a telephoto lens, came out properly, although the image was indistinct and not really conclusive, the "jinx" which has bedevilled Fortean researchers for many years, and in many continents, struck again; and David Clarke's camera malfunctioned, causing pictures which were seriously double-exposed. They were, however, probably the most convincing pictures yet obtained of the mysterious creature of Falmouth Bay.

It should also be remembered that whilst such respected authors as Michael Bright, and practically every other author who had written about the subject of British sea serpents had quoted Mawnan-Peller who claimed that:

"In January 1976 a strange (and, so far unidentified) carcass was discovered on Durgan Beach, Helford River, by Mrs. Payne of Falmouth. For a while it was thought that the monster was dead"

Everyone in the field were overjoyed at the discovery of this wonderful piece of evidence and nobody actually thought to investigate it further, or to ask Tony Shiels himself about it.

By the time that I was first investigating the Morgawr phenomenon in Cornwall during the summer of 1994 the belief that there had been a genuine monster corpse washed up rotting on a Cornish beach, and that only stupidity on behalf of some un-named 'powers-that-be' had prevented science from getting their sticky fingers on a wonderful piece of cryptozoological evidence had become entrenched in the canon of fortean belief. Like so many entrenched beliefs, fortean or otherwise, the truth, though far stranger in some respects, was far removed from what had been written in so many books and magazines on the subject.

A few weeks after the initial discovery of the headless carcass on Durgan Beach, the *Falmouth Packet* reported that a young naturalist living locally believed he had found the answer to the mystery:

The mystery of the bones of Durgan Beach may have been solved this week by 13-year-old Toby Benham, a keen student of skeletons. Toby believes the bones found at Durgan by Mrs Kaye Payne of Falmouth, come not from a 20 foot sea monster as suggested, but from a whale.

He came to this conclusion because he thinks that the bones form part of a skeleton he discovered on nearby Prisk Beach just after Christmas. Toby studied the Packet's photograph of Mrs Payne holding a bone from the beach, and he is convinced that it is one of those he saw.

"I am sure it is from a whale, " said the young naturalist emphatically. His explanation for their appearance at Durgan is equally emphatic. Storm tides swept them around from Prisk, he says. The original skeleton was about ten feet long, and the skull, which is now one of the prizes in Toby's collection of bones, looks like that of a whale. He said the skull had what appeared to be blow holes and it seemed very similar to pictures he has of whales' heads.

Unfortunately, although several books report Mawnan-Peller's description of the finding of a "carcass" on the beach; none, that I have been able to find, have reported the fact that the "carcass" was actually a headless skeleton, and that there is every likelihood that the skeleton itself was actually that of a whale. Only one book actually acknowledged the whale theory, and that was *Monstrum* by Tony "Doc" Shiels; and, for reasons known only to themselves, the fundamentalists among the world of Forteana have decided to take it upon themselves to ignore everything that Doc ever says!

"Of course it was a bloody whale," Tony blustered at me one night as we were sitting around the kitchen table drinking rum out of coffee mugs. "Here, I'll show you" and he rushed away from the table into the dark interstices of the next room from whence he emerged a few minutes later clutching a colour transparency showing a pretty teenage girl clutching what was undoubtedly one of the vertebrae of a dead whale. "My daughter, Lucy," he barked at me, before changing the subject and demolishing the rest of the bottle of rum.

However, having been caught out once already by the oft repeated assertion that the carcass was indeed that of an unknown animal we embarked on a quest to see if we could get hold of Toby Benham and the elusive whale skull. By dint of some major detective work we managed to track down Toby's mother who said that, unfortunately, Toby was no longer living at home. As, by this time he would have been nearly as old as me this did not come as any great surprise, but we asked diffidently, whether there was any chance that his mother knew what had happened to the elusive skull. Of course she did, she told us. When Toby had grown up and fled the nest he left the skull behind, and for many years it had been lying open to the weather in his mother's garden where it doubled as a door stop and a somewhat macabre garden ornament. After some years she had got tired of it and donated it to a local educational institution.

Three weeks later, in a dusty cupboard of a locked classroom in a local college, this is where we found it. The proprietors of the college were happy to let the CFZ have it as a specimen for our nascent collection of cryptozoological memorabilia. And so we carried it gingerly out to our van and took it home, which is where it resides to this day. We had it identified by an expert at Plymouth Aquarium and by Dr Karl Shuker who both correctly stated that it was the somewhat damaged skull of a pilot whale, thus vindicating what Tony Shiels had stated all those years before.

Many people have claimed that all the sightings of the Falmouth Bay monster can be directly linked with Tony Shiels. This is clearly not the case.

In 1996 local author Sheila Bird wrote a letter to the *Falmouth Packet:*

For anyone who has actually experienced a sighting of the strange marine creature which has popularly become known as Morgawr, the monster of Falmouth Bay, japes and jokey reports of sightings are particularly frustrating in that they discredit genuine reports and reporters, and thereby discourage serious investigation which could possibly lead to a scientific breakthrough.

This being the case I have decided to place on record my sighting of this creature off Portscatho on 10 July 1985, which I did not report at the time, for it coincided with the launching of my book Bygone Falmouth, and I was reluctant because it might have been interpreted by some, as a joke to create timely publicity.

Having just met my brother, Dr Eric Bird of Melbourne University, who is a scientist and who had flown in from Australia on that day, we were relaxing on the clifftop to the west of Portscatho at about 8.00 p. M. , when he leapt to his feet and exclaimed at the sight of an unfamiliar, large marine creature with a long neck, small head and large hump protruding high out of the water, with a long, muscular tail visible just below the surface, propelling itself in a north-northeasterly direction just offshore.

Drawing the attention of two passers-by with binoculars, we were able to scrutinise the grey, slightly mottled creature closely and observe that there was either another hump at the base of its spine, or more likely that the muscular rhythms of the tail created the appearance of a hump. The tail seemed to be about as long as the body and the creature was an estimated seventeen to twenty feet in length.

For several minutes we were able to observe this graceful creature, with its head held proudly as it glided swiftly and smoothly on the glassy surface of the water, illuminated in the clear evening sunlight.

There were a number of birds wheeling around and a couple of boats in the vicinity, but all seemed oblivious of one another. Suddenly the creature submerged; it did not dive, but dropped vertically like a stone without leaving a ripple ...

Alison and I visited Shiela Bird in the early spring of 1996 and we were both impressed by what a solid, sensible and down-to-earth woman she is. We spoke to her at length about her sighting and she told us again how she had agonised for months over whether to make her sighting public. Reading between the lines it seemed as if she was scared that she would be linked with all the media furore that had surrounded Tony Shiels's antics. Tony had become notorious across the country after the Morgawr sightings especially after his revelations that some of his magickal experiments were conducted by/with skyclad (naked) witches who happened to be his own daughters. His antics even made the national newspapers with *The Sun* describing the Shiels clan as "The Weirdest Family in the Land".

Twenty years after appearing all over the fortean and paranormal press in the guise of Psyche the skyclad monster invoking witch, Tony's daughter Kate wrote:

Some serious feminists, deeply involved in the women's movement have been rather critical about allowing myself to be photographed nude in those days. They see it as a kind of exploitation, cheap cheesecake, or something of the sort. I disagree. As well as being a witch, I was in show business. I always retained full control during the photo sessions, and most of the photographers and reporters were a wee bit scared, afraid and in awe of the Shiels clan.

Nothing was ever published without my permission. If anyone was being exploited, you could say that the witches exploited the press. Yes, I know some people are shocked by nudity when it is associated with witchcraft. They see it as utterly wicked and depraved. I feel sorry for those small-minded puritans.

They must live horribly frustrated lives. I feel free to do whatever I wish to do, so long as it harms no one. I see nothing harmful in those photographs. For one thing, they help to dispel the popular notion of a witch as an evil, ugly old hag. That is just one aspect of witch nature, as perceived by man.

I have only met one of the naked witches: Miranda only became involved in Tony's invocational activities relatively late in about 1980; but, in a quiet Cornish voice, she explained to me that witchcraft was women's magic and women's power. I am sure that she is right. Since I first became involved with Tony Shiels I have made friends with a number of people within the pagan community. I even share a house with one, and although I remain a Christian, I have nothing but respect and admiration for sincere neo-pagans who are only trying to live their lives in the way that they see fit.

However, I have a sneaking suspicion that Sheila Bird would not have seen it like that, and would have been horrified at the thought that anyone, especially the British media, would link her with such arcane goings on. I remain convinced that she is a sincere woman who saw something very strange in the sea that July day in 1986, and her testimony remains one of the best accounts on record of Morgawr the sea dragon.

As my investigations into Morgawr the Sea Dragon and the grotesque Owlman of Mawnan we were reached their height, I was once again dragged into the debate surrounding the existence of Mystery Cats in Cornwall.

On January 12th 1995 Angela Browning, Junior Agriculture Minister and MP for Tiverton (Beast of Bodmin territory) launched an official investigation into the beast of Bodmin. Good news, we all thought until we discovered that the budget was a meagre one. This was just about enough to finance Zoologist Charlie Wilson, a consultant with the Wildlife agricultural Development Advisory Service and Mammal biologist Simon Baker in their investigation.

After six months, the experts published their findings in a report which in the best traditions of the British Civil Service concluded that there may, indeed, be a Beast of Bodmin. . . and equally, there may not. In the wake of these gloriously fence-sitting deliberations the long hot summer of 1995 suddenly started to become highly peculiar.

Being seen in certain quarters as somewhat of a pundit on matters crypto, not to mention zoological, I was approached by a number of newspapers and a couple of radio stations for my views on the MAFF report.

It was my first experience of how newspapers have a distressing tendency to write the stories *they* want to write, and to misquote the poor blasted interviewee with liberal abandon. I was impressed and almost immediately decided on pursuing a parallel career as a journalist. One front page surpassed themselves when under the headline "Report on Beast Slammed" they claimed:

John Downs [sic] *a specialist in the research of mystery animals yesterday described as 'rubbish' the controversial Government report which could find no evidence of a Beast of Bodmin Moor.*

Although much Government paperwork is indeed 'rubbish' I am not in the habit of saying so in public, especially when, as in the case of the MAFF report, the video evidence that they had examined was palpably of domestic cats. The MAFF report was well written and well argued and merely said that they could find 'no evidence' of a big cat living in the area. It was therefore up to someone else to try and do the Government's work for them!

It seems to me that all one has to do to get in the media eye is to criticise the Government on the front page of *The Western Morning News* because within days I was inundated with approaches from newspapers, TV and radio.

It was my appearance on one of the radio stations which lead onto the next chapter in the story.

I have always had an excellent ongoing relationship with Gemini Radio in Exeter, and at that time in particular with one of their star D. J's, an Australian geezer called Steve Browning. It was no great surprise, therefore, when one evening a day or so later he telephoned me to ask me to appear on his show. I spoke for about fifteen minutes, live on air, on the subject of mystery big cats in the South West and mentioned that what "we really need is a specimen"

Half an hour later someone, identifying himself only by his Christian name, which he asked not to be divulged telephoned the radio station and claimed that three animals including a pregnant female had been shot He gave no further details, and as at the time I was elsewhere I knew nothing about it until the next morning. .

My family keeps very late hours and consequently I am a late riser. I was awoken at about 8. 30 AM by a telephone call from Steve Browning. He told me about his mystery caller from the day before and almost immediately put me on air. I appealed for the mystery caller to phone me back. I promised on air that I would respect his confidentiality and that, if he could get me the carcass of one of these cats, there was every chance that we could clear up a large part of the mystery. Later that day I repeated the same appeal for the 'Western Morning News and on both occasions I took the unprecedented step of publishing my telephone number.

I had two telephone calls. One from an undoubtedly sincere, possibly mad, and somewhat annoying woman who claimed that the animals were sent by God as a manifestation of His angels, and that by encouraging people to desecrate the corpse of an angel I was committing an unthinkable blasphemy. I thanked her for her advice and a few minutes later I received a call from someone who was obviously so drunk that he had difficulty in stringing words together. He burbled and swore at me for about a minute and then hung up.

A couple of days later, however, after another yet another appeal on the 'Steve Browning Show', I received another telephone call, and this one appeared, on the surface at least, to be the genuine article.

For many years there have been persistent rumours of a government and military cover up regarding the big eats seen on

Exmoor and Bodmin. I have tended to disregard these reports as merely paranoid conspiracy theorising. After all - unlike, at least in theory, the question of UFOs - the matter isn't of the slightest significance to defence, and would appear to have no security significance whatsoever. I had never been able to see any real reason why any such cover up would or should take place. This telephone call, for the first time; gives a reason why such a cover up might have taken place!

I am taking a totally neutral position as regards this report. The caller seemed plausible enough, although extremely paranoid. He was also obsessed with Princess Diana and was claiming that when he had been a Royal Marine he had been part of a detachment of security services sent to protect HRH whilst she was paying illicit visits to the home of her lover, Major James Hewitt, in the Devon village of Bratton Clovelly. It must be said, in his defence, that he told me this some weeks before the liaison became public knowledge. It was certainly the first that I had heard of the scandal that was later to rock both the nation and the monarchy!

I mention this only because it does, to a certain extent at least, establish his *bona fides* as a Royal Marine and presents some corroboration for the story that he was to tell me. My informant claims that when the Royal Marines made their well-publicised, and apparently fruitless hunt for the Beast of Exmoor in the mid 1980's, that he was a sergeant in charge of one of the small reconnaissance parties. He also claims that the marines were also searching for the beast in another unspecified location in the South West He further claims that the search for 'the beast' was not the primary aim of the exercise, but that security implications forbade him to tell me what the Marines were REALLY doing there.

Over my last decade as a fortean pundit I have met a number of ex-military personnel, (or more accurately people *claiming* to be ex-military personnel) who have claimed to me that something unpleasant to do with National Security has happened on Exmoor over the last twenty-five years. One middle-aged man called Derek even claimed to have been part of a crack squad of specialist soldiers sent to the Somerset border to retrieve a crashed UFO. The fact that he was an undeniable alcoholic who seemed to have got involved with the CFZ and its sister organisation The Exeter Strange Phenomena Research Group purely with the idea of trying to seduce some of the more athletic male students who came along to our monthly meetings, must make one question the motivation behind his disclosures.

However, a couple of old friends of mine had also been involved in the 1985 and 1987 searches and, try as I might, I was unable to catch my mystery telephone caller out. It does appear that he was a part of the second expedition in the mid spring of 1987 and was probably stationed near Rackenford. Unlike the stories weaved drunkenly to us by Derek, this tale does, I believe, stand up to a certain degree of scrutiny.

The main claim of my mysterious caller is that three animals *were* shot at unspecified locations, and that at least one was shot on private ground by a party who were not only trespassing but had not been given permission to carry firearms. He claimed that a relatively junior officer had panicked and that the cover up had been perpetrated further up the chain of command in order to 'save face'.

My personal thoughts are that this is real life not 'the X Files' and that while 'the truth is out there'; it is probably far more prosaic. I did, however, tell him that I would be very interested to receive a corpse, or even the skull of one of these animals. He chuckled and said that he would see what he could do.

True to form, three days later, after another late night I was woken up by another telephone call. This time it was Joan Amos. She told me that a skull - possibly that of a big cat - had just been found on Bodmin Moor.

It is now a matter of public record that on 24th of July 1995, just a few days after the publication of the MAFF report 14-year-old Barney Lanyon-Jones and his two older brothers found what they at first thought was a strange-looking rock in a shallow stretch of Bodmin's River Fowey near Golitha Falls. When they fished it out of the water, it appeared to be a skull - apparently from a large felid. The lower jaw was missing but the skull possessed a pair of prominent upper canines.

It appeared that the original owner of the skull had been a young female big cat, and initial reports were that it was either a leopard or a puma. Although 'Doc' Shiels and others had told me that *'there are no such things as coincidences"* I immediately thought that the whole affair *was* too good to be true. For the world to believe that only a fortnight after the apparently damning (in reality no such thing), MAFF report, a genuine beast would allow herself to be conveniently decapitated in the vicinity of one of the areas best known beauty spots was asking one to suspend disbelief to a ridiculous extent

The telephone was red hot (figuratively) for the next three days. I told one close friend that I was sure that the skull had come from a mounted specimen and joked that I wondered which of the interested parties in the North Cornwall area had an old leopard skin rug in their loft!

The experts from Regent's Park did not agree. Giving the lie to the oft repeated accusation that "proper" zoologists are always sober and sensible in their judgements, whilst cryptozoologists are a bunch of loonies who will believe *anything*, on 1st August, Douglas Richardson from London Zoo examined the skull and pronounced it to be most likely a leopard's skull. So excited was Richardson by the discovery that he told the press that he was hoping to raise up to £10,000 to mount an expedition to catch any big cats lurking on the Moor.

Both Karl Shuker and I remained unconvinced. This was, after all, the third such skull to be found in the southwest. Two schoolboys found the first one from Dartmoor in 1988. Earlier in 1995 one of the schoolboys, now grown up, admitted to my then wife that whilst the skull *had* after all been found where they claimed at Lustleigh, it had been wrapped in a plastic bag. This effectively makes a nonsense of all the wild claims that have been made for this piece of evidence.

The second skull, was discovered in several pieces by Lynton builder Barry Hanks while walking his dog near Brendon, Exmoor, during late August and early September 1993, and was apparently derived from a wall-mounted tiger head. However, when Doug Richardson got more and more excited about the discovery at Golitha Falls and announced that the skull was from a recently dead animal, and still had particles of flesh adhering to it, my conceptions of reality were overturned completely, and I decided to drive into Cornwall myself, and to go and see the good doctor.

We phoned the Shiels residence and he boomed down the telephone to me that he would be delighted to see us as long as we brought some booze with us. We happily agreed and set off on our voyage of discovery into the ancient Celtic kingdom of Kernow.

Bodmin itself had a very weird atmosphere.

One of the pubs in the high street had several little huddles of serious looking men all discussing *'THE beast'*. There was a persistent rumour that the army had been called in to track the animal, and the usual paranoid nonsense about creatures escaping from government genetic research laboratories was being aired. From what the drinkers were saying you would have been prepared to believe that Dr Mengele had just been made the head of "The good ol' Min of Ag and Fish" and that somehow the whole thing was all their fault

On the way out of Bodmin towards Falmouth we passed two army trucks full of soldiers in full battle dress. They had camouflage make up on their cheeks and carried guns. I don't know what, {if anything) their presence signifies, and I suspect that they were perfectly innocent 'Territorials' out on an exercise. However it all added to the oppressive aura of high strangeness that surrounded us on our journey.

The outside wall of a public lavatory in a car park in Bodmin Town Centre had the spray-painted graffiti: "HOW LONG BEFORE A CHILD IS KILLED?" and the graffiti on the bridge, which spanned the dual carriageway, was even simpler: "MAFF IS MURDER". Feelings were running high.

Two days with 'Doc' restored my sanity. We discussed cabbages and kings, drank some wine, and did a live phone-in to Gemini Radio from the public bar of *'The Seven Stars'* in Falmouth.

As we were driving home Doug Richardson announced that he was seeking backers for another investigation into the Bodmin creatures. Several magazine and newspaper reports said that he intended to kill the animal. I strongly believe that if there is an animal, its danger to human is minimal and that its danger to livestock has been greatly exaggerated. For several days some colleagues and I started serious plans for a rival expedition of our own.

At that time Richard Freeman was just an anonymous voice down the telephone, but I called him in Leeds and asked whether he would be prepared to help carry out an investigation with three aims. Firstly to try and capture a live specimen before Doug Richardson and his pals from the Zoological Society of London. Secondly to attempt a study into the danger (if any) posed by this creature to Cornwall's ecology and biodiversity (not to mention its farming industry), and thirdly to try and establish once and for all what the creature actually was.

The sightings continued, and for an entire week I was inundated by hysterical telephone calls from members of the public either claiming to have seen the creature or worried that they and their kith and kin were in imminent danger of disembowelment from the claws of a mysterious felid. I made careful notes of the first type of report and politely told the second type of caller not to be so bloody ridiculous, whilst Richard Freeman and I hurriedly put our plans into motion.

My anonymous informant telephoned back and said that the discovery of the skull was a direct result of my appeal on the radio and in the newspapers. I had asked for a skull and some acquaintances of his had delivered. When I made the original appeal I was expecting that if I were successful I would have to collect a gruesome parcel wrapped in a bin-bag from the car park of some Cornish country pub. His acquaintances (and by inference his one-time colleagues), he said, had merely decided to he a little more flamboyant about it!

The inference was, although I have to stress that he did not actually say this, that the skull was of one of the creatures shot in the mid 1980s. The truth was somewhat different, although I still think that my appeal for a skull had been instrumental in the events that lead to the discovery at Golitha Falls.

A few days later a rather shamefaced Doug Richardson announced that the British Museum (Natural History) had found the egg cases of a tropical insect inside the cranium and that the apparently fresh flesh was a result of the dried tissue left inside a skull when a corpse is prepared for a skin rug being reconstituted when the skull was soaked in river water.

The matter was over for the time being and everyone except Doug Richardson had a good laugh about it. The only person that I felt sorry for was young Barney Lanyon-Jones, the schoolboy who had found it originally. He looked so disappointed that it was obvious that he, at least had not been responsible for the hoax. For hoax it undoubtedly was.

One swallow does not make a summer, and three hoaxes do not disprove a mystery cat. Something was and still is out there, and the whole truth is stranger than it might seem. However, as in the aftermath of his humiliation Doug Richardson quietly forgot about his plans for an expedition to shoot the beastie and therefore as its life was not in imminent danger Richard and I decided to postpone our big cat hunt until the summer of the next year (1996) so that we would have more time to prepare.

At the now defunct *Zoologica* exhibition in Sussex that September I finally met Doug Richardson face to face. He seemed a nice enough bloke but was (quite understandably) loath to talk about the events of the summer. I offered to buy the skull from him as a *memento mori* for the CFZ collection but he told me that it was going to be auctioned for charity. I never heard anything about the matter again.

Then, in the early autumn of 1995 we received word of what is, to date, the most recent sighting of the Mawnan Owlman, took place, allegedly, at the end of the summer of 1995 and is chronicled in a letter sent to Simon Parker, the night editor of the Western Morning News in Truro. It reads:

Dear Sir, I am a student of marine biology at the Field Museum, Chicago, on the last day of a summer vacation in England. Last Sunday evening I had a most unique and frightening experience in the wooded area near the old church at Mawnan, Cornwall. I experienced what I can only describe as 'a vision from hell'. The time was fifteen minutes after nine, more or less, and I was walking along a narrow track through the trees. I was halted in my tracks when, about thirty metres ahead, I saw a monstrous man-bird 'thing'. It was the size of a man, with a ghastly face, a wide mouth, glowing eyes and pointed ears. It had huge clawed wings, and was covered in feathers of silver/grey colour. (sic). The thing had long bird legs, which terminated in large black claws. It saw me and arose, 'floating' towards me. I just screamed then turned and ran for my life.

The whole experience was totally irrational and dreamlike (nightmare!). Friends tell me that there is a tradition of a phantom 'owlman' in that district. Now I know why. I have seen the phantom myself. Please don't publish my real name and address. This could adversely affect my career. Now I have to rethink my 'world view' entirely. Yours, very sincerely scared... 'Eye Witness'.

By this time my life was no longer my own. The long, hot summer of 1995 with all its attendant high strangeness changed my life forever. My mental illness, which was still untreated, was completely out of control, and my life was becoming so bizarre that I had difficulty in knowing what was real and what wasn't. I found myself living in a universe where all the established laws of physics, and more importantly the established moral certainties, which had defined the first of 35 years of my existence, were no longer in place. As I got deeper and deeper into the miasma of weirdness surrounding the events at Mawnan Old Church I became more isolated from those around me, and although I did not realise it at the time my behaviour became untenable. I was drinking heavily and subsisting on lethal cocktails of various narcotics. It was not until many years later that I realised what had been happening. The pressures and strains which had beset my marriage from its beginning had overtaken me. I was so unhappy with my life that I retreated into a self-made cocoon of noxious chemicals. The only times that I came alive when I was on stage with my band or when I was on the track of unknown animals.

In what, looking back, I can only see as a tremendous error of judgment, I acquired a manager who had his own agenda - an agenda which had very little to do with my aims, objectives or philosophies. When I sacked him just before Christmas 1995, I made a tremendous effort to put my life back on track, but it was too late. My career as a cryptozoologist had finally taken off. The magazine was selling well, and I was even beginning to get paid for writing articles for books and magazines. But my personal life was a mess. As my relationship with Alison disintegrated, I threw myself into my work. I released an album called *"The Case"*, during the closing months of 1995 and a four-track EP six months later. Both were heavily influenced by Tony Shiels who not only made a guest appearance on the former record, but designed its cover.

I did not realise it at the time, but I was running on empty. My marriage was a sham (although I didn't realise it), and increasingly I was using drugs and alcohol to get through the day. Alison and I argued incessantly, and one night in March 1996, I woke up at midnight to find her fully dressed, bags packed, and in the process of leaving me. I broke down in tears and begged her to reconsider. She reconsidered, and for a few more months our marriage tottered on. I was one of the featured speakers at the 1996 Unconvention that April, and I found to my great joy that I was now well and truly part of the British fortean establishment. However, Alison wasn't. She found herself less and less involved, and despite all my efforts, as I gained the fame that had so long eluded me, she felt more isolated. I felt angry that she was withdrawing from me - becoming cold and distant just as the goals we had both worked towards for so long were becoming within our grasp. I was so scared of losing her that, rather than address the problem in a sensible, adult manner, I retreated further into alcohol- and drug-fuelled psychosis. Still, my researches into *The Owlman and Others* continued apace and I found myself in a place that I had never had to go before. As I began to draw putative links between the Owlman apparitions and the more gruesome aspects of the history of that part of southern Cornwall my dreams became filled with visions of tortured children sacrificed to an implacable bird-god. My life became a living hell, and to my everlasting shame I took out my frustrations upon those I loved most.

On 28th July 1996 Alison and I had a bitter argument about a trivial matter. I fell asleep. When I woke up - an hour or so later - she and Lisa were gone. I never saw Alison again, but the Exeter grapevine informed me that she had gone straight to the arms of Nigel Smith, my one-time keyboard player who had always annoyed me by his habit of snapping my braces.

CHAPTER NINE

A NEW ORDER

Even now, over seven years later, it is difficult to write about the events of that horrible summer. Marriage had not been what I expected it to be. All the way through our relationship I had found myself making compromise after compromise, and going without the things that I believed that I should have expected in a vain attempt to make the relationship work. Looking back, I'm certain that Alison found herself in the same dilemma. However, by the early 1990s I truly believe that we had reached a sort of consensus reality - a situation where, although neither of us had got exactly what we wanted, that we were both reasonably content. It is only now that I am beginning to realise the extent of my mental health problems at the time. Not only must I have been hell to live with, but I was also in a position where I truly did not know what was happening around me. I knew that there were times during our relationship that both of us had been unhappy, but truly it had never entered my head to leave Alison, no matter how bad the relationship had got. It never occurred to me, in a million years, that Alison would ever leave me. It was unthinkable.

As a fortean I had spent much of my career writing about situations when the unthinkable had indeed happened. Now, with a bizarre twist of irony, I found myself and us that situation. And I had no idea how to deal to it.

It is frightening how often in life, one seemingly insignificant decision can have such remarkable ramifications and repercussions that it truly does stand up as an event of almost quantum significance. As soon as I realised that Alison and Lisa had left I panicked. I had absolutely no idea what I was going to do. I adored my wife and daughter, and in many ways I felt that I had given up large amounts of what I wanted to do with my life in order to do my best to provide for them both. Now they were gone, and I had absolutely no idea what to do. The one thing I did know was that I didn't want to be alone and so I telephoned Graham Inglis - the only friend of mine whom I thought might be available to spend some time with me.

I am not going to pretend that I remember much about the first few hours after I discovered that Alison and Lisa had left. It is one of the best things about the human psyche that one's brain somehow manages to blot out the memories of the worst times in one's life. I knew then that I was in deep trouble. Despite all my prayers I had no communication from my wife. I did, however, hear from my mother-in-law. She soon dispelled any illusions that I might have had that a reconciliation was possible, or that she or the rest of Alison's family might act as some sort of conduit for negotiation. She made it very plain that Alison had made her aware of certain aspects of my lifestyle both before and during my marriage, and that they were prepared to use the information as leverage against me in order to make the inevitable divorce as easy for Alison and as nasty for me as possible.

I have no intention of getting into recriminations. In many ways the breakdown of my marriage was my fault and even if it wasn't, now - the best part of a decade after - it is pointless to rake up the past and reopen old wounds. I have never actually recovered from the appalling trauma of my divorce, and I doubt whether I ever shall. However, as far as this book is concerned at least, one of the greatest and most positive knock-on effects was that the Centre for Fortean Zoology was forced to adapt itself to my new life. If I am honest, I can now admit that if it hadn't been for my divorce, the CFZ would have trundled along quite happily publishing a magazine every three months and the Yearbook once a year. But, if I had remained reasonably happily married, it would never have been any more than that. As it was, I was forced to make the CFZ financially viable, and, as such, we were to eventually become the biggest and most active Cryptozoological research organisation in the world. The seeds of that expansion were sown on the night of the day that my wife left me.

Graham turned up about half way through the afternoon, and stayed for nearly three weeks. During the first night that we spent drinking whisky and waiting by the telephone for a call which never happened, we got to know each other far better than we had in the previous eight years of our friendship. To me, Graham went from being an amiable geezer who used to let me rehearse in his flat to being the one person in an uncertain universe that I could rely on. The two of us got gloriously and thoroughly drunk. At that time I was still convinced that my wife would return to me, but for the first - and by no means the last - time in my life, Graham urged caution. He pointed out that even if Alison and I were to get back together, it was pretty obvious that something had to change. I explain to him how cryptozoology in general, and the CFZ in particular, had become of paramount importance to my life. We decided that whatever was going happen, Alison was unlikely to want to resume cryptozoological activities, and although through the haze of time and alcohol I can't really remember how it happened, I do remember that when we woke up - with stinking hangovers - the following day, Graham had become the deputy director of the Centre for Fortean Zoology.

The events of the next week proved that Graham's forebodings were true. A few days later I received a letter from Alison asking for divorce, and when the papers were served me from her solicitors they cited my unreasonable behaviour as grounds for the dissolution of our marriage. I was shocked to read that one of my pieces of unreasonable behaviour was to have wasted time and money on unworkable schemes and projects. These projects were my musical career and the Centre for Fortean Zoology.

Within days the people who had been *our* friends began to polarise into two armed camps; her friends and my friends. It was then that something cracked within my head and I entered a place that I had never been before; indeed a place that I never even knew existed. My perception of reality altered completely. In many ways it has never recovered.

As each day another one of my former friends would desert me I felt more and more alone. Graham, and a few others stood by me, but slowly and inexorably my world fell apart and was replaced by a new and nightmarish landscape of unbelievable anguish. I found myself experiencing emotions which were so intense that there are no words to describe them, and even now I don't really know what they were. For the first time in my life I began to hallucinate without the aid of psychotropic chemicals and I saw visions and heard voices that are impossible to describe with any semblance of accuracy.

My true friends rallied around, and each night for a month one of them stayed in my house essentially on 'suicide watch'. By this time the constant security blanket of alcohol, valium and prozac was beginning to take effect, and I went about my daily routine like a zombie. My nights, however, were horrific, and my dreams were populated by monsters, daemons and the faces of friends of mine who had died many years before.

The next six months were particularly difficult. I had practically no money, and was faced with the imminent probability that I would lose my house and therefore my animals and whatever of my possessions I could not move into a bedsit. In order to survive I sold most of my possessions. My record collection went first - a priceless collection of over 5000 LPs, which had taken 20 years to amass, was scattered to the four winds. It is, I think to Graham's and my credit that the CFZ publication schedule went on pretty well without a break. Graham had spent some years working as an administrator for the Department of Transport and he worked long and hard to transfer the CFZ membership list on to our antiquated computer. It seems amazing - looking back only seven years - to realise that at this stage we didn't even have a PC. We had two ramshackle Amiga games computers, and somehow - between the summer of 1996 and the end of the following year - we managed to put out six issues of the magazine, two yearbooks, and my first two Cryptozoological books - "*The smaller mystery Carnivores of the West Country*" and "*The Owlman and Others*". The darkest time for us was just before Christmas 1996 when we were forced to sell large portions of my cryptozoological library just in order to print and distribute the December issue of the magazine. Looking back, I realise now that neither of us knew what we were doing. Graham's new database had a number of teething problems, and over the first year that he took over the administration, between us we managed to make a complete hash of the book orders and resubscriptions. During this time many people who had been supporters of the CFZ since its inception decided that they had had enough and left.

On Christmas Eve, I sat up in bed cuddling Toby. My dog had become increasingly important to me during these months. I had always had a tendency toward anthropomorphism and treated him a more like a little person in a fur coat than a pet animal. He slept in bed with me each night, and I would have long conversations with him. That evening I held him tight and I remember saying to him (and my cats, Carruthers and Isabella, who sat inscrutably at the end of the bed), are that it looked very much as if I was not only going to lose my house but that my dreams of becoming a professional cryptozoologist were also over. I have no way of proving this, but I am convinced that Toby - in his own peculiarly doggy way - turned round to me and said: "Don't be daft Dad, something will work out - it always does".

And he was right.

As the date for my divorce hearing rumbled slowly closer, my wife, her family and friends, once again made it perfectly obvious that they were prepared to stoop pretty low in order to secure our divorce on as favourable terms - for them - as possible. I found myself in a position where in order to protect my ageing and ailing parents from witting or unwitting injury during the fall-out from this particular explosion, I was no longer able to confide in them to any major degree. Even so, my mother had a nervous breakdown, from which she never really recovered, and was subsequently stricken down by breast cancer - from which she *did* recover - for a few year,s at least. Unable to confide in my own parents because of the enormity of the situation, I found a father figure in a very unlikely place. In many ways Tony "Doc" Shiels - the Wizard of the Western world - became a father to me between the closing weeks of 1996 and the spring of 1998. This may well explain what happened next!

1997 will go down in Fortean history as the year when - for a few short months - forteana became bankable. It was the 50th anniversary of the so-called Roswell incident when something had crashed into the desert in New Mexico and kick-started an entire industry of people who wanted to believe. At one time there were 11 monthly newsstand magazines on fortean, and more specifically UFO related subjects. At that time I had never shown more than the slightest interest in flying saucers, but I was practically bankrupt and had a litigious ex-wife threatening to force me to sell my home. So I became a UFO expert. I went into W H Smith's and bought a copy of each of the aforesaid magazines. During one intensely tedious weekend I read them all cover to cover, and on the following Monday I telephoned each of the editors and introduced myself as one of the world's leading UFO investigators. It says a lot - I think - about the gullibility of the UFOlogical establishment that not one of them questioned my statement, and that by the end of the day I had regular work in five different magazines. Two months later, the money started coming in and I was not only solvent, but in my own little way I was famous.

1997 was a particularly strange year. In many ways it was wonderful - I had plenty of money, my future was secured, and for the first (and only) time in my life women seemed to be queuing up to go to bed with me. I spent the first few years after my divorce in a miasma of alcohol and promiscuity, revelling in my newfound fame. Although I was desperately unhappy at losing my wife and my daughter, I was too busy to grieve, and I will be first to admit that I found great comfort in the arms of a succession of dodgy women and an even greater succession of bottles of cheap wine.

Against my better judgment, I even found myself becoming interested in the UFO phenomenon. I think that it was because I had had my personal objective reality overturned in such a dramatic way, that it spurred me on to investigate areas of forteana that I had not previously done.

I also became very interested in crop circles. Whereas if I had actually thought about the subject before (and most of the time I hadn't), I had assumed that they were all fakes made by enterprising art students, now I wasn't so sure.

Several years before I had appeared in a number of episodes of a Westcountry TV series called "Mysterious West". It was my TV debut and one which, furthermore whetted my appetite for television work. As a somewhat unwanted side-effect of my new found media exposure upon the small screen, I was figuratively inundated with stories of high strangeness from across the region. It got to the stage that I was unable to go into a pub without a total stranger coming up to me and regaling me with stories of witchcraft, ghosts and things that went bump in the night. This was, as one can imagine, an invaluable source of new stories for me to investigate, and, as part of my new-found status as a bachelor, Graham and I decided that we had to make use of this treasure trove of new source material.

We decided, one drunken night, that it would be a good idea if we were to start a generic research group for the Exeter area by which we could recruit new blood into our research team (which at the time only consisted really of the two of us). We also had a 'covert agenda' (to steal someone's phrase).

We had every hope that amongst the influx of keen-eyed researchers that we fondly hoped would wend their way to our door in search of the answers to the great mysteries of the universe would be attractive young ladies who would find a grossly overweight (and soon to be divorced) fortean researcher to be a peerless companion for romance and wild adventures. Of course, it didn't work out like that.

By default, Graham had become my business partner, and over a series of drunken brainstorming sessions we formulated the rough framework of our future activities. One of the first things that we started was the Exeter Strange Phenomena research group (our late night brainstorming sesh coming up with the initials E.S.P. which we thought was an exceptionally funny pun - which over the next two years no-one ever seemed to understand). We announced the formation of the nascent group in the Exeter *Express and Echo* in early October, and, to our immense gratification, we received a number of telephone calls from interested people who wanted to come and see us and discuss their experiences.

Unfortunately, none of them were young nymphomaniacs with an irresistible attraction to overweight divorcees.

In January 1997, Graham and I were approached by a reporter from the local BBC Radio station who wanted to interview us in our capacity as founders of the Exeter Strange Phenomena Research Group about our involvement with paranormal research in the area. Always having an eye for the main chance we made a tentative enquiry about the possibility of us having a regular spot on the station. This is the sort of approach that we make all the time, and so we were actually extremely surprised (as well as gratified) when, a week or so later, we had a telephone call from Janet Kipling - the, the host of the station's weekday afternoon programme - asking us whether we would like to have a regular spot on her show. Would we? Of course we would, we replied joyfully jumping at the prospect of an unprecedented degree of access to the hearts, minds and wallets of the BBC Radio Devon listenership! So, early in February we made the first tentative broadcasts of our show "Weird about the West", which soon become a popular part of the station's output!

What we didn't realise at the time, was quite how much credibility this new found position would actually give us. As representatives of the BBC (albeit unpaid and rather unconventional ones) we could open doors that had previously been closed to us and could have access to people who would previously never have bothered to listen to us. Because on the whole (apart from the cost of the license fee and the odd error of judgement *vis a vis* Michael Barrymore or an Australian soap opera) people trust the BBC, they trusted us and we soon became the repository for an unprecedented number of stories concerning UFO reports and other incidents of high strangeness in the area. Slowly, as we collated these reports on our various computer files, a strange pattern began to emerge and we realised that these incidents were not, as we had originally thought, isolated occurrences, but more a part of a greater and far more perplexing whole.

On the eighth of May 1997 I joined the ranks of those cryptozoologists that no-one will ever believe again because they have (more by accident than by design) seen one of the very creatures that they have dedicated their lives to searching for It was about a quarter to eight in the evening and I was driving along the narrow roadway between the village of Warleggen and the dual carriageway when I saw a creature cross the road about thirty feet in front of me.

I watched it for about four seconds before it disappeared and I realised that I had joined the privileged ranks of those fortunate enough to have *seen* 'The Beast of Bodmin'. Although I had seen what I believe to be a mystery cat about ten years previously in the New Forest, there is the world of difference between the vague felid shaped shadow which vanished after a few seconds into a hedgerow in the middle of the night, and what I saw the other evening on Bodmin Moor. For a start, I can make a positive identification of it species-wise. It was a puma!

Although I didn't see its head, the creature I saw was about two and a half feet tall with strong gracile legs and extremely large paws. It was about four feet long with a long curved tail, about two feet long, behind it. The animal was a dark, muddy, chocolate-brown with lighter coloured under parts. The end of the tail was clubbed and either dark brown or black. The ground on which I saw it was dry and it left no footprints nor were any hair samples left on the gorse bushes through which it walked.

My camera was in its bag on the back seat of my car, but I was too shocked to use it. Like Dinsdale, Sanderson and others, I am sure that without concrete evidence no-one will ever believe it. But it happened. So there! I spent several days agonising about whether I should make my sighting public, or whether it was merely a private gift to me from the Gods of

Cryptoinvestigative methodology. Ironically, it was a quote from the "Father of Cryptozoology", Bernard Heuvelmans, that made up my mind for me. In 1968 he wrote:

I have spent much time in the last few years eagerly scanning the sea and even the dark waters of Loch Ness. 'And what if I should see one?' I thought and it was not a comfortable idea. For if I should have the luck I had longed for so much, it could only seem too good to be true, and my whole book would he suspect. I should have to make a bitter choice whether to sacrifice the book upon which I had spent so many years' work, or to keep my mouth shut about a report which would be of unusual value coming from a professional zoologist who had made a particular study of the problem.

I decided that Professor Heuvelmans was being too cautious. After all I don't believe that the hypothetical existence of Big Cats on the British moorlands would stand and fall upon whether anybody believed my testimony. The case for 'The Beast of Bodmin' and its ilk was far too strong for that. And if my own personal and professional reputation was so fragile that it could be destroyed if people chose not to believe my eyewitness testimony, then I was in the wrong job and should really have been contemplating a career move.

I thought with some fondness about what Heuvelmans had written so many years ago, and over the next few weeks I concocted a fantasy wherein the kindly old zoologist, who has, after all helped me several times during my career, did manage to achieve his ambition in a scenario similar to the main character in Robert Heinlein's *The Man who Sold the Moon*. This was nothing more than a fantasy but if only for the sake of the pioneering zoologist to whom my colleagues and I owe such a debt that it might be true!

So I wrote the story up in my monthly column *The JD Files*, for the now-defunct magazine *Uri Geller's Encounters,* emailed it off to Paragon Publishing in Bournemouth, and told them to follow the advice of the Duke of Wellington and "Publish or be damned". They published - I wasn't damned, and I continued my life as a jobbing cryptozoologist very much as before.

At the end of May, Graham and I, in our official capacity as representatives of the British Broadcasting Corporation made three daily appearances at the Devon County Show. We were part of the BBC's "Roadshow" which was, like such events the world over primarily designed to provide cheap entertainment for the hoi polloi. There were Spice Girls look-alike contests where prepubescent girls were encouraged top perform high-kicks and pelvic thrusts to the soundtrack of inane pop music. There were vulgar party games featuring balloons and more inane pop music and there were chances for the aforementioned *hoi polloi* to win prizes consisting of mugs, T Shirts and pens emblazoned with the logo of the aforementioned British Broadcasting Corporation.

There was also (feeling somewhat like the proverbial fish out of water) me, Graham and Toby the Dog doing a series of live question and answer sessions and providing a chance for the general public to talk about their experiences in the wacky world of the paranormal. Getting well and truly into the spirit of the thing Graham was wandering around the audience dressed as a 'Grey' alien and I was giving away prizes donated by those terribly nice chaps at *"Sightings"* magazine (a UFO magazine - now deceased - that I was working for at the time). A splendid time was had by all, and much against my better judgement I was actually beginning to enjoy myself.

Several members of the public joined us up on the stage to tell us of their experiences, which were mostly uninteresting in the extreme, and our forty minutes were soon up. Several interesting things, however, happened that day.

Firstly, as we were packing up our things and preparing to leave the County Showground an elderly farmer came sidling up to us with an embarrassed and rather sheepish look in his eye. He refused to tell us his name or give us any means of contacting him again, but he wanted, he informed us, to tell us his story.

He, apparently, owned a small farm in the east of the county (he was reluctant to tell us exactly where), and over the previous few weeks he had been experiencing some very strange things. A bachelor, he lived alone, but, or so he claimed, every night for some time, as he was lying in bed, he had heard the unmistakeable sounds of someone walking around on the flagstoned floor of his kitchen in what sounded like hob-nailed boots. His kitchen was directly below his bedroom and the sound, he said, was unmistakeable.

On several occasions he had gone down to investigate, and although on one occasion he had seen what he thought was a shadowy figure flitting away into the darkness he was not sure whether this had been the result of his imagination working overtime.

He had also seen strange lights hovering over a field of barley about a hundred yards from his farm, but a few nights before approaching us things had taken a sinister turn. In a scenario horribly reminiscent of one that Graham and I would encounter on the Carribean island of Puerto Rico some eight months later, he visited his chicken run one morning to find about two-thirds of his fowls dead, with no apparent injury.

I pricked up my ears at this. "Were any of the birds outside the coop?" I asked him, wondering whether the attack (if indeed attack it was) would prove to have followed the scenario so familiar from having read accounts of chupacabras attacks in Central America. "How the hell did you know that?" he muttered suspiciously and left. I gave him one of our business cards in the vain hope that he would get back in touch with us, but he has never done so.

We were slightly shaken by that, so we made our way home feeling slightly chastened, On our way back, we had to stop for petrol and in a spirit of slightly fortean *caprice* Graham dressed back in his alien costume and went to pay for the petrol and cigarettes in the guise of a 'Grey' from Zeta Reticuli. It says something about the times we live in, I think, that no-one paid him the slightest bit of notice.

The third main event of that momentous day took place when we got home. There waiting for us on the doorstep was a tall, thin chap with a big nose and greyish hair. Graham went on ahead to make sure that he was neither a debt collector or some hired lackey of my ex-wife's solicitors because,e at the time, my divorce negotiations were entering a very sticky and unpleasant stage which was to culminate in her having a warrant issued for my arrest. As I lurked sheepishly in the car park Graham strode intrepidly ahead to see who our mysterious visitor was. I could see them conversing together but it was too far away for me to hear anything that they said. Then I could hear Graham starting to laugh. He then turned around and gave me a friendly thumbs up gesture. It was obviously OK to proceed.

As I walked up to my front door Graham introduced me to our sinister looking visitor. It was a bloke from Exmouth whose name was Nigel Wright. He had heard us on the radio, and he had even bought one of our magazines in a local shop, which is how he knew our address. He was, or so he claimed, a keen amateur researcher into UFOs andf the paranormal. He had never seen a UFO (something that was to change over the course of the next three or four months), but as a child he had encountered a number of ghosts. He was willing to work for nothing and he wanted to join our investigative group. "Yeah, why not?" we said, and with this dull and rather inauspicious beginning a relationship was forged which has lasted ever since.

Against my better judgement I found myself becoming interested and - slowly - ever more involved in the search for unidentified flying objects. This was just as well, because the summer of 1997 saw an unprecedented number of UFO reports coming in across parts of East Devon. A couple of years later Nigel and I wrote a book - *The Rising of the Moon* - which chronicle the events of that particular summer and attempt to place them into some sort of context.

The events of the summer proper started on Wednesday the sixteenth of July when a well-known Devonshire businessman and philanthropist who has asked to remain anonymous was sitting, with his wife on the balcony of his house at West Hill (an affluent suburb of the small market town of Ottery St Mary) at about 22.35 when they noticed a bright orange-white light to the south west. Around it were four smaller white lights that moved rather erratically. They watched it for a while before it flew off towards the north. However, this was just the start. Over the next seven weeks, literally hundreds of UFO reports came in. As someone who strictly did not believe in such things, I found my belief systems increasingly under threat as the witnesses began to include my friends, lovers and - on the 12th August myself.

That night, the Exeter Strange Phenomena research group held a skywatch at various locations across Devonshire. Whilst Graham manned the Exeter location the rest of the core team, together with five other members of the group, and Janet Kipling, from BBC Radio Devon, were on Woodbury Common.

I arrived at about quarter past nine with a friend of mine. It was in fact the first time that I had visited Woodbury Castle for many years and I took the chance to look around. Dusk was falling as my dog and I wandered around the walls of the ancient earthwork. It was very quiet and very still. It was the sort of heavy summer night that one usually only experiences in the tropics and there was a distinct feel of thunder in the air. I climbed to the top of the ridge, and as Toby half heartedly ambled after rabbits (who paid no attention to him whatsoever), I looked over towards the great mass of Haldon Hill on the other side of the Exe Estuary and wondered what the night ahead was going to bring.

The air was rich with the scent of gorse flowers and the little chirping sounds made by grasshoppers and other small insects. For a moment I allowed myself a brief daydream, mentally substituted the sound of English grasshoppers for the strident squeaks of crickets and tree frogs, and it was like I was back in Hong Kong as a small boy.

Just for a moment I could imagine that instead of the Exe estuary I was looking out over the myriad of tiny islands in the bay of Hong-Kong and that the lights from the town of Topsham way below me, were in fact the lights of dozens of little junks embarking on nocturnal fishing expeditions. For the first time in many months I felt happy and I drifted on a cloud of self-indulgence until my reverie was shattered by the sound of approaching cars and the arrival of the other members of the team.

I called to Toby who had found something incredibly interesting to sniff at, and wandered purposefully back down to the car park. There were tiny pin-pricks of light on some of the bushes as I passed and I realised, much to my delight, that for the first time in nearly three decades I was seeing glow worms.

The intrepid investigation team unloaded their equipment, mounted telescopes and video cameras onto their tripods, opened cans of beer and waited expectantly for something to happen.

Nothing did and it started to rain.

There was almost 100% cloud cover in North and West Devon and so our Bideford, Totnes and Tavistock groups decided to call it a night but at Woodbury we still had about 40% visibility and so despite a light drizzle we struggled on. At about eleven (unfortunately just after Janet had concluded her interviews with us and gone home), all seven of us saw what seemed like a very dim blue-white star moving very erratically just within the burgeoning cloud cover. We watched it for several minutes, and then, as now, the best visual analogy that I can give is that it looked like a quasi-stellar version of the whirligig beetles that whizz around on the surface of ponds and slow moving streams during hot summers.

Half an hour after our sighting, two young men, walking on Exmouth sea front saw two red lights behaving erratically. I met one of them at the BUFORA conference at Sheffield and he told me that they were "whizzing along just above sea level". His mate works for BAe, saw it in more depth, but refused to talk to our researchers even with confidentiality ensured because he works on government defence work.

At midnight on the 12th-13th, DJ John Pierce said on Gemini Radio that there were power cuts in the Budleigh area that SWEB couldn't explain. I rang one of my contacts at Gemini the next day and they told me that one of the Torquay area transmitters had been struck by lightning. Although we can confirm that we saw thunder and lightning over Torbay on the previous night from our vantage point high up at Woodbury castle there does seem to be a minor mystery surrounding the whole affair. Graham rang SWEB on the 13th August at 19:45 and they denied that anything of the sort had happened happened.

The 'lightning strike' had occured at approximately the same time as we had seen the strange blue light in the sky, and at the same time another one of our group who was in the Torbay area, was trying to contact us on her mobline 'phone and found that for some inexplicable reason that she was unable to get any reception.

As we were at the skywatch itself, Jan was getting repeated interference on his car phone with which he was trying to maintain contact with the other groups carrying out their skywatches up and down the south coast of England.

One of the more bizarre episodes that happened to us during the long hot summer and autumn of 1997 was what my friend and colleague Jan Scarff dubbed "The Case of the Weird Warbling Whatsit of the Westcountry".

Graham was on holiday in Cornwall with his Mum during the last week of September, and therefore missed all of the excitement. I feel sure that had we had him available with his level of technical expertise, the situation, which eventually arose, would never have happened.

He was on holiday and so I did the Weird about the West radio show accompanied by Jan Scarff. Our guest was a zoologist who was talking about strange and anomalous appearances of animals in the British countryside. This was an area with which, in my capacity as Director of the Centre for Fortean Zoology, I am very familiar. We managed to conduct a pleasant if unremarkable show and then went back to my house to drink tea, smoke cigarettes and listen to a new CD that I had just bought by Scott Walker - an artist of whom I am inordinately fond.

I can't really remember how Jan became part of the ESP investigation team. I think that he just heard us on the radio one day and then turned up at one of the meetings. Her certainly predated Nigel as a regular in the ESP camp, but unlike Nigel he has a job in London much of the time and is thus unable to spend anything like the amount of time working with us on ESP investigations as I suspect that he would have liked to.

It so happened, however, that he was working relatively civilised hours on a job in south Devon during the spring and summer of 1997 and was therefore, for a few months at least, able to be part of the fun and games that were afoot. It is lucky (if, indeed there is any such thing as 'luck' which I personally doubt), that he was available to join in the events of that summer because with hindsight I doubt if we would have managed without him.

We were sitting at home with Toby the Dog, relaxing and listening to Scott Walker's inordinately glorious voice when the telephone rang. It was the bloke who had been our guest on the afternoon's show and he had a peculiar incident that he wanted to share with us. It appears that just after we had finished the broadcast one of the people who had been listening to us telephoned the BBC studios, not realising that our guests habitually join in the show by telephone, and asked to speak to him.

More by luck than for any other reason she managed to get hold of his telephone number and rang him to tell him a most peculiar story. The lady lived at Clyst St Mary (a little village just outside Exeter) who had been hearing strange bird calls outside her window in the middle of the night, every night for the previous five weeks.

He was convinced that the matter was a strictly paranormal one, and outside his remit, which was purely zoological in nature and so he passed the case over to us, wished us luck and rang off. We immediately rang the old lady in Clyst St Mary.

Luckily for us, it transpired that she had managed to make a cassette recording of one of these episodes of strange bird calls, and she played it, first to Jan and then to me, down the telephone. It sounded like nothing I had ever heard before, although it was mildly reminiscent of the weird call of an Albatross, but even though Albatrosses have been known to venture into the Northern Hemisphere on odd occasions the chances of one alighting outside a lady's bedroom window at precisely the same time each night and issuing forth unearthly cries for a precise number of times before dissappearing every night for six weeks was so unlikely as to be statistically impossible.

We decided to visit the scene of these events, and in the words of the characters from a dozen third rate US TV cop shows "stake out the joint". This we did on the night of the following Friday, accompanied by Dave Hopkins - a keen ornithologist, whom we brought along not just because he is good fun, but because we thought is it WAS some strange bird making these noises then he would be the person in our team most likely to know what sort of bird it was.

According to our witness these noises always occured at four minutes past two in the morning, and so we began a long and lonely vigil in the car park of the boozer opposite her house. Curious, the pub landlord stood outside with us giving us coffee and telling us ghost stories. Apparently a bar manager several years before had hung himself and ever since there had been a string of poltergeist reports and even the occasional sighting. Some of the more superstitious bar staff refused to work after hours alone.

Although we started the evening in high spirits and an atmosphere of hilarity had prevailed, by the time two o'clock approached we were actually getting quite scared, and when all the owls in the area started to hoot and screech we were quite un-nerved, but unfortunately we heard nothing even approaching the noises that had been played to us. Feeling somewhat deflated we all went home, but the next day Jan telephoned me to tell me that much to his surprise, the lady had reported hearing the same noises as usual on the previous night, and had even been watching us wandering around the garden at the same time as she had heard them. This was getting very strange indeed and when, on the next two nights (saturday and sunday) she produced tape recordings of what was apparently the same sound, we decided that there was only one thing that we could sensibly do - we had to go to her house, at four minutes past two, wait in her bedroom and see what happened.

Understandably she was loath to have a whole bunch of quasi-fortean weirdoes trampling around her boudoir and therefore it was only Jan who visited her laden with paranormal investigating equipment the following night. As the hour of two approached the atmosphere in the house became strained and tense, and by two o'clock you could, (in Jan's words) "cut the atmosphere with a knife".

Four minutes later the unearthly sounds started. Jan, together with the lady's son Paul, rampaged around her bedroom and eventually found the source of the noise.... it was a novelty Japanese watch with an alarm consisting of the electronically generated sound of a cock crowing.

The mystery was solved, but there is an object lesson here for us all. During the days before we knew what had actually caused these sounds I appeared on the BBC Radio and played the tape, voicing my opinion that here MIGHT be a genuine paranormal occurrence. As it was, it was nothing of the kind, but if I had not come public here in this column with the truth of the matter "The Case of the Weird Warbling Whatsit of the Westcountry" could well have passed into the canon of fortean literature as a genuine unsolved mystery.

One wonders how many other well known cases have equally prosaic explanations?

The really important thing here, however, isn't the fact that we solved a minor fortean mystery and in doing so managed to get a couple of figurative feathers in our collective cap, because, let's face it, whatever kudos we might have gained from doing that was lost by playing the recordings of a novelty Japanese Alarm Clock to a hapless reporter from BBC Radio 4's Today programme in the guise of being evidence of a genuine paranormal phenomenon.

No, the real importance of this episode is that it is a great indication of our collective mindset at the time. By the time that we became embroiled into this particular adventure we had been in the middle of a UFO flap of epic proportions for nearly two months. Then - at the end of September it all stopped.

In the closing sequence of the 1969 film '*The Battle of Britain*' the fighter pilots, who for about six weeks had been engaged in a titanic struggle against the overwhelming odds of serried ranks of incoming Luftwaffe aircraft, are sitting outside the Nissan huts of their airdromes on the south coast of England waiting for an onslaught that never came. The pilots were tired, pale and drawn, and could not really believe that The Battle of Britain was over.

On a personal level, one Tuesday morning at the end of September 1997 I knew how they felt. For weeks I and my gallant (if slightly eccentric) investigation team had been receiving nightly reports of UFO activity in the East Devon area. Nigel, Graham and I, in particular had been averaging three hours of sleep a night, and I had been resorting to tranquilisers to get me to sleep during the few times when the telephone was not actually ringing. As I slowly woke up - my head still fuzzy from Valium, and with cramp in my left foot, from where my dog Toby had been lying asleep on it, I slowly began to realise that the telephone hadn't rung since the previous day, and that I had been asleep for nearly fourteen hours. For the time being, at least, the East Devon UFO flap seemed to be over. I stretched, yawned and went back to sleep.

During the four months leading up to the end of September we logged about forty different incidents involving anomalous arial activity, involving a total of one hundred and twenty six witnesses, but the greatest concentration of this acticity was between Sunday 27th July and Friday the 15th August during which at least fifty individuals saw a variety of different objects in the sky, and suddenly it was over. We are all relatively sober and level headed infividuals and I would not like to say that we were clutching at straws but on one level at least I am sure that we were.

It was a time of immense change for all of us. At the time the Exeter Strange Phenomena Research Group was the largest and most active that it had ever been and there were half a dozen people working with it who have not been named in the text, not because I want to denegrate their contribution towards our research but because they have since drifted away, and we have lost contact. Being (usually at least) a relatively ethical writer I do not want to be in the position of dragging people who would probably not want it into the glare of publicity just for sake of a complete narrative.

The fact that so many of the people who were working so hard together during the summer and autumn of 1997 are no longer in contact with each other is actually, I believe, quite important. We were like old army buddies who had fought a long campaign together and who, after demobilisation would never see each other again.

The affair of the 'Weird warbling whatsit' was like the final skirmish before the cessation of hostilities.

I know, or at least I THINK that I know, that these events were an enormous psychological watershed in all of our lives. The members of the team who usually had normal and fairly mindane existences were actually quite worried at the imminent end to this brief period of excitement in their lives. For two months they had been giving and receiving telephone calls at all hours of the night, camping out at Woodbury Castle to watch the sky, and collating evidence that we all believed was going to lead to something fantastic. As it turned out we were right but not in the way that we all thought!

I am certain that for these people, the idea of returning to a normal suburban existence was too much to bear and that this is why we leapt on the idea of the 'Weird Warbling Whatsit' with such gusto.

For me, however there was a whole different range of stresses which were making the imminent end of the excitement of the summer seem like an insurmountable obstacle. By this time my divorce had come through but although, on paper |I was a free man the reality of the situation was something else entirely. This is not the time or place for recriminations, but sufficient to say that the emotional strain of the divorce and the resulting pain that it had caused to me and my family was too much to bear. There were complex financial settlements to consider, and it so happened that with what some people would no doubt refer to as life's little ironies, and others would call the Gods of chaos playing silly buggers with me, for the first time in many years I was beginning to make some money with my writing. At the time that my wife and I separated I was earning practically nothing and we had mounting debts. I was therefore faced with the very real possibiltiy that my new found success as a fortean spokesman and writer would be negated by the perfectly legal fact that the woman I was not living with was entitled to half my new found income.

Things started to get very nasty and at one time I was even threatened with imprisonment if I did not comply with certain requests that I felt to be unreasonable. This was too much for me to deal with and I slipped very quickly back into the dark morass of psychosis.

I didn't want to admit it to anyone but I was hallucinating nearly every day. Each night the voices in my head got louder and more insistent and again I found myself facing an abyss that was so unlike anything I had ever been prepared to deal with before that I really didn't know what to do. My only life-line was my involvement in the incredible events of the summer, and the thought that they were rapidly coming to an end which would leave me with nothing in my life apart from writing to earn money that I probably wouldn't be allowed to keep was a horrific prospect.

After well over a year of waiting I had finally been accepted for a twelve-month course of psychotherapy at Wonford House psychiatric hospital in Exeter. Everybody warned me that this was likely to be extremely harrowing and although at that time I would have done anything to get rid of the crushing weight of despair and the mocking voices and visions which tormented every waking and sleeping moment I was not looking forward to it. The idea of life without any excitement, cameraderie or fun was a daunting and abominable prospect.

So for all of us, I think that the fact that, for a while at least, we were taken in by the peculiar case of the 'Weird Warbling Whatsit of the Westcountry' is quite understandable, even justified. The important thing is that this should really be seen as an object lesson for all wannabe forteans. We had a bloody good team of reasonably hard nosed investigators who are not prone to jumping to conclusions. But we did; and if it can happen to us it can happen to anyone!

In October 1997 Nigel Wright submitted the following report to us:

"Approximately three weeks ago, two young men were swimming in Otter Cove. As darkness drew in they decided to make for the shore and change to go home. As they got changed, one of them looked out to sea. He saw what he described as a 'greenish' light, under the surface. He called to the other young man and they both watched as this light 'rose' to the surface of the water. The next thing they knew there was a very bright light shining into their faces. They turned and fled the scene".

On the cliffs above, the mother of one of the young men was waiting to collect them in her car. Frightened, they told her of their experience, only to be told that she, too, had experienced something strange that evening. Driving towards Otter Cove about ten minutes before she had seen a strange animal like an enormous cat which she described as being "all lit up inside itself". The strangeness doesn't end here, however.

The next day a dead pilot whale was washed up on the beach nearby.

The following report from Nigel is taken from the files of the Exeter Strange Phenomena Research Group:

To see any of God's noble creatures come to a painful, and sad end, is never a nice thing. However, sometimes we can learn from the way in which the animal met its end. This may very well be the case is this instance. One of the largest of all the world's creatures, dead, and without any apparent cause for its fate

It was about 6.30 p.m. when I got to hear of a dead pilot whale, which was washed ashore at Otter Cove. Now, not being a zoologist, I decided to phone Jon, to obtain his advice on how to treat this news. He asked me to go straight down to the cove and try to obtain some photos of the creature, along with some samples. I must admit that the very idea of being so close to this dead leviathan of the ocean was not really something that I was looking forward to. For a start, I had heard of the really quite disgusting smell that was supposed to emit from such things. Take it from me, this much is true, my nose can testify to this fact. Also, I am quite a sentimental man, and to look at this mammal, as it lay sadly still and yet so complete, on that cooling summer beach, was a sight that almost brought me to tears.

The first thing that stuck me, as I looked on at this scene, was how perfect the carcass was. There was no decay or huge chunks torn from it. Then, as I wandered around it I noticed that there was only one external wound, in the area of the genitals a large round incision, the size of a large dinner plate, was cut right into the internal organs of the mammal. The sides of this incision were perfectly formed, as if some giant apple corer had been inserted and twisted around. From the wound hung some of the internal organs. I quizzed the official from English Heritage, who is responsible for the disposal of the carcass; he informed me that no natural predator, or boat strike, would have caused this wound. As I looked at this sight, the first thing that came into my mind was how this looked just like the cattle mutilation cases of recent times. Could this be just a coincidence, I was not certain at that time, I decided to phone Jon again, so I rushed off to find the nearest phone box!

Have you ever noticed a funny thing about persons who have a great knowledge of their particular subject. They have a knack of sounding very calm and collected, even when you are tiring to tell them something that is, to you, so very exciting. This is the position I found myself in, that night, as I stood in that phone box. Jon remained very calm and collected as I recounted the details of the strange wound that I had seen on the creature. In the quiet, restrained tones of a college professor, he just said Um! Rather interesting". That was it, no outpouring of wild excitement, or ranting at the top of his voice, praising my having found the lost conclusive proof of alien involvement. No, just three little words. However, little was I to know, that this was indeed, a significant moment in our investigations into the mysteries that surround this part of our coastline.

Later that week, we had the photos back from the lab, we compared these photos to the ones of classic cases from the U.S., of cattle mutilation. As if to confirm my initial thoughts, the type of wounds were very similar. This similarity remained just an oddity, in what was up to then, a very odd year. Then, early in 1998, I attended a UFO conference, at this, I was informed of another set of events, which in themselves, which was strange enough, but when placed with this sad case, was enough to ring alarm bells in Jon and my minds.

There were no signs of injury to the beast except for a circular hole, apparently incising its genitals and anus. As many UFOlogists know such injuries have been reported on domestic and wild animals, often in conjunction with flaps of UFO activity. It is important to note that the zoologist from 'English Nature' who examined the creature was at a loss to explain such peculiar injuries. The fact that a marine mammal exhibiting such injuries is found in conjunction with UFO activity, is, we believe, at least partly significant!

What compounds the strangeness of this episode is that ten years before, almost to the day, another whale was stranded in the area. This time at Otter Cove itself. The Exmouth Herald for September 25th 1987 reported:

Please could we have our whale teeth back

Callous looters hacked off the lower jaw of a rare whale washed up near Exmouth to steal its two front teeth. After the 20-ft long Cuvier's beaked whale was found dead at Otter Cove on Monday, Exeter's Royal Albert Museum and the British Museum in London sent experts to retrieve it for research. But during Tuesday night, the whale floated back out into Lyme Bay because nobody had secured it. In the meantime, Customs officers who had arrived to take charge of the carcase on Tuesday mornmg found that the teeth which are Government property were missing.

Mr. Kelvin Boot, from the Royal Albert Museum in Exeter, said: "This whale is one of the rarest as far as beaching goes. There are no records of one being stranded in Britain this century. There was a sighting in the 1960's, but that is not like having the actual whale to investigate. It is a very significant find. Perhaps we should have chained it to make sure it didn't float away, but I am confident that it will turn up again on a beach along the coast. The Marines are on stand-by to tow it in as soon as it is sighted.

We will then dissect the whale, taking samples of various organs to check for heavy metal pollution in the sea and to discover what it has been feeding on. So little is known about this particular beaked whale. I just hope we can get it back. We may never get the chance again.

Fortunately for the scientists the whale obliged on Thursday morning, when it was washed up at Budleigh Salterton. Mr. Keith Green, an Exmouth-based Customs and Excise officer, said:" We would like to hear from anyone who has any information on the whereabouts of its teeth - they are still the property of the crown. All whales, porpoises and dolphins stranded on the British coast are the property of the Receiver of Wrecks, a department of the Customs and Excise service.

Under its rules, the mammals' teeth have to be removed and sent to the British Museum to establish the age and sex of the whale.

Here, we would like to note that whereas the newspaper's conclusion that the lower jaw was hacked off by souvenir hunters is probably correct, this IS remarkably reminiscent of another scenario commonly reported in UFO-related animal mutilations. The coincidence between the locations and the timing (as we shall see there were UFO reports in 1987 as well) is worth remarking upon.

As Nigel pointed out, they would have, made spectacularly uninteresting souvenirs, and having come face to face as it were with another suppurating cetacean ten years later, he feels it unlikely that any but the most psychotic of curio hunters would have summoned up the intestinal fortitude to hack the jaw off the great beast. I have to agree with him, and would add that the task would have been a particularly onerous and time-consuming one, and would also add that Otter Cove is a particularly isolated spot that can only be reached by driving through the grounds of a local holiday camp.

If the mutilation was carried out at night (which it would have to have been in order to escape the prying eyes of gleeful holiday makers) it would seem almost impossible (having visited the location) that:

a. The operation (which would have needed a chainsaw to complete) could have been carried out without attracting attention.

b. That the perpetrators (whoever they were) could have taken the immense jaw up the treacherous cliff path without having incurred an unreasonable degree of danger.

or

c. Anyone would have bothered.

One is also left with the inarguable fact that this species of beaked whale has no teeth in its bottom jaw. Therefore if person or persons unknown had removed the bottom jaw - and it appears from everyone that we talked to that this was the case, it could not have been done to remove the teeth!

Even if it were not for the undoubtedly interesting fact that:

A. The Beaked whale was washed up on the same beach as the UFO sightings.
B. Both whales exhibited apparently inexplicable mutilations
C. The whales were washed up ten years apart and according to David Bolton at the Royal Albert Museum in Exeter, apart from two small dolphins there are no other records of cetacea strandings from Lyme Bay
D. Both strandings coincide with other episodes of high strangeness,

the stranding would have been interesting anyway. The combination of all these factors is an irrisistible one!

Another important thing, which happened during 1997, was the entrance of Richard Freeman into our lives. I had known him vaguely for some years - he started subscribing to *Animals & Men* some time during 1995. He wrote - proudly - to us that he was just about to commence a Zoology degree at Leeds University, and we heard from him - by letter - every few months for the next couple of years. We actually met him in the flesh for the first time at the 1996 Unconvention. At the time, Alison's and my marriage was in end game and although Richard and I chatted in an animated and friendly fashion for an hour or two, nothing much came to pass. When he heard that Alison and I had separated, he wrote me an incredibly kind and affectionate letter, and by telephone and mail, our relationship strengthened. He came down to Exeter at the end of 1996 to see the New Year in with us, and in early 1997 we did a television show together. We soon became very close friends, and Richard was a regular visitor to the CFZ during the year.

It soon became apparent that he was no ordinary zoology student. He was (and is), a Goth - one of that peculiar band of young people with a predilection for doomy music, black clothes and graveyards. He was a practitioner of ritual magic, and during the summer of 1997 he carried out an extraordinary experiment during which he managed to create the tulpa or thought-form of an enormous spider in a cellar in Leeds. He was also possessed of a strange and bizarre sexuality and had a predeliction for being beaten up by specialist prostitutes. He also had - and has - a marvelously surreal sense of humour, a wonderful sense of the absurd, and a brilliant if erratic mind which is capable of feats of lateral thinking which are far beyond the minds of most mortals - including myself. Without either Graham or I noticing, Richard soon became part of the CFZ family - and the aforesaid CFZ family was a far richer and better place for his arrival.

1997 ended with the CFZ (and me in particular) in a much better state than we had been a year before. We were back on track, I was not going to lose my house, and best of all, Graham and I were just about to leave the country for our biggest adventure yet - chasing vampires around Central America.

CHAPTER TEN

SOME CORNER OF A FOREIGN FIELD

A s the summer of 1997 slowly drifted towards the season of mists and mellow fruitfulness, Graham and I were presented with a new challenge. It all began with a phone call from a bloke called Tom Tanner. In September 1997 - just as Graham and I were getting over the tumultuous events of the UFO-ridden summer we had a telephone call. It was from the aforementioned Tom - a researcher for AVP Films (a documentary company working for Channel 4 in the UK). He asked us whether we would be interested in a journey to central America in search of the chupacabra - a semi legendary vampiric entity which had - allegedly at least - been responsible for some appalling predations on the domestic livestock owned by farmers in the region.

I had always been somewhat sceptical on the subject. After all - as anybody who has read this memoir so far will know - I am essentially a Zoologist, who has become embroiled in matters paranormal much against my better judgment. The whole idea of the chupacabra was ludicrous. It was described as being something like a 4 ft-high kangaroo, with no tail, and with weird spines up its back. In one of my less guarded moments I described it as being like a sonic the Hedgehog on acid, and the best part of a decade later I cannot think of a better description. The fact that it looked like an artist's impression of a malevolent alien, and that it came to international media prominence of the same time as the global proliferation of interest in such things which accompanied the 50th anniversary of the so-called Roswell incident (see the previous chapter), did nothing to raise my belief in the phenomenon. However, remember that at the time - although I was on paper at least one of Britain's foremost fortean investigators - I was, in reality, on the dole with practically no money, so the opportunitiy of spending a large chunk of the forthcoming winter in the Caribbean together with my best friend, seemed too good an opportunity to pass up. Were we going to go to Puerto Rico, Mexico, and Florida in search of a semi legendary entity which looked like a badly designed computer game? Or were we going to spend the winter in relative penury in cold, dank, Exeter? For heaven's sake - it doesn't take a genius to work the answer that question out!

So, after a particularly strained festive season spent with my parents in North Devon, it was with a relatively positive outlook that Graham and I took the afternoon train from Exeter to Heathrow Airport. It was the beginning of one of the greatest adventures of our lives.

The seats on the train itself were uncomfortable enough, and the bloke sitting opposite me was reading one of the tackier of the UK tabloid newspapers which proclaimed (on its front page no less) the story of a hapless traveller who had been deemed too large to be allowed onto a transatlantic air flight. This served to inflame my paranoia again to an unacceptable degree, and by the time we arrived at Reading Station in order to catch the 'courtesy coach' (a particularly inappropriate name, considering that it was an hour late and the driver was both rude and uninformative) to Heathrow Airport, I was in a state of considerable paranoia for which there only seemed to be one sensible cure - alcohol!

We eventually arrived at a cheap, comfortable and singularly unimpressive motel on the outskirts of the Heathrow complex where we were to meet the camera crew. When we arrived they were nowhere to be seen, and so Graham and I showered, made ourselves reasonably personable and retired to the bar to await their arrival.

Then happened one of the quasi-fortean coincidences that seem to occur more often within the fields of cryptoinvestigative methodology than to those mortals who do normal jobs for a living. We were sitting, drinking beer, at a small round table a few yards from the bar when I heard a vaguely familiar voice. I turned around, and there - admittedly looking somewhat older but eminently recognisable was someone whom I hadn't seen since I was a young boy in Hong Kong. I went over and introduced (or should that be re-introduced) myself, and when he had got over his obvious surprise that the seven-year-old schoolboy in shorts had turned into a bearded giant of 20 something stone, he and his wife joined Graham and me at our table. We had a long and animated conversation about things about which Graham neither knew nor cared but the good fellow took it all in good part and we passed a very convivial couple of hours.

There was still no sign of the camera crew.

Quite a lot of beer, a large meal and a bottle of undrinkable 'wine' (which tasted like a cross between pickled onion vinegar and sherbet) later we were a little bit sozzled and there was no sign of our soon-to-be traveling companions. By midnight, as we were just about to retire to our separate beds (the bar having closed and the facilities for amusement offered by the hotel being somewhat limited) we heard the unmistakable sounds of a party of guests arriving at the hotel and attempting to get some sense out of the slightly retarded night porter.

Staggering around from the conservatory in which we had been drinking, talking and generally wasting an evening we discovered that it was indeed the three members of our team that we had been eagerly awaiting, and we immediately offered our skills as beasts of burden and helped them unload their hire car. We offered to buy them a drink but they said, quite rightly as it turned out, that there would be plenty of time for that in the weeks to come and that having finished filming in the North of England at tea time, and then having driven all the way to London, and then with an early start the next morning, the most sensible thing to do would be to get a relatively early night.

Staggering into breakfast like a pair of two toed sloths on Methaquaaqualone we eagerly (or as eagerly as one can at 6.30 in the morning) awaited the "Full English Breakfast" that the hotel menu had promised. After hanging around for ten minutes we were informed by a particularly taciturn waiter that the chef was ill and that we would have to break our fast with some spectacularly unattractive cornflakes and some even less appetising fluids which proclaimed themselves to be 'coffee' and 'orange juice'.

The three members of the crew whom we had met briefly the previous night then came into the breakfast room, looked somewhat annoyed at having to put up with the singularly unattractive menu offered to us, grabbed cups of what the hotel staff still insisted was coffee and joined Graham and me at our table.

They introduced themselves. First to arrive was Nick the cameraman. Over the next few weeks we discovered what an exciting career he had enjoyed so far. When someone casually mentions "having been in Bolivia before Christmas" and talks about the difficulties and privations involved in filming an ascent of Mount Everest for six months at a time, and all without any trace of self consciousness and without even the slightest hint of being a poseur, one can only be in awe of the bloke. I think that I can truthfully say that if it weren't for Nick we wouldn't have survived the trip. There are various incidents recounted in the following pages (and quite a few which have been left out in order to protect what remains of our tattered reputations), which we just wouldn't have got through without Nick's good-humoured and kindly assistance.

A few minutes later Dave, the sound man entered. Another quiet, unassuming bloke with a broad smile and a quietly acerbic sense of humour. Over the next few weeks we were to get to know him as well as we did Nick. Dave had the unenviable task of having to record all the sound for the documentary team. As this involved having to attach microphones to me and Graham, and therefore laid us open to electronic eavesdropping at any time - and also considering that Graham's and my conversation, when we forget that we are likely to be overheard, does sometimes border on the scatological, means that Dave should really be (if there were such a thing) be nominated for whatever the cinematic industry has as its equivalent of the Purple Heart for services over and above the call of duty.

Finally Warren joined us. I have never been any good at judging ages of people but I reckon that he was probably the youngest of the team, (either sitting at our table in London or awaiting our arrival in Puerto Rico with figuratively baited breath). He soon proved himself to be a wizard with gaffer tape and superglue and to be the best technician that I have ever worked with. Over the next few weeks he came to remind me of another Dave - the backline technician with whom I had done so many UK tours with *Cockney Rebel*, and whose quiet good humour had managed to deflect many a storm upon the ocean of a low budget rock and roll tour during the early 1990s. (See my book *Road Dreams* (1993) for details). This expedition was costing a great deal more money and the stakes were far higher, but Warren managed to keep the whole show figuratively (and sometimes literally) on the roads. Thanx pal. If it weren't for you the film would probably never have been made.

Giving up 'breakfast' as a bad job, we loaded the enormous number of ungainly packages, parcels and bundles onto the crew hire car, and as they drove off towards Heathrow Terminal Two, Graham and I boarded the so-called courtesy coach and made our way towards the same destination. Making our way through the cavernous concrete tunnels, which surround the singularly unattractive aviation conurbation that is Heathrow, we felt that the journey was starting properly at last.

Ironically, it was getting all our luggage (and the camera equipment) through customs to get it out of England that was the most arduous administrative exercise of the whole journey. I had imagined that entering Mexico would be more difficult. I had been led by many people to expect a country where I assumed that half the officials would either be open to (or looking for) bribes, and quite prepared to make imaginary obstructions in our path if they didn't get them. I was wrong. Entering Mexico and even the United States was a doddle compared with leaving England, and to this day I am really not quite sure why. I am sure that there is a perfectly rational explanation - probably something to do with the Inland Revenue (or some similar government department) wanting to make sure what was taken out of the country was for legitimate use abroad and not for illicit sale. However, this account is about our search for the grotesquely surreal blood-sucking vampire of Latin America and not for the whys and wherefores of the laws surrounding import and export from the United Kingdom, and so in the interests of brevity (and not boring all my readers stupid with unnecessary information) I feel that we should leave the subject and get on with the journey.

We negotiated Emigration and received our boarding passes. This is where Graham and I made our first mistake. We made straight for the duty free shop where I bought four hundred cigarettes and half a bottle of whisky and Graham bought enormous amounts of rolling tobacco. Unfortunately he neglected the extra cigarette papers. In most of the places that we were to visit, these essential items of equipment are seen as items of dope smoking paraphernalia, and are therefore either illegal (as in Puerto Rico) or extremely difficult to buy (everywhere else). So Graham's stash of Golden Virginia was pretty well useless, and as far as I know was largely intact by the time we finally re-entered the United Kingdom three and a bit weeks later.

What we shouldn't have done was to drink the whisky immediately, but in a spirit of bonhomie and good humour it seemed like a good idea at the time. Graham and I were mildly pickled by the time the aeroplane took to the air at about ten thirty in the morning and by the time we were half way across the Atlantic, and had drunk large amounts of the free booze kindly laid on by those jolly nice chaps at American Airways we were cheerfully, if slightly noisily drunk! Then a rather sexy stewardess who (although she was far from being in the first flush of youth) smiled sweetly at us and asked us whether we wanted to buy any duty free products. As we had finished our whisky it seemed a good idea to spend $20 US on a litre bottle of Jack Daniels which we proceeded to drink until the jolly nice stewardess politely came up to us and took the bottle away from us promising that we could have it back when we arrived in the land of the free. Perhaps the fact that we were singing cheerfully and making a series of biologically detailed comments about President Clinton (who at the time - as always - was involved in allegations of a sex scandal) had something to do with it, or perhaps it was the fact that drunkenness on an aeroplane is actually a federal offence according to US law!

We weren't actually causing any trouble. I very much doubt whether we were causing any annoyance whatsoever to the other passengers, but although Graham and I have got an enormous capacity for alcohol (at least compared to most normal mortals), it is only right and proper that the powers-that-be should have assumed that we were going to cause trouble, even though there was no way in reality that we were actually going to. We then decided to go to sleep and when we awoke the 'plane was just about to make its long descent through the clouds towards the Florida coast.

For reasons completely unknown to me it seems that American Airways do not operate scheduled flights between London and either Mexico City or San Juan in Puerto Rico, so on each journey we had to go through Miami. Miami Airport, (which we visited four times in three weeks) is a particularly unprepossessing facility and is hardly likely to make anyone - least of all me - look upon the United States with a less jaundiced eye.

We managed to become separated from the rest of the crew as we tried to negotiate American Immigration. Unfortunately we managed to get in completely the wrong line and a process, which should have taken about fifteen minutes, took nearly an hour! Certain unkind rumours amongst other members of the team later in the journey suggested that this was because we were too drunk to know any better, but I maintain still that the real culprits were the Immigration Officers to whom we spoke to first of all, who spoke hardly any English and mistook our statement that we were traveling TO Puerto Rico as a claim that we were actually residents of the island (this despite our UK/EEC passports), and then became quite unpleasant when we tried to explain the true state of affairs to them.

OK, the fact that Graham went off for a cigarette at precisely the wrong moment and then ended up in yet another wrong queue also didn't help, but on the whole the mistakes were not of our making. We eventually managed to negotiate the Immigration procedure and found the rest of the crew - who by this time had become convinced that Graham and I were stumbling around drunk somewhere else in the airport terminal and were therefore going to make them (and us) miss the next 'plane to Puerto Rico. We managed to board the next aircraft with about five minutes to spare and I THINK that we managed to convince Nick and the others that the delay really hadn't been our fault. I hope that they believed us.

The aeroplane taking us from Miami to Puerto Rico was a very much less ostentatious affair than the one in which we had traversed the Atlantic. The upholstery on the seats was far more shabby, the stewardesses less plastically attractive, and the food far less wholesome. Graham and I felt at home almost immediately. As we relaxed into our seats the 'plane took off and flew slowly across the Caribbean towards Puerto Rico. Being an internal US flight the alcohol was no longer free and so I surreptitiously poured Jack Daniels (from what was left of the litre bottle that we had been given back by the aircrew of the previous aircraft upon our arrival in Miami) into the complimentary glasses of Diet Coke, which we were given. Graham wisely decided not to drink any more whisky.

Unfortunately, although (as I have stated already) Graham and I both have a fairly masterful capacity for alcohol, I am much larger than he is, both in frame and weight, and I have also been a whisky drinker for longer than he has. Graham has an incredibly fast metabolism and is therefore very skinny. When he tries to match me drink for drink with whisky (especially as he prefers it with a much larger ratio of whisky to coke than I do), he has been known to come a cropper. He therefore switched to beer whilst I flew over the moonlit Caribbean in a haze of blended Kentucky spirit.

By the time we finally landed at San Juan airport we were both sober - well relatively so, but whereas I knew what to expect, Graham was less prepared for the wall of heat that hit us as we disembarked from the aircraft. Graham was dehydrated and felt decidedly unwell. Indeed, he remained under par for several days, but I felt immediately at home. I had forgotten the glorious essence of a tropical night; the coppery taste, the sound of crickets and tree frogs, and the rank smell of unwashed humanity and cooking food from the semi-legal food stalls manned by hawkers which sprung up like mushrooms alongside most of the roads.

All my worries about not being able to deal with the tropical heat vanished immediately and I luxuriated in the heat and the ambience of a place which although diametrically on the opposite side of the world to the place where I had been brought up was in essence so close to it that it immediately felt like home.

As we collected our baggage from the revolving carousel the three remaining members of the team, who had already been on the island for a week, turned up to greet us. Graham and I had met all three before.

First was Tom, the researcher who had originally contacted us nearly six months before. We owe him an enormous debt of gratitude because if it weren't for him we wouldn't have been there in the first place. Like the other two team members who were waiting for us at Puerto Rico airport he had a dreadful sense of humour but was (and presumably still is) an efficient and reliable researcher.

The second on the scene was Marcus. A cheerful bloke with a passion for birdwatching and a shock of unruly hair. He was the producer of the film and although he had a fair amount of artistic input his main job was to deal with the money, the administration and the more complicated aspects of the project in order to free Graham and me to hunt for vampires and the rest of the crew to make what we all hoped was going to be a wonderful movie!

Finally Norman arrived. He is one of the foremost documentary directors in the UK, and although we had our differences at various times during the trip he is a man for whom I have a great deal of respect and with whom I very much hope that I will be working again in the future. He looked uncannily like an older version of the young John Lennon (if that isn't too much of a mixed analogy for anyone to grasp) and he had an impeccable taste in music and drinks, introducing me both to *Radiohead* and Margaritas (one is an English rock band and the other a cocktail consisting of Cointreau, tequila and lemon juice - I leave it up to your powers of deduction to work out which is which).

This was the crew with whom our entire existence over the next three and a bit weeks would be spent. We loaded the thirty odd items of luggage into the two surprisingly spacious Japanese mini-vans and made our way across San Juan to the hotel. At night, San Juan, or at least the parts through which we had to drive, looked like any other touristy and Americanised resort city across the world, and with the air conditioning on in the car we were safely cushioned from the outside world, but as we pulled up outside the hotel and disembarked again the heat hit us again and we were soon enveloped in the all encompassing womb like ambience of the tropical night.

The procedure of checking into the hotel took a surprisingly long time, but eventually we found our rooms, discovered how to work the air conditioning and then together with the rest of the crew we walked three blocks through the tropical night to a bar where we drank a rather pleasant beer from the Dominican Republic called *Presidente*, and discussed our plans for the next weeks filming.

I spent much of the first two days sitting in the Plaza San Sebastian - in the middle of old San Juan - doing the occasional piece to camera about what we hoped to achieve on our journey, and spending the rest of the time watching and filming the local wildlife - in particular the ubiquitous Boat Tailed Grackles - birds a little larger than a starling with glossy plumage and peculiar boat-shaped (as the name implies) tails. These were by far the most common indigenous species of bird there, and they never ceased to amaze me with their apparently fearless antics. They begged for food amongst flocks of feral pigeons and seemed to occupy an important niche in the local ecological infrastructure.

Later in the day, Graham arrived. Whilst I had been doing endless, slightly stagey pieces to camera about my hopes and expectations for the forthcoming trip he had been 'chilling out' in his hotel room drinking the local brew and watching a TV movie called *Confessions of a Mad Housewife*. Such are the privations of life on a cryptoinvestigative expedition.

We also managed to visit a gloriously rococo (or baroque - architectural terms have never been my strong point) pleasure gardens in what used to be the grounds of a Palace built by a Spanish Emperor whose name I have shamefully forgotten. We spent a cheerful hour or so watching birds (the feathered variety) in surroundings which were again very reminiscent of those from my childhood. The Emperor's gardens were irresistibly reminiscent of what the Botanical Gardens in Hong Kong looked like when my mother used to take my brother and I there in the mid 1960s. Crumbling Victorian Colonial architecture covered with undergrowth and vines, reminiscent of Kipling's poem about the Karella vine. When I visited Hong Kong again in 1980, the Botanical Gardens had been modernised out of all recognition, and whilst it is certainly a boon for the animals that had been kept there in a small zoological exhibit, no longer to be kept in conditions of smelly squalor, (the Orang Utan exhibit in 1980 was particularly spectacular), something, to my mind at least, had been lost when the decaying splendour had been replaced with neat walkways and concrete pillars. I hope with all my heart that the Emperor's Gardens in Old San Juan are left to decay in magnificent peace!

During previous trips to tropical countries I had become fascinated by geckos. They are peculiar little lizards who live off a diet of small invertebrates and scraps of food discarded by creatures (often humans) further up the food chain than themselves. I had forgotten that there are no true geckos in the new world, but instead their place within the zoological infrastructure was taken by various species of Anole. Known as 'new world chameleons' (because they have a limited ability to change colour in order to adapt to their environment, these little lizards were everywhere, and for several days both Graham and I spent many hours videoing them (for no real reason apart from the fact that they were there to be filmed).

I was endlessly fascinated by the way that they extended flaps of skin across their throats as a cooling mechanism, and also as part of complex courtship rituals. Although I had seen various species of *anolis* in zoos and pet shops, they looked completely different in the wild. In the same way that Guinness DOES taste completely different in Dublin, these tiny lizards are seen at their best as part of their natural habitat, and shouldn't really be kept in tanks.

One of the best sites for Anole watching was in the immediate vicinity of a peculiar piece of statuary in the square next to the Plaza San Sebastian. Although I never managed to ascertain what it was supposed to represent, it looked for all the world like a half used Doner Kebab in a particularly sleazy back street kebab shop, and soon became known to many wags amongst the crew as the 'monument to the unknown kebab'.

A more disturbing local monument, and one which was all too reminiscent of a particularly unpleasant scene from a John Waters movie was the Teddy Bear Bar - a ramshackle pool hall, the outside of which was covered with crucified soft toys. Having always found the images of the crucifixion to be particularly disturbing, I was quite perturbed by this monument to Latin American tastelessness. Wondering whether there was any significance to this appalling edifice we asked two of the locals, who were lounging about outside. Stinking of cheap rum and marijuana they explained to us that the only rationale for this deplorable edifice was that there was something similar in New York City, and that the brother-in-law of the proprietor had returned from the Big Apple determined to do something similar for San Juan.

With the bonhomie of winos the world over they asked us why we were filming the Teddy Bear Bar. (As a complete film crew - all with English accents - accompanied us, one could hardly blame them for their curiosity. In appalling Spanish we explained that we were from the UK making a documentary about *El Chupacabra*. One of them nodded sagely and pointed towards a wall behind us on which was spray-painted a rough depiction of a goat. "*El Chupacabra*," he chuckled.

It was a symbol that we were to see painted up upon walls across the island over the next week and was just one symbol of how this collective fear had managed to imbue itself into the consciousness of the islanders.

On our third day we went into the heartland of the island and commenced our investigation proper. We had been given a guide and interpreter by the benevolent local police force - his name was Rueben, he was a native of New York and he had been working in Puerto Rico for several years. He was to be an invaluable guide to us over the next few hours, and, like so many of the people that we were to meet over the next few weeks during the short time we knew him, we developed a close bond and became quite fond of each other.

The first witness, who by English standards at least, seemed to live in dreadful poverty, was in fact a policewoman and quite well off by the standards of her village. She told us in a mixture of Spanish (translated by Rueben) and extremely hesitant English, how about eighteen months or so before, she had been hanging out her washing on a line in the back yard - in reality an area of wasteland decorated by pampas grass and the stumps of two moth-eaten banana trees - when she had seen a spinning red light in the sky several miles away between two mountains.

Within days she had experienced a series of attacks on her poultry that were kept in a ramshackle (but extremely secure) coop underneath the house. Here, I should perhaps explain, that the house in which she was living had been built on the side of a steep hillock, and the back part of the house was raised from the ground on stilts. The chicken coop was therefore at ground level between them.

She told us how on several occasions she had found members of her flock, outside on the ground although they had previously been locked into the coop for the night. On each occasion, the corpses were totally exsanguinated (presumably through two puncture marks on the neck) but were otherwise unharmed. On one of these occasions she and her brother had seen the animal that they believed was responsible. It was bipedal and looked a little like a kangaroo with spikes sticking out of its back. It had a reptilian face and slit eyes. She drew us a picture which showed a creature remarkably similar to the drawing made so familiar by Puerto Rican UFO researcher Jorge Martin.

She told us how some of the chickens had been covered with a revolting layer of slime which she assumed was saliva. This facet of the Chupacabras attacks has been noted elsewhere, and many researchers have hypothesised that this slime is in fact some kind of anti-coagulant which is used - like that in the saliva of a vampire bat - to aid the exsanguination of the chupacabra's victims.

She also drew our attention to an ancient thorn tree just beyond the perimeter wall which surrounded her property. The creature had disappeared into the undergrowth here, she told us, but as it did so it rubbed itself against the tree leaving a revolting stain as if it had been covered with ink. This was too good an opportunity to miss, and so the intrepid team - well, Graham actually, as he is more limber and supple than yours truly - climbed over the wall and negotiated the steep slope to the base of the tree. At the bottom of the slope was what looked suspiciously like an open sewer, and I was very glad that it was Graham, not me who had to avoid falling headfirst into it.

Graham eventually reached the base of the tree, but much to my disappointment he said that there was no sign of any discolouration or stain upon the bark. Mostly for the benefit of the ever-watching cameras (but partly in a vain attempt to secure some sort of specimens) he scraped some bark samples from the base of the tree where our witness and her brother claimed that the stain had once been, and, to preserve some semblance of scientific integrity, took a second bark sample from another part of the tree for use as a control sample.

He then negotiated the slippery slope up to join the rest of us, and we went on to visit our next witness.

We didn't have far to go. She lived next door. She, too, had seen a mysterious creature but was afraid and refused to talk to us. According to Rueben she was a refugee from Colombia and spoke only her own peculiar dialect of Spanish. She was, he claimed (and I have no reason at all to disbelieve him), both highly superstitious and distrustful of both the police and the media. The political background from whence she had come made this last statement highly believable.

She did, however, provide us with a potentially exciting piece of evidence. Although she did not want to talk to us, she was willing to give us a sample of what she claimed was chupacabra dung.

Highly excited I asked for more information, but was somewhat deflated when, on her instructions (shouted through the barred screen-doors as all the way through our conversations she refused to come outside), Rueben took us to a particularly dry and desiccated piece of ground about fifty feet from the front of her house, and pointed skeptically down to the ground below us. There, coiled malevolently were what I assume were some enormous worm casts. Again, more as a matter of form than for any other reason I took some samples (noting some peculiar indentations on the dry ground next to them) and carried them in a specimen jar to the lady of the house who confirmed (through Rueben) that yes, this was what she meant, and would we please now leave her property.

There was obviously nothing more that we could get out of her. I noted at the time, however, that although what we had collected were almost certainly worm casts, the ground on which we found them was baked solid with the sun and was as hard as concrete. When you add to that the fact that during the rest of our stay on the island, although I examined every piece of waste ground that we passed I never saw any other worm casts even remotely resembling the so-called chupacabra dung of Dorado, it is, perhaps fortunate that I took my specimens back to England with us.

Rueben then told us that a few miles away there was a government research station where the corpses of chupacabra victims were taken for analysis and he offered to drive us there. We eagerly agreed, and Graham and I hopped in the back of the police car, and sirens blaring we made our way towards trhe next stage of our investigation.

Unfortunately, when we got there it seemed that our luck had run out. Civil servants are civil servants the world over, and whereas the meek little clerk on the reception desk had been only too happy to talk to his amigo Rueben about the tests that his laboratory had carried out, when he turned up complete with sirens blaring and two van loads of strange Englishmen brandishing TV cameras he decided that discretion was the better part of valour and that he had better refer the whole affair to his supervisor, who in turn referred us to the director of the establishment who was (surprise surprise) playing golf for the day and was therefore uncontactable. The fact that the two security guards who accompanied him pulled guns on us as soon as I began to argue was an added incentive to us to forget about the whole matter.

Giving the whole affair up as a bad job we decided to break for lunch. We said our farewells to Rueben (after filming several establishing shots of him and us driving along in the police car), and as he disappeared off for his afternoon shift we went off to lunch at a particularly fine seafood restaurant on the cliffs overlooking the Atlantic Ocean.

That afternoon we visited a house owned by a man called George who appeared to be a local small-time gangster.

According to the information that we had been given, there had been an attack on over thirty cockerels that had been co-owned by George and his next door neighbour. I will be the first to admit that I have a typically English middle-class stance towards bloodsports and those who practice them, and therefore my sympathies were not altogether with the bereaved farmers. George was the sort of wide-boy who, in he had been English would have lived on the outskirts of somewhere like Harlow New-Town making a living from selling 'dodgy motahs' and 'bent MOTs'. He was not an immediately likeable person but once we had by-passed his air of bravado we could see that he really was frightened. His business partner Oscar described how he had found the birds found killed and drained of blood and how there had been a trail of three-toed footprints leading across the surface of the yard. We examined one of the chickens and there were indeed two massive puncture wounds on the neck and thorax, and the body appeared bloodless. We took feather samples from around the area of the puncture wounds, hoping that subsequent analysis would show some evidence of the mysterious slime (theorised by some to be an anti-coagulant) which has been reported on so many of the chupacabra's victims.

In what - with hindsight - I can see was a remarkable oversight, we had no dissecting implements with us. Neither did we have any formaldehyde, nor indeed anything else that we could have used to preserve soft tissues (unless we were to do so in my precious bottles of duty-free buttered rum). I conducted a makeshift autopsy using a penknife that my ex-father-in-law had given me, and some plastic knives and forks of the sort that people use on picnics. Over the years I have cut up a lot of different animals ranging in size from a woodlouse to a dolphin (which will be described later on in this book). I have never conducted an autopsy on a human, but during my tenure as a nurse I have seen, and handled, human corpses and have assisted in the laying out procedure that takes place whenever a person has died in hospital. I am not squeamish, and although I am not qualified in any proper sense of the word as an anatomist, I do have a certain working knowledge of the internal organs of many species of animal. I can truthfully say that I have never seen a corpse quite like this.

During my childhood in Hong-Kong I examined freshly dead - and not so freshly dead - animals of all types. One thing that they all had uncommon, as all animals which die in the tropics do - is that within minutes of death the micropredators move in. Invertebrates such as blow flies, burrowing beetles, myriopods, Sexton beetles and worms of various types attack the corpse before it is cold, laying their eggs on the surface of the skin, and in some cases burrowing deeper within the body of the animal to feast on the flesh inside and to lay their eggs in order to secure the future of the next generation of their species.

As the unfortunate chicken whose corpse I was now handling had been killed at least 24 hours previously, and had been lying on the ground under a bush since then, I was confident that when I opened it up I would find it a wriggling mass of creepy-crawlies. I was completely wrong. There was absolutely nothing there. The body was completely drained of blood, and there was no break in the connecting membrane between the thoracic and body cavities. When I opened up the body cavity I was appalled to find that the liver was missing. I re examined the body closely. Apart from the two puncture marks in the neck and thorax I could find no other entry or exit wounds. A close examination of the skin found no signs of micro predation at all. The feathers had been fairly seriously chewed at by feather mites, but when I examined a couple of the living fowl which were still awaiting their fate in the cock-fighting arena, I found that to all intents and purposes, at least one species of feather mite seemed to be well-established in the smallholding as the living specimens exhibited the same degree of feather mite predation as the corpse. I asked Graham to go back under the bush from which he had retrieved the corpse to look for any signs of blood or body fluids on the ground. He agreed, albeit reluctantly, because he was otherwise engaged - taking surreptitious video footage of the ample buttocks of the numerous buxom Puerto Rican lasses who were milling about, hoping to get on television. He searched the area under the bush thoroughly and assured me that as it was all very fine and dry dust, any fluid that had been spilled would have shown up immediately.

The problem of the lack of micropredation worried me. In the corner of the farmyard was a rotten log. I kicked it apart and was reassured to see that it was full of small invertebrates of the sort that one would normally have expected it to attack the corpse soon after death. There was also no shortage of flies. One of the policemen we had met that morning had told us that the nickname for Puerto Rico amongst some of his colleagues was "*Isla des Moscas*" (Isle of Flies), rather than the more picturesque "Island of Paradise" which was emblazoned upon all the literature available from the island's tourist board. The only hypothesis that I was able to come up with was that, somehow, whatever had caused the death of the animal had tainted the flesh to such a degree that even the most seemingly insignificant micropredators would ignore it.

That thought chilled me to the marrow, and that night I had great difficulty in getting to sleep.

The next day we had been scheduled to visit a complicated cave system deep in the forests in the mountains and around Aguas Buenas. However, we spent a fruitless morning hanging around in the town square waiting for our contact to turn up. The only person to arrive was the local mayor. No-one in the crew was expecting him, and to this day we have no idea why he arrived at the time that he did. I have a sneaking suspicion that it was because he possessed the unerring talent that is seemingly possessed by politicians everywhere - he had a nose for a good photo opportunity and he availed himself of it. I suppose shaking the hands of two scruffy geezers from England made a difference from kissing babies, and probably won him just as many votes!

Eventually we managed to find our way out of the town, and we made our way through several acres of dusty plantain plantations before we reached what was obviously some sort of Government Depot. It was a low, white bungalow with a red tiled roof and reasonably well-kept gardens that would not really have been out of place in the suburbs of a

Westcountry seaside town like Falmouth. Unlike any suburban villas in southern Cornwall, however, a chain link fence surmounted by rolls of barbed wire surrounded it, and the machine pistols on the belts of the two enormous, uniformed security guards struck a jarring note.

As Tom and Marcus negotiated some complicated deal with the folk from the Civil Defence Graham and I filmed the local lizards that were larger and slightly more fearsome in appearance than those that we had seen in the relatively civilised lowlands of San Juan and its environs. Whilst I was stalking a particularly recalcitrant anolis specimen round and around the tattered trunk of a tall palm tree, Marcus and Norman summoned us, instructed us to get into the van, and together with a large and battered jeep the three vehicles proceeded in some sort of a convoy down a dusty road towards where we were reliably informed, the 'Batcave' could be found.

From what I could gather from the conversation taking place in the front of the van, we were able to drive a certain distance along the road, but would be unable to go any further than a pair of impressively locked and bolted gates, some eight foot tall, that loomed in front of us.

I am not sure what happened next because as has been related at various instances during this narrative, my knowledge of the Spanish language is limited to "*Dos Margueritas por favor*" and "*Hijo de Puta!*" ("Two Margueritas please" and "Son of a Whore!" respectively). During the next few weeks my knowledge of the language increased slightly, to the extent that when we were in the Mexican desert a week or so later I was able to ask exactly how many animals had been killed in a particular Chupacabra incident, but even then, the Spanish for "How much do we have to bribe you in order for one of your guys to take a pair of bolt cutters and cut your way through these chains so we can make a documentary without having to pay an exorbitant sum of money to whichever of the local big bosses wants to charge us for filming here?" was a task far beyond either Graham's or my limited competence.

This is, however, what I gather was being negotiated, and, I suspect (but neither know or care) that some money changed hands, because eventually a tall, ageing and slightly fearsome bloke in a red singlet took a pair of bolt cutters and together with a motley collection of Civil Defence bods (who seemed to materialise as if from nowhere), cut through the bolts allowing us access to the nature reserve (or whatever it was) from whence the forces of law and order had attempted to exclude us.

It was bloody hot. In fact, although I had rapidly acclimatised to the heat on the island, this was probably the hottest day that we had during our stay and before we had even started (what we were reliably informed was) the thirty minute walk to the 'Batcave', my shirt was sticking to my back, and although I still had my trusty Panama hat on my head (it had been bought for me three days before on Norman's insistence that together with an extravagantly phallic cigar it made me look something like Orson Wells), I was beginning to feel too sweaty to be able to preserve the natural dignity of an Englishman abroad. I therefore did what I thought was an extremely clever thing and figuratively hitched a lift (OK I just climbed aboard) the jeep which was taking the equipment over the bumpy roads of the national park (which were far too rugged for the civilised and slightly effete vans that we had been travelling in) to our destination.

"That was clever," I thought. I was convinced that the so-called half hour walk would be completed in about seven minutes slightly bumpy travel, whereupon I could regain my composure in the shade of a convenient tree, and thus look fresh and rested by the time we were ready to film us 'arriving' at the "Batcave".

However the best laid plans of '*Animals & Men*' tend to go (as we said the following week in the desert) "Prickly Pear Shaped".

The 'Batcave' wasn't a half hour stroll from the locked gates as we had been led to believe but was a forty five minute climb up a rocky hillside that sloped at an angle of over forty five degrees in front of us!

I have never made any secret of the fact that I am extremely physically unfit. Let's face it, when you are the size that I am, to try and do so would be a singularly pointless exercise. For too many years now I have eaten too much, drunk too much, smoked too much, ingested too many chemicals and taken practically no physical exercise. Now, suddenly, I was to regret these excesses with the very real possibility that this hillside before me was to be my nemesis.

As a child in Hong Kong I had spent many hours playing on hillsides like this and so the terrain was not at all unfamiliar. However, the prospect of clambering up a slope, the prospect of which was making younger and far more physically fit members of the film crew wince in anticipation, reliving experiences from my childhood thirty years before was not something that I was relishing. However, I was damned if I was going to let anybody realise, and so as far as possible I tried to be 'ahead of the field' as it were and to treat the whole affair with as much nonchalance as I was able.

OK, my stance as leader didn't last more than five minutes and the ascent took me a fair bit longer than it took some (but not all) of the rest of the party, but I did it, and I eventually reached the summit with my honour (and my Panama Hat) relatively intact. About half way through our ascent there was a loud tooting noise from the open area at the bottom of the hill, and, looking down, we could see that reinforcements - in the form of another four Civil defence bods (two of them female) was at hand. This brought the total number of our party who were trespassing upon the Parks Department property to about sixteen.

The two female Civil Defence volunteers were a shapely and beautiful lady called Isabella. She moved with the lithe grace of my cat (with the same name) at home in Exeter, and a wonderful lady called Maria. She was about half my height and of roughly the same build and physical characteristics, making her somewhere between sturdy and circular.

The two of us hit it off immediately, much to the ribald delight of the assembled party, and we flirted outrageously for the rest of the day as we courteously helped each other up slippery rock faces and into the cave. By this time it was starting to rain and the rocks were becoming slippery. As we approached the entrance to the cave it became apparent that all was not well.

A torrent of muffled curses from the technicians at the top of the hill and inside the cave mouth where they were sheltering from the burgeoning rainstorm told Maria, Graham and me that something was amiss. Knowing that, whatever happened, Norman would want to film our final approach to the cave, I sat on a comfortable rock about fifty yards down the hill, offered a cigarette to Maria, lit one myself and stared into the middle distance waiting for something to happen.

Graham went ahead to recce the situation and found out that there was some unexplained fault on the cables which were an integral part of the lighting rig. There was also a second incipient problem. The entrance to the cavern was so small that until we had access to some proper lights it was problematical whether I would be able to get in through the tiny gap. Warren was dispatched down the hill to find a replacement cable and a selection of necessary repair tools, and I still sat on the rock musing on the utter ludicrousness of the situation.

To have made it up the hill unscathed and without even having been particularly more out of breath than the rest of the party was, to me at least, a seriously impressive achievement and I was feeling rather proud of myself. I looked forward to my return to the UK if only so I could tell friends, family and psychiatrists about how I had managed to slay one of my own personal dragons. However, having managed to slay the dragon and lay it (figuratively at least) at my feet and those of my dusky (if rotund) maiden Maria, it seemed as if the whole episode had been completely pointless. If we were not able to actually get into the cave then we might as well have stayed back in the hotel watching "Confessions of a Mad Housewife" on Cable TV.

My mildly pointless reverie was shattered by the arrival of Graham who had been examining the entrance to the cave and was somewhat amused to find out that the Civil Defence folk were using what looked suspiciously like a petrol bomb to illuminate the dark cavern. He followed up this piece of information with an obscure reference to my collection of Irish Rebel songs, which I had taken half way across the world to listen to in my hotel bedroom each night, and then disappeared off into the undergrowth with a cackle.

Within minutes Warren arrived back with the necessary bits of kit and within a very short length of time the essential repairs had been carried out and we were ready to resume filming. Maria and I climbed up the last fifty yards and hugged each other as we reached the summit. We then disappeared into the murky depths of the cave.

Filming being what it is, however, this was far more complicated than it appears. We actually had to go in through the entrance of the cave on five separate occasions being filmed from every conceivable angle before we were allowed to actually enter the cave and explore.

Whereas, as one might expect, we found absolutely no evidence that these caves were haunted by El Chupacabra we did find evidence that showed WHY the local people, riddled as they were by a mixture of peasant superstition, Santeria madness and Roman Catholic guilt could well believe that these caves were, indeed haunted by a monster.

There was evidence that the cave was quite well frequented by the local populace as the walls were covered in graffiti of various types. Even with my limited knowledge of the language it was obvious that ninety percent of what was written on the walls was of the "Ramon Loves Dolores" ilk, but it was equally obvious that other inscriptions were nothing of the kind.

One of the most annoying things about our whole trip is that neither my photographs or Graham's video tape of the carvings that we found inside the cave actually came out. Time will tell whether the Channel Four footage shows anything recognisable, but within only a few yards of the entrance of the cave was a little niche in the rock where it was obvious that candles had been placed in the near past. Above the burned-out candle stubs was what was obviously a fertility symbol carved into the rock. It looked (and this is from memory) very similar to the familiar image of the *Sheela Na Gig* which is found over much of the Celtic world, except for the phallus sticking out of the top of its head. This hermaphroditic deity was obviously a figure of some respect amongst the local people. We asked our valiant guides for an explanation but none was forthcoming although I remain convinced that they knew a great deal more than they were letting on.

There was other evidence that this cave had been used for ritual magick in the relatively recent past, and there was also no doubt that the cave was the haunt of at least three species of bat, one of which was a vampire. Graham was happily filming a cluster of these tiny chiropterids high in one of the niches of the ceiling of the cave above us, when he was startled by a stream of unpleasantly warm liquid pouring down the back of his neck. If anybody was ever in any doubt about Graham's qualifications to be the deputy director of the world's greatest Cryptozoological research organisation, the fact that he has been pissed on by a vampire bat is - I think - a good enough qualification for anybody.

Another species of bat that inhabited these caves was evidently a fruit eater because our guides pointed out some pale and anaemic plants that had apparently grown from the seeds of the Moca plant - a favourite food of the bats that had been excreted onto the ground below their roosts. I collected specimens of some of these Moca nuts and eventually I managed to get them back to the UK. In the early summer I shall try to germinate one of them.

Another of my specimens from this part of our journey was less lucky. In a cleft in the rock I discovered a peculiar looking snail whose shell appeared very much in the guise of a flying saucer. I collected several of these creatures over the next few days, and although my original hypothesis - that they had evolved this peculiar shape so that they could live in the crevasses in the walls of these mountain caves - was disproved when we found specimens of the same species in the open ground at El Yunque rain forest two days later, they were interesting specimens. However, closer examination proved that the snail from the caves was larger, flatter, and unlike its purely vegetarian cousin was habit eat both meat and bat droppings.

I named the two mysterious molluscs Norman and Marcus, after our beloved Director and Producer and managed to keep them alive for several weeks. Unfortunately, however, they expired soon after I got them back (probably totally illegally) to the UK. Sad but true. However, six and a half years later I returned to Puerto Rico, and when I came back to Britain there was a plastic box containing eleven of these singular snails in my hand luggage. We hope that they will be the nucleus for a breeding programme at the CFZ.

After about an hour filming in the caves, our guides pointed out that the rain was coming in quite strongly by this time and by using a series of graphic pieces of pantomime they pointed out that furthermore the rocks on our descent back to the truck would be treacherously slippery if we left our descent much longer. There was a third aspect to our predicament which lent urgency to our departure - it was getting dark. The climb up had been difficult enough in broad daylight but, to go down through a burgeoning sea of mud in the gathering gloom seemed to be an exercise, which was designed to stretch intrepidness beyond reasonable limits, and so we all elected to leave.

Much to my surprise, the descent was somewhat easier than the climb had been and I got back to the bottom of the hill safe and sound to a barrage of cheers from the Civil Defence folk who, by this time I think, had actually got quite fond of me and were busy teasing Maria and me about what they saw as our burgeoning romance. We drove back up the track to the gates and the road with me and the chap in the red singlet (whose name, it turned out was Ernesto), sitting in the front and everyone else packed like sardines into the back. Ernesto sang as he drove, and tried to teach me a complicated refrain of a song (which I later found out) was a lament for someone whose sweetheart had died of an unspecified disease. It was quite a cheerful tune, and although the words were quite beyond me I picked up the melody easily enough and we warbled our way up the hill. My attempts to teach Ernesto *The Rocky Road to Dublin* were almost as successful and although no-one else in the vehicle knew what we were doing we enjoyed ourselves.

When we returned to where we had left the other vehicles the Civil Defence Volunteers invited us to join them at a roadside bar which was, as far as we could gather, their social club. There those who could play pool challenged the locals to game after game of what I must admit I have always seen as a remarkably uninteresting exercise, and the rest of us drank smoked and ate tortillas.

When it was time for us to leave, the men in the party all either hugged me or shook my hand and Maria kissed me goodbye. Joking apart, there was a definite attraction between us and I felt a slight tinge of regret as I realised that I would probably never see her again. Feeling like that most rakish of cryptozoologists - one with a girl in every port - I got into the van next to Graham, waved goodbye to our new-found friends and let Marcus drive us back to San Juan.

The next day we were up in the mountains again with another group from the island's Civil Defence Squad led by a bloke called Ishmael. I have done him a great dis-service. On the face of it he was surly and uncommunicative, but when I returned to the island in 2004 we met again, and I found out that he had merely become completely fed up with the attitude of so many western camera crews who were determined not to take the chupacabra affair seriously. During the week that Nick Redfern and I spent with him in 2004 we soon became quite good friends, and my initial feelings of hostility towards him vanished like the boojum at the end of the poem. As the roads climbed higher it began to rain, and for the first time since we had been on the island we began to feel chilly, but eventually the little convoy of two vans, Rosario's car and the pantechnicon from Hades pulled into a grassy space beneath another hillside, and shuddered to a halt. The mountain loomed above us through the misty rain and, although it was not as immediately impressive as the place we had visited on the previous day it had a far more forebodeing air about it. We disembarked, and almost immediately began our ascent. Unlike the previous day the level of communication between us and our guides was not as easy, and whereas Maria, Ernesto and their friends had been solicitous and supportive of us, here (although this may have just been my paranoia) I felt that our guides were not only sure than "The Fat Gringo" was not going to make it up the mountainside, but were amused at the thought that I wouldn't make it up.

Being a bloody-minded bloke, this made me even more determined to make my way up in as unscathed a manner as possible and also to accept as little help as I could in doing so. Ismael led the way slashing wildly from side to side with his machete as he cut through the undergrowth. The rest of us made our slow ascent up an almost impenetrable slope of boulders, and uninviting undergrowth.

As we climbed the hillside it became rapidly obvious why this place had attracted such an unsavoury reputation. Not only was the terrain itself treacherous in the extreme but, from what I could gather from our guides, it was beset by poisonous snakes of a gigantic size (despite the claims by academics, who should - I think - be believed that there are not only no poisonous snakes on the island but that the largest Puerto Rican snake - The Puerto Rican Boa - only achieves a length of 90 inches) and even the plants were dangerous. Nearing the cave, which was our apparent destination, I discovered a disgustingly beautiful pink parasitic plant which looked like something that could only have been invented by someone like Michael Moorcock. It was an almost translucent pink colour and was slowly and inexorably choking the life from its host.

I paused to look at it and reached out to touch it gingerly. One of our guides shouted at me to stop, but it was too late. As my arm brushed against it I felt a mild stinging sensation, and by the time that we had eventually climbed back to the bottom of the hill my arm was coming up in purplish white blisters. The plant was so beautiful, but so evil looking I managed to get Graham to film it before our guides destroyed it and trampled its remnants into the rocks below. As the crew clambered past us to set up the camera and sound equipment at the mouth of the cave in order to film the final bits of our ascent I sat on a rock to survey the scenery. It was dank and depressing. For the first time during our journey I was wishing I were somewhere else.

The crew seemed to take an interminable length of time to set up their equipment, but finally they finished and Graham and I climbed up the final few yards to the mouth of the cave where, according to Norman's instructions we were supposed to say something profound. I was in a filthy mood by this time, and in no state of mind to be a performing seal for the cameras and so as I finished the ascent I muttered "I wish Sick Tim was here" (a reference to a second-hand car dealer in Torquay who had the biggest collection of hard core pornography that I have ever seen). But Graham - equally disgruntled and as always the master of understatement climbed to the top of the rock, stood atop like a predatory bird, shaded his eyes to look around at the aeons-old rock formations that surrounded it, and summed up his feelings in two concise words: "Interesting stratigraphy!" Norman put his hand over his face and groaned in despair, as the rest of the crew fell about the place laughing. Neither comment summed up the ethos of Livingstonian adventure that Senor Hull had in mind, and for some reason neither made the final edit of the film.

The blokes from the Civil Defence Force glowered at us with disinterest and seemed completely nonplussed by the antics of these loco gringos who had travelled half way across the world to stand on the top of a mountain and talk crap to each other!

Needless to say, although we examined the caves in some detail, there was no evidence whatsoever that this was the lair of a humanoid quasi vampiric entity, or of anything else larger than a domestic cat for that matter. One of the strangest things about Puerto Rico is that no-one seems to know exactly what native mammals there are. Neither the British Museum (Natural History) or the Biology department at Managuez University on the island were able to help me in my quest for a species list, and although a book about the local avifauna stated that there were twenty two indigenous mammal species on the island (of which six were extinct), and which included sixteen species of bat, a more detailed species list was not forthcoming.

Logic dictates that there are probably a few small rodents as well as bats which are indigenous to the island, and I have since found that there are several introduced species, including Asian monkeys (escaped from serum laboratories), mongooses (introduced many years ago to keep down the local rat population), and at least one species of South American opossum (introduced for no apparent reason), but like so much about the island its mammalian fauna remains a mystery. Certainly apart from the bats (of at least three different species) that we saw at Aguas Buenas none of us saw any wild-mammals on the island during our stay. The week before we had arrived Norman saw what he thought was a mongoose at El Yunque but even this was a fleeting glimpse from out of a car window.

There was only one memorable incident during our perilous descent down the mountainside. Ishmael, our intrepid leader had been showing off his agility to impress the fat gringo (who he was sure would fall down a crevasse). At one point he was balancing perilously on a rock making great show of indicating to me the safest route that I could take, when he fell head over heels into a gap in the rocks from whence he had to be rescued by two of his cohorts who giggled and winked at me as they passed him the rope to climb out with.

Needless to say I managed the descent, through landscapes reminiscent of those created by Lord Mongrove in "*Dancers at the End of Time*" unscathed and we soon reached the flat grassy area at the bottom of the hill which is where I noticed the aforementioned blood blisters on my fore arm.

Retreating to a bungalow about fifty yards away, Graham and I hosed ourselves down to remove the last vestiges of whatever poisonous juices had been left on our bodies from our encounter with the virulent parasitic plant on the mountainside, and then we retired to investigate a small stream which flowed down the edge of the grassy field.

Before leaving Exeter I made sure that I had packed a small fishing net in my suitcase and here was my first chance to put it to use. As anyone who has ever known me will affirm, I have an irresistible fascination with investigating ponds and streams. My mother contends that I was doing it as a toddler, and as I approach my fortieth year on this planet, I see no indication that this trait of my personality is going to change.

Darting around the tiny drainage stream I met some old friends.

When I was a child in Hong Kong I used to visit a location, known amongst the local European youths as "Tadpole Pond". There was something about the ethos of ex-pat life in the mid 1960s that prompted us to give a suburban 'home-countiesesque' name to what was essentially a concrete basin built by the Japanese during the Second World War as a source of water for military vehicles. Situated on the hillside above Lugard Road on what was then called Victoria Peak, but what has now probably been given a name far less rediolent of its imperial past when it was the home to generations of senior British Civil Servants, this tiny oasis of water no more than ten square feet in area was the home for a bewildering variety of animals and plants.

I used to mount various fishing expeditions there and night after night I would return home to our flat at Peak Mansions, a mile or so away, clutching various small wriggly things in jam jars, most of which were then deposited in a large aquarium tank in the family hallway.

Probably the most frequent species to be found in my catches were little grey fish that we called "Guppies" although we knew that they were no such thing. In fact it was only many years later that I discovered that they were Mosquito Fish *(Gambusia affinis)*. This species, which is native to the southern states of the USA, has been introduced over much of the world as a control against mosquitos. A typical report comes from Utah where the species has existed now for over six decades:

"In the past years there has only been one type of successful biological control which was the introduction of the mosquitofish, *Gambusia affinis*, a small guppy-like fish that eats mosquito larvae, thus reducing the mosquito populations. In the thirties, the mosquitofish was introduced into the Saratoga warm springs at the north end of Utah Lake. Since that introduction, the tiny fish has established a surviving population in the lake and some of its small tributaries.

At the beginning of each mosquito breeding-season, areas are evaluated for the use of *Gambusia* as a control. Gambusia are planted in ponds, marshes, drains and ditches where the water will not dry up completely, thus killing the fish. Over the years an overwintering population has been established in many aquatic habits throughout the county.

Biological control with the use of *Gambusia affinis* is a working control method. It would be hard to estimate what the mosquito population might be if it were not for the help of this tiny frequently overlooked friend and ally."

I suppose that I shouldn't have been particularly surprised to find a thriving population of these charming (but surprisingly aggresive) little fishes in the drainage stream high up in the Puerto Rico mountains.

I was interested to find out how long these creatures had been living in Puerto Rico. Walter Courtenay, the American Ichthyologist, told me via email that:

"*Gambusia affinis* was introduced into Puerto Rico around 1923. The reference on this introduction is: Hildebrand, S.F. 1934. *An investigation of the fishes and fish cultural possibilities of the fresh waters of Puerto Rico, with recommendations.* Typewritten report to Commissioner of Agriculture and Commerce, Puerto Rico. 38 pp".

We caught one, filmed and photographed it and then let it go again. It was actually months later when I realised the significance of my fishy encounter. Although most of the fishes in the shoal were normal gambusia, a significant number of other fish swimming alongside - whilst obviously closely related - were morphologically different enough to be classified as a different species. Seven years later, despite enormous efforts on my part, I have not be able to identify them and can only conclude that they are some type of mutation amongst the Gambusia population which appears to be unique to the mountain streams which run off from the El Yunque rain forest.

Later that day I encountered another strange fish - which coincidently was also very similar to one that I had known in my childhood. We were sitting on the banks of the slow-moving river that runs near to the town of Canovenas, which has been noted for the last decade as being the epicenter of chupacabra activity on Puerto Rico. Norman had decided in his infinite wisdom to interview Graham and me separately before we left the island. We both realised that he was doing his best to get each of us to slag the other off for the cameras. As we had singularly failed to catch the chupacabra during our week-long sojourn (as I had been quite certain that we would), and as - due to a series of misadventures - many of the planned encounters with chupacabra-related celebrities had singularly failed to happen, and thus both Graham and I had flatly refuse to attend a cockfight, there was a marked lack of action in the film so far. Norman was determined to change that by staging a fight between Graham and me. We were equally determined that this was not gonna happen.

While Norman interviewed Graham with a series of leading questions designed specifically to provoke conflict between us, I got bored and went off to investigate the aquatic life of the river.

As anyone who has known me for any length of time will tell you, there is an innate attraction between me and running water which has taken up large parts of my life since I was a small child. I have never been able to pass a river or stream without inbvestigating its depths, net in hand, in search of whatever fauna and flora lurk within. This little river was no exception.

I rolled up my trouser legs and went paddling. Unlike the situation in the rain forest high above us there was no shortage of small life in the water. I noted at least three speies of fresh water shrimps and several species of tiny armoured catfish. I have been an amateur aquarist for many years and it was an extraordinary experience to see Corydoras catfish - little creatures commonly kept as pets, and on sale in high streets across the United Kingdom in the wild. In the deeper water to my right I saw some larger fish but most interestingly from my point of view - I caught a lamprey.

Lampreys have always been of particular interest to me. They are amongst the most primitive of vertebrates and have fascinated me now for nearly three decades. The Encarta Encyclopaedia describes them:

Lamprey, common name for any of about 40 species of smooth-skinned, eel-like, jawless fishes. Lampreys are widely distributed in the streams and seas of temperate and subarctic regions worldwide, except for waters off southern Africa. Adult forms of parasitic species live on the blood of fishes and sometimes devastate fisheries. Like the related hagfish, the lamprey has a pistonlike tongue that creates suction when the mouth is placed against an object. Numerous small teeth on the mouth and tongue pierce the flesh of fishes. The animal has no bony skeleton, its chief support being a flexible cartilaginous rod.

All lampreys breed by ascending freshwater streams to spawn once before wasting away and dying in two to three months. Eggs hatch in two to three weeks. The blind and toothless larvae burrow in the mud, straining water through their mouths to capture small life forms for food. The larva is so unlike the adult that scientists formerly believed it to be a member of a special genus (Ammocoetes). It remains in the mud for at least four years before undergoing a metamorphosis and departing for its adult habitat. Adults are about 91 cm (about 36 in) long.

The problem is that like any cursory description this one leaves out more than it includes. I find these tiny creatures fascinating and their macabre zoology perfectly mirrors the lifestyle of the more esoteric paranormal entities that I have also dedicated much of my life to searching for. I seem to have an innate fascination for blood-suckers (whether they be of the undead or the parasitic type), and the fact that I found a well-grown lamprey in a stream in chupacabra country seemed like a good omen for the next part of our journey.

I watched it for about ten minutes. It was about eight inches in length and an olive greenish colour. It hung on to the algae covered rocks with its sucker, and moved like a tendril of some bizarre water weed in the current of the stream. It was perfectly adapted to its environment and I wished that I could have stayed there longer to observe it. It is one of the worse parts of going on expeditions is that whilst you are in a certain place your time is so limited that you are unable to carry out all the tangential investigations which tempt you at every turn. One such tangential investigation that I was forced to forsake was that of the musical aspects of the Santeria cults on the island and another (and probably more important) was the ecology of this peculiar little jawless fish.

It was only when I returned to the United Kingdom that I realised quite how important my sighting had been because, search as I did, I was unable to find any references to Puerto Rican lampreys in any of the available literature either in zoological libraries or on the Internet. I spoke to some of the local people on the subject but none of them had more than the slightest inkling what I was actually talking about. This shouldn't really have surprised me because as I have noted in my memoir of the expedition, the people of Puerto Rico are not noted for their zoological knowledge.

I contacted Dean A.Hendrickson, Curator of Ichthyology at the Texas Natural History Collection (a division of Texas Memorial Museum) to see if he could help me solve the mystery of the Puerto Rican lamprey:

Dear Sir,

I am a zoological researcher from the UK. I was in Puerto Rico earlier this year and I caught a lamprey in one of the lowland streams near Canovenas. I was unable to identify the species.

I have been unable to find a species list of Puerto Rican fishes, and I would be grateful if you could tell me what species of lampreys live on the island.

Yours sincerely,

Jonathan Downes
The Centre for Fortean Zoology

One of the most fantastic things about the advent of email for the fortean (or indeed any other sort of) researcher is that it gives you almost instant access to information. When I was writing *"The Smaller Mystery Carnivores of The Westcountry"*

(1996) I was reliant on writing letters and sending them the 'old fashioned way'. In many instances this would mean a delay of two or three weeks in order to gain even a tiny and relatively unimportant piece of information. When you consider that this was usually when the letters were written to people who were not only living in the same country as me but often only within thirty miles of my house, you can imagine my frustration. The advent of the Internet has allowed almost instant access to information. I emailed Dean Hendrickson at lunchtime, went out to do my weekly food shopping, and had the spark plugs on my car changed, and by the time that I returned his reply was awaiting me. It was, however, not as helpful as I had hoped:

I too don't have ready access to any "fishes of" publications for Puerto Rico, so can't help with the lamprey (I'd be interested to learn what it turns out to be, however).

I then contacted another renowned American Ichthyologist, Karsten Hartel, who replied to me:

Dear Jon:

There are no records of lamprey from the Caribbean that I know about, especially in fresh water. Was the specimen an adult? If so how big? Did you save the specimen? I'm quite sure the specimen must have been an eel of some kind.

I'm sending a copy of this to Dr. Hensley at UPR.

My reply was simple:

Hi

The lamprey was an adult rather than an ammocaete. It was very similar in appearance to the European Lampetra planeri although a little larger. It was about seven inchews in length and about half an inch thick, and olive green-brown with black eyes, a sucking, circular mouth, black eyes and a row of gill slits. I observed it sucking onto a rock in the strong current in the middle of the river. Unfotunately I did not secure the specimen as I did not realise that it was anything unusual. I was making a documentary for British TV on a completely unrelated subject.

I would, however, be interested in descriptions of whatever freshwater eels there are in the area, but I am certain that it was not an eel.

Jon Downes

In the absence of any other information I have to therefore conclude that the CFZ may indeed have come across a new species of animal during its sojourn on the Island of Paradise - a hitherto unsuspected species of petromyzonid. However the search amongst the internecine archives of the sacred groves of academe continues and we hope that the mystery will soon be solved. If not, it will be one of our first priorities on our return to the island, for return we are most definitely going to do.

A few days later we flew to Mexico.

I fell in love with Mexico within minutes of landing. The ethos of the place was completely alien to anywhere else that I had ever visited, and its bizarre range of cross-cultural influences made it a fascinating and bewitching land. I was immediately entranced and became determined to find out as much as I could about its culture and its history. Almost uniquely, however, amongst places that I visited I found it impossible to find a guidebook of any substance written in English. Despite the popular conception of Mexico as a third world country in social and economic thrall to its northern neighbours, Mexico is fiercely independent. English is not only very much a foreign language but also it is one that is rarely if ever spoken.

For reasons best known to themselves the travel agents back in the UK had booked us into a particularly seedy hotel in one of the worst parts of town. As we drove through the scenes of urban deprivation of this particularly insalubrious portion of Mexico City (which were slightly reminiscent of some of the seedier locations in one of the Batman movies) all of us were feeling somewhat perturbed.

When we finally pulled up at the hotel to be greeted by a Neanderthal thug twirling a nightstick impressively as he glowered in our general direction, and when we realised that this was the security guard cum hall-porter, the crew as a man refused to stay there. Graham and I kept our peace in the back of the car and let the others fight our battles for us, but were greatly relieved when after about ten minutes of negotiation in Spanish between the crew and one of our swarthy drivers (whose brother in law was apparently the concierge at a better hotel somewhere else in the city), we drove off in search of pastures new.

An hour or so, (and three hotels later) we eventually ended up at The Imperial Hotel in the middle of Mexico City. According to its web site it was...

Inaugurated in 1904 by President Porfirio Díaz, the hotel was considered one of the most elegant in the city and was for a while one of the tallest buildings!

During his period in office (1914-20), President Venustiano Carranza lived in the hotel, and a few years later one of his successors, Alvaro Obregón, was assassinated shortly after leaving the premises for an engagement.

Years later the building became the offices for the American Embassy (now situated in Rio Danubio, further down the Reforma).

Renovated many times in its lifetime, the building opened its doors once more, as a five star hotel, in 1989.

However this luxurious edifice was a long way from the popular conception of the conditions that two intrepid cryptozoologists should have been living under during their expedition to "The Ends of The Earth" and it was this dichotomy between reality and perception that was to cause poor old Norman Hull a number of headaches over the next week that we were in the country. How could he portray us as intrepid when we were having twenty-four ounce steaks, cactus salad and glorious red wine sent up to our rooms by room service? However all this was in the future. We had just arrived in a new country and as he had promised me back in London it was time to introduce me to possibly the greatest piece of Mexico's cultural heritage - The Margarita!

Graham and I soon became addicted to this glorious concoction, and on our return to the UK we were determined to recreate our culinary experience. By dint of trial and error we eventually managed to achieve an approximation of the drink that we had grown to love so much on the opposite side of the Atlantic Ocean.

However we must now go back to the bar of the Imperial Hotel in Mexico. Graham and I were sitting in a happy daze of tequlia and waiting for something to happen when suddenly we noticed that our party had been augmented by an extremely pretty girl of indeterminate years (but some years younger than me). She had shoulder length curly hair of a bronzeish hue and was carrying a clipboard. It turned out that she was Gina - our Mexican travel guide, interpreter and general Ms Fixit who was to be an integral part of our adventures over the next few weeks.

Graham and I were feeling reasonably intrepid at this point and so, eschewing further alcoholic indulgences we decided to leave the rest of the party in the bar and to go wandering through the streets of Mexico City. For reasons partly to do with an innate caution and mostly to do with laziness we didn't bother to roam more than a couple of blocks from the hotel, but even this was a journey fraught with adventure (albeit adventure of a relatively restrained type).

As we wandered through the dark streets, deserted apart from small gaggles of slightly disturbing looking youths with Zapata moustaches and skateboards who seemed to melt into the darkness at our approach we began to grok Mexico City in its fullness.

It was incredibly quiet. Despite being before midnight in what is after all the biggest city in the world, and also being in an area full of hotels, bars and restaurants there was hardly any noise. Even in Exeter at 'chucking out time' the streets are full of gangs of noisy and relatively cheerful revelers waiting for their taxi home or queuing up outside a mobile hamburger stall, and having just flown from San Juan where the noise and smell of the tropical night in a city full of nightlife was all pervasive this was mildly disconcerting. Whereas in Puerto Rico the streets would have been full of people sitting at pavement bars listening to an addictive mixture of Latin American rhythms and quasi-European pop music here the only people to be seen were the aforementioned groups of youths who despite their fearsome appearance (fearsome, that is, to two 'locos gringos' from Exeter who had been forewarned by the tourist guides that Mexico City was full of pickpockets and footpads), seemed more wary of us than we were of them.

It was only days later that we realised that our appearance - two wild eyed Europeans, both well over six foot in height, (most of the locals were significantly shorter than us), one grossly overweight and the other sporting the sort of crew cut usually associated with convicts or football hooligans - must have been off-putting to say the least. Whereas after a few days in the country we would cheerfully wish the people we met *"buenos noches"* (in appallingly accented Spanish), on our first night in the country we were slinking around nervously and must have presented a most fearsome, nay offputting appearance.

Another reason for the almost unearthly silence was the complete absence of wildlife noises. Everywhere else that I have ever been in the tropics the sounds of crickets and treefrogs is an all pervasive background to the nighttime experience. Here, despite being well within the tropical regions there was nothing. Whether this absence of zoofauna was due to the pollution (apparently some of the worst in the world) or the cold (despite being in the tropics it was decidedly chilly - probably because we were so high above sea level) I don't know but during our time in Mexico City itself we saw no insects or herpetofauna at all.

The only animals that were to be seen were several packs of (what we can only assume were) semi-wild dogs, which seemed to be found wherever we went in the city. Even these peculiar long-haired canids, which were like a cross between a husky and a chow, were spectacularly inactive. They just sat there and did nothing with aplomb and flair.

Graham has a great fondness for domestic cats and dogs, and I know that he had found the generally poor condition of the cats which roamed the back streets of Old San Juan particularly distressing. As always when confronted by a dog or a cat his first instinct was to run up to it to make friends. As we were passing down the left hand side of the "Plaza de Revolucion" Graham caught sight of a group of three or four of these shaggy street dogs enjoying a dust bath beneath the branches of a rather shabby looking bush. He went across to introduce himself to them, and to this day I don't know whether it was his incipient good sense or my cry of "Don't be a bloody fool - Rabies!" that deterred him from making what was potentially a very stupid (and potentially fatal) mistake.

During our first days in Mexico we met and interviewed a number of chupacabra experts and one thing soon became very obvious. The tradition of vampiric attacks on livestock in Mexico went back hundreds of years, and it has only been in the previous two or three years that they had been attributed to the chupacabra. Indeed, even the earliest so-called chupacabra attacks had been blamed on a mysterious winged big cat, and it was not until after the events of 1995 when the - by now - ubiquitous image of the kangaroo like creature from Puerto Rico was splashed across the world's media that anybody (mostly self-styled UFO experts), started to draw the inference that the two sets of incidents were even slightly related.

It was only days later that we realised that there had been an important piece of evidence staring us in the face all along. Dotted across Mexico City are some glorious pieces of baroque architecture including some extraordinarily ornate pieces of sculpture. In several locations there are statues of Mexican Military heroes who presumably occupy the same place in the pantheon of military history of their country as do Nelson and Wellington to the British. In at least three locations these statues are flanked with statues of lions like those at Nelson's Column in London. Unlike those at Nelson's column they sport stylised wings and strange manes similar to the mohican haircut once sported by a Scottish bloke called 'Wattie' who used to sing with a long defunct punk band called "*The Exploited*".

Before dismissing this connection we should, I think, examine the possibility that these statues are renditions, albeit stylised, of a REAL creature. The two features, which set them apart from any of the KNOWN species of New World felid, are the Wings and the Mane.

Although my friend and colleague Dr Karl Shuker has successfully shown that there is some substance to the folkloric accounts of cats with wings, (they are in fact cats suffering from a rare and obscure skin disease), no-one has to my knowledge at least ever suggested that this condition has ever effected any of the larger felids. The wings, might, however be a heraldic stylisation.

Is there any evidence that there are (or have ever been) any MANED big cats in the new world? Certainly neither pumas nor jaguars sport such an adornment. American cryptozoological researcher Mark Hall has produced quite a body of evidence to suggest that the long extinct American Lion *(Panthera leo atrox)* may have survived to the present day in parts of North America.

It is very tempting so theorise that we are looking for a new species of flesh and blood felid. A bona fide cryptid that has eluded recognition by the scientists of orthodox zoology and which has come back from a primordial past to attack livestock in present day Mexico. It seems more likely, however, that the heraldic beasts that can be seen by every visitor to Mexico City are more likely to be a stylised representation of one of the archetypes from the Mexican psyche than an accurate depiction of a living creature. The link does, however remain and it is very notable that the animals described to us as being responsible for the earliest chupacabra attacks in the country are so similar to those which have been immortalised in statuary across the nation's capital.

After a few more days in the flesh pots of the capital the expedition moved down to the Puebla Desert, where we uncovered what was possibly the most unpleasant piece of evidence that I have ever found in a crypto-investigative mission.

On our last evening in the capital as we were driving back through the traffic jams of a Mexico City rush hour we were stopped repeatedly by small children who tried to sell us knick knacks, cigarettes, sweets and comic books. They would rush up to the car each time we stopped at a traffic light, rap on the window with a stick and thrust their wares in for our perusal. One of the most commonly seen items of merchandise was a crudely made rubber facemask of a sinister looking bloke with a tiny moustache. We asked Gina - our very attractive young interpreter - who this was, and she replied with a smile that "You ask many Mexicans and they will say that THIS is the REAL chupacabra". It was a crude caricature of former president Carlos Salinas de Gortari - who had absconded to Dublin some eighteen months previously with his young mistress, leaving the country very nearly bankrupt.

This led onto a discussion about Mexican politics where Gina tried to explain to us the genesis of the FZLN Separatist movement under the notorious Subcommandante Marcos (more of whom later). I have always been interested in political folksongs and I asked Gina whether there were any FZLN folk songs. She didn't know what I meant, so in an attempt at illustration I told her a little about the 'troubles' in Northern Ireland and sung her a few bars of a song called *Rifles of the IRA*:

"In Nineteen hundred and Sixteen, the forces of the crown,
For to capture orange white and green bombarded London Town,
and in 'twenty one, Britannia's Huns, were up to earn their pay
when the black and tans like lightning ran from the rifles of the IRA".....

She quickly got the point and sang me a verse of a song which I believe was entitled *"Hang El Presidente"* (or something of the sort), and I was amused at the thought that if the TV cameras had been on us each of us had committed high treason by the laws of our own countries. On our return to the hotel I tried to persuade Norman Hull that a re-enactment of this episode would make a fine addition to the TV show but he was unimpressed.

Tired and hungry we dropped Gina at her flat and the rest of us went back to the hotel where we ate a huge meal, drank too much beer and eventually retired to our rooms. When I entered my abode I noticed with a smile that my snails were happily climbing over the makeshift cage that I had made them out of two Imperial Hotel cut-glass punch-bowls, and it wasn't until after I had showered and was just about to go to sleep when I realised that the red light on my telephone was flashing signifying that there was a telephone message for me.

I accessed the answerphone message, which turned out to be in very broken English from someone who didn't give either a name or a return number. From what I could gather he was claiming that he had information about the famous Mexico City UFO videos that had been made famous the previous year. He was claiming (or at least this is what I THINK he was claiming) that the Government who were desperate to convince the gullible peasantry that the "Space People" were on their side rather than on the side of the FZLN Separatists had fabricated them. He said that he would telephone again but needless to say he never did.

The first part of our journey to Puebla was unspectacular. We drove through miles upon miles of drab, uninteresting suburbs which got more drab and uninteresting the further we journeyed. Then, imperceptibly, we entered some equally drab and uninteresting countryside and, although the back of the Chevrolet Suburban was cramped and uncomfortable, I fell asleep. When I awoke we were approaching the mountain pass, which drives through the foothills of the volcano Popocatepetl. As the road climbed higher it twisted and turned through the foothills of the two mountains and all of a sudden the scenery changed. The lower reaches of the volcano were covered in peculiar stunted trees, which if it hadn't been for the fact that they all sported straggly "beards" of Spanish Moss and strange epiphytic plants (that I think were orchids) looked for all the world like the strange stunted oak trees that are found by the roadsides in my native North Devon. I have no pretentions of any kind to being a botanist so whether like their Devonshire counterparts their peculiar appearance is caused by the relentless buffeting of the wind, or whether it is an inevitable by product of the thin, black volcanic soil and the sulphurous atmosphere I don't know.

Whatever its provenance, the landscape is unforgettable, and to be driving through it on the way to interview people who have had first hand experiences of vampires which have turned innocent farm animals into "bloodless zombies" is one of the fondest memories that I have gathered over the last thirty nine years! There are times that I wish that I had not turned my back upon the more conventional aspects of the work ethic, and that I long for a respectable middle-class existence in suburbia, but moments like this re-affirm my faith in my chosen path and remind me that when I had a "proper" job and an "ordinary" existence I hated it, and that the way I have decided to live my life is, indeed, the right one for me!

As we drove down the hill on the other side of the pass we could see the City of Puebla spread out below us. Legend has it that Puebla's founder, the Bishop of Tlaxcala, saw the city's site revealed to him in a dream and I will refrain from saying that it must have been a pretty dull one, because whilst the major part of the city is unremarkable some of the older bits, especially the churches and monasteries are remarkably beautiful,

I am afraid, however, that most of my impressions of Puebla were not particularly favourable. At the centre of the town was a huge public square in which was a large car park surrounded on three sides by cafes and shops. It was uncomfortably hot and, I am afraid to say, completely unremarkable. We stopped for lunch, and then made our way through dusty streets, each completely indistinguishable from each other to an expensive looking motel complex situated on the outskirts of the town. This was the Hotel El Mesón del Angel, where we hung around in the car park waiting for our next contact - a vet called Soledad de la Pena.

After we had been waiting for about half an hour there was a screech of brakes and a large American pick-up truck (or jeep - I never know the difference between them) pulled into the dusty car park. I had spent the intervening thirty minutes watching lizards and humming birds and trying not to think of cold drinks and a soft bed, and was shaken out of my self-indulgent reverie by Tom who came to tell us that both our next witness, and our new car had arrived.

For reasons partly to do with budgetary constraints and partly to do with the film director seeing the obvious comic potential in the scenario of "fat bloke in small car", it had been decided that we were going to be driving a tiny WV Beetle during our stay in Mexico. To be fair, the VW Beetle is almost the national car of Mexico - indeed I believe that it is the only country that this classic car first commissioned by Adolf Hitler six decades ago is still manufactured. (Here is should state for completeness's sake that a scathing comment on one VW web site was that one correspondent heard that you couldn't legally export the Mexican VW's to the USA "because they don't pass the pollution laws and the five mile an hour crash test". At the time we thankfully were unaware of these strictures and so we blithely got in and drove away. There was a slight problem almost immediately. Although I had just about mastered the skill of driving on what was for me the "wrong" side of the road whilst in Puerto Rico I couldn't find reverse gear and so for several days the only way that I could get the car to go backwards was to stop, get into neutral and have Graham push me backwards!

Norman, being the fine director that he was (and is) found this seriously funny and made us do it for one particular sequence as we were pulling up outside Soledad's house. This led to his second major mishap of the expedition. The first had taken place on our last day in Puerto Rico when, just before filming the interview with Graham as I was wandering about the lowland river looking at "lampreys that don't exist" he fell into the river spoiling his camera and one of the walkie-talkies. On this occasion he was meticulous in setting up the shot he wanted. He carefully positioned the camera and sound equipment and placed Warren at a point about ten yards out of shot to show us where to stop. We drove into shot and out again as requested, shuddered to a halt at exactly the right place, whereupon I switched off the engine and Graham disembarked to push me backwards. This all went perfectly until Norman failed to signal for me to stop in time and I almost ran him over, knocking him to the ground!

Luckily no harm was done to him, and apparently the rushes of that particular sequence caused great merriment to everyone concerned once the film arrived back in England. The edited version of this sequence looked great and made it to the final version of the film. However the light amusement of the day was over and we were ready, after what had, by anyone's standards, been a most grueling day, to get on with the veritable meat and potatoes of investigation for Soledad de la Pena - a vet who had examined three sheep which in Jaime Maussan's words had been turned into "bloodless zombies" by the chupacabra.

As always it took an inordinate length of time to set up all the equipment in Soledad's sitting room. She lived in a very modern 'ranch-style' house that unusually for all the houses that we visited during our three weeks away from home was actually relatively familiar in both architectural style and furnishing. It could have been the abode of a relatively well to do vet (with mildly alternative tastes in furnishing and decoration) from anywhere in the world. Soledad herself also looked refreshingly familiar; a smartly dressed middle-aged woman with collar length hair wearing jeans and cowboy boots. She chainsmoked and passed around bottles of chilled lager and little glasses of Mezcal as a chaser. (For those not in the know Mezcal is a similar drink to Tequila but somewhat heavier and more potent).

Eventually the crews were ready for us, and I interviewed her (using Gina as a translator) and she told us a remarkable and chilling story. From what I could gather at the time, and from what I've been able to corroborate in the intervening years, in the years immediately following the departure of President Carlos Salinas de Gortari, the social and economic structure of the country changed dramatically. As far as I have been able to ascertain massive loans from the International Monetary Fund and from foreign investors flooded into the country's Exchequer and set Mexico firmly on the road to solvency. I believe that one of the conditions of these loans was that the Mexican government would set up the first proper welfare system for the country's farmers. One of the new benefits of the system was that farmers could claim a modicum of insurance when their stock had been killed accidentally. As a result of this state appointed vets such as Soledad de la Pena would visit farms where such deaths had taken place in order to validate the insurance claim process.

Apparently in the July of 1996 she had been called to a smallholding owned by a farmer called Dom Pedro. A mysterious predator had attacked three of his sheep, but unusually for alleged chupacabra victims at least one of them was still alive. By the time she got to the figurative scene of the crime it was at least twelve hours after the attacks had taken place and what she found was so shocking and disturbing that if it had not been for the fact that we saw actual video evidence of her examination of the hapless beasts we would most certainly not have believed her.

Even now I find this episode, perhaps the most disturbing one that I have ever investigated, and certainly the most inexplicable because I can come up with no biological explanation whatsoever for the evidence that she found.

The sheep that was the subject of the video had been completely drained of blood. The video shows Soledad putting her hand (encased in a white glove) through an enormous hole in the chest of the creature and apparently reaching into the thoracic cavity itself. As she withdrew her hand, the glove had no more than tiny traces of blood upon it. She told us, in a tremulous voice that the animal had been entirely drained of blood. Because of the total exsanguination the animal's heart was not beating, and the animal was not breathing however, in defiance of all the rules of biological science it was still alive.

She noted that there were two holes, one drilled completely through the bones of the rib cage and that certain of the internal organs (and here my lack of Spanish was a great disadvantage because Gina's English was not up to my asking complicated pathological questions) including (as far as I could gather) the liver itself! The autopsy report had been given to Jaime Maussan who was planning to publish it together with other documents relating to the case.

She told me that she had no explanation for this at all, at least not one that fitted within a recognised framework of known physiology. She was particularly interested in this case because she was not only a vet but was also a recognised expert in UFOs and other paranormal phenomena. After we had concluded the interview and she had shown us the videotape of the unfortunate sheep she then showed us a selection of video tapes of UFOs flying over Popocatepetl itself.

Then came the jackpot. Although we had only been scheduled to film with her for a couple of hours and had intended to spend the rest of the day driving south towards Jalapa to rendezevous with Dr Palmeros, she offered, completely out of the blue, to take us to Dom Pedro's farmyard itself, and although Norman was initially loath to deviate from the present plan he reluctantly agreed to go. I am very glad that he did so because the film we took there proved to be the highlight of the resulting documentary.

Soledad took us by a circuitous route to one of the less salubrious suburbs of Puebla where the attack had taken place. As we drove towards Dom Pedro's farm, I, for one, was appalled by the level of poverty I was seeing. In my native North Devon there are some relatively disued farm tracks, which are full of potholes and have deep gullies where successive generations of tractors have eroded the primitive road surface. In Mexico we found ourselves driving down a very similar road but this was actually the main street of this particular suburb. We noted several dead dogs lying beside the road, and in one particularly insalubrious byway we saw what looked suspiciously like an open sewer. Later, after we had met, interviewed and said our goodbyes to Dom Pedro. David Hall was in the car with us as we drove up and down the road recording wildtracks to go over a montage of GV's (general views) of the area. He asked us to talk about what we saw and was (I am afraid) mildly appalled when I said that it was by far the biggest shithole that I have ever visited. I found it impossible not to be appalled at the squalor and level of poverty that some of these people had been forced to live in. I know that David thought that I was being overly judgmental but I wasn't. I have been to some pretty squalid places in my time, but there was something about the sheer desolation of this particular suburb of Puebla that affected me badly.

It seemed somehow more desolate and forlorn than any other Third World township that I have visited. I am used to the uncomfortable sights of a community living in appalling poverty. However, in my experience, wherever you go - somewhere - you will see a spark of passion, or ingenuity, or one of the other things that defines the human condition. Here - although it was pretty enough in parts - the whole community had become shrouded in an indefinable air of menace, horror, and despair. At the top of the street you could see two small children - little girls aged seven or eight - plying their trade as prostitutes. The people shambled up and down the street with dull, dead eyes as if they were privy to an appalling secret, which has too much for them to bear, and too much to even share with anyone else. The only sign of affluence that I saw that afternoon was a fleeting glimpse of a large black Cadillac with four motorcycle outriders. It was - so we were told - the parish priest (a Roman Catholic of course) and his 15 year-old mistresses paying an ever-so-brief visit to their flock.

Dom Pedro's house was, at least from the road, one of the best-kept and nicest abodes in the village. It was a long, low building painted the sort of washed out green colour that in England at least is usually associated with hospitals for the criminally insane, but which under the searing tropical sun was surprisingly attractive. There were various flowering shrubs growing outside and the flowerbed, which ran in a narrow strip against the wall, was well kept and colourful. As we turned into the farmyard itself, however, it was a different story. The biggest and most noticeable feature of the vista, which greeted our gaze, was a huge steaming dung heap upon which a motley collection of bantams and domestic fowl scurried about busily. Along one side of the farmyard (which was no more than thirty square yards in area) was an extremely squalid cow shed in which several scrawny Friesian cows, covered with scabs and galls and with some rather unpleasant looking growths on their udders stood nervously chewing at some straggly pieces of hay.

In one corner was a tiny brick cell with a barred gate as a door in which a large and sullen pig stood chomping at the metal door and scowling menacingly at us. There was hardly enough room for it to turn around, and although I ceased being a vegetarian several years ago, all my very British views on animal welfare came to the surface. However, we were not only strangers in a strange land but we were guests in someone else's farmyard and it was not my place to bring my middle class English views on the subject to bear.

Perched on a strange brick platform about ten feet above the pig was a scrawny looking dog which whined and yapped unhappily at us. I looked at it sadly and thought of my own dog Toby far away in Exeter, and whatever guilt I had been feeling about having left him in kennels for three weeks whilst Graham and I gallivanted around Central America vanished out of the figurative window.

In the event there was little that Dom Pedro could tell us that we had not already gathered either from Soledad or from Jaime Maussan, but it was both awe inspiring and surprisingly unnerving to actually be in the location that the attacks had taken place. Probably the most important thing about our visit was the sight of the huge painted crucifixes which even two years after the event were still bedaubed over the walls of the farmyard. Later we found that although the attack at Dom Pedro's had been an isolated one the whole community had been affected by the collective fear of such a horrific event and most of the other houses in the immediate vicinity were also daubed with similar crosses. My Spanish is (as anyone who has read this narrative so far will be aware) pretty grim, but even I could understand when told that the huge white crosses were *"por protectione de vampiros"*.

Wondering about the official viewpoint of the local church to these attacks (something which for various reasons we didn't have the chance to explore in more depth) I asked Dom Pedro who had advised him to paint the crosses on the wall. I had assumed that the parish priest had been responsible, but we were told that the villagers had all decided upon this action for themselves and that the established church had refused to get involved.

We finished filming and out of the corner of my eye I saw Dom Pedro's wife approaching us with a huge jug of milk and some glasses. Having seen the condition of the udders of the poor unfortunate cows in his farmyard I decided that discretion was the better part of valour, and managed to (in the best traditions of tabloid journalism) "make my excuses and leave" before being put in the position of having to cause great offence by refusing the proffered drink. I disappeared off to a far flung corner of the yard ostensibly to take photographs leaving the rest of the assembled company to drink the milk (which was apparently delicious but which I suspect caused a number of stomach upsets amongst various members of the crew).

After we said goodbye to Dom Pedro came the tedious business of filming endless establishing shots and scenic views of me and Graham driving up and down the street, and doing our best to avoid the potholes. By this time I had managed to master the controls of the car reasonably well and had even managed to get into reverse gear without difficulty. For the sake of the record I would like to say that the piece in the finished film, which appears to show me grinding the gears in a dastardly fashion, was in fact Nick Plowright and was done purely for effect. Never mind, in view of everything that Nick did for us during our three-week adventure I forgive him entirely because it did make for an extremely funny sequence in the finished film!

During our desultory drives around the back streets of Puebla, Graham and I noticed several stray dogs which looked suspiciously like coyotes and had such a mean expression on their jowls that even Graham was not tempted to try and make friends with them. By the time we had finished it was approaching dusk, and as Graham and I were parked up, having a crafty smoke and gazing out of the window at the huge volcano silhouetted against the most glorious sunset that I have ever seen (Graham with customary drollness describing it as "interesting particular distribution from the volcano"), we heard the most extraordinary noise. From somewhere behind us came the loud rattling of an internal combustion engine, which sounded like it belonged to an entire division of Armoured Cars. Overlaid on top of this unholy row was the sound of someone shouting excitedly in Spanish. It sounded like a call to arms, and mindful of the then current political situation we swiftly wound up the windows (as if that would have done us any good against a hail of machine gun bullets) and looked around nervously.

Instead of an approaching armoured column manned by an elite squadron of FZLN guerillas all armed to the teeth and ready for action we saw a dilapidated estate car with a rough and ready loudspeaker lashed to the roof. In the back were some open crates containing a selection of rather dusty fruit and vegetables. It was no armed insurrection, merely an itinerant greengrocer going about his lawful (and presumably legitimate) business.

I looked at Graham and grinned. "Truly", as I told Marcus later that evening during our journey back to civilisation, "we were, as the name of the series that we were contributing to proclaimed at the ends of the earth".

As always, when I was being particularly pompous (which with hindsight I think that I most probably was), Marcus brought me down to earth with a bump! This time he did it by pointing out, on a street corner only a few yards away from us, a sight which could have come from any of half a dozen places in my home town of Exeter - a very suburban and ordinary looking kebab shop. We all laughed and drove back to the hotel.

We spent several more days in the vicinity. I would like to say that we are engaged in hardcore Cryptozoological activity, but in fact we were involved in the very tedious process of making a documentary film. We had a number of amusing misadventures, which are chronicled, in my book *"Only Fools and Goatsuckers"*, but for the purposes of this narrative only one more thing of any great importance happened during our stay in Mexico. It was on our last day - as we were driving back to the capital.

As we were driving through the outskirts of the Puebla desert on our way back to Mexico City, there was a strong wind blowing off the high sierras, and we were soon driving through the middle of a dust-storm. Obeying the worst precepts of "Murphy's Law", the car began to shudder and an ominous bumping could be felt as we drove along. Pulling rapidly into the roadside verge - a swathe of sun-baked earth littered with empty oil-cans, we quickly disembarked to investigate. Our front, right hand tyre had developed a puncture and was completely flat.

Well, that's what is supposed to have happened. What ACTUALLY happened was that we were driving along through a dust-storm as previously stated when Norman (in his infinite wisdom) decided that what this film needed was a sequence of Graham and me changing the tyres of the aforementioned VW beetle in the equally aforementioned dust-storm. He therefore ordered us to stop and let down the tyres of the car!

Changing the tyre of a VW Beetle in the middle of a sandstorm (especially when none of the tools that the car-hire firm had provided were the correct ones) is a task that I do not recommend to anyone, but eventually we managed it, and caked with dark brown dust we eventually got back in the car and resumed our journey.

We found a small garage where, more by luck than by judgment, we managed to get our tyre re-inflated. By chance two of the four mechanics had actually seen El Chupacabra and lived in a village where there had been a number of attacks. They took us to the village where we spoke to a number of witnesses who told us accounts remarkably similar to those that we had heard in Puerto Rico. It was only as we were driving away that we realised that these attacks had happened at exactly the same time and on the same date as those in Dom Pedro's farmyard.

Two youths who had been hanging around at the garage offered to take us to the village of Tlaloxitcan where the attacks had taken place.

During our journey (which took approximately forty minutes) we unravelled the details of the attacks. The modus operandi was exactly the same as with the other attacks that we had investigated both in Mexico and in Puerto Rico but with one important difference. For the first time, although the corpses were exsanguinated the blood of the innocent victims (thirty animals belonging to ten households) had been scattered on the ground. We were perplexed by this anomaly until we discovered that the village where these attacks had taken place had one important difference to the site of any other chupacabra attacks that we had investigated - it was an Indian village rather than one populated by descendants of the invading Spaniards. Even many hundreds of years after their arrival there was still a surprising degree of segregation in many parts of the country.

The importance of the ethnic origin of the people of Tlaloxitcan is that because of their cultural background it would seem logical that they were closer in their belief system to their Aztec ancestors than to that of the invading Spaniards. As we have seen the sun was the most important single facet of Aztec belief, and it was also the deity to which they carried out their most well known rites - those of human sacrifice. The ethos of blood sacrifice is an integral one within Aztec iconography, and it is, I believe, important that blood was spilled in a ritualistic manner in conjunction with the only chupacabra attacks that we were able to investigate that had taken place within a predominantly non-Hispanic community. It is important, however, to examine the cultural importance of human (and animal) sacrifice within Aztec culture because it is completely different to other rites of human sacrifice performed across the world.

It was our last day in this magnificent country. As we drove back to Mexico City we could see the silhouettes of the cactuses against the setting sun. Behind us was the immense volcano belching tonnes of gas and dust into the atmosphere above us and we really did feel that we were at the ends of the earth.

I would like to end the story of our sojourn within the mountains of the Emperor with that final thought, but life being what it is, the real story ends with somewhat of a pratfall. We arrived back in the capital very late and re-occupied our original rooms at the Hotel Imperial. I had been feeling a little off colour all day. It was the result of the windburn from the dust-storm which had given my face the hue of an alcoholic beetroot and also (or so I believed) the result of what felt like half a tonne of the local alluvial soil blocking my sinuses.

I have inherited several things from my Mother. It was she who read me the Allan Quatermain stories by the renowned (and now sadly considered to be politically incorrect) Victorian author Henry Rider-Haggard when I was a child. It was as a direct result of these stories of high adventure (and a smattering of quasi-forteana) that I embarked on my chosen career. (Apparently according to the folklore of my family, it was her obsession with these books that made her persuade my father, half a century before I went to Mexico to take up a career in Her Majesty's Overseas Civil Service - leading to my childhood as an ex-pat and my love for the tropics). However I also inherited a susceptibility to head-colds from her - one genetic trait that I could have done without.

What I thought was sinuses blocked from the dust storm turned out to be an incipient and very nasty cold which left me feeling feverish, unwell and bad tempered for much of the rest of our journey - but that (as they say) is another story altogether...

Chapter Eleven

The Embarrassing Years

After leaving Mexico, we spent a week in Florida. Then, in mid-February we flew back to the UK. We had only been away for less than a month, but if a week is a long time in politics, then three weeks is an eternity in fortean related publishing. When we left England, I had been earning a lot of money, my interminable divorce was finally settled, and in the bizarre world of forteana I was not only somewhat of a star, but I was one of the few people making a living out of it. When I returned, suddenly - due to the vagaries of the publishing world, and the BBC - I wasn't a star any more, and most disturbingly, despite having just completed an expedition to the ends of the Earth, I was skint again. All four of the magazines that I had been writing regular columns for had gone out of business, and for reasons best known to themselves the BBC had decided to replace our regular radio show with the inane drivel of a wannabe breakfast TV presenter and a golden oldies playlist.

For some reason, the malaise didn't stop there. It seemed - for quite some time - that whatever project we undertook was doomed to failure. My mental health began to deteriorate again - partly as a reaction to the fact that everything around me that I had worked so hard to achieve seemed to be going pear-shaped, and partly because the horrors of the previous two years which had been assuaged by the fact that I had hardly stopped working during 1997 and early 1998, came to the front of my mind as I suddenly found myself with no money and very little to do.

As my mental health deteriorated, so - in many ways - did my public persona. Between 1998 and 2000 I did a number of things of which I am not proud, and in many quarters, and I stopped being regarded as the *enfent terrible* of contemporary forteana and began to be seen as an annoying drunk. This is why this chapter is named as it is. Sir Winston Churchill called the middle volume of his autobiography - the one covering the years when he was not in political office - *The Wilderness Years*. At least on the whole, during this time *he* behaved like a gentleman. Much of this period - though often highly enjoyable at the time - is, in retrospect, merely embarrassing.

At the end of 1997 I was wildly excited to receive an offer from - what I thought was - a *bona fide* publishing company to reprint my book about the Cornish Owlman. Sadly, the company turned out to be a homemade exercise run by a man who had very different ideas to me about how my *magnum opus* should be packaged and publicised. I would like to stress, that unlike other people with whom I was to do business during the embarrassing years, the managing director of this publishing company was not a crook. Not at all. But we were singing from a completely different set of hymn sheets, and when my long-awaited first "proper" paperback book appeared I was appalled! The front cover picture bore no resemblance to the creature that had been seen in the woods surrounding Mawnan Smith, and was so garish that one bookshop which was run by friends of my parents refused to stock it, claiming that it was semi-pornographic and looked like a bad horror comic. In view of this, then it is probably fortunate that the publisher - for reasons that I still don't understand - had decided to omit my name from the front cover. He had also done a hatchet job on the editing, and large chunks of the narrative were either missing, or had been scrambled to such an extent that the book made no sense whatsoever.

However, worse was to come. At the 1998 *Fortean Times* Unconvention, I met Mark Chorvinsky for the first time. I had always been an admirer of his work with *Strange Magazine*, and had looked forward to meeting him. I gave him a copy of my book, and all hell broke loose.

We parted on good terms, and I went off to my hotel room with my then girlfriend for some illicit lechery and to plunder the mini bar. The next morning Mark Chorvinsky was livid. He hated the book and took grave exception to everything I had written about him. He seemed to think that somehow I was casting doubts on his ability and professional reputation as an investigator. "Of course I'm not, dear boy," I said in the calming Old School voice which usually manages to soothe our transatlantic cousins when their feathers have been ruffled. "I'm merely reaching a different conclusion to you." But it was no good.

On his return to the United States he sent vitriolic emails to various correspondents, including. I believe some Internet discussion groups, and from what I can gather told everyone that he could that he regarded me (and presumably still regards me), as some sort of fortean antichrist for daring to claim that he might have been mistaken.

I couldn't be bothered to join in the mudslinging because not only was he not the first person to attack me in print that year, and he certainly wouldn't be the last, but I really didn't care. After all, despite the highly dubious provenance of the Mary F. photographs, there was still a reasonably good body of evidence to support the hypothesis that there was indeed some strange creature at large in the waters of Falmouth Bay.

Then, within weeks, a Scandinavian Lake Monster enthusiast called Jan Ove Sundburg launched a premeditated and vicious attack on me over the Internet. His initial posting to the CZ newsgroup read:

There's also a darker side to cryptozoology, at least to the European one. Since it now is an "official secret" that Mr. Jonathan Downes is, and this is very much in his own words, living off beer on his expeditions, I feel I need to discuss this with the list.

It is truly a pity in itself that Mr. Downes doesn't realize that he's a shame for his country, Great Britain, but the real danger is two-fold:

First, we will never be able to approach science as the laymen we are, with the problems we have with the unknown animals we're searching for, as long as anyone of us is drunk or drinking, even bragging about this, while representing the cryptozoology community.

Second, people watching us; the media, locals and other interested people, will draw the wrong conclusion that we're all the same as Mr. Downes - a wild bunch of beer drinking hooligans, that doesn't care that much about what we came for.

What concerns me the most is the scientists. Many of them are irritating prejudist's, [sic] but they're not our enemies and if we really want to get somewhere within the boundaries of our subject, we must get a foot inside their door, to consult them for the knowledge we don't have ourselves.

There's a rotten apple in every basket, as the saying goes, but if we don't watch it this rotten apple will soon spoil the entire harvest.

This was completely unprovoked and unfair. I have never made any secret of the fact that I drink, but I have also never - to this day - drunk alcohol whilst in the field, and I am certain that alcohol and drugs have never affected my professional behaviour or conclusions. Luckily, the Cryptozoological establishment of the time agreed with me, and Sundberg was ejected from the newsgroup and universally shunned for some time to come. Later that year he led an expedition to a monster-haunted lake in Norway, which ended in acrimony and accusations of fraud. I was not there, although I know people who were, and so I will not comment further. However, to have two vitriolic attacks on me in such short succession hurt badly, and contributed to my slow and inexorable decline.

One good thing did come out of the *Fortean Times* Unconvention of 1998. Richard Freeman had been spending so much time with the CFZ that we mutually decided that when his university course finished in the early summer, he would move to Exeter as a full-time director of the organisation. In the spring of 1998 Richard, Graham and I were involved in another fiasco - an abortive documentary about big cats, which turned out to be a ludicrous waste of time and money.

In the late spring, a few days before the chupacabra documentary was broadcast on UK Channel 4 television, I split up with a girlfriend whom I had been dating for about six months. It was the final straw for me. I decided, that if women were not going to treat me with any respect, then why the hell should I have any respect for them? In a move which now fills me with the utmost embarrassment, together with several colleagues and friends - including Richard, but not including Graham who always thought it was a vulgar and ungentlemanly pursuit - I embarked on an odyssey of sexual promiscuity whose only aim was to win a competition. Points were awarded to those people who had performed a specific sexual act, and the winner - at the end of the year - was awarded a lucrative prize of a crate of alcohol. Richard (largely because of his adventures with ladies of negotiable virtue) won the first year's competition, but in 1999 and 2000 I was the winner. Surprisingly, during these two years, I was also in a tumultuous and ultimately fruitless relationship with a married woman who shall - to spare her blushes - remain nameless. Whilst appearing to be a pillar of respectability, she had - in her youth - been a notorious criminal, and had spent some time in prison. And, although I hate to admit it, this factor added a certain *frisson* to our relationship. I was on a fast downward spiral of self degradation and alcohol abuse, and would probably have become what Jan Ove Sundberg had accused me of, if it wasn't for the fact that during these years I was too drunk - most of the time at least - to go out into the field and actually achieve anything.

Richard finally joined us in early July. Graham and I drove up to the north of England to collect him. We spent the weekend at a pagan camp in Bridlington where the great and good of the Neo-Pagan movement sat around drinking beer, smoking marijuana and listening to talks on broadly pagan or Fortean subjects. My then girlfriend (the one time notorious criminal), and I larged it up all weekend and she revelled in her new position as the First Lady of Forteana. I gave talks about the Owlman and the chupacabra expedition, and apart from that the weekend was only notable for the fact that Graham got laid, and another friend of mine - a well-known academic - distinguished himself by drinking so much that he was doubly incontinent in his tent. I still have a piece of video of him crawling about on all fours, appallingly befouled and screaming *"Take this you bastards"* at members of the Inner London Education Authority (his employers), that he fondly imagined were following him about, and spying upon his antics whilst he was in his cups.

Massively hungover, Graham drove us back to Exeter, and only informed us later that he was so tired and so under the influence that he had fallen asleep twice whilst driving down the motorway at nearly 100 miles an hour, and that even whilst he was awake he was hallucinating so much that he couldn't even see the road.

As I have already told, I had become an acknowledged UFO expert purely because I needed the money to pay for my divorce. On the whole I had nothing but contempt for most of the people within the UFOlogy community. the more I looked into the subject, the more that I found the that the extra-terrestrial hypothesis was complete nonsense, but despite it being against all logic, a ridiculous number of people still believed in it. Even though if there were no longer any magazines dealing with the subject - at least not any that were prepared to pay for articles - I was still (much to my surprise), viewed as a famous UFOlogist, and from there it was a short step to appearing at conferences and lectures around the world, and by the end of the 20th Century I had written or co-written no less than five UFO related books. It had been easy to become seduced by the subject, but like an unwilling mistress of an unattractive married man I wanted out. I just didn't know how to do it.

In my defence, I did try to put a new spin on the UFO subject. I was prepared to prostitute myself to some degree by appearing at conferences aimed at ETH true believers, but in the books I wrote about the subject, I made every effort to take a new and fortean angle on the subject. In the spring of 1998 my publisher asked me whether I would write a UFO book. He wanted another one of the "blah blah blah alien bases, blah blah blah government cover-up, blah blah blah Roswell" books which, at the time, were so prevalent on the shelves of bookshops at the time. I persuaded him that, together with Nigel Wright, I should write a book about the 1997 UFO flap, which had taken up so much of our time during the summer of the previous year. I don't know how, but I sold him on it. Nigel and I sat down to write the book - in fact I wrote most of it, but could not have finished it without Nigel's sterling research and his voluminous library of newspaper clippings. The book was nearly finished, when Richard Freeman and I came up with a new theory. Sadly - mainly due to my error, and with no malice aforethought - Richard never got the credit for coming up with his share of it.

I had been aware of the theory about window areas for years. The term was first coined by John Keel who postulated that phenomena such as mysterious animals whose existence could not be explained within conventional zoological terms of reference, UFOs and even ghosts and other apparitions were in fact inhabitants of another dimension who/which were only visible in this one by means of some mysterious trans dimensional portal or window. He postulated that these 'windows' only occured in specific places, and his term 'window areas' has become part of the accepted parlance of the fortean researcher, and as far as I was concerned it was (and is) indisputable that some areas do seem to have a far higher prevelance of fortean phenomena than is the norm.

During my career as a fortean researcher I have visited several of these places. There is a specific slice of southern Cornwall, which is undoubtedly a 'window area', and I have described the gamut of high strangeness that has occurred there in *The Owlman and Others* as well as in this book. The island of Puerto Rico is another, as are parts of Mexico and as we collated the enormous amount of data that went into *The Rising of the Moon* there seems little doubt that several areas in South East Devon, including Littleham, Woodbury Common and parts of Lyme Bay itself are another ones.

What common factors (apart from having more than their fair share of quasi fortean occurences) are there between these different areas?

We were faced with a large amount of apparently heterogenous data and Richard and I found ourselves in the position of having to take a step back and examine the data in some depth.

The first thing that is apparent is that the events in south-east Devon during the summer and early autumn of 1997 cannot be seen in a vacuum. As we have shown, such spates of apparently disparate phenomena are well known within the canon of fortean literature. Over the years I have been involved in investigating several of them, most notably the events of the long, hot summer of 1976 in southern Cornwall, which are described in an earlier chapter.

I noted in *The Owlman and Others* how Mawnan Smith, and in particular the areas adjacent to Mawnan old Church were surrounded by a particular sinister reputation. This is neither the time nor the place to sift through every peice of evidence that we uncovered during our research for *The Rising of the Moon* but Nigel and I found that Exmouth had once had a similar reputation as a place where things "weren't quite right".

There are other links as well. Both areas are predominantly rural, with agriculture, fishing and tourism being the major economic forces. Both areas are adjacent to the sea and both areas have large numbers of ancient archaeological sites in the vicinity. Both areas have an interesting range of wildlife living there, and as I showed, there are other links as well.

For the moment, however, it is important to examine one of the most important links, because, apart from the animal mutilations and the UFO reports, both areas have reports of zooform phenomena - in Mawnan Smith, the eponymous Owlman and in Exmouth/Littleham/Woodbury we have various four footed furry feinds; the strange beasts of Hullham Rd and the animal that was "all lit up".

The examples given in this book are just a few of the many zooform phenomena on record. They are often linked with a specific geographical location such as a church (Owlman), a mountain (Am Fear Liath Mor), or a road. Graham McEwan recounted one particularly interesting incident in his book *Mystery Animals of Britain and Ireland* (1986):

On the night 0f the 21st January 1879, a man was driving his cart home from Woodcote in Shropshire to Ranton in Staffordshire. At I0.00 p.m., as he was crossing a bridge on the Birmingham and Liverpool Junction Canal (now part of the Shropshire Union Canal), about a mile from the village of Woodseaves, a horrible black creature with enormous shining eyes jumped out of the trees by the roadside and landed on the horse's back. The man tried to push it off, but his whip just went through the creature and in his fright he dropped it. The horse broke into a gallop, the creature clinging to its back. Eventually though, the phantom vanished and the exhausted horse and its terrified owner made their way home, stopping to rest at an inn in Woodseaves where the man described his ordeal. He was so shocked that he spent the next few days in bed. His whip was found next day at the spot where he had dropped it.

The story has an interesting postscript. A few days later, after a garbled version of the story had been circulating, the witness's employer, Mr B., was visited by a policeman who was investigating a report that he, Mr B., had been attacked and robbed on the Big Bridge on the night of the 21 January. Mr B. described the true incident to the constable who responded, in a disappointed manner: Oh, is that all, sir? Oh, I know what that was. That was the Man-Monkey, sir, as does come again at that bridge ever since the man was drowned in the cut [canal].

Mr B. described his employee's frightening encounter to the folklorist Georgina F. Jackson just a week after it happened.

Ape and monkey ghosts such as 'The Man Monkey of Staffordshire', and, more appositely, the ghost ape of Marwood in Devon and 'Martyn's Ape' of Athelhampton in Dorset (which although they are explicable within the terms of purely regional folklore as 'animal ghosts') exhibit in my opinion, characteristics analogous to those exhibited by the smaller BHM phenomena of parts of the United States.

Unlike the phenomena in America, however these British phenomena each have a convenient little folk story to explain their presence in the occult infrastructure of the region. The Ghost Ape of Marwood was, when alive a pet of a local landowner who one day grabbed the landowner's young son and climbed a tree with him, refusing to come down, whereas the well known spectre of "Martyn's Ape" is supposed to have its origins in the unfortunate pet of an earlier female scion of the Martyn family who was either accidentally walled up alive during building work, or entombed (also alive) when the daughter either committed suicide in a locked, secret room or was walled up by an unforgiving parent, (depending on which account you read).

It is my supposition that rather than the apparitions being a result of these, rather far fetched stories, the stories were rather invented by local people to explain the sightings of monkey shaped apparitions, or small BHM as we should really refer to them, that had been seen in the vicinity since times immemorial.

We noted earlier in this chapter that Exmouth and Mawnan Smith both have gained extremely bad reputations. This is something which can be noted in a number of locations where Zooform Phenomena are prevalent.

* In *The Owlman and Others* I described how the zooform entity known as The Jersey Devil had arisen to haunt a place whose reputation was already so evil that the original inhabitants had named it popuessing (place of the dragon), but this is a scenario that one can note again and again.

* In *The Mothman Prophecies* (1973), John Keel notes that the mothman appeared at a disused ammunition dump, and was also a precursor to the disaster at Point Pleasant bridge.

* The Nahanni River valley in Canada is known as Headless Valley. Early in the 20th century the Nahanni became a land of mystery and legend. Tales of gold deposits lured prospectors, and when the headless bodies of some of these adventurers were discovered, legends of fierce natives and mythical mountain men grew. In recent years, however, there has been little trapping and prospecting, which may still be partially in response to the old legends. It is a well known site for Bigfoot reports.

* Doone Valley in North Devon is not only a place with a grim reputation and an unpleasant history but as we have seen in chapter two of this present volume, it is the reputed haunt of a local werewolf.

Littleham is not only the epicentre of the 1997 outbreak of high strangeness, but it is one of the oldest parts of Exmouth.

According to *The Winchester Chronicle* (1001).

And thence (i.e from Hampshire) *they* (The Danes) *went westward until they came to the Defnas (men of Devon), and there to meet them came Pallig, with the ships that he was able to collect; for he had revolted from King Aethelred in spite of all the treaties he had made, and notwithstanding that the king had well endowed him with landed estates and gold and silver (.........) And thence they went to Exanmouth (mouth of the Exe), so that they disposed themselves in one course upwards until they came to Pinhoe.......*

From Florence of Worcester's translation of the word Exanmutha, (ostium fluminis Eaxse) it is clear that he considered it as meaning merely the mouth of the river, and not a town of any kind. However as J.B.Davidson suggested (1898) the available evidence suggests that there was some sort of settlement there even at this time. As the Danish ships were left moored in the inner bay of Exanmutha whilst the harrying of Devonshire, and most particularly the Battle of Pinhoe, was going on, it is at least probable that a few dwellings stood on the shore of the bay, but there can be no doubt that the village, if any, formed a very subordinate member of the manor of Littleham, in which it stood. For many years it was Littleham that was the centre of the social and economic infrastructure of the area and that its place was only usurped by Exmouth several hundred years later.

Exmouth didn't even have a church of its own until two hundred years after Littleham, and three hundred years after Edward the Confessor (1002-1066) had granted the deeds of the Manor of Littleham. As recently as 1830 Exmouth was still very much a 'poor relation' of Littleham and the situation may have continued even more recently than that. Now, however it is merely a suburb (and not a particularly prepossessing one) of Exmouth.

A similar scenario can be presented *vis a vis* the other epicentre of episodic high strangeness back in 1997 - Woodbury Castle. Although it was originally completed in about 300 BC the Castle was still in use and of strategic importance as recently as the Napoleonic Wars between 1798 and 1803.

For many years, therefore, Woodbury, like Littleham was far more important as a social, cultural and spiritual centre of activity than it is now, and this is, we believe, extremely important, for this is the greatest thing that the places which appear to be the epicentres of an unusual degree of quasi-paranormal activity have in common.

* Littleham. The spiritual, social and economic centre of the area, only usurped by Exmouth after the rise in popularity of sea-side holidays made Exmouth reasonably popular as a resort at the end of the eighteenth century. Exmouth was also relatively isolated until the advent of the railway in 1861, and until at least 1830 it was the superior parish in Ecclesiastical terms.

* Woodbury. One of the first locations on the east side of the river Exe. It was the most important settlement in the area until the Middle Ages, but even as recently as the Napoleonic Wars it played an important role within the socio-economic and military-industrial infrastructure of the area. Now, however, it is deserted.

Compare these two locations with the other epicentres of broadly paranormal activity described in earlier chapters:

* Puerto Rico. Once the last refuge of the Carib Indians, it was the political centre of the region for many years because of its integral place within the Spanish Empire in the Western Hemisphere. Now it is a shadow of its former self - politically it is neither independent nor an integral part of the United States. Now it is only visited by western journalists in search of the chupacabra and emissaries from the mainland of the United States intent on discarding their industrial waste.

* Mexico. Once the centre of Montezuma's mighty empire, even after the Spanish invaded it was a powerful and large nation. Now, having lost Colorado, Texas and New Mexico to the United States it is a country on the verge of penury whose ex-President absconded to Dublin with most of the contents of the National Treasury and his beautiful (if dumb) mistress. The Aztec Empire is now a haven for Child Prostitution and Drug Money.

* Falmouth Bay. Once a thriving sea-port, recession after recession has meant that it is now visited mostly by tourists and the once proud seafaring industries are very much on the wane. Falmouth is no longer a mighty sea port and the whole area is rapidly diminishing in importance.

* Mawnan Smith. A great blow was stuck to its spiritual heart - Mawnan Old Church, when it was reconsecrated (see *The Owlman and Others*). Further damage was done to the area with the wave of redundancies in the rural industries over the past thirty years which have meant that once thriving agricultural communities are reduced to a shadow of their former selves.

At last we have a link between the areas which demonstrate an unusual level of fortean phenomena. It may not be the definitive link, it may not be the only one, but it is, for the moment at least, all that we have, and it provides us with an extremely useful like of investigation.

During the summer and autumn of 1998 Richard and I believed that we were beginning to reach at least a partial understanding of these window areas if we approached them from a phenomenological viewpoint.and that far from digressing up a varying number of blind alleys during our search for the truth.

We believed that we have formulated the beginnings of a theory which can explain the nature of not all, but a large proportion of anomalous phenomena, and especially those which cluster in so-called 'window areas'. However, to do so, we must first examine the work of some unjustly ignored scientists.

Wilhelm Reich was a Freudian analyst born in Austria in 1897 and spent much of his life trying to prove the energetic reality of the "Libido" which Sigmund Freud had coined. Reich worked on his own version of biophysics for many years but by 1933 he had to leave Germany as Hitler's Nazi regime and the threat to his own well-being increased. Eventually after moving to Oslo he moved to the United States in 1939. Using what was, for his time at least, a high quality microscope, Reich observed that under high magnification he could see that what appeared to be luminous blue/green globules, which were released by decaying food. He described these as some form of biological ether. He likened these globules to Bions, which were named and researched by H. Charlton Bastian, a contemporary of Louis Pasteur. Reich claimed that the particles he could see in the microscope were actually an unidentified energy or radiation form, which in turn caused conjunctivitis and skin tanning. Reich named this energy 'Orgone'.

Reich was not the only researcher to hypothesise a measurable 'life energy'. Franz Anton Mesmer (1734-1815) had similiar ideas. He theorised a connection between Newton's theory of "universal gravitation" and the power of the human mind and body. Newton had commented the body contained an invisible fluid that responded to planetary gravitation and Mesmer believed that a body's well-being depended upon whether the body's "animal gravitation" was in harmonic alignment with the planets and chose the term "animal magnetism" for life energy.

Baron von Reichenbach (d. 1869) also hyothesised an electro-magnetic life energy "Odic Force." He conducted thousands of tests with more than hundred sensitive people and he developed a comprehensive theory concerning this energy, much of which was contained in a book called *"Researches on Magnetism, Electricity, Heat, Light, Crystallisation and Chemical Attraction, in their Relations to the Vital Force."* Which was translated into English by Prof William Gregory and first published by Taylor, Walton and Maberly, London, 1850.

This concept of a measurable 'life energy' is nothing new. These three scientists were, however the first to attempt to codify it. This 'life energy' (call it what you will) is of course what priests and magicians have been using for centuries. The savants of every culture have developed effective and complex mechanisms to create and project this energy. Various cultures have used everything from human and animal sacrifice, chanting, and emotional build up in congregations or magical groups, walking in circles, sex magical practices, and other rituals. In The Bible, for instance, you will find no less than 23 passages that tell how to sacrifice animals. In most instances the Shaman or priest used energy that was available and accumulated it up for release in a religious-magical operation.

However, can be seen from the experiments described by Alexandra David-Neel, and those described by Richard in his book *Dragons: More than a Myth* it does seem that it is possible to create a tulpa or thoughtform that can achieve some degree of independent existence.

We now have to ask whether it is possible for a thought form to be inadvertantly created in a spontaneous act as a by-product of magickal and religious ritual activity? Or, possibly, whether a tulpa-like being can be created as a necessary by-product of social religious and/or magickal behaviour. If one person - albeit a medium can do it - maybe we should hypothesise the synergistic effect (on an etheric level at least) of generations of people who worship and perform rituals in the same place.

Both Woodbury Common and Littleham have been used for two, if not three, groups of religious practises:

1. The Druid religion of the Celts
2. Christianity

and possibly

3. Contemporary Wiccan and Neo-Pagan worship and although the practitioners of each religion would be aghast at the suggestion at in many essentials at least, their religious practises were much the same.

* All three religions are based on prayer and ritual
* All three religions deal with a triune deity
* All three religions have a ritual roughly analogous to the rite of Holy Communion

Unlike Wicca and the religion of the Druids, Christianity, however, is not, except in the most abstract and metaphysical way, a religion whose devotees or priests consciously attempt to create thought-forms. However, as we have shown, the 'life-force' (by whatever name you like to call it, is a necessary, nay a logical by product of ritual and religious activity, and as David-Neel and Evans-Wentz have both shown, under certain circumstances this life-force can achieve an independent (or quasi-independent) existence, even after rituals lasting days, hours, or weeks. Imagine, if you will, a life-force created without form as an unconscious by product of the prayers and rituals of worshippers over many centuries.

How many times have you gone into a church or some other building and said 'this place has a good feeling about it?'

Imagine if you will that the creation of a life force, is a necessary side effect of worship, and that if such rituals are, as was certainly the case in all the areas that we have discussed, carried out over a period of many centuries, then an extremely powerful tulpa-like entity is a logical result. Indeed, if Evans-Wentz is to be believed there can be little doubt about it.

However, there is are great differences between a tulpa created as a conscious act of will by a skilled magician and our hypothesised Odillic Life-Force entity created as a necassary but unconscious by-product of years of ritual and worship.

* The tulpa is created with a specific goal in mind or to carry out a specific task. Our hypothesised Odillic Life-Force entity has no such goal. Although we can have no more than the most minimal understanding of the natural history of a life-form (if indeed it can be described as such) which is completely unlike any other that we have ever studied, it would be reasonable, I suspect, to suggest that such an entity would not stray far from the place where it was created.

* The tulpa is created with a specific form. In *Magic and Mystery in Tibet* Alexandra David-Neel describes how she created the tulpa of a jolly and fat monk. In *Psychic Self Defence* Dion Fortune described creating a fearsome wolf. However, if our hypothesised Odillic Life-Force entity has been created in the way that we suggest, then it would be unlikely to have a specific form. It would just exist.

How many times have you gone into a disused church or a ruin and said this place feels evil?

To study the natural history of an entity whose nature we do not even pretend to understand, and whose existence is hypothetical is an almost impossible task. However it is this that we now have to do.

As David-Neel, Evans-Weltz and other sources quoted in this book have implied a tulpa needs constant nurturing in order to grow. This implies that its source of energy; its food (if you like), is emotion. If one takes this line of thought and extrapolates it together with what we already know (or guess) about our hypthosised Odillic life-force entity it makes perfect sense.

If, as we have hypothesised, such a creature (and although I don't like using the word 'creature' I can't think of a more apposite term), is nurtured by the emotions dissapated during prayer and religious ritual, then it is logical to suppose that it could also feed from excessive outpourings of emotion from other sources. Having been both a drug user and having suffered for many years from a debilitating mental illness I can testify to the immense outpourings of wasted emotion that each condition can produce.

I do not know whether the food needed by these creatures is chemical (the endorphines or pheromones produced by people and animals in extremis, in agony, in ecstasy or in prayer) but I believe that these creatures will, like any other living thing, do whatever is in their power to provide themselves with sustenance.

I believe that the perception of these creatures is inherently linked with the part of the psyche awakened during the psychedelic experience and that in many ways the two scenarios can be linked. I would suggest that these creatures can produce situations whereby a human or an animal can produce the emotion (or chemical by-products of same) that is necessary for its well-being. This would explain how so many fortean phenomena are strangely religious in nature. It would explain visions of the Blessed Virgin Mary and the great Icons of other religions, which on occasion appear to unwary believers in a semi-corporeal form.

It would also explain, how in places where religious activity has continued for so many years the level of quasi-fortean phenomena is so much higher.

Why do such phenomena appear in cycles - in Lyme Bay, Woodbury and Littleham, cycles of about ten years?

Maybe that is when the 'creature' gets hungry.

Richard and I were blown away by this theory, and so - it must be said - was our publisher. We spent much of the autumn and winter of 1998 writing the book which eventually contained this Unified Fortean Field Theory of everything, and as a 1998 slowly turned into 1999 we look forward to the new year, and the publication of what we truly believed would be a ground breaking a book in the annals of Fortean Research. It was published in March and completely ignored by everybody - even the fortean press and sold so little to do that already shaky relationship between the publisher and me broke down entirely and we parted company in a very acrimonious manner.

In the late spring there were a number of UFO reports across south Devon, there was a spate of mutilated dolphins found washed up on the south Devon coast, and as always some the UFO fraternity were convinced that they had been attacked and butchered by aliens from the planet Zog. We had been interested in cetacean mutilation since the events of September 1997, and Richard, Graham and I went to investigate. We were certain that we were not going to find that the bodies had been mutilated by "precision laser equipment", as had been claimed by certain so-called fortean researchers, but we decided that if we were to carry out an autopsy on one of these poor creatures then we could put the matter to bed once and for all.

Thanks to a helpful representative of Brixham Seawatch, a local cetacean conservation group we were able to examine the corpse of one of these creatures in situ, and for the first time we were able to perform a detailed autopsy. What we found was conclusive but it unfortunately seems to have nothing to do with either UFO phenomena or any other mystery.

Our findings were as follows:

1. Despite reports in certain areas, the head of the animal had not been removed with a single clear cut (reminiscent of a laser according to one source). The head had obviously been 'sawn' off by two or more strokes of a serrated, cleaver type instrument. There were saw marks on the blubber and on the cervical vertebrae and the patterns of the cuts through the blood vessels to the head all confirmed this.

2. We removed the lungs. If the animal had either drowned there would have been seawater in the lungs. If the animal had been asphyxiated, for example, by staying under water with its blowhole closed, the capillaries in the lung itself would have burst and there would have been excess blood in the interior of the lungs. Despite the fact that the lungs were completely intact and undamaged there was no excess fluid inside.

3. There was, however, an excess of blood in the body cavity itself, which is consistent with the animal having been concussed.

4. On the tail of the animal, just below the tail flukes were marks of what appears to be nylon rope, probably from a net.

Our conclusions are that the unfortunate animal had swum into drift nets, probably placed illegally by Cornish Crab fishermen, and became entangled. Whilst still alive, the fishermen, unwilling to damage their nets, bashed the dolphin over the head with an oar to stun it, and sawed its head and some of its fins off, before throwing it back into the water.

Thursday 29th April 1999 was a particularly sad day. Our next door neighbour - a lady of whom we had all grown particularly fond - had died and we had to attend her funeral, at which I read the eulogy. After the funeral none of us felt able to do any work, and so all three of us retired to our rooms to be alone with our thoughts and our memories.

The next day was Bealtaine.

The name of the fertility festival of Bealtaine means "good fire", and bonfires were once used to mark the symbolic return of the summer sun and renewed life. The Celts have a God named Bel, meaning "Lord", who is known as "The Bright One"

- a God of light and fire. Beaten celebrates the return of the light and its life-giving force upon the Earth.

Bealtaine is a powerful holiday, filled with legend and tradition that goes back farther than most recorded history. One of the most famous is probably the Maypole, a tall pole of oak adorned with a hawthorne garland and many brightly coloured ribbons. The ribbons would be held by the many participants who danced their way around the Maypole in opposing directions, weaving in and out until the people were almost arm in arm and the Maypole was woven with bright springtime colours from top to bottom. The Maypole is actually a symbol for fertility of the land, and the ribbons being wound represent the movement of energies between the Earth and the Sky (The Goddess and the God) that causes the plants to grow and the world to re-awaken.

Besides being a celebration of the fertility of the earth and the renewed growth of crops, what we must realise is that the cycle of planting and growth does not only pertain to physical plants, but also to our spirituality as a whole. Bealtaine should be a time to plant the seeds of spiritual growth and development in us all, praising the God and Goddess for the great gifts they have given us all.

I am a Christian, not a Pagan, but many of my friends (including Richard) are devotees of the old religion and I have always been particularly interested in the rituals of Celtic Paganism. Months before, the Exeter Strange Phenomena Group, which Graham and I had founded in the autumn of 1996 had agreed to stage a Bealtaine ritual in Mawnan Woods with the intention of attempting to invoke the grotesque Owlman which has been reported there for over twenty years.

Various members of the Exeter Strange Phenomena Group decided to come along for the ride, and veteran Australian cryptozoologist Tony Healy co-author of a remarkable book called *Out of the Shadows* also accompanied us. Tony had arrived in Exeter that afternoon. We had met him at the Unconvention, and as is our custom we had invited him to stay with us for as long as he wanted.

One of the less well publicised roles of the Centre for Fortean Zoology is that it acts as a flop house for visiting forteans from around the world and at various times one can find several well known members of the fortean and cryptoinvestigative communities wrapped in blankets or sleeping bags on my sitting room floor. Tony - by the way - stayed on and off for three months.

One of the party was a long haired and bearded young man wearing a ragged Medieval Court Jester's outfit. Perhaps appropriately, he answered to the name of 'Jester', an ex-road protester who together with Daniel "Swampy" Needs was one of the few members of this itinerant though well meaning community to reach a level of notoriety in the national press. Clad in his eponymous costume he had spent the months leading up to the evictions as a merry maker and a jester whose role was to keep the spirits of the beleaguered protesters uplifted and to bait the oncoming forces of law, order and destruction. As a result of his activities he was charged with several public order offences but that, like so much hinted at in this book is undoubtedly another story!

When the road protest finally finished 'Jester' hung up his cap and bells and returned to his studies of folklore and the occult and, more by luck than by judgement ended up at one of the meetings of the Exeter Strange Phenomena Group in early 1999, where he soon became a fixture.

He had read my book about the Owlman and was determined to help us in any way during our attempts to invoke the beastie. Together with Richard (in the guise of 'Muzzlehutch the Magician' he performed a theatrical and exciting ritual in the woods below Mawnan Old Church to the rapturous applause of the rest of use who looked on in awe.

This is not the time nor the place to describe the ritual in any detail., but it seemed to work because over the next few months Owlman activity seemed to start again. The most important aspect of that was the following email which we received with a few weeks of the ritual:

In early July, we received the following email. In view of the history of hoaxing and surrealchemical shenanigans surrounding his Owliness I include it here with no comment apart from the obvious one that IF it is true it turns much of what I have written and said publicly about the phenomenon in recent years completely on its head.

My Experience of 3/7/1976
Sally G

Pembroke, Wales
July 2000

To whom it may concern,

Writing this down isn't going to be the easiest thing that I've ever done, so I'll try to get it over with as quickly as possible. I have reluctantly decided to speak on my experience, for reasons that I won't go into here. This is the first time that I have thought about any part of what happened during that summer in years- It took me quite a while to really forget about what I saw, and I suppose you could say that it had a definite effect on the way that I lived my life for a number of years following the event. I am a 38-year old career woman who has quite enough going on in her life without dredging up a very upsetting incident that happened 24 years ago. This is certainly the first time that I have written any of this down, and probably the first time that I have wilfully remembered it in any detail since I was a teenager. I recently mentioned it in passing to someone whom I am very fond of, and he suggested that I contact you, having found you on the net. I am aware of some of the bits and pieces that have been written about my experience in the intervening years, and by-and-large I have no complaint. I remember Mr Shiels as being quite concerned about my friend Barbara and I at the time. He seemed like a nice man.

I have read the essay on your website concerning the incident. There are a couple of indiscrepancies that you weren't to know about that I should probably clear up. My name wasn't really Chapman at the time- it was W***, although I told Mr Shiels that it was Chapman. Babs gave her real name. You'll probably understand why I did this. I was still VERY upset when Babs and I were walking on the beach the next day. Babs was much more grown-up than me at the time (and probably still is). She was calming me down, trying to make me laugh, because I hadn't slept a wink the night before. She walked up to Tony and told him what had happened. I have no idea how she knew of him, but I gather he was a bit of a local character. I didn't really know that part of Cornwall at all.

He had some paper and pencils on him, and had us draw it. He helped me so much that day without even realising it-I remember him making me giggle a bit, and he was so cheery that he really snapped me out of it. I don't think either drawing was particularly good- I'm not really sure that it was as OWLLY as our pictures suggested. I've just realised that I've been stalling actually describing what happened when we were in the wood that night. This thing STILL has an effect on me all these years later. It was probably around 9.45pm when we saw it. We had made tea with a little camping stove, and I seem to remember that we were talking about school and boys. There was a boy at home that I was very interested in, and Babs wanted to know all about it. Neither of us had had boyfriends before at that point. It was still light. I seem to remember that it hadn't rained for ages, and the woods were very dry and crunchy, if that makes sense. The noise was so abrupt in the quiet of the woods that we both jumped up together. It was a kind of hissing. I don't know, I can't really remember. It was loud and sudden. We both looked over into the wood, and there it was.

I had been to see a horror film in Plymouth a few months before, a werewolf film with Peter Cushing. This was the first thing I thought when I saw it, I thought it was the werewolf. The face wasn't really like an owl, thinking back. It was like a frowning, sneering black thing. The eyes were burning, glaring and reddish. I don't know if it had fur or feathers, but it was gray and grizzled like the werewolf in the film. I remember hearing Barbara start to laugh, but it was a sort of choked, panicked laugh. Tony Shiels did us a great favour by playing down our fear when he talked about what happened to us later on. I think when we saw him that day on the beach that he must have known how upset we really were.

I knew right away it was REAL. It wasn't like a monster in the films that look rubbery and fake. It just looked like a very weird, frightening animal, as real as any animal in a zoo. It looked flesh and blood to me, but there is simply no way it could have been. It couldn't have been something that was born and grew. No way. I have no idea what it was. My head hurts even thinking about it.

It was more frightening than I can really describe. I remember blood rushing to my head, making it pound. It just stood there for what might have been a minute. I'm not really sure how long. Barbara was laughing, but it was more like a sort of breathless hysterical sound by now. I wanted to run but couldn't. It was so EVIL, intensely so. When it moved, that nearly did it, I nearly started running. It's arms or wings or whatever went out, and it just rose up through the trees. Straight up through the evergreens, it didn't flap, it didn't make a sound. Then, weirdly, I thought 'costume' for the first time, because the legs looked wrong. They looked like a kind of grey trouser material, certainly unnatural. I can't be entirely sure now. And then the feet. Black, hooking things. I have no idea how it had managed to stand up on them. They were like an earwig's tail-piece.

It's difficult trying to remember exactly what happened next. The wood was quiet, but it felt as if it, the thing, could appear again at any second. I think I had nearly fainted at one point. Babs was the same. We were shaking like leaves. I was thinking that someone was going to come out of the woods laughing at their trick, but really I knew that it couldn't possibly have been a trick. On one level, my mind simply wasn't accepting it. It still doesn't in a way. That's how I got over it, I think. By pretending that it hadn't really happened. As I mentioned earlier, in some ways I lost a lot of years to it. Somehow, shaking and crying a bit, we got packed up. That was the worst time, waiting for it to come back. I don't think that I could have coped seeing it again. My mind was POUNDING, ballooning. I don't know how it could have disappeared like it did. The woods weren't that thick. Not thick enough to hide what I can only think of as a monster. I know that sounds silly, but it is perhaps the most apt way to describe it. It seemed to just vanish, like a ghost.

We were originally going to walk back to Babs' home, near Gweek, but it was pretty much dark by now. Obviously as an adult you question why you stayed out, but that's what we did. We moved camp to a place where the woods were thinner, as I recall. I didn't sleep a wink, and neither did Babs I suppose. Yet somehow I knew it was gone for good. The atmosphere was lighter somehow, there were bird noises coming out of the trees, calls and the like. The night crawled by, and eventually it started to get light. We made tea at about six or so, and went for a walk down on the beach around nine. We met Tony Shiels, and told our story.

I really don't know why I decided to write all this down, after so many years. As I have said, someone close to me thought that I should come clean. Actually, doing so has affected me less than I thought it was going to. Reading over it, I feel a little embarrassed. It doesn't seem possible now. I have no idea why or how it happened. I never expect to.

I moved with my family from West Hoe in Plymouth in 1980 to Surrey, and then on to Pembroke to work in a creative role in 1989. I believe that what happened in July '76 shaped my life for years afterwards.

My good friend Barbara emigrated with her husband to Australia in 1987. I haven't spoken to her in many years, but I think that I would hear if anything had happened.

That's about it, really. For what it's worth, I haven't been to Cornwall since I was a teenager. Whatever happened that July is firmly in the past, and I intend to leave it there.

I know exactly what she means!

I don't know whether it was psychic backlash, but as will be seen, the next eighteen months were uniformly awful. Despite a string of media appearances and successful books we were dogged with financial and emotional problems and, by the end of the year, we had definitely had enough. On New Year's Day 2001, together with two very powerful witches from Yorkshire, I took part in a nine hour ritual to break the spell once and for all. At the time of writing at the very end of January 2004, the spell seems to be working but one thing is certain.

Although it is certain that the story of the Owlman of Mawnan ain't over yet, my investigations into His Owliness ended with writing this chapter. I await further developments with interest but, like Sally G., my involvement is firmly in the past - and I, too, firmly intend to leave it there.

In August 1999 I flew to America for the second time in two years. In my suitcase I had seventy-five copies of *The Rising of the Moon*. I was a special guest at the International UFO Congress in Nevada and I was faced with the almost insurmountable task of trying to convince an audience of true believers that everything they knew was wrong!

My problems were compounded by my new job. I had been appointed the Editor of a magazine called *Quest*. I wasn't to know that the organisation that published this and other titles was highly dubious and that I was to find myself in the uncomfortable position of being an apologist for a man of doubtful financial morals, and I ended my tenure as Editor having to explain to a plethora of disgruntled contributors, including the brightest and best of the fortean establishment, some very close friends, and my own father, why they were never going to be paid for their work.

Indeed I spent a large proportion of my time at the International UFO Conference in Nevada apologising to ex-contributors for the non-appearance of remuneration for articles that my predecessors had written for the magazine in its previous incarnations. I finally managed to extricate myself from the mess just before Christmas but my reputation had been irrevocably tarnished by my association with Top Events and Publishing Ltd of Tarporeley, Cheshire, and if I am honest I don't know whether it has ever entirely recovered.

Even worse, *Quest* had always featured a mish mash of esoteric nonsense of the kind propounded by people like Erik von Daniken in the late 1960s. It was a horrible mish mash of crap, alleging that God was an astronaut, the pyramids had been built by extra terrestrials with sophisticated anti-gravity devices and similar nonsense. I felt dirty by association. I have always abhored the mindset that tries to make an alternative religion out of paranormal research, and here I was propogating pernicious nonsense to a generation of true believers. I didn't tell anyone, but on the long plane journey from Los Angeles to Heathrow I decided that I was going to retire from fortean research. I felt that I had alienated myself from the people in the community for whom I felt regard, respect and affection, and I could no longer countenance being part of the world in which I had come to live.

Of course, my brave resolution was not to last. As soon as I passed through immigration at Heathrow Airport, a pair of wannabe TV moguls met me for a pre-arranged 'power breakfast' that I had completely forgotten about. As my dear friend and colleague Graham grabbed my suitcases and passed me a cigarette we were whisked into the airport coffee shop to swig coffee, munch on waffles and discuss our next project.

Like all the other projects I was to be involved with over the next eight months it was a self-deprecating joke. I no longer felt confident or capable enough to do any serious fortean research, and so, almost as a gesture of ironic self-destruction I undertook a series of stupid projects whose main aim was to deflate the self conscious miasma of arrogance which I felt had come to surround my serious work.

Three days after my return from America we started filming a low budget spoof of the then trendy Blair Witch Project for HTV. Based loosely on the folklore surrounding sightings of a strange monkey-like creature in the woods surrounding Brassknocker Hill near Bath, I made sure that *The Brassknocker Hill Project* was a knockabout romp of slapstick silliness, homosexual innuendo and stupid in-jokes. It certainly had nothing at all to do with mainstream cryptozoology and it infuriated every cryptozoologist who saw it. I just laughed. We had been paid three hundred quid for it. I didn't give a damn anymore and I wanted the whole world to know it.

The next three projects; a somewhat scatological book of semi-fiction called *The Blackdown Mystery* in which I lampooned the then current UFOlogical mores with a string of drug jokes; a CD of novelty songs with fortean themes featuring my band *The Amphibians from Outer Space* by this time *sans* the keyboard player who had absconded with my wife, and with the addition of the legendary British Fortean, Rev. Lionel Fanthorpe; and a ridiculous art movie based around my most notable literary success *The Owlman and Others*.

Billed as a cinematic adaptation of my book, it was in fact no such thing. A homage to Tony Shiels and to another great inspiration of mine, film-maker John Walters, the movie, which was eventually shown for the first time at the 2000 Unconvention at the Commonwealth Institute in Kensington High Street, London, was like nothing else ever made in the annals of forteana. One of my friends from America told me, after she saw it that it "sucked worse than any other movie I have ever seen," and was somewhat nonplussed when I told her that this was, after all, the reason I had made it in the first place.

What I was not prepared for was for the film to be a success. Much to my surprise it was. One review read:

A co-production with Limited Talent Productions, it's a pseudo-documentary loosely based on the book of the same name by Jon Downes and is a blackly comic romp that sees the author and his girlfriend retrace the investigative steps in the book. Involving sea serpents, gay cowboys, wizards, mad lemonade selling tramps, transsexual nazis, inbred yokel mobs, lesbian witches, and other assorted perverts and nutters, it is a trash cinema classic in the same league as Phil Tucker's Robot Monster, Edward D. Wood JR's Bride of the Atom and John Walter's Multiple Maniacs.

Other reviews were equally enthusiastic and compared the film favourably with the horribly over-hyped *Blair Witch Project* which had no jokes and cost nearly 50 times as much to make, despite being the cheapest budget hit film on record. Unfortunately, our plan to make a silly movie that would detract from all the attention that had been given in recent years to the Owlman phenomenon failed badly. By CFZ standards at least it was a great success and gave us even more media attention, which was ironically the very last thing that we had been looking for.

It was essentially just a very silly spoof art movie with little relevance to the main body of the research that the CFZ both collectively and individually has carried out into the Owlman Phenomenon. What it did do, however, almost as an afterthought, was provide my first (and only until this book) public claim that Tony Shiels had been responsible for all the original sightings and that the phenomenon proper had not started to appear until some years later after people had started to believe in the stories that had originally been produced as a joke.

At the end of 1999, we were approached by N.M News of Solihull to work on their new project - a national Sunday newspaper with an ethical 'green' remit. From the start I had grave reservations about the project and felt that it was too idealistic to succeed. However, we were all willing to try, and our brief sojourn with the project (which only lasted eight or nine issues) finally gave us enough money to set the CFZ up properly. From being a rather grubby and sordid bachelor pad, we invested time and money, acquired a housekeeper and eventually made some semblance of order out of the ongoing chaos.

By this time I was earning quite good money as a straight journalist dealing in environmental matters and I was determined to put my involvement with UFOlogical matters and, more particularly the new age fringe belief systems behind me. I was determined to reinvent myself, and although I continued publishing *Animals & Men* - it was more for sentimental reasons than anything else. I didn't realise it at the time but my attempts to reject and ridicule my past achievements were pathological to a disturbing degree.

As I mentioned earlier, Tony Shiels had become somewhat of a surrogate father to me during the horrors of my divorce. We fell out mildly during 1998 but have since made friends again. My relationship with Tony had two major effects on my life. The first was that I - for a while at least - adopted his methodology of surrealchemy, lexilinking, and general tomfoolery. Although I no longer adhere to those disciplines, I am very grateful to him for having introduced me to ideas and concepts which broadened my mind to a far greater extent than drugs ever had, as well as owing him - almost certainly - my life, because it is almost certain that I would have killed myself if it had not been for his love, strength and support during those horrible times.

However, also as a result of my adulation of the man, I began to affect an interest in all things Hibernian. Unfortunately, as well as getting hold of a large number of CDs of Irish music, for a while I also espoused the cause of radical Irish politics. To this day I believe that the Irish nation has received a very poor deal at the hands of the British. However, these days, I no longer give my support to those who desire to solve the problems of the Emerald Isle by violent means. However, back in 1998 and 1999 I read as much as I could about the history of the Irish armed conflict. I was - and still am - appalled at the civil rights abuses which my country has perpetrated against the Irish Catholic population, especially as in many cases it was purely because the ruling Conservative government in the UK could not function without those few precious extra votes from the disgustingly corrupt Ulster Unionist Party. I was disgusted to discover that the country of which I am so proud to be a citizen, was castigated by international courts on so many occasions for the sort of human rights abuses that - if you are to believe our present government - only take place in the fundamentalist Muslim or Third World countries.

Although I never joined Sinn Fein, I was - and still am - a member of the Wolfe Tone Society, and I made several generous financial donations to the prisoners' wives Welfare Fund. However, on a couple of occasions my involvement with "the lads" crossed the border from being a concerned humanitarian human being, and bordered on being something far more sinister.

It seemed like a jolly jape when, in December 1999, in my music column in *The Planet on Sunday* - I made the live album by Irish rebel band *Athenrye* my record of the millennium. This prank - for a prank is all that it really was - very nearly had some serious repercussions for me. A week or so before Christmas, together with Graham and the ever-faithful Nigel Wright, I travelled to London to review a couple of concerts by the band. In my innocence I had supposed that they were some sort of Irish version of one of the left-wing folk singers - such as Leon Rosselson - who appear at art centres up and down the country singing songs about how their grandfathers got beaten up during the General Strike. The truth was far more sinister. Although the band could not have been nicer to us, it was somewhat distressing to find that we were the only English people in the audience. Furthermore, the audience was not the middle-class folkie intellectuals that I'd imagined, but a band of crewcutted, tough young men who regarded us - quite understandably - with enormous suspicion. Graham and I got happily and cheerfully drunk - oblivious to the fact that Nigel was getting ever more frightened and that the toughest and most sinister members of the audience paid no attention to the fact we knew all the words to the songs and were beginning to look (as Nigel said later), as if they were planning to forcibly remove us and probably our kneecaps.

Then it happened. The band were halfway through a particularly stirring number which exhorted the British Army to "go home", before they made them. The melodies stopped, and soon all there was in the crowded room, which 250 tough young men - some often wearing black balaclavas and with suspicious-looking bulges in their coat pockets - dancing stationary, and bobbing up and down on to the martial drumbeat and the rhythmic bass guitar. The drums continued, and the crowd began to chant "I - R - IRA - blow the British scum away", and then at that point Graham and I began to get nervous. And then the chanting stopped - as the drums and bass continued, Terry Manton the lead singer approached the microphone.

"You know that all British journalists are lying scum", he started, and my heart dropped. I looked around me nervously, hoping that although some of the crowd knew that I was English, that none of them knew that I was a journalist. Then Terry continued:

"But there are a few British journalists who have deep inside them beating hearts of bold Fenian men. There are three of them here in the audience tonight - Jonathan Downes, Graham Inglis and Nigel Wright. This song is dedicated to them and to the *Planet on Sunday* - it's called *S.A.M Missiles in the Sky*"

I gave an audible gasp of relief, I looked at Graham and he was grinning back at me. When the song finished, Graham and I left the dancefloor and returned to our seats do find ourselves being treated like heroes by a group of very violent looking young men. They all bought drinks for us, and at least two convicted murderers shook us by the hand.

I found out later that my review of the album, together with a photograph of me and Graham surrounded by a group of men wearing balaclavas and presenting the closed fist salute of the Provisional IRA appeared on a number of republican websites and may well have appeared in *An Poblacht*.

Although it would be amusing to find out what of the elderly, and rather inept managing editor of the *Planet on Sunday* would have thought about having his eminently dull but respectable newspaper cited as being recommended reading for the young terrorist, we soon realised that we had - by our naivety and stupidity - not only put ourselves in a potentially life-threatening situation, but had also laid ourselves open to some gravely serious repercussions from the British Government.

There was one - mildly curious and slightly fortean - repercussion from this unfortunate incident. A UFO researcher called Barry King, had for some years, been circulating an irregular (and almost illiterate), newsletter which contained lists of UFO researchers whom he claimed the British Government had opened files on. In common with most people within the UFO community (at least those with any sense), I had always felt that Barry was an amiable but harmless fruitcake. In April 2000 - four months after our unfortunate run-in with the boys from the old brigade - my name appeared on that list for the first time. I am certain that there is nothing that I have ever written or investigated within the world of UFOs, which could possibly lay me open to any form of government investigation. However, it is almost certain that being a journalist on a national newspaper with known terrorist connections would mean that there would be a number of files on me. The fact that Barry King included my name on his list four months after my only overt involvement with terrorist politics indicates that perhaps he should be taken more seriously in future.

To be quite honest, my involvement with the Provisional IRA began and ended with being bought a drink by one of the Aldershot pub bombers. However, like my equally unfortunate - but luckily less dangerous public flirtation with extreme right-wing politics, although my sympathies are with are those who seek a political solution to the Northern Irish issue, my public espousal of terrorist chic was not much more than it just another symptom of my deep unhappiness with myself, and my desperate search for a new and satisfactory identity.

In January 2000, I embarked on a course of group psychotherapy, which I hoped, would have remarkable affects on my life. It certainly did, although not in the way that either I or the medical professionals who overlook my progress had hoped. I fell in love with one of the other members of my psychotherapy group, and embarked on a torrid, and emotionally devastating love affair, which was to last for the next ten months.

For the first and only time in my life I had found a partner with whom I felt totally emotionally and physically satisfied. For us, the well-known term 'a whirlwind romance' was entirely apt. Sexually, romantically and emotionally I was at peace for the first time in my life. However it was too much, too soon and as events proved, deciding to marry a woman that one has met in the outpatients department of a psychiatric hospital is not necessarily the best idea that I had ever conceived.

We had at least two insurmountable problems. Although I had renounced recreational drugs several years before I still drank heavily whereas Linda was a chronic dope smoker. She was also a devout Roman Catholic, and found my Zen pantheistic approach to Christianity too much to deal with, whereas I found great problems in dealing with her adherence to what I considered to be dangerous superstitious nonsense. The relationship was too intense to last, and we were both too fragile to make it work, and in the autumn we fell apart with devastating results.

The year 2000 had been a particularly horrible one anyway. Toby, the CFZ Dog and probably the best friend that I have ever had died of cancer in June at the age of sixteen. With his death a large part of my life was over. He had been my constant companion since he was six weeks old, and had been the one constant in a life of turmoil. The night before he died he was too weak to walk and we had to carry him to my bedroom, where he slept on my bed has he had done all his life. I knew that he would have to be put to sleep on the following day, and as Linda, Toby and I lay in bed together, I was crying like a grief stricken baby. Summoning reserves of strength that neither he or I knew he had, he pulled himself up to the top of my bed to lick my face and comfort me, as he had done every time I had been upset for the previous sixteen years. The following day I watched helplessly as the vet administered the lethal injection and I knew that my life would never be the same again. Within two or three weeks my two elderly cats, Isabella and Carruthers, whom I had kept for an equal length of time also died and I was totally alone.

By the late summer of 2000 my life was completely out of control. My house/the CFZ (for they are one and the same), had seemed to have become a drop-in centre for every drug addict, transsexual, pervert, Satanist and general loony in Exeter. Somehow these weirdoes had wormed their way into my household where they stayed, drinking my wine, eating my food and bleeding me dry. At the time Graham was so disgusted with these people that he just kept his distance, not realising that the situation was totally out of my control and that I hated these wasters being there as much as he did but that I just didn't have the emotional tools to get rid of them.

On one occasion, Linda and I had gone out shopping, and returned home to find three total strangers sitting on our sofa together with a girl who was a vague acquaintance of mine. She greeted me with a broad grin and announced to me proudly that they had decided that they were going to turn my house into a pagan women's space. I tried to explain, kindly, that I was not a pagan, nor a woman, and that this house was *my* space - but they just accused me of being sexist, and ranted for half-an-hour through the open window at me after I politely asked them to leave.

On another occasion two women with serious psychological problems had somehow invited themselves to stay. One was a friend of another friend of mine to whom I owed money, and so I felt beholden to allow her to stay on my sofa until we found her a place to live permanently, and the other was a friend of Graham's. As I often did in those days when life got too much for me, I had spent several days in bed lying in the darkness waiting for the pain to end. My good friend Nick Redfern - a renowned UFO author - had come down for a visit, though I had completely forgotten his imminent arrival. The first thing that I knew was when his jovial face peeked around my bedroom door, and he asked me in his broad Brummie accent, "Who the fuck are those two mad bitches sitting drinking Special Brew on your doorstep?"

Blearily, I heaved my immense bulk into some semblance of a sitting position. "What do you mean?" I asked. He told me - while trying to bite back the streams of hysterical laughter - that there were two strange women; one immensely fat and the other almost skeletally thin, one with a strange squawking voice that sounded like a castrated turkey, and the other brandishing the remains of a mobile phone. Apparently they were both dead drunk, in a state of semi undress, surrounded by empty beer cans and a veritable mountain of cigarette butts, shrieking at the top of their voices about the fat one's recent sojourn at her Majesty's pleasure for stabbing her ex-boyfriend. Apparently, Nick thought that even by CFZ standards (as they were at the time), that it was a bit much, to have two drunken mad women screeching about stabbing people whilst sitting on on the doorstep of what was supposed to be the world's leading Cryptozoological research institute.

The brain-damaged woman stayed with us for a few more days during which she started to exhibit some ludicrously paranoid affectations. She became convinced that she had been hounded out of her home in the north by neighbours who were convinced that she was a "pee-dee-o-phile", and that these aforesaid neighbours were now hiding outside my house whispering abuse at her every time she left. She used this as an excuse to stay at the CFZ long after she had outstayed her (very limited) welcome.

Even Graham was not immune to the madness of that horrible summer. Although he was disgusted with me for allowing this ongoing freak show to continue at mine - and the CFZ's expense - he too was drinking far too much, and his behaviour sometimes took a strange and disturbing turn. One evening in August Richard and I were summoned to Graham's flat by an almost incoherently drunk phone call from his girlfriend. Apparently, Graham had had an accident and needed to go to hospital, but was refusing to go. Richard and I drove round to Graham's flat post-haste, to find a scene which looked as if the Manson family had been holding a genteel *soiree*. There was blood everywhere. The bedclothes were soaked in blood. There was blood soaked into the floor. The sink in the corner of the room was smashed, and there were bloody handprints all over the walls. Sitting in the middle of the bed, wearing nothing but a *Hawkwind* T-shirt and a pair of grubby underpants was Graham - out of his brain, with an alarming gash on his right knee. He was cheerfully singing an out of tune version of *"Masters of the Universe"*, and waving his hands around wildly to the music, oblivious to the fact that every time he moved another spurt of blood would pour out of his kneecap. To cap it all, he had painted toenails. "What the fuck has happened here?" we asked, and were answered with an incoherent tale about how during a play fight, things got out of hand and his girlfriend had whacked him on the knee with a teacup, which then broke.

I telephoned the ambulance and despite Graham's protests, Richard and I bundled him in. Leaving his girlfriend to tidy up the mess, we followed the ambulance to hospital in my Mercedes. The events of that evening - in the accident and emergency room at the Royal Devon and Exeter Hospital, Wonford - will be etched in my memory for all time. Graham was insistent that there was nothing wrong with him, and that I was just "laying my trip on him", by insisting that he stay in hospital to be seen by a doctor. He got more and more noisy, and verbally abusive so that the senior nurse on duty took me to one side and threatened to call the police if I didn't calm him down. Graham then removed his underpants and started wandering around the main triage area of the emergency room demanding to know where the bar was. I cajoled him into putting his underpants back on when - after a wait of nearly three hours - the duty doctor arrived. His name was Boris. He was from the Ukraine, and he could hardly speak English.

"...but what can I'd do with this silly man's when he is so drunks that no nurses is going to come and helps me?" he asked me with deep, eastern European conviction. Graham then removed his underpants again and started to sing. With my fingers crossed behind my back, and omitting to mention the fact that I had actually been struck off the Nurses Register over a decade before on mental health grounds, I assured him that I was, indeed, a nurse and more than qualified to help Dr Boris in the necessary task of removing a number of shards of broken, grubby crockery from the wound in Graham's knee, assessing the damage, if necessary applying a venous clamp, and stitching up the wound.

Dr Boris looked unconvinced.

" but how is you going to - how do you say - making him a lie-down? He is a singing and a dancing....."

By this stage Graham was convinced that he was actually at some sort of a rock festival and was dancing manically in the corner to music that only he could hear...

"Like this", I said, and with a silent plea that Graham would forgive me in the morning, I punched him on the jaw, and knocked him on to the gurney. Back in the days when I had been a nurse I had been taught some totally illegal methods for subduing a violent patient. I sat on Graham's chest, with my forearm against his throat and remembered everything I had been taught, and from then on the procedures went relatively according to plan, and Graham even began to sober up and co-operate. I eventually got him home just after four in the morning.

Life continued to get weirder. When my 41st birthday party came along, the police were called twice because of the noise, there were an inordinate amount of drugs and alcohol consumed, and two of my less attractive party guests (who had never actually met before that evening), gave a live sex show in my garden shed. Another party guest entertained the revellers with accounts about how she had recently taken to picking up geriatric, alcoholic tramps who were sleeping rough in the graveyard opposite her flat, and bringing them back to her abode for group sex. She told us proudly that one of the tramps had given her anal warts and had then proceeded to defecate in her bath. She also claimed that her father was determined to sabotage her burgeoning career as an artist by masturbating all over her most prized paintings, and how - one night - she had been so drunk that she had started to eat what she thought was cold fish and chips, only to find that it was a piece of dog excrement wrapped in newspaper. Could my life get any worse?

Sadly, yes it could.

I battled unsuccessfully with ill health, and Graham's ex-girlfriend Tracey (with whom I had also enjoyed a very brief affair) killed herself. Money, emotional and health problems proliferated until none of us knew what the hell was happening. I was pretty well bed-ridden and worse, I had become completely addicted to the medication I had been prescribed and essentially I was a junkie. I was abusing my pain killers to a ridiculous degree. I discovered that in a world where I had nothing, the addictive alkaloids from the opium poppy provided a short term solace so irrisistible that I gladly fell deeper and deeper into a morass of drug dependency.

On Christmas Eve, I took an overdose of various pharmaceutical opiates. It was the second time in my life that I have ever made a proper suicide attempt. It wasn't a cry for help. I had just had enough. Luckily I was horribly and messily sick everywhere. I woke up on Christmas morning feeling horrible, but at least I didn't want to die anymore. I celebrated the anniversary of the birth of Our Lord by being repeatedly sick secure in the knowledge that it couldn't get any worse. That night, drunk to hell, I dreamed about my sojourn in Nevada.

I dreamed about the desolate beauty of the desert. I dreamed about the happy day I had spent in the National Park with my friend Kay. I dreamed about the hummingbirds that busily glided between the wisteria flowers - apparently floating in the air. I dreamed of the buzzards that circled endlessly in the eggshell blue sky above the lonely red sandstone mesa that towered high over the gambing resort where I had stayed. And I dreamed about sitting in a darkened bar with a gaunt man with a big nose and wild staring eyes who told me with a smile. "You gave a good talk and it's a good book and you're a nice guy but until you go back to the beginning you'll never be happy".

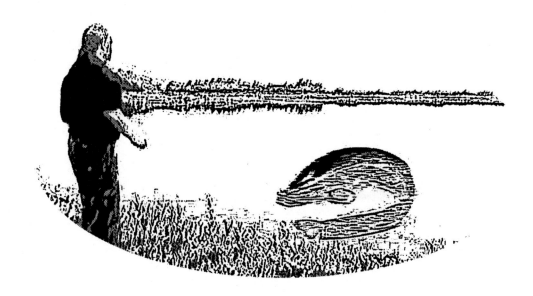

Chapter Twelve

A Golden Dawn

And from then on, it all started to get better again. In the second week of January, after nearly five years away, my daughter came home. This isn't as dramatic as it sounds. Although I never heard from Alison again after the day she walked out (I saw her in the street couple of times and we pointedly crossed the road to avoid each other), Lisa had resumed contact with me back in the summer of 1998. We had seen each other for short periods of time every two or three months and it was obvious that she - like me - had serious mental health problems. However, one night early January she telephoned me and asked if she could come home. I was overjoyed.

As winter began, tentatively to turn into spring, I was on the road to recovery. I had spent the long winter nights thinking about my encounter with Rueben and I realised that he had been right. It was time for me to go back to my roots.

The first February of the 21st Century was a strange one indeed. Rural England, (and although I live in the city I am near enough to the country to consider myself rural), was reeling from an epidemic of foot and mouth disease. The fog of a Devonian winter evening was mixed, literally, with the pall of smoke from the vile funeral pyres of tens of thousands of slaughtered animals. The newspapers and saloon bars were rife with horror stories of the crude and inhumane methods of slaughter employed by the rank amateurs who had been drafted in by the Ministry of Agriculture to cull these poor unfortunate creatures. As one drove through the Devon lanes the fields on either side of the roads were empty. Large tracts of the countryside were cordoned off and rural England was under seige.

Most of my books over the last decade or so have described my search for the England of my dreams. I was brought up in Hong Kong during the last days of the Empire on which the sun would never set, and so was approaching puberty by the time I came to live in the English countryside for the first time. Perhaps this is why I fell in love with it. Like all my love affairs it was ultimately doomed, as I searched in vain for the English countryside about which I had dreamed and fantasised whilst in the tropical splendour of the Hong Kong archipelago. I had been writing about my love affair with rural England for years, and perhaps it was because everywhere I looked, I saw the object of my desires lying raped and ravaged like the victim of some horrible bout of ethnic cleansing that I started thinking about writing this book. Rueben would, I was sure, have been proud of me.

There really isn't much else to say about 2001. With my renewed role as a surrogate father to bolster me up, I had quit using opiates by the early spring. There were some serious issues between Graham and myself, but they were not to be sorted out for another year or so. 2001 was spent picking up the pieces from the disastrous previous year. Richard and I worked very hard writing articles for any magazine that would have us, just in order to carry on producing *Animals & Men,* promoting the Weird Weekend (our annual convention which had begun in 2000), and the CFZ Yearbook. Together we watched in horror as the airliners crashed into the twin towers of the World Trade Centre, and together we worked to ensure that the Centre for Fortean Zoology - my precious creation that had so very nearly perished in the previous year - would survive into the new millennium.

When Tracey died, we had adopted her dog, and despite my silent promise on the day that Toby died, there was once again the sound of doggy footprints padding up and down the wooden stairs of my house. Once again there was a CFZ dog - and all was really right in the world. About the only good thing which had happened in the dreadful year of 2000 was that Richard travelled to Thailand to make a documentary about the Naga - a semi legendary giant snake - for the *Discovery Channel*. His trip was a resounding success, and together we made as much capital as we could out of it. As soon as I was well enough to travel again Richard and I - both together and separately - hit the road and appeared on lecture stages all over the country. These days I was sober most of the time, and although there was the odd late-night drunken sing-song during residential conferences such as LAPIS, my hell-raising days were mostly behind me. I bought a new suit, had a haircut and did my best to present the CFZ as a respectable and reputable organisation. In the early summer our good friend Nick Redfern left us. When I had appeared at the International UFO Convention in Nevada, all I had got out of it was an enigmatic meeting with a man who looked like a fictional character by Robert Heinlein, a drunken blow-job from a woman who should have known better, and a reputation as somebody who didn't believe in the ETH, and refused to play the American new-age game at any cost. When Nick made his second appearance there in the spring of 2001 he met the woman who was later to become his wife. He moved to Texas in the early summer and married her in the autumn. Sometimes fairy tales do happen.

2002 started badly. After a holiday in Spain with my father, my mother was taken ill and rushed to hospital. It was a reccurrence of the cancer, which had stricken her down some years earlier. After a six-week illness she died in early March. I was desolate because I adored my mother, even though we had drifted apart in recent years.

My mother's death gave me somewhat of an intimation of my own mortality. My health had been gradually deteriorating for years, and whilst by the spring of 2002 I was relatively drug free, and I was no longer consuming alcohol by the bucketload, I was still far from well. What was worse was that I had been forced to accept the position that whereas none of the things that were wrong with me were actually going to kill me, I was never going to recover from them, and I could look forward to the rest of my life spent as some sort of an invalid. This idea didn't thrill me overly, and so I decided to do exactly what I had always done during my adult life. I ignored the problem and got on with something else.

During the long, hard weeks at the end of winter and the beginning of spring whilst my mother lay in Barnstaple hospital slowly dying, Richard and I took it upon ourselves to reinvent the CFZ. We decided that whereas we were now a reasonably well-organised publishing company that put out regular issues of a reasonably literate magazine, and the odd book here and there, it was time for the CFZ to progress onto the next level - that of a *bona fide* field research organisation. We realised with horror that apart from Richard's week long sojourn to Thailand with the *Discovery Channel*, in the autumn of 2000, and a few days spent cutting up a dolphin here, or chasing big cats there, we had done no real research whatsoever for years. Indeed between 1998 and 2002 my entire life had been spent battling my personal daemons, or earning a living. This was not what either of us wanted when we had set out to become Fortean Zoologists, and so we resolved to do something about it as quickly as possible. My mother died at the end of March and the whole of my family - those of us who were left anyway - gathered for the funeral together with what seemed like hundreds of mourners from across the world.

On the morning of the funeral I stood outside the old, grey stone church at Clovelly and watched the serried ranks of mourners march wearily through the lych gate. Although spring was undoubtedly upon us, it was a cold day and the thin drizzle coated my glasses as I stared blankly into the middle distance. The daffodils - one of my mother's favourite flowers - peeped bravely above the grey-green grass, and despite the rain a lone cock blackbird was singing defiantly. I was gagging for a cigarette, and feeling abominably sorry for myself. I had adored my mother, and it was her early tutelage into the ethos of Rider-Haggard and Edgar Wallace that had made me into what I was eventually to become. As the surprisingly tiny coffin was carried into the main aisle of the church my mind was miles away. I was not listening to my brother's intonation of the funeral service. I was not listening to the eulogy. Except in the most basic physical manner I wasn't even in the church. I was a seven-year-old boy walking hand in hand with my mother along Lugard Road on Victoria Peak. We were in search of butterflies, caterpillars and tadpoles. We were living in a surreal enchanted summer, which has never really ended.

That night, lying on the mattress on the floor of my increasingly lonely little bedroom I wondered what I was going to do next. For the first time in months the fruit of the poppy coursed through my veins, caressing my battered synapses with the waters of lethe. But even in my befuddled state I knew that opiates were never gonna solve the problem of what I was going to do next. Then it came to me. A few weeks earlier Richard and I had received the following news story as an email:

The monster of the mere
Feb 14 2002

Liverpool Echo

IT sounds like an unlikely fisherman's tale.

But the manager of the Martin Mere nature reserve in West Lancashire is convinced there is something large lurking in the deeps. Some creature, say staff at the reserve, is responsible for dragging fully grown swans into one of their lakes.

And it could be a monster fish the size of a small car, a kind of cross between Jaws and the Loch Ness Monster. This is one theory which might explain the sight of a swan being pulled underwater.

Several visitors witnessed the swan trying to flee the grasp of a giant underwater predator on Thursday night. In an earlier incident, the 20-acre lake where swans gather was left deserted as they all refused to go on to the water.

"Something is completely spooking them," commented reserve manager Chris Tomlinson.

"On two occasions, both Thursdays, January 17 and February 7, something in the water has caused the 1,500-plus wild wintering swans to completely disappear".

Centre manager Pat Wisniewski adds: "Whatever it was out there last night must have been pretty big to pull a swan back into the water. Swans weigh up to 13 kilos".

Pat added: "This could be an extremely large pike, or a Wels catfish. Both conceivably could survive in the rather murky, de-oxygenated water for years and grow to an extremely large size".

Four years ago Pat spotted something that appeared to be the size of a small car circling the mere just below the waterline of the lake, which is four metres deep. One theory is that something may have made its way into the mere through its drainage system many years ago as a juvenile and remained there ever since having grown too large to escape.

Visitors to WWT Martin Mere are asked to keep their eyes peeled for the monster.

For some reason that story had intrigued us both. We included it in the issue of *Animals & Men* which we were working on at the time, and when we attended the *Fortean Times* Unconvention in early April we met a young man from Liverpool who had done a little bit of preliminary investigation into the subject.

He was a strange looking fellow with dark, malevolent eyes that seemed to sink far deeper into his face than anyone could have imagined. He wore a T.Shirt which proclaimed "I fuckin' hate everyone and everything", and when I commented wryly to him that I could empathise, as I felt like that some mornings, all he could do was mutter' "it's ironic innit?" at me, in a pugnacious manner which suggested that he actually meant every word of it. He was far from being the most prepossessing person with whom I have ever had a fortean meeting of minds, and he could tell us nothing concrete to help us in our quest, but he muttered "fukkin Martin Mere is a weird place man", enough times that we decided that not only were we gonna have to agree with him but that it was about time that we went up there ourselves to decide for ourselves.

However, things aint always that easy.

I had always been rather scared of swans - ever since an unfortunate incident in my childhood, soon after I returned to England. For the first few months that my family spent in the UK, we lived in a village called Whiteparish in Wiltshire. My mother's parents were still alive then - during the early summer of 1971 - and a tiny cottage which had once been owned by Lord Nelson's lover Lady Hamilton, became a family base from which my father and mother and my brother and I commuted every few weeks down to the West Country in search of somewhere permanent to live. Personally I enjoyed this sojourn in Wiltshire very much indeed, and thus began a love affair with the area, which has continued to the present day.

On one fateful Tuesday morning, my family was in the pretty little market town of Andover. It seems amazing in these days where horror stories of abducted children, and sex offenders running rampant around our society, but my parents had left me (aged 11), and my brother (aged 8), to our own devices, feeding bread to the ducks and coots, in one of the pretty little parks which are dotted around the town centre, by the side of the river. This is the first time that I had ever encountered a swan. I was perfectly aware of what ducks were like - I had seen several species in Hong Kong, but as far as I was aware, these beautiful birds, which swam in majestically up and down the water, were merely large ducks. How wrong I was.

Drawn to us by a apparently limitless supply of pieces of bread, we were soon surrounded by water birds of all shapes and sizes, clamouring for our largesse. Slowly, and majestically, one of the Mighty Swans swam slowly towards us. It was obvious - with hindsight - that he was the king of the river, because the serried ranks of small birds, which had gathered around us, parted - as if by magic. I was entranced by the beauty of the giant bird as it swam slowly towards me. It was one of those magical moments when time seems to go in slow motion, and for what seemed like hours (although it was only a few minutes), the colossal water bird and I looked each other in the eyes as we grew slowly closer. Suddenly the spell was broken. The great swan gave a most un-regal squawk, and rushed towards me. It grabbed the bag of bread out my hand and knocked me over, bruising my leg badly, as it pushed me aside with its mighty wings. There was a god almighty splash, and with the merest flip of its other wing - almost without noticing what it was doing, it pushed my little brother into the river.

Ever since then I have treated swans with the utmost respect, and the idea that there was a mysterious predator lurking in a Lancashire lake, strong enough to be able to pull one of these mighty birds beneath the surface, was an exciting one.

It was another seven or eight weeks before Richard and I were able to travel to Lancashire and discover quite how weird the place was for ourselves. Within days of my mother's death my father started to go downhill badly. It is not surprising really. He and my mother had been childhood sweethearts in the early 1930s, and except for a few years during The War - and its immediate aftermath - when he had gone to Sea, they had been together for nearly seventy years. I know how desolate I had been when Alison and I had parted after only twelve years, and I could only imagine at the whole that he must have been feeling in his life.

Strangely, however, something wonderful did come out of the appalling emotional psychodrama of my mothers death. My father and I - who had sadly always had a difficult relationship - slowly and surely became friends. I telephoned him every day, and despite years when we both did our best to ignore the others existence, we became closer and a very real bond was established. I like to think that this was my mothers final - and possibly greatest - gift to us both, because the relationship that I then began to develop with my father was very special and became ever more important to me.

Because of his own deteriorating condition he decided that he no longer wanted to drive the elderly Jaguar that my mother had given him for a 40th wedding anniversary present. He diffidently asked me whether I wanted to take it over?

Of course I did. I loved that car.

And so, although I still had no real visible means of support I found myself driving an elderly, but undeniably aristocratic looking dark-blue Jag, which was a vast improvement on the succession of old bangers that had been the CFZmobiles ever since its inception.

About a month after the Unconvention we held our third annual 'Weird Weekend', and partly to mark the 20th anniversary of the first record that I had released, and partly because it seemed like a good idea I managed to get my band out of rehab long enough to play their first gig in six years. Before we played, I sat in the bar with my old pal Marcus Sims (the bass player), and we reminisced over what a long, strange trip it had always been.

At that time there seemed to be a plethora of pop groups who were pretending to be mentally ill. Madness had always been a favoured *leitmotif* amongst certain sectors of the rock and roll establishment, but with *The Amphibians from Outer Space* it had not been an affectation; it was a grim and somewhat uncomfortable reality. Marcus had spent a considerable time in Tone Vale Psychiatric Hospital near Taunton, my own struggles with reality have been documented at length in this book, Dave the drummer was a serious depressive and my darling daughter Lisa had her own daemons to battle on a daily basis. Three middle aged men and a young woman staggered onto the stage, and despite the fact that we had only rehearsed twice (in my sitting room without either amps or a drum kit), and had not actually played together with amplifiers since we recorded the *Weird World* album at Channel House studios in Bristol with Lionel Fanthorpe during the summer of 1999, we played - though I say it myself - a blinding 50 minute show. We just about managed to stay in tune, and despite my admitted shortcomings as a lead guitarist, we managed to pull it off. After eight or nine of my songs, I grinned at Marcus, grabbed the microphone, and started to taunt the audience:

"Do you assholes want us to go through our programmed set and act real slick? Or do you just want a 20 minute version of *Louie Louie*?"

The audience - most of whom were too young to know that I was quoting Iggy Pop from thirty years previously - started to howl as we thundered into the greatest and dumbest riff in rock and roll. True to our boast we kept the three-chord monster going for nearly twenty minutes until I turned my amp up to full volume, knelt down in front of it with my guitar and started to produce wave after wave of deafening feedback. I left the stage as the band continued to play, and the ear-splitting screams of feedback rent the air. Richard - dressed, as always, in black - took my place on the stage and started to scream a Lovecraftian invocation to the eldritch Elder Gods. The audience looked stunned, but realising that they had been present at a very special and invocatory occasion began to scream applause.

I disapeared to the other bar with my cousin Pene and a few close cronies, where I was joined by Marcus and Dave. We set out to drink the night away, but I have a sneaking suspicion that Richard's mock comedic invocation somehow struck a chord with a giant beast living deep in the murky waters of a Lancashire lake. For deep in Martin Mere something was stirring.

A few days later, Richard and I set off to see if we could find out what it was.

Still getting used to the luxury of driving a Jaguar rather than an old banger, I drove northwards in a daze. Never having been someone who enjoyed motorway driving, once we had passed Bristol, we took the back roads and drove relatively sedately through the Worcestershire countryside on our way north. I first fell in love with the English countryside in 1971, and - unlike many of my later amours - my affections have proved to be permanent. However, I do not think I have ever seen my beloved look so delightful as she did on that late spring day as we drove towards our Lancastrian nemesis. The May blossom was fully out, and the hedgerows were a riot of muted but gay colours.

There is something particularly special about the spring flowers of England. As I write this chapter I am sitting in semi-rural Illinois - two years to the day after the events I am describing. I can see for the first time a transatlantic spring. There are flowers, there are birds and butterflies but they are different ones and look oddly alien to my anglophilic eyes. Because the CFZ is getting ever more complex and demanding I can never get any of my own writing done at home, and so Graham packed me off for a fortnight to America to finish this book. I am progressing at a rate of knots, but as I look out of the sitting room window here in Marshall, IL, and I see an American Robin - a peculiar bird the size of a thrush which is totally unlike its British namesake save for its reddish breast - engaged in a tug of war with a particularly recalcitrant worm, and a large and pugnacious swallowtail butterfly patrolling the herbaceous border like a stealth fighter in the skies above Basra, I suddenly feel a pang of homesickness. May is the most beautiful time of the British year, and for the first time in 34 years I am not in England to see it.

Casting my mind backwards twenty-four months I can relive our journey northwards in my minds eye as it if were yesterday. By lunchtime we were driving parallel to the Long Mynd; that mysterious chunk of prehistoric Shropshire made famous by Childrens author Malcom Saville. The peak of one of the hills was shrouded in a grey mist; unusual on such a balmy day when the rest of the sky was a translucent, robins egg blue. I pointed out this to Richard as we drove by, telling him the legend of The Devil's Chair - the name given to this rocky outcrop.

According to legend, the rocks of the Devil's Chair were brought there by the Devil himself. Curiously, perhaps, he was carrying a load of stones in his apron and apparently travelling across Britain from Ireland, when he fancied a rest. As the legend goes, the Devil was actually planning to use his load of stones to fill in the valley on the other side of the Stiperstones, which is known as Hell's Gutter. Unfortunately for him, as he got up after his rest on the highest rock of the Stiperstones, his apron strings snapped and the rocks tumbled out. Instead of picking them up, the Devil left the rocks scattered all over the ridge and the legend has it that you can smell the brimstone on them in hot weather.

On the longest night of the year, according to legend, he sits on his chair and summons all his local followers - dark-witches and evil spirits, mainly - and they choose their king for the year. However, he is said to visit the area regularly, and whenever he is in residence, the Devils Chair is shrouded in the grey mist as it was on the day we drove past.

I do not enjoy driving any more, but *this* was an idyllic drive. Pausing only to make a detour to Nick Redferns fathers house in Walsall to collect some camera equipment and a faz machine, we drove further north and eventually found ourselves approaching the little town of Southport just before dusk. We found our hotel, ate an enormous repast of Chinese food washed down with beer, and retired to sleep for the night. I had insomnia and sat up in bed typing what was to become my book *The Monster of the Mere* onto my newly acquired laptop, as Richard snored away in the bed opposite me, dreaming of Gothic amazon women.

The next few days were taken up with explorations. Western Lancashire is a peculiar place. We discovered that the lake now known as Martin Mere was relatively new, and had only been constructed in the early 1970s, although it was on the site of part of what had once been the biggest stretch of fresh water in England. Until the end of the 18th Century Martin Mere - five miles long and two miles wide - was an immense stretch of water, with a rich and proud legacy of folklore and quasi-forten phenomena. It had dragon legends, a tradition of human sacrifice, a mermaid, and even had links with King Arthur! According to some legends it was the lake where Sir Launcelot - the son of the King of France - had been taken to safety upon his fathers untimely (and nasty) demise. In his adult like he had taken on the name Launcelot-du-Lac (Launcelot of the Lake), and this was THE lake!

This part of Lancashire really has very little relationship to the rest of the county. It is all reclaimed land for one thing - being largely the quondam lake bottom of Martin Mere, and is as flat as the Lincolnshire Wolds. It has a strange ambience about it, so strange in fact that as soon as you enter the area it feels like you have suddenly been transported into another space and time. This is not unique in England. When Alison and I were travelling into Cornwall every few weeks during the autumn of 1995 and the spring of 1996 to meet 'Doc' Shiels and go chansing His Owliness we both remarked on the fact that whereas both sides of the 'official' border between Devon and Cornwall were much of a muchness, there was a spot on the A30 - somewhere just before Launceston - that the whole ambience of the countryside changed imperceptably and that suddenly you felt that you were in a different part of the space-time continuum.

Richard and I spent a blissful three or four days exploring the region. We visited Martin-Mere itself and spoke to Pat Wisniewski the warden. We became convinced that there was 'something' in the lake, and were overjoyed when Pat gave us permission to come back with a proper investigation team. About the only thing that marred our trip was the fact that for most of this leg of it we were based in Blackpool.

You will remember that during my stay in Mexico I had annoyed one of my fellow travellers by referring to a tiny village in the Puebla Desert - with its open sewer, dead dogs, child prostitutes and appallingly corrupt village priest - as "the biggest shit-hole I have ever visited". I would like to retract that statement. I have now been to Blackpool.

In my 2002 book *The Monster of the Mere* I describe our first impressions of the town. I do not think that there is anything if I can say here to improve on the description:

Richard and I gazed out of the window in horror as we cruised round and round the filthy streets looking for somewhere to park. "This is everything that's wrong with Britain today lumped together, multiplied by ten and put in the same place", growled Richard as another gang of drunken louts with skinhead haircuts, ear-rings and tattoos, false plastic breasts and cans of lager lurched across the road in front of us, as their girlfriends staggered on behind. He told me how, in the late 1970s, his grandfather had described seeing groups of small children playing in the sea at Blackpool while lumps of human faeces floated around them.

Family groups of the most horrific looking people were everywhere. The very people who you see on every television programme about the dangers of paedophilia, marching up and down clutching badly spelled placards and threatening to 'torch the gaff' of someone they believe to be a 'nonce' just because he has a passing resemblance to someone whose features appeared in a badly printed photograph in The News of the World were there with their children. Their little girls wore the sort of revealing clothes that as a parent myself, I would shudder at an eighteen year old wearing.

I am no feminist, but I try to treat everyone with respect regardless of age, sex, colour or creed. However, I would argue that for a woman of any age to be wearing skin-tight pink silk trousers and a tiny pink crop top, made of a sheer material which not only plainly revealed her erect nipples, but was obviously designed to do so, and emblazoned with a motto reading "I'm a sexy bitch" is inappropriate. It is demeaning not only to herself but to all members of her sex. When the person wearing it is no older than nine years old it beggars belief. When her sister - older , but still obviously under the age of consent - is wearing an equally revealing outfit and a T Shirt proclaiming her to be a 'Porn Star' one really does feel that one is losing grip on reality.

I feel like little Bobby Zimmerman writing "A Hard Rain's Gonna Fall" as I try and give you just a few of the impressions we gathered of this disgusting cess pit of a town.

* We saw women in late middle age wearing enormous cowboy hats covered with red glitter, pink fairy wings, and T Shirts reading, Kiss me, spank me, F*** me.

[AUTHOR'S NOTE: The word F*** is what was printed on the T Shirt. As regular readers of my work will know, I am quite prepared to use the old Anglo-Saxon word 'fuck' where it is appropriate. To use an F and three asterisks is merely vulgar]

* We saw a group of drunken lads in their late teens or early twenties staggering about in the gutter. One was dressed as a circus ringmaster, one was dressed as a clown, one as a gorilla and one as the devil

* We saw gangs of drunks with the cross of St George painted on their faces, standing in a line as they urinated in the gutter as their jeering girlfriends stood by watching

* We saw a joke shop which sold sex aids and children's toys side by side in the window.

The streets were full of rubbish, the sea looked like an open sewer, the gutters were full of a river of piss and vomit in which MacDonalds wrappers floated merrily, and the air stank of grease, cigarette smoke, sweat and decay.

It was a filthy place, and I have seldom enjoyed a stay anywhere less. Martin Mere, however, was a completely different experience. It was one of the most beautiful places that I have ever been. It had an amazing history. Once upon a time it had been the largest lake in England - some five miles long, and three miles across. However, land was at a premium, and at the end of the 16th century plans were made to drain the lake. By the mid-19th century, the largest lake in England was no more. In its place where acres upon acres of rich verdant pasture - reclaimed land which was excellent for farmers because in the main it consisted of the rich silt from the bottom of the vanished lake. The area was riddled with weird folklore. The lake had once been the haunt of a Mermaid, and there were even stories of weird pagan cults who had practised human sacrifice.

Although the lake had been drained, the resulting land was still well below sea level, and at least once a decade, there was severe flooding. In the 1960s Sir Peter Scott brought a large part of the area, and started to refill the lake. It became the property of the Wildfowl and Wetlands Trust, and remains as a nature reserve to the present day. It was here that the mysterious predator was said to lurk and prey upon the majestic swans and geese. We made an appointment to see the Senior Warden - Pat Wisnieski. He was a lovely bloke - a few years older than me, and with a wicked sense of humour. Could we, we asked, come up to the lake with a full investigation party?

"Yeah, why not" he said. And the die was cast.

Nearly two months later we were back.

SEARCH FOR GIANT PREDATOR WITH TASTE FOR SWANS:
Hunt goes High Tech for Mystery Monster

Experts from Exeter will spend four days using specialist equipment to discover whether Martin Mere really does hide a monster. Attracted by reports in The Advertiser earlier in the year about the possibilities of a wels catfish or a giant pike attacking birds the sleuths will be gazing over the waters of the wildfowl reserve's biggest lake. The Centre for Fortean Zoology will be unloading infra-red cameras and sonar equipment tomorrow ready for its vigil. Martin Mere's centre manager Pat Wisniewski said the intention was to use fish finding radar-like equipment to try to trace large bodies of fish in the lake as well as to tow a baited line in the hope that anything rising to it could be photographed and identified just in case the mystery monster, which was seen dragging a thirteen kilo swan underwater is a wels catfish as has been suggested. The team will be using infra red sights to watch over the lake overnight for any nocturnal fish. At the moment there are no big stocks of visiting birds and most of the resident birds have finished breeding so there is nothing to be harmed out there.

It is an ideal time to do it, said Mr Wisniewski.

Angling experts were divided as to whether the waters of swan lake were deep enough to hide a giant catfish which can grow to 62lbs in Britain and reportedly 202 lb abroad, or whether it was a large pike trying to attack a swan.

The expedition was a resounding success but it was marred by personal problems. Graham and I were hardly speaking to each other. Our relationship had deteriorated to such an extent that it was obvious that something would have to be done, or else we would either come to blows or - at the very least - have to end both our professional and our personal relationship.

Graham had been a pillar of strength to me for years and the two of us had been through a lot. However, when he had initially become involved the CFZ had been a far looser, laid back and less professional body. Over a period of years the demands on us all became far more onerous, and Graham - who had joined a very *lasseiz faire* and laid-back bunch of groovers - was unprepared for the new and dramatic change in direction brought on by Richard and me almost overnight in early 2002. He was also tired of the madness at the CFZ.

Although I hadn't realised it at the time, he was greatly disturbed by the *milieu* of strangeness that had surrounded us all during 1999/2000. As already chronicled, the years of madness and excess had taken their toll on me to such an extent that I ended up attempting to take my own life. So blind I had been to the rest of the omniverse that I hadn't noticed the effect that my mental and physical decline had taken on Graham.

The events of the spring of 2002 had been the last straw. For years the Unconvention had been our major fundraiser for the CFZ, and each year we spent an inordinate amount of time and effort preparing for it. This year we had been hit by two trajedies. My mother's death, and a serious bout of ill health suffered by Richard's father which necessitated Richard spending ten days away from the CFZ in his hometown of Nuneaton. Both these unfortunate events took place during the time when we would normally have been manufacturing books and magazines for sale at the Unconvention.

It is completely because of Graham's sterling efforts that we managed to get enough stuff together for the event. He worked some immensely long hours and we managed to - against all odds - turn in a respectable performance. Then came the Weird Weekend, and by the time we returned to Martin Mere in July Graham was exhausted and well overdue for a break.

This was probably not the best time for Richard and I to spring the whole new rebranding of the CFZ upon him.

But that is exactly what we did. And I have regretted it ever since.

There were four of us, in two cars, who drove along the enchanted lanes that led across the quondam lake bottom towards the waterfowl reserve. The fourth was our newest recruit; John Fuller.

'Black John', who got his name because a) he is black and b) his name is John, joined the CFZ as part of the Right Honourable Tony Blair's 'New Deal' programme aimed at reducing the numbers of adult unemployed. He came for six weeks, and over two years later he is still here. He is a strange chap.

Rastafari is a religious movement, predominantly of black people who know Africa as the birthplace of Mankind and the throne of Emperor Haile Selassie I, a 20th Century manifestation of God whom they believe had lit their pathway towards righteousness, and is therefore worthy of reverence. Rasta, as it is more commonly called, has its roots in the teachings of Jamaican Black Nationalist Marcus Garvey, who in the 1930s preached a message of black self-empowerment, and initiated the "Back to Africa" movement. Which called for all blacks to return to their ancestral home, and more specifically Ethiopia. He taught self-reliance "at home and abroad" and advocated a "Back to Africa" consciousness, awakening black pride and denouncing the white mans Eurocentric woldview, colonial indoctrination that caused blacks to feel shame for their African heritage. "Look to Africa", said Marcus Garvey in 1920, "when a black king shall be crowned, for the day of deliverance is at hand". Many thought the prophecy was fulfilled when in 1930, Ras Tafari, was crowned emperor Haile Selassie 1 of Ethiopia and proclaimed "King of Kings, Lord of Lords, and the conquering lion of the Tribe of Judah". Haile Selassie claimed to be a direct descendant of King David, the 225th ruler in an unbroken line of Ethiopian Kings from the time of Solomon and Sheba. He and his followers took great pride in being black and wanted to regain the black heritage that was lost by loosing faith and straying from the holy ways. Sellasie was proclaimed by many of his followers to be the next best thing to a 'living god', and this divinity was extended to others in his family.

In the early 1960s, one of Haile Sellasie's nephews had been stationed in London as a Naval Attache; representative of the tiny Imperial Ethiopian Navy. There he had met and fallen in love with an Englishwoman. The result was Robin John Haile Fuller, Crown Prince by birth, rock music archivist by inclination, chef by training and fundementally unsuited to working for any normal employer. I had known him on and off for years, having first met him when Alison and I used to sell him Led

Zeppelin bootlegs at record fairs in the late 1980s. With hindsight, it seemed inevitable that he would end up working at the CFZ.

Marcus Garvey would have been appalled. As well as taking over the onerous duties of printing and manufacturing our books and magazines, a living godhead - the embodiment of the divine consciousness - was now to be found making tea for a middle aged and somewhat cynical scion of the now defunct British Empire. John is a remarkable man. Not only does he accept the 'wings and sparrows of outrageous fortune' at the CFZ with calm good humour, but he is the person most responsible for having dragged us from the realms of pure chaos into something approaching sense and order.

The tiny convoy - my Jaguar and Graham's battered Volvo - pulled into the dry grass of the Martin Mere nature reserve car park soon after lunch. We must have looked a rum crew. Richard, having eschewed his usual gothic garb for black jeans and a *Half Man Half Biscuit* t-shirt, and me wearing a pair of rather nasty blue shorts. Graham and John looked quite dapper but nothing could remove the wild, almost feral, look in Graham's eyes as he did what he always does when you put him in a new place; looks around to make sure he knows where the exits are.

The Lake itself was somewhat of a disappointment. Only an acre and a bit in size, at its deepest point it was only eight feet in depth.

Baron Georges Cuvier (1769-1832) possessed one of the finest minds in history. Almost single-handedly, he founded vertebrate paleontology as a scientific discipline and created the comparative method of organismal biology, an incredibly powerful tool. It was Cuvier who firmly established the fact of the extinction of past lifeforms. He contributed an immense amount of research in vertebrate and invertebrate zoology and paleontology, and also wrote and lectured on the history of science. However he has been held up to ridicule in the eyes of cryptozoologists because of what Bernard Heuvelmans called his 'Rash Dictum'. "There is," the Baron said in 1812, "little hope of discovering new species." Over the next century a whole procession of the world's largest and most exciting new species were discovered.

The phrase 'Cuviers Rash Dictum' has entered the canon of cryptozoological research. One Wednesday at the end of July in 2002, 'Freeman's Rash Dictum' did likewise. The first thing that we did - after unpacking our equipment and installing ourselves in the bird hide where Pat had said we could make camp for the next few days was to have a cup of tea. While John put the kettle on and I started to write up the days events on my laptop, Graham and Richard went for a walk round the perimeter of the lake; something that took in the region of twenty minutes. They reappeared looking hot and cross. The lake, Richard informed us in his most gothically petulant manner, was only "a shallow puddle full of bird shit", and there was no way that there was any large creature hiding in there, and that this whole episode was a "waste of fucking time." He swallowed down his tea and went off in a huff.

Less than five minutes later he was back! He had seen the monster!

Whilst walking around the Mere's edge, Richard came upon a massive fish basking in the shallows. Its black, oily, scaleless back bore a small dorsal fin. Disturbed, the massive animal made off and dove in a tremendous swirl to reappear briefly further out close to a small island. It dove again amidst a huge disturbance. Its length was hard to estimate, as only the back broke the surface but if it *was* attacking swans, the team agreed it would have to be around 8 feet long.

Richard - probably in an attempt to redeem himself following his 'rash dictum' - suddenly became incredibly enthusiastic. He wrote more in the expedition log on my laptop than anyone else had. He wrote cool, calm, zoological sense. However, on occasion he allowed his imagination to run away with itself. Even before he came to live at the CFZ he had become enormously enamoured of a friend of mine - a young lady called Ally. Although this attraction was - and still is unrequieted - she's quite fond of him and rather than do what any sensible person would and tell him to snap out of it, she strings him along - albeit unconsciously - by being nice to him in a slightly vague and new-age manner. Richard's Goth pretensions have been chronicled elsewhere in this volume, and so no one will be particularly surprised to hear that one of his log entries for the Saturday read as follows:

Conducted search of the north end of the island, ground baiting as we went. Saw large fish - but not the target - surfacing eight times. Went back home, asked Little Ally to marry me. She said yes and we now live in a castle with me as her foot-worshipping chattel...

That night we got our own back. As Graham muttered about his need for headspace and went off to do his own inimitable thing, John, Richard and I sat down and ate Chinese food. It was the first time that John had realised quite how besotted Richard was with the object of his affections, and, without meaning to, John and I started to goad Richard as to how far he would go to make her happy. The most ludicrous example that I came up with, was asking him whether he would be happy to be positioned in an upright 'begging' position, with his forelimbs in a rat-like posture, whilst being pulled around in a little metal cart on wheels, with his only nourishment coming from a plastic tube attached to her bile duct. John looked aghast at this, but then neither of us were particularly surprised when he said that the only thing he would not do for her was to give up cryptozoology.

We saw the fish again the next day and made four definite sonar contacts. After a process of scientific detective work we deducted that it was a wels catfish. The wels, sheetfish or European catfish (*Silurus glanis*) is indigenous to continental Europe east of the river Rhine; it appears to be particularly common in eastern Europe, especially in the basin of the river Danube. It has a slimy, scaleless, elongated body and a broad, flat head with a wide mouth. Writing in *Naturalised Animals of the British Isles* Sir Christopher Lever notes that it has a "distinctly sinister appearance". He goes on to describe the creature in some depth:

The head, back and sides are usually some shade of greenish-black spotted with olive-green, and the underside is yellowy-white, with an indistinct blackish marbling; the head and back may sometimes be a deep velvety black and the sides occasionally take on a bronzy sheen. Two long barbels depending from the upper jaw, and four short ones from the lower jaw, help to give the catfish its name. There is no adipose fin, but an enormously elongated anal fin: a tiny dorsal fin is situated half-way between the bases of the pectoral and pelvic fins. The largest authenticated wels, taken from the river Dnieper in the Ukraine in the southern U.S.S.R., measured over 16 ft (5 m) in length and weighed 675 lb (306 kg); elsewhere in Europe and in England, however, the wels seldom exceeds 5 ft (152 cm) in length and 25 lb (11 kg) in weight.

The wels is a solitary fish. It lives mostly in the still, deoxygenated waters of lakes, marshes and lagoons, but can also be found in the lower reaches and backwaters of slow-flowing rivers. Unusually for a catfish it is tolerant of both heavy industrial pollution and salt water and is found naturaly in the brackish water of certain parts of the Black and Baltic Seas. Wels are nocturnal, choosing to feed after dark. They are voracious predators, especially when adults. Lever lists prey species as including: "turbot, bream, crayfish, eels, frogs, roach, tench, ducklings, goslings and occasionally water-voles.".

But how did an animal from Eastern Europe get into a man-made lake in Lancashire? The evidence available to us leads us to conclude that Frank Buckland of the Acclimatisation Society may have introduced the giant fish to Lancashire after his visit to Southport in the 1870s. Frank Buckland was a remarkable man and one of my all-time heroes. His mission in life was to introduce the strangest animals that he could find from around the world into the British countryside, and then when he had succesfully acclimatised them to their new conditions, he would kill and eat them.

We discovered that he had been a close confederate of another eccentric landowner who had been pivotally involved with both the construction of the Leeds-Liverpool Canal and the public aquarium at the Southport Wintergardens. We discovered that the aforesaid aquarium was one of the most sophisticated in the country at the time and had even managed to breed American alligators - no mean feat even today. We know that Buckland had been involved with the succesful introduction of wels into other parts of England, and it was no great leap of the imagination to hypothesise a scenario whereby Buckland and his cronies had introduced young wels fingerlings into the Leeds-Liverpool canal.

According to our hypothesis, one of these remarkable fish had survived, and during one of the occasions when the canal broke its banks (as it had done regularly over the years), had swum into the interconnecting waterways which criss-cross across the marshes which make up the Wildfowl and Wetlands Trust reserve. From there it swam from pond to pond, until - during the floods of the previous year - it had eventually arrived in the lake itself.

We believed that Richard and John Fuller had encountered the biggest and the oldest fish in England. We were feeling rather pleased with ourselves after having conducted a reasonably successful investigation but we were not at all prepared for the torrents of media attention we were to get as a result. To date we have not had anything like it before or since. Just typing +Martin_Mere +Monster into an Internet search engine produces over 20,000 results!

A typical news story read:

Hunters believe they have spotted a mysterious giant fish thought to be responsible for attacks on at least two fully-grown swans.

Sightings of the creature, dubbed the Monster of Martin Mere, were reported earlier this year by visitors to the bird reserve at Burscough, Lancashire. Now a four-man team from the Exeter-based Centre for Fortean Zoology say they have seen a "very big fish" during a 24-hour watch at the Wildfowl and Wetlands Trust beauty spot. Organisation members, who claim to have pursued vampires in Mexico, dragons in Thailand and skunk apes in Florida, have launched a four-day operation in an attempt to crack the mystery of the fish.

They are spending four days at Martin Mere using infra-red cameras, military-style night lights and "fish finder" sonar equipment in a bid to find out more about the mystery beast. Director Jonathan Downes, who said he was somewhat sceptical upon first hearing reports of the fish, believes the monster may be a Wels catfish that could have been born during the reign of Queen Victoria. Native to mainland Europe and introduced into parts of the UK in the late 19th Century, Mr Downes said the Wels catfish is the largest freshwater fish in the world and can reach a length of 16 feet. The "eight-foot fish" was first spotted on Thursday by team member and qualified cryptozoologist Richard Freeman, who is hoping to capture the creature on film.

He said: "I have seen something black and shiny snaking around in the water in almost the same place as the original sighting several months ago. It certainly looked like a Wels catfish.

"I can't say for sure that it was a Wels catfish. But if a pike had attacked the swans there would have been wounds. This thing seems to come up underneath and drag its prey down under the water.

This was only one of many. Things got completely out of hand when I was interviewed on the subject for a radio station claiming to be 'The Voice of Free Iraq', and when the announcer on the evening news on BBC Radio 4 announced a peace accord in Northern Ireland, a bomb outrage in the Middle East, and four blokes seeing a fish in Lancashire in the same breath! It was undoubtedly our first big media success, and we made as much capital as we could out of it. It led to our setting up the first proper CFZ press office and the first media mailing list, and these steps - together with the other new administrative procedures that had been instituted when John Fuller came on board - came a long way to dragging us kicking and screaming from being a bunch of eccentric anarchists, to being (as we are today), the worlds largest and best respected cryptozoological organisation.

But we still had an almost insurmountable problem to overcome. Graham's and my relationship had pretty well reached breaking point, and despite doing our best to appear *ad idem* for the multitudinous media photo shoots, we had come to a point where we needed to do something quickly if our relationship was going to survive at all. I remember telling Richard at the time that my relationship with Graham in August 2002 felt pretty much like my relationship with Alison had done in the days and weeks before we split. We were inexorably heading for disaster and neither of us knew what we were going to do about it.

I think that it is a tribute to both of us that we came through this crisis. Graham took a week off work so we could both decide what we wanted to do, and during this week we both listed the issues that caused conflict with the other. On his return to work we sat down, and over a period of a couple of days we reached an accord that has - broadly at least - worked ever since. The wonderful thing was, however, that we not only repaired our working relationship but became friends again, and our friendship was deeper and stronger than it had been before.

In the meantime the media circus surrounding the Martin-Mere affair showed no sign of abating, and I found myself with more than enough material for the book that eventually became *The Monster of the Mere*. I soon began to realise that there was a socio-psychological process at work here. In the same way as Michel Muerger had shown that most large bodies of water had been imbued with monstrous properties by the folk who live alongside it, I soon began to realise that a similar mechanism seems to take place in smaller bodies of water.

No less a personage as Colonel John Blashford-Snell, who had become our Hon. Life President upon the death of Bernard Heuvelmans a year or so before had told the story of a small village in the home counties which had a village pond haunted by a 'killer perch', which had required the Army to move it.

My burgeoning theory was confirmed a year later when we were called into action to investigate sightings of a crocodile-like creature in a small pond adjoining a housing estate in Cannock, Staffordshire.

The affair started with the following email message from Nick Redfern. He may be living in Texas now - living proof that one can take the boy out of the West Midlands, but the fact that he still keeps a finger on the pulse of the event's of his hometown, prove that one may not be able to take the West Midlands out of the boy!

It was a story from the Wolverhampton Express and Star dated Jun 16, 2003, 14:13:00

Mystery as 'croc' spotted at pool

By Faye Casey
Jun 16, 2003, 14:13:00

A Staffordshire community was today trying to unravel a pool monster mystery after reported sightings of a 7ft "crocodile" type creature rising from the deep.

Police officers, RSPCA inspectors and an alligator expert from Walsall were called to the pool in Roman View, Churchbridge, Cannock, on Saturday afternoon when reports of the sighting were first made.

They searched the area and found nothing, coming to the conclusion that the creature must have been a fish or possibly a snapper turtle.

But locals are not convinced and youngsters have designed their own "croc on the loose" posters to stick on lamposts.
One man, who did not wish to named, said he called the emergency services because what he saw in the pool was not a large fish. He and members of his family had being feeding the swans when the creature emerged.

"We were there looking at the two swans and their baby cygnets," said the man. "And there was a commotion in the water and lots of turbulence. "It was far too big to be caused by a fish. As the creature went past I saw it had a flat head, a 5ft long body, and 2ft tail. It was not smooth and was moving in a snaking action - my initial reaction was it was a crocodile or alligator and so I called the police."

Linda Charteras, from nearby Cheslyn Hay, was also feeding the swans on Saturday afternoon.
"I saw the creature first - a large pool of dirt came up. It looked as though it was after one of the cygnets. I saw its head and long nose and thought there was no way it was a fish," she said.

Natalie Baker, who lives on nearby Nuthurst Drive, said her children and their friends had been designing the posters. "There has got to be something in it for the police and RSPCA to come out."

But despite growing local interest in the creature - a group were out with their binoculars scanning the water last night - the RSPCA say it is highly unlikely the beast was an alligator or croc.

Nick Brundrit, field chief inspector for the RSPCA, said the team kept up observations at the pool for around an hour and a half on Saturday, but there were no obvious signs of an alligator-type creature.

He said the sighting was more likely to be a group of basking carp swimming together, or possibly a snapper turtle.

Following on from the excellent preliminary fieldwork carried out by Mark Martin, the main CFZ expedition finally reached Cannock in the early afternoon of 21st July. After a rendezvous at our digs the Exeter contingent and Mark Martin drove in convoy to the pond at the end of Roman View. No matter how many times one carries out an expedition like this to finally see the location of a series of mystery animal reports for the first time. The pond where the crocodile had been reported was surprisingly wild looking - an oasis of sanity in an increasingly desolate and unattractive West Midlands Environment.

Especially considering that on the far side of the pond from where we set up our temporary base camp, a new section of the M6 was under construction and what looked as if it had once been a virgin woodland on the hillside opposite had been flattened in order to build a featureless and rather nasty out of town shopping centre, the ground immediately surrounding the pond looked even more inviting.

A wide range of butterflies and other flying insects fluttered, hovered, and buzzed their way around the thick vegetation., which was about 800 yards long and 300 yards across was fringed by reeds and bullrushes. A contemplative looking heron sneered down at us from a large bush at one end of the pond, and - indeed - most of the weekend there gazing down at us with a particularly supercilious manner. The pond was also home to a pair of swans and their three cygnets who cruised up and down the water like majestic galleons were and totally ignored us for the duration of our stay.

From CFZ HQ in Exeter came me, Richard Freeman (who had only been back in the country for four days after his first expedition to Sumatra), Graham Inglis, John Fuller, and Nigel Wright (on his first CFZ expedition for some years). We were joined by the aforementioned Mark Martin, Peter Channon (from the Exeter strange phenomenon group), Chris Mullins (from *Beastwatch UK*), Neil Goodwin (from Mercury Newspapers), and Wilf Wharton (the CFZ Wiltshire representative soon to be emigrating to the Antipodes). Much to my amazement, everybody turned up roughly on time, and after three short briefings:

1. Me (giving a general overview)
2. Mark (giving the background to the case)
3. Richard (giving a brief list of do's and don'ts of crocodile handling)

we went to work.

I split the available personnel into three field groups.

1. THE BOAT TEAM (Mark and Graham)
2. THE AWAY TEAM (Richard, Wilf, Chris, Neil and Peter)
3. THE SHORE TEAM (Me, John and Nigel)

The initial idea was that the boat team would spend Monday and Tuesday carrying out intensive sonar sweeps of the lake with the intention of determining the depth any large fish or errant crocodilians. In the meantime, the shore team would scour the shoreline in search of signs of a large beast and also to determine the entry and exit points of the pond.

Even as John, Graham and Mark struggled to get our trusty dinghy *The Waterhorse* (named after Tim Dinsdale's boat), inflated and onto the water, the first set of eyewitnesses arrived. They were a motley gaggle of teenage boys who came up to us, and in thick Brummie accents asked "whether we were here for the crocodoile, loike?"

We replied in the affirmative and they told us that they had also had an encounter with a scaly creature in Roman View Pond.

Richard interviewed them:

RICHARD FREEMAN: I gather that you've actually seen this animal and fed it. Could you please tell us exactly what happened?

LADS: we came down at just after the RSPCA had been here. We saw what looked like the animal in the water and so Elliot went and got some chicken and we lobbed it into the water to feed it. Some of it went too far away. But then we threw one-piece and it landed just next to it and there was a massive splash and we could see both the head and the tail.

We actually thought that we had seen two of the the animals in the water but then remembered that there is at least one massive pike in here and that the other animal was a fish.

RICHARD FREEMAN: And what did this animal look like?

LADS: It was dark and about 5 ft long including the tail.

RICHARD FREEMAN: Did you see scales or ridges on the tail or anything like that?

LADS: We didn't see its tail properly but there did seem to be a few spikes.

RICHARD FREEMAN: And have you seen the animal since?

LADS: No. We stopped coming down here after the TV people had been. We have been told to keep away from the pond by some of the local residents.

(There then followed an amusing teenage rant about one of the women whose house overlooks the pond and whom the gang of lads seem to to cordially dislike, before Richard managed to bring the conversation back on course)

RICHARD FREEMAN: Do you know anybody else who has claimed to have seen it?

LADS: Yeah, a couple of our friends.

(Although we asked them whether these other youths who had allegedly seen the creature could be brought to us, they singularly failed to arrive)

LADS: One of our friends had been out walking her dog and spotted it. This was the first time that it was seen. Also a lot of kids from our school have been bunking off at lunchtimes it and coming down here. Some of them say that they have seen it. One day we came down and there were about 50 kids sitting on the bank.

RICHARD FREEMAN: Do you know whether it has ever been seen on land?

LADS: Not to our knowledge. No.

RICHARD FREEMAN: Does anybody - not necessarily you - have any ideas about where it might have come from?

LADS: We were told that it might have been a pet that got too big and was thrown out...

RICHARD FREEMAN: There seem to be a lot of little streams and pipes which come in and out of the pond. Do you have any idea where they go to?

LADS: not really.

RICHARD FREEMAN: Prior to this there has not been anything odd reported in this lake before?

LADS: I don't think so. I seem to remember that there was some speculation about something in this pond a few years ago but can't remember the details.

NB: It should be noted that we have a record of the names of the teenagers in the group we have not publicised them here for reasons of confidentiality

The group of teenagers went about their business, and we went about ours. However, at least at first some of the other local residents were not as friendly. From the moment we arrived the net curtains began to twitch and soon a procession of local residents walked past this - nonchalantly - to find out what we were doing. Nigel spent much of his time in conversation with these people, explaining the details of our mission and reassuring them that we were perfectly harmless. There was one slight problem however. Despite having made every effort to contact the owners of the pond (we had even instituted a search with HM Land Registry), we had been unable to find them. After we had been at the pond for less than an hour, one irate local who claimed to be a friend of the owner approached us in a combative and pugnacious manner. For a brief few moments if looked at us if we were going to be embroiled in an unpleasant scene. However, John Fuller and I managed to calm the situation down, and the man disappeared reasonably mollified.

Finally we managed to get the boat onto the water and the away team was dispatched to the far side of the pond. Then paydirt! Nigel, by luck more than by judgement, ran into the Lady whose family had been renting the property for 38 years. She could not have been more helpful and despite the fact that we were trespassing on her property she granted us permission in writing to carry out whatever investigations we felt necessary.

At about 6.15, after a series of false alarms, Mark Martin in the boat had a sighting of what appeared to be the 18-inch long dark blackish green head of a large animal. It was not a positive sighting of a crocodile but it was the best that we had managed to achieve. At the same time, the away team found an area of flattened reeds, which had looked as if a large animal, had it made itself comfortable after emerging from the waters of the pond. Unlike other such areas around the shores of the pond there were no downy feathers from one of the swans, and as the area of flattened vegetation was too big for any known mammal species from the area it seemed quite possible that this had been the resting place for our mystery crocodilian.

As soon as we had permission to survey the pond and its surroundings and we were no longer conducting a covert operation we laid a series of navigation lines across two sections of the lake. We took a series of sonar readings to determine the depth of the lake along the lines and found to our surprise the depth of the lake seemed to change by the minute. The next day we found that the lake was fed by a series of sluice gates from connective channels which criss-cross the entire area. We discovered that the bottom of the lake was mostly fairly thick silt, and found that the influx of water from the north end was causing waves in the silt itself, which meant that the depth of the lake fluctuated in some places from between 2½ and 4 ½ feet.

Then in the early evening, John Mizzen, one of the original witnesses who had been interviewed by Mark Martin turned up. Richard spoke to him:

RICHARD FREEMAN: Basically, can you recount the story from scratch?

JOHN MIZZEN: We were over on the other side of the pond feeding swans when about five feet from the water's edge my daughter-in-law was looking down this way while I was looking at the lake. She saw the - what ever it was - and said "That's never a fish". It then swam along the water's edge where I reckon that the water is no more than two feet deep and it was about 5 ft long and that's including the tail. When it got 5 or 10 feet away from us, it came up and broke the surface. It was about 5 ft long and that is including a tail of about two feet. Its head was flat, as was its jaw and its nose, and it was dark greenish black in colour and about 18 inches wide. The tail had a scaly appearance, and then it went underneath the water and we just lost contact with it. It had been on the surface for about three or four seconds and in that time it covered about 15 to 20 feet.

RICHARD FREEMAN: On its head, did you notice anything about the eyes?

JOHN MIZZEN: I didn't see anything of that - not the eyes sticking out of their head or the water or anything. I only saw it from behind and the surrounding parts to its eyes were not visible as far as I could tell.

Later that afternoon at Richard spoke to a number of other elderly gentleman who requested anonymity. One of them told us that there been a series of incidents at a slaughterhouse which was on the shores of one of the other ponds connected to Roman View Pond by a watercourse. Apparently this establishment - which dealt predominantly with the despatching of elderly and ill horses - supplied meat to local zoos. Some of the meat was hung in a concrete pits in order to prepare it for consumption by zoo animals. Whilst it was hanging something had taken enormous bites out of the carcasses. On another occasion a horse was attacked. Apparently, in the vicinity there is a training stables at which horses learn to draw old-fashioned hearses. One of the ways that they trained these animals to walk slowly is to swim them in another of the local ponds, which is connected by a watercourse to Roman View Pond itself. One one occasion whilst one of these horses was swimming, it was attacked by something. When they got it out on to the bank it had a massive bite on one of the back legs. It was 8 to 10 inches deep and went right down to the bone. The horse was immediately taken to the knacker's yard and shot.

By this time it was beginning to get quite late in the evening, and so the team then decamped to the local pub by way of one of the most unpleasant tasting fish suppers that it has been my misfortune to eat. Later in the evening as it was approaching dusk we returned to the pond and spent three hours searching the the surface of the pond with three one-and-a-half million candle power spotlights. The away team, with head torches strapped on, scoured the bank, and out in the middle of the lake Mark and Graham sat patiently in the boat waiting for a scaly monster to surface.

Needless to say all these searches were fruitless and at about one in the morning we packed up for the night.

The next day the CFZ posse was all up and about relatively early. After an excellent breakfast we arrived at the lake soon after 10. Within 20 minutes everybody else had joined us (except for Wilf who had been forced by pressure of work to drive down to the south at the end of the previous night's escapades).

In many ways the second day was a slight disappointment after the adventures of the first., it seemed like that, although when you look back if he is now easy to see that we achieved even more. However, at the time it didn't feel like it. Whereas on the first day we had been rushing about and we had even logged a sighting, much of the second day was spent hanging about waiting for something to happen.

The boat party continued their sonar sweeps of the lake while the shore party continued their their explorations of the bank in search of footprints and signs of crocodilians. Sadly, no such signs were found. Indeed, although on the previous day, we had managed to log one pretty good sighting by Mark Martin, today we had none at all. However, this did not mean that the day was a complete waste of time.

In the original newspaper report a local lady called Natalie Baker, as saying that her children and their friends had been so excited by the media activity following the initial crocodile sightings that they had spent some time making coloured posters of the animal as part of a school project. Now, Nigel has been working with and for me and nearly seven years now, and over the years I have asked him to do some extraordinary things for me. I have never before said to him "Dude, I want you to find me a little girl who draws pictures of crocodiles". But I did, and - not at all to my surprise because over the years I have known him I have come to rely on his powers of deduction a great deal - he not only found me the little girl, but managed to persuade her to give me one of the aforesaid posters. Flushed with success after that particular triumph, Nigel and I went off in order to try and solve another mystery, which - we felt - was likely to have a pivotal importance in solving the case of the Cannock crocodile once and for all.

Richard and I have been members of what I like to call the "UK Animal Mafia" for some years. This is a weird sort of freemasonry that consists of people on the fringes of the pet trade, the zoo trade, and the Professional Zoology trade. These people - even when it would seem that they have completely opposing agendas - often co-operate to a surprising extent. One of the foremost members of the Zoo Mafia in the Midlands had warned us about the activities of a particularly unscrupulous reptile dealer who was - allegedly at least - operating in the Cannock area. Nigel and I left the shore party and the boat party doing their own respective things and went undercover.

It was surprisingly easy to track this fellow down. He had left a trail of debts a mile long, and whenever we went we couldn't find anybody who would say a good word about him. We found the shop where he had once operated a business, which - according to one of our informants - had been closed down on animal welfare grounds. We spoke to his erstwhile landlord and found that when he closed he had left large sums of money owing. We found that he had then set up business under another name in another part of town, but this too had gone the way of all flesh. After two failed businesses, we discovered that the person question had most recently been sighted working part-time for a pizza delivery company, and selling the remnants of his stock through small ads in the local paper.

Although we cannot prove it, we were convinced that this discovery had essentially solved the provenance of the Cannock crocodile. It was obvious that somebody had been dumping exotic reptiles in the district. Only a couple of days before we arrived the *Wolverhampton Express and Star* had carried a story about a large common snapping turtle which had been captured in a local brook. Although the newspaper report claimed that the turtle - named "Lucky" - by the RSPCA inspector who captured him could have been over 20 years old and had "probably lived most of his life in the wild", having inspected the brook in question, and furthermore knowing that when snapping turtles achieve the size of the specimen fished out of this tiny brook in Staffordshire they are very sedentary creatures who on the whole sit on the bottom of a stream waiting for something to swim into the open mouths, I feel that it is far more likely that "Lucky" was dumped into the stream in question within the last few weeks.

Feeling rather pleased with ourselves for having completed what we regarded as a rather tidy piece of detective work, we returned to the lake. We discovered that in our absence the CFZ operatives whom we had left behind had discovered some useful data about the age of the lake. Apparently it had begun life as a pit from which locals dig coal. When the coal petered out in the mid-1930s it had begun to fill with water. However, it was a long and slow process, and it wasn't until after the war that the water was deep enough to swim in. We also spoke to one of the head honchos of the local angling society and we discovered that although there were some very big carp in the pond, the largest pike that anyone had managed to catch was only about 9lb in weight. However, according to the local water bailiff there was at least one massive pike weighing in excess of 23lb and probably more than three and a half or four feet in length.

The shore team had also managed to identify a number of other small ponds in the area and had found of that most of these were interconnected - either by culverts or by open-water courses. One of the strangest things that we discovered was that somebody had been dumping koi carp into several of these ponds. At the time, I wrote a column for *Koi Carp* magazine, and so, with these very limited credentials, Nigel, Richard, John and I paid a visit to a small koi farm about half-a-mile away. They too had heard the stories about koi carp - some of them quite sizeable and worth quite a lot of money - being dumped into these local ponds. But they were completely unable to let us know who had been dumping them and why.

The next day we found ourselves in the middle of Cannock Chase, and deep in conversation with the local wildlife officers who told us that koi had also been turning up in isolated ponds across Cannock Chase as well. It seems as if there is some kind of strange Piscine Johnny Appleseed at work doing his best to stock of the waterways of the West Midlands with these large, ornamental fish.

Back at the pond we were ready to do a reconstruction of the original sighting by John Mizzen, Linda Charteris and her children. Some time before we had instituted the practice of performing reconstructions of sightings filmed from two or three different angles much in the manner of the BBC television programme "Crimewatch". We have found that using these methods is an invaluable tool in field investigations, and although we had already interviewed both John and Linda in some depth, as had Mark right at the beginning of the investigation, we decided to carry out one of these reconstructions are at the pond. We filmed it from three angles - Neil on one side, Mark on the other and Graham filming POV crocodile from the boat. It is always interesting carrying out up one of our "Crimewatch" reconstructions and we have never yet done one where we didn't learn something new.

John Mizzen is probably one of the most professional and accurate eyewitnesses that it has ever been my pleasure and privilege to work with. During our "Crimewatch" reconstruction we discovered that his estimates of the distance that the crocodile had been from the shore and our measured distance differed by only a few inches.

After the "Crimewatch" reconstructions, we slowly began to break camp. John and Neil lit a barbecue which had been donated to us by Chris Mullins and soon the fragrant smell of slowly charring burgers drifted over the evening wind. Someone produced the remains of a bottle of Scotch and Nigel appeared from Sainsbury's with two dozen bottles of beer. The CFZ drank, ate, and watched the sun go down. Neil disappeared back to Liverpool, and the rest of us went down the pub. Tomorrow was another day and we had another investigation to undertake.

Unfortunately, we had not caught a crocodile. From the eye-witness descriptions Richard and I are fairly convinced that we are talking about a spectacled caiman of between 3 and 5 ft in length. Sadly, it was unlucky, and nobody managed to fish it out of the pond or one of the connecting streams. It was doomed to a slow and ignominious death as soon the first chills heralded the advent of the season of mists and mellow fruitfulness. And all because of some stupid selfish bastard who wanted an exotic pet!

C'est la vie. Unfortunately!

Chapter Thirteen

Tales from the North

Once Graham and I had sorted out our problems with each other, life at the CFZ resumed on a reasonably even keel. However, within a couple of weeks of our return from Martin Mere, in the summer of 2002, Richard and I found ourselves off on another adventure.

Back in early June, I had been idly flipping through the news pages on Teletext when I came across a truly weird tale. A wallaby had been found decapitated and exsanguinated in what that sounded suspiciously like the well known scenario familiar from cattle mutilations. I was immediately struck by the similarities to the series of wallaby attacks that took place at Newquay zoo in the mid 70s. This new outbreak had taken place in Loftus on the borders of north Yorkshire and Cleveland.

We rang Loftus police station and spoke to PC Eddy O'Hara who had been working on the case. PC O'Hara confirmed the story and told us that a local vet was going to perform a post mortem on the animal and had it in deep freeze. We suggested that the CFZ should come up to Loftus examine the cadaver and help in the case. PC O'Hara seem glad of the help and was happy to pass on the details of the animal sanctuary were the attack had taken place.

We rang the owner of the Hope animal sanctuary. On the telephone he sounded like a charming - if slightly dotty - middle aged man with a passion for animals. He was also glad of our help and told us what had happened. He had found two dead wallabies over several days. The first had no marks on the body and was unfortunately buried. He found the second, a female albino wallaby a few days latter. This animal was missing its head and right fore leg. It was lying in the paddock and strangely there was no blood anywhere. None of the other animals had made any noise and the owner and his family heard nothing on the night of the attack. He seemed convinced that devil worshippers frequented the woods that backed onto the sanctuary. He told us that a freind of his from a neighbouring village had told him some satanists were arrested in the woods and he was convinced the wallaby was the victim of ritual sacrifice.

We had planned to travel up to Loftus and investigate but fate had an ace up its sleeve. We were contacted by a company called Making Time who were making a tv show for UK Living called *Scream Team*. The idea was to take six good looking young people and ferry them round the country in a bus investigating spooky things. The group had spent nights in haunted houses and had camped out in woods rumoured to be the haunt of devil worshippers (not the ones at Loftus). Making Time wanted the *Scream Team* to be in on the case and help with the investigation.

So, eventually we found ourselves in the in the Spa Hotel, in the delightful seaside town of Saltburn by the Sea. It was the night before my 43rd Birthday. I telephoned my father that night from my room in the hotel and he asked me how I was planning to spend my birthday. I think that it says a lot about my improved relationship with my father that, when I replied that I was going to spend it cutting up a dead wallaby, he didn't balk, and merely wished me many happy returns of the day.

This was our first experience of what was to become known as 'Reality TV'. On paper the idea seemed fine; take a bunch of kids who were interested in the paranormal and were aged 19-30, shove them in a Scooby Doo style bus and travel around the country with them investigating mysteries. However, the reality was completely different. On the whole, the 'kids' had been chosen for their looks rather than their investigative acumen, and they were mostly jobbing actors and actresses who saw this as a good career move.

That evening Richard went out on a pub crawl with them, while I sat in the bar of the hotel with my old friend Davie "Geordie Dave" Curtis. I first met Dave at a UFO conference in Lytham St Annes during the winter of 1999. Together we caused a swathe of mayhem from which British UFOlogy has never quite recovered. Indeed, Andy Roberts, the wittiest commentator on the British UFO scene, wrote:

"After dinner we all decanted into the piano room for a few hours of the most bizarre UFOlogical post gig 'fun' I have been present at, and I've been at a few. Simple Beatles songs soon gave way to rock standards belted out by a man who I spoke to much but know only as Dave from Geordieland, aided and abetted by a freeflowing permutation of Jon Downes, Nigel Wright, Sir Malcolm of Robinson, and many others including Miss Bott on backing vocals. Louie Louie, Stand By Me, *all the UFOlogical classics were trotted out and then it was into Irish rebel songs such as the touching version of* The Armagh Sniper *delivered by Jon (bar bill for the night £65.00) Downes, now doing a passable imitation of Citizen Caned... the most responsible of us such as Posh UFOlogist, Nick Redfern, merely looked on in disbelief..."*

That was only the beginning. In the intervening years Davey and I had become firm friends, and with our common interests in Keelian UFOlogy, drink and Irish rebel songs, we became regular fixtures at UFO conferences around the country. He had joined us on our investigation into the giant catfish at Martin-Mere for a few days, and slowly but surely he became a permanent fixture in the cryptozoological madness of my life.

He and I sat happily in the bar and put the world to rights while Richard did his best to impress the aspiring young actresses of the *Scream Team* posse. The next day we left for Loftus and the animal sanctuary. It spread for around an acre and consisted of home made enclosures constructed from sheds, ponds, paddocks and even an old caravan. The enclosures were well maintained and reasonably spacious. Inmates included stray dogs and cats, seagulls, a cormorant, polecats, wallabies, sheep and goats, rabbits and a llama.

This is where things started to get weird. The first great surprise was the proprietor of the sanctuary himself. Far from being the gentle, elderly middle-class man we had imagined he turned out to look like a cross between "Big Daddy" (the well known 1970s wrestler) and rap star Eminem. Thick-set and burly, he wore a string vest and had short, bleached hair with a tiny, dark-brown 'tail' at the name of his neck. He was obviously a very genuine guy, however, and cared deeply for his charges and was visibly very upset at what had happened. The weirdest thing, however, was the sanctuary. He claimed that it was financed purely by donations and money raised from car boot sales. I gave up trying to finance the CFZ like that years ago, and his menagerie put ours to shame. Something didn't add up.

We took a group of the *Scream Team* 'kids', and examined the perimeter fence of the property. The fence was mostly makeshift and could have been breached easily. I had always been interested in the assertions made by the original investigators at Newquay Zoo in 1978 that there was a notably higher level of background radiation in the paddocks where those wallabies had been butchered. However, a sweep with a Geiger counter revealed no abnormal radiation levels that are often associated with the classic cattle mutilation scenario.

That evening we then took the defrosted wallaby carcass to the Beck Veterinary practice in Whitby. Here, the highly helpful vet, Simon Beck had agreed to let us use his surgery. The first vet to whom the carcass had been entrusted had not got around to doing the post mortem so Simon and myself got to work on it. All six of the *Scream Team* (including a very squeamish and vegetarian Amy; a luscious and pneumatic blonde with the facial expression of a startled squirrel monkey), squeezed into the small surgery together with the camera crew, sound, director, and producer.

The wound on the neck and forelimb was indicative of a blow from a heavy, sharp object such as a hatchet or machete. The trachea was neatly severed at one of the rings suggesting the head was yanked off after the initial blow. The blood vessels contained a lot of blood, suggesting the animal was alive at the time the wounds were inflicted and had not been mutilated at a later time. This also contradicted the early stories that the body was drained of blood. The pelt was removed to facilitate examination of the skin. A bruise was found at the base of the spine, indicating that a blow was dealt there, perhaps to incapacitate the animal.

The organs were all present. Lungs and heart were full of blood indicating a struggle at the time of death. The intestine contained no trace of drugs or indeed anything untoward. There was no evidence of sexual motive. Simon Beck proved to be a first rate pathologist. It was a pleasure to work with him and all present learned a lot of practical skills from his dissection techniques

The conclusion that we reached was that a gang of several men had killed the animal by cornering it, striking it at the base of the spine and then holding it down whilst the fatal blow was dealt. It is likely that the body was held up by the tail and the blood caught in a bag. The head and forepaw were never found. There was no evidence of occult or ritualistic activity and the men who did this were not drunk or on drugs. The killing was carried out with co-ordination. It seemed that the killing was a deliberate act of malice with someone who had a grudge against the owner.

The following day we reported to PC O'Hara and told him of our findings and showed him the photographs of the post mortem. He agreed with our theories of the gang with a grudge. He and WPC Rachel Dick told us that they thought it was an out of town group who were responsible, as the local thugs would have soon been exposed by gossip in the small community. Despite some side-splittingly amusing stories of inbreeding and bestiality in nearby Skinningrove they had never come across devil worship.

In Richard's words: "Next day we took a look at the woods in Loftus. Unless empty beer cans and not so empty rubber johnnies are artefacts of the great beast, then there was no evidence of unclean rites wherein naked acolytes prance 'neath the gibbous moon whilst daubing themselves in wallaby blood."

We then spent the next couple of days relaxing with Dave and Joanne Curtis in Seaham on Sea, before returning home. The *Scream Team* were on their way to the next adventure in ghost-haunted Edinburgh.

If the intervention of the CFZ on the side of the forces of law and order has helped the police in their attempts at catching the killers then we will have done a good day's work. Although it seems that in this instance the motivation of the killers was malicious, studies in the United States have proven that a significant number of serial killers and serial sex abusers started off their careers ill treating and killing animals. We, therefore believe that our expertise in profiling perpetrators of animal mutilations is of very real social importance.

We then returned home, and a week later caught a train to London where Richard and I were to appear on yet another 'reality TV' show. This is where disaster struck!

The show was called *Diners*, and in theory at least it seemed like a fantastic idea.

The basic concept of the show was that people - even interesting people - talk in a more interesting spontaneous manner when they are relaxing with friends over a meal, than they do when plonked into the sterile and artificial surroundings of a television talk show. Therefore, thought some bright spark at the BBC, wouldn't it be a great idea to take a selection of interesting people, put them into one of London's best restaurants, ply them with good food and wine, and allow them entertain the world with their scintillating conversation. Yes, it was very good idea. However, the BBC being the BBC, what was actually delivered was a long way from what had been promised.

When Richard and I were first approached for the show, we were delighted. It sounded just the sort of thing that we would enjoy. We are both lovers of good food, and it seemed like this was a perfect opportunity to proselytise on behalf of the CFZ whilst being paid and fed. They promised to put us up in one of London's best hotels and Richard and I were looking forward to the prospect immensely. However, even before we went to London, alarm bells were beginning to ring in my mind. The show was being augmented by an in-depth website, and both Richard and I readily agreed to give an interview to the show's researcher to provide ancillary information for it. What we were not prepared for, however, was for two or three hours grilling about our personal lives in the most impertinent detail. They wanted to know our family histories, medical records, and the details of our love lives in excruciating thoroughness. When the researchers started to ask me the details of my divorce settlement I got angry, and was minded to pull out of the whole project. It was only the fact that Richard was so much looking forward to it that made me rein in my temper and continue. I wish that I hadn't been so considerate.

We arrived in London in high spirits, but these were soon dampened. The high quality hotel turned out to be one of the nastiest, drabbest, grubbiest, and most uncomfortable travel-lodges in the teeming metropolis. The staff were surly, the rooms uncomfortable, and the service non-existent. That evening - not in the best of tempers - we sat around in the bar waiting to be collected. The transport taking us to the restaurant was very late, and by the time we finally got there we were ravenously hungry, tired, disgruntled, and not prepared for what came next.

By the autumn of 2002 my physical condition had deteriorated badly. I had permanence and debilitating sciatica, and several other arthritis related conditions, which meant that I always had to walk with a stick, and I could not stand up for any great length of the time. During our tortuous conversations with the BBC researcher I had explained this, and was therefore both surprised and angry to find that I had to stand in a queue for 45 minutes before being allowed into the restaurant. We had also told the BBC researcher that Richard was allergic to seafood. Imagine our dismay, when we found out that Richard was unable to eat 75% of what was on the menu. What was left was badly prepared, insubstantial, and frankly rather unpleasant yuppie fodder. I have a constitution like that of a cast-iron rhinoceros, and can eat - and have eaten - pretty well everything, and even I balked at most of what was on offer. The restaurant itself was designed like a school refectory and had the ambience of the main bus station in Birmingham. The service was disinterested and the whole evening was rapidly turning out to be a disaster.

Richard and I were both tired after a long, and hard summer of investigating. We were not in the mood to be pissed about by people of the ilk of those we were dealing with - both behind, and in front of the camera. Although we bravely tried to talk interestingly about cryptozoology - as we had been contracted to do - as course after course of inedible crap was served to us, washed down with the sort of wine that one can pick up for a couple of quid at the local supermarket if one is prepared to risk a stomach ulcer, we began to play up. And by golly, when Richard and I decide to play up, we do so with a vengeance.

About two-thirds of the way through the meal - when we were presented with tough, and slightly rancid tasting main courses - we both lost our tempers. The vinegary wine may have tasted disgusting but there was nothing wrong with its alcohol content, and whilst I wasn't particularly drunk I had had enough to loosen my tongue, and Richard was as pissed as the proverbial tailed salamander from the family Trituridae. When viewing the eventual TV programme, I look bored and vacant, and am heard to say " I'll be glad when this is fuckin' over", a couple of times, but on the whole I acquitted myself reasonably well. Richard, however, who had been looking forward to the evening far more than I had, went crazy. He swore, cursed the BBC, insulted the antecedents of the director-general, moaned - loudly, and with perfect justification - about the food, the restaurant, the production team, and the fact that the BBC had axed his favourite television programme - *Doctor Who* - over a decade before. He swore with a colourful and prurient imagination, which made one look upon the English language with new respect. After about an hour of this, we tore off our lapel microphones, made rude gestures at the hidden cameras and stormed out.

Some weeks later, Nick Redfern likened our behaviour to the notorious incident in 1976 when the *Sex Pistols* celebrated the release of their first single by appearing on a TV show fronted by the late Bill Grundy.

On December 1st 1976, less than a week after the release of single *Anarchy In The UK,* the legendary punk rock outfit appeared on the live, early evening local London magazine show *Thames Today,* and in doing so propelled themselves to fame and fortune, while simultaneously burying the career of the shows host Bill Grundy.

Intended as a probing interview designed to investigate the blossoming moral abyss which was Punk, the segment degenerated into farce when the allegedly boozed-up Grundy goaded the already sweary Pistols - Johnny Rotten, Glenn Matlock, Paul Cook and Steve Jones, joined by an entourage which included Siouxsie Sioux - into ever more hilarious outpourings of half-mumbled profanity.

The episode has become legendary and was an undoubted career boost to the iconic punk band. However, we had been working hard for years to rid ourselves of the image of being a bunch of beer-swilling hooligans. We had never really deserved that appellation, but after Sundberg's unprovoked attack on me four years previously the subject of drinking and wild behaviour still occasionally reared its head.

In the event, nothing untoward happened at all. The programme was eventually broadcast on a minority cable channel which nobody much watched. I doubt whether it would have had an adverse effect upon our careers, because by this stage both Richard and I were pretty well established at the top of the Cryptozoological tree, and the astounding revelation that we sometimes drank hard liquor and used profane language would have surprised absolutely no one. We both went through agonies, however, hoping that my elderly father, and Richard's elderly grandparents (not to mention my brother, a priest), would not get to hear of the episode and be embarrassed by us.

The next day I awoke in my uncomfortable hotel room bed feeling absolutely lousy. My head was spinning, and I was hallucinating. We managed to negotiate breakfast and find our way back to Paddington Station, where - by the statue of the little bear made famous by Michael Bond - I collapsed. The worst bout of depression that I have ever suffered hit me like a ton of bricks. How I got back to Exeter I don't know, but when I got home Richard and Graham put me to bed and I stayed there for the next three months.

The history of my bipolar illness has been chronicled elsewhere in this book, but this time it was different. Not only was it far more severe than anything else I've experienced, but for the first time I was no longer a chronic substance abuser, and also for the first time my life wasn't in chaos. It is only with the benefit of hindsight that I realise that my previous bouts of depression had been confounded by the problems that were in my life at the time. I was always in debt; I was always in some emotional turmoil either about my marriage or about some girlfriend or other. I had always - until then at least - been to a greater or lesser extent under the influence of alcohol or drugs. I had then so always tried to seek chemical or alcoholic solace in order to deal with my illness.

This time was different. I was relatively solvent, my affairs were in order, they had no pressing debts, no lunatic girlfriend, and moreover my drinking was at a minimum and I was drug-free. The irony is that the simple fact that my life was relatively under control, that I was happy and healthy most of the time threw this appalling bout of depression into sharp bass relief.

The worst thing about trying to describe an attack of manic depression to someone is the word itself. Depression implies that you are depressed or unhappy. When you have nothing much to be unhappy about then people tend to give you very little sympathy. This is totally unfair. A serious bout of depression shuts down all your mental and emotional processes. Just doing normal day-to-day activities like walking to the bathroom takes up more emotional and mental stress than - on a normal day - would carrying out an intellectually wearing task writing an academic document. You cannot handle even speaking to people. One afternoon in mid October I made the ultimate effort and came downstairs. It had taken the whole day to do this. I saw John Fuller for the first time in weeks, and he asked me a perfectly natural question. "Are you going to get Graham to get some more tea bags?" he asked. This was too much for me to deal with. I screamed, burst into tears and ran upstairs again.

I am amazed that Richard, Graham, and John managed to deal with the situation as well as they did. Working at the CFZ is not easy at the best of times. Doing so when the boss is completely insane is damn near impossible.

The only person with whom I could have any sort of conversation was my daughter Lisa. Somehow we resonate on a far more primal level than I do with anyone else in the world, and basically she took over looking after me, while Graham, Richard and John kept the the CFZ functioning.

My psychiatric nurse visited, and my doctor prescribed me some new medication - almost as a last resort. Over the years I had been tried out on over a dozen different mood stabilisers and anti-depressants. None of them had worked, and in many cases the side effects had been appalling. One drug made me so hypersensitive to sunlight that my body was covered with suppurating pink rashes. Another gave me heart failure. This one - much to my surprise - actually worked and took away much of the pain, but left me as dysfunctional as an infant or an opium eater. For three months I lay on my bed, looked out of the window and prayed for it all to end.

By the beginning of December I was beginning to feel better, and whilst I was still too unwell to leave my bedroom, I could - at last - read again. During the weeks leading up to Christmas I read Douglas Botting's biography of my hero Gerald Durrell. With my brain cells fried to hell it was a long, slow and laborious process but I found that every page was fascinating. I had not realised it, but Durrell's life had paralleled my own in so many ways. However, he was a giant of a man in every way, and without him conservation as we know it today would not exist. Compared to him my achievements -

and even those, which I hope that the CFZ will manage in my lifetime - are very minor indeed. The irony is, however, that in the same way that there are definite parallels between his professional life and mine, our private lives, and in particular our strengths and weaknesses are very similar. Like me, he was terminally bad at relationships. Like me, he had probably married the wrong woman (the first time at least), and, like me, his wife had eventually left him because of his increasingly bizarre behaviour. However, in his character flaws - like everything else - he was bigger and better than me. He drank himself into epilepsy and eventually to death, had wild and untreated fits of mood swings and depression and whilst he was capable of great generosity and love, he was also capable of being viciously mean spirited. However, he was aware of his faults and remained remarkably modest about his achievements.

It was reading Botting's book that prompted me to resume work on this present volume, and also give me inspiration for how I intended the CFZ to continue. I was quite upset when I read about how Durrell had tried to rewrite history in the wake of his first wife leaving him. Jacquie Durrell had been an intrinsic part of the first years of Jersey Zoo (now the Durrell Wildlife Preservation Trust), but Gerald had done his best to write her out of history. As this book has shown, Alison was intrinsically important in the setting up of the CFZ, and although we are no longer in contact with each other, one of my main reasons for writing this present book was to make sure that her place in Cryptozoological history was assured. As I read the account of Gerald's life, I was convinced of two things first of all I was not going to drink so much that I lost control of my bowels, developed epilepsy, and finally died of a buggered liver, and secondly that we were in a unique position. The CFZ should not only look for unknown species of animal, but it should put into place the mechanism for ensuring that once these new animals were discovered, that they should be protected from extinction. In our own little way - with the formation in the summer of 2004 of our first nature reserve, and with our collaboration with Chester Moore in his work with a the highly endangered red wolf in Orange County, Texas - we are beginning to make steps in the right direction.

But at the very end of 2002 something very weird was happening.

In the northern forests of Europe an ancient 'creature' has lived for centuries. It inhabits that twilight world between wakedness and sleep. Sometimes it emerges, following its own agenda, and going about its own business. Occasionally, it encounters one of its own kind, and even more occasionally it comes into contact with the strange bipedal creatures which inhabit what they like to think of as the real-world. The northern forests have changed mightily over the years, where once there were nothing but trees, and where once only the spring waters emerged from the living rock, the newcomers - mankind -have built their own peculiar dwellings, and etched their own peculiar essence upon the land. Many of the Forests have been cut down, and replaced by roads, concrete, Tarmac, and industrial waste. The land, which was once traversed only by forest walkways, is now criss-crossed by pulses of electromagnetic radiation. Strange patterns are forming, and a new, and some people terrifying, presence has emerged from his ancient sleep.

Far better-known than the strange denizens of the pine forests of northern England is Bigfoot, the semi-mythical man beast of the North American forests. He has become a cultural icon the Loch Ness monster has for the Scottish Tourist Board. Bigfoot has been used to to sell everything from chocolate to motorcars and soft drinks to cigarettes he's even featured in a soft porn movie. But towards the end of the year 2002 newspaper headlines all over the world claimed that Bigfoot was dead!

Ray Wallace, one of the most controversial figures in American cryptozoology, died in November. In 1958 his construction company had been working at Bluff Creek in California. One of his employees found strange footprints apparently belonging to a giant ape. As veteran American Fortean Loren Coleman wrote in Wallace's obituary:

Wallace was to be involved with the local tales of hairy giants for the rest of his life. Allegedly in the later in the 1950s, for example, Wallace offered to sell Texas millionaire Tom Slick a captured Bigfoot. Wallace failed to produce the creature when Slick came up with an offer. Down through the years, Wallace would carry on pranks, be tied to carved fake Sasquatch feet, and produce and try to sell dubious photographs and films. He was a great letter writer and would pen long passages to magazine editors about this photographs or telling of how he knew a Bigfoot was nearby guarding a mine full of gold. After awhile, most Bigfoot hunters and researchers took Wallace as merely a spinner of fanciful tall tales. Through his contributions to Strange Magazine, *the* Track Record, *and indirectly to* Fate Magazine, *Wallace relished keeping his name in the limelight of the Bigfoot mystery.*

Although it is indisputable that Wallace was responsible for some a pretty hefty hoaxing, in my opinion at least it would be facile to dismiss the whole bigfoot phenomenon as merely been the result of one man's mischievous sense of humour. Tabloid newspapers, however, love to see things in a black and white and love it even more if they can accompany it with a picture of a woman with big tits. Bigfoot is dead! said the newspapers, and it was almost as if the phenomenon wanted to prove the legions of hack journalists wrong. Because I seriously doubt whether it is entirely a coincidence that only two days after his death the first newspaper report in the UK surfaced describing an encounter with what some unknown media scribe described as "The Sherwood Forest Thing".

Scottish Fortean researcher Mark Fraser described the initial encounter:

"The Sherwood Forest "Thing" has apparently been sighted for many years and has now become part of the local folklore. One day, after hearing about the creature, two men, along with two friends, took it upon their selves to actually go out and hunt "the thing" down. The four men drove deep into the forest and lay in wait for the creature.

"After about an hour they heard the sound of heavy footsteps approaching. As the steps grew louder and closer, the driver switched the lights of the car off. In the darkness, the men could now see two glowing red eyes, at about 8 feet from the ground, moving towards them from the depths of the forest. As the eyes and footsteps moved closer to the men, fear finally took over. The companions deciding not to hang around, restarted their car and drove off. As the vehicle moved away, the men could just make out a large, dark shape move up into the trees."

And this was only the beginning. Over the next weeks and months the United Kingdom was to be the host for the biggest flap of man beast sightings ever recorded outside Asia or North America.

As a cryptozoologist I have always been particularly interested in the accounts of European man beasts. Because of their very unlikliness, within a zoological framework at least, they have to be seen as part of a pan-global phenomenon. Such creatures have been reported from every continent - even Antarctica - and to my mind at least, they can be divided it into two rough camps. These two divisions are not absolute and it would be an unwise man who would even attempt to claim that they were.

Some of the animals of this type, which have been reported across the world, appear to be *bona fide* cryptids: flesh-and-blood creatures whose existence has not yet been accepted by mainstream scientists. The yeti, for example, is to my mind at least a flesh-and-blood animal. I believe that there is every likelihood that an evolved descendant of *Gigantopithecus blackii*, a creature from the Pleistocene epoch has survived to the present day. Its fossils have been found alongside those of animal slaughter like the giant panda and other creatures, which can still be found in the remote forests of China. Logically, there is no reason what so ever, that it could not have survived alongside them. Smaller mystery primates from the forests of Indo-China are also almost certain or to be flesh-and-blood creatures. Explorer Adam Davies, brought back hair samples from the forests of Sumatra, which for have been analysed by reputable scientists. The results of these tests seem to indicate that the Orang Pendek of Indonesian folklore is living, breathing, a creature closely related to the orang utan.

Other mystery hominids are more speculative. I have grave doubts whether Bigfoot actually exists in a flesh-and-blood form. Unlike the yeti in Asia, there is no fossil record to support the existence of such creatures and the fact that they have repeatedly been seen in conjunction with UFOs and other quasi Fortean phenomena, tends to suggest to me that they are not physical entities.

Several other well-known mystery hominids can, I feel, be put firmly into this category of Zooform Phenomena. The Yowie of Australia, for example, is another creature, which seems unlikely to exist within a strictly zoological frame of reference. My main reason for this assertion is that with the exception of a very few a small rodents there are no known placental mammals south of the Wallace's line which divides Australiasia from Indonesia. Man brought the only placental mammals, which do exist there. It is perfectly feasible that man brought rats and mice, and their faithful dingo hunting dogs with them. The idea that they also brought viable breeding population of shambling primitive hominids with them as well is frankly absurd. But people have been reporting such things in the wilder parts of Australia and even in New Zealand for many years.

The man beasts of modern Europe present a slightly different problem. Unlike their spiritual cousins in Australia, North America, New Zealand, and the shambling a hairy brute once reported in the vicinity of a scientific research station in the depths of Antarctica, there is a viable fossil record of the non-human primates in various parts of Europe including the United Kingdom. The only problem with the man beasts of the UK and other parts of northern Europe being *bona fide* flesh and blood carbon-based life forms is one of sheer logistics. Britain is simply too well-explored to harbour a population of cryptic higher primates. Nevertheless, over the past 1000 years, such things have been seen occasionally in the wilder parts of our sceptred isle.

In recent years sightings have tailed off. In the mid-1990s there was a series of sightings of man beasts in the wilder parts of central Scotland. These were definitely paranormal in nature. They were seen in conjunction with UFOs, and in one case one was seen running very fast alongside a moving car. Such running men are a well known part of Scottish mythology. Perhaps the most famous is Jack the runner-a phantom that haunts the long driveway leading to Glamis Castle, the ancestral home of the late Queen Mother. This ancient castle is also home to another legendary monster. According to the burgeoning folklore on the subject the wife of one of the 19th century Earls of Strathmore gave birth to a hideously deformed son who lived to an extraordinary age.

Such entities are not really the domain of the cryptozoologist. They harbour an intense and enduring fascination for me and for my colleagues, but they are really outside our remit. However, the accounts of wild men across the country have fascinated me for years. On 7th April 2002, newspapers across the country carried a photograph of what purported to be a bigfoot type creature photographed in the Highlands of Scotland. Sadly, it turned out to be a hoax, albeit a very good one.

When the first accounts of the "Sherwood Forest Thing", emerged in late November 2002, many researchers that were working within the Fortean zoological communities believed that it would to turn out to be another hoax. How wrong we were. As of the year slowly ground to its end, more eyewitness account came in of sightings of similar creatures all over the country. Man beasts were seen in Sussex, in Lancashire, in Scotland, and over what is euphemistically described as the festive season a proliferation of sightings occurred in the vicinity of Bolam Lake in Northumberland.

A few weeks before Christmas the veil of horror that had enveloped me for so many months began to lift and I began to take an interest in my life and my work again. Coincidentally - although as my old mentor Tony Shiels once told me "There's no such thing as a coincidence" - Just as I was beginning to take an interest in the outside world again, the spate of British man beast reports began to arrive first on a weekly, then on a daily, and finally on an hourly basis in the in box of my Outlook Express email programme.

The night before New Year's Eve, I was lying on the mattress in my bedroom listening to a bootleg CD by the Grateful Dead and the night of my 40th birthday suddenly squirmed its way into my consciousness. I remembered my conversation with Reuben. Finally after a wait of four years I realise that the time had come for me to test my theory and to prove to myself that not to anyone else whether or not my earlier research into the Owlman and other Zooform entities had been a valid or whether I had just wasted 10 years of my life. For the first time in four months I began to get enthusiastic, even excited, and I realised that the next great adventure in my life was about to begin.

I sat up in bed. A friend of mine had given me a bottle of whisky for Christmas. These days I rarely drink spirits, but I poured myself a healthy dollop of Scotch, added a minimal amount of Diet Coke, and drank a silent toast to the strange man who looked a little bit like the bass player with *Quicksilver Messenger Service*. I swallowed my drink, turn out the light and willed myself to sleep. I had a sneaking suspicion that I was going to need all the reserves of energy that I could muster.

The next day I woke up with a mild hangover, but happier than I had been in months, and for the first time in ages I was fired with enthusiasm about a new and exciting challenge that had arrived, as if out of the deferred, in order to start the new year with a bang for me and my colleagues.

I bounced out of bed, and immediately started to take stock of the available evidence. Over the next few days I began to collate the sightings that there had received and I made contact with several researchers who had been in dealing with the subject.

During what is euphemistically known as the festive season, Richard always goes back to the Midlands to visit his friends and family. Lisa and I stay at home, tending or the family dog and cats, and trying not to drink too much. I always find Christmas a spectacularly annoying time of the year. I have never really understood why one has to celebrate the birth of Our Lord by getting spectacularly drunk and loading oneself up with so many debts that one has to spend the rest of the year paying them off. By about the 28th of December I am always spectacularly bored. My friends and colleagues are always away, none of the businesses, periodicals, or people for whom I do consultancy and writing work are ever around, and there is only a limited amount of entertainment that can be garnered from the parade of third-rate crap which is splattered all over the television networks. The advent, therefore, of a new and exciting quest was just what are the proverbial doctor would have ordered if he hadn't been proverbial.

Usually, when embarking upon a major investigation with the Centre for Fortean Zoology, I consult with Richard before I take any action whatsoever. I have a tremendous faith in his Zoological and Fortean judgment, and - let's face it - he's such a crazy son of a bitch, with a unique and surreal sense of humour, that planning an expedition, a film, an excursion, or even a trip to Sainsbury's is far more fun with him than without him. However, on this occasion, Richard was delighting in the fleshpots of Nuneaton and I was so excited by this potential new adventure that I decided to do a large proportion of the groundwork by myself. Thus it was that on his return to Exeter, early in the New Year, I was able to present him with quite an impressive dossier of data.

I have described my researches into the Cornish Owlman earlier in this book. In the varying editions of my book on the subject, and also - I suppose - in the ludicrous art movie that I made about the subject I have explored the possibility that the Owlman had its genesis in a complex practical joke on the part of the notorious Irish wizard Tony Shiels. over the years my theorising has grown more and more complex, and I have adopted some of the ideas of what Tony himself gave me. These include the concept that the Owlman was somehow a quasi-physical manifestation of Loplop - the bird-headed *alter ego* of Surrealist painter Max Ernst. After all, Max had done some of his most famous work while staying in that particular part of southern Cornwall in the 1930s. Surely it couldn't be a coincidence that in the very woods where he first gambolled in surrealistic eroticism four decades before, a birdman so similar to his exquisite corpse *alter ego* appeared at the very season of resurrection in the year of the artist's death?

Over the years as I distanced myself from the events in the haunted woods of southern Cornwall, I came to the conclusion that Tony had probably invented the original sightings. Whether he had done so as a homage to his surrealistic mentor, or as part of some strange self-publicising a practical joke I didn't know - to be quite honest I didn't care. What I was certain of, however, was that over the years the rich will artistic vision whether it had been Tony's or that of his mentor had achieve to a certain degree of objective reality. Tony admitted to me that in his opinion the this Owlman would never have come into existence if he hadn't read John Keel's momentous book, *The Mothman Prophecies*. Whether this was an admission on his part that he had indeed made the whole thing up, or whether as I sometimes believe in the deepest and darkest stillnesses of the night, he meant that in some way that the effect of this remarkable book on Tony, who is by anybody's standards a remarkable man, had produced a Surrealchemical event on some quantum level which had brought this strange phenomenon into some degree of objective reality I still don't know. It doesn't really matter. The fact is that for over a quarter of a century the woods in that part of southern Cornwall have been home to a strange, unearthly, and sometimes malevolent being.

Could Ray Wallace's death have sparked off something similar in the global *zeitgeist*?

We liaised with Geoff Lincoln, who had worked on the Bolam phenomenon. We gave him our planned arrival time, and asked him up to see if any of the eyewitnesses would be prepared to speak to us. Much to our delight, five out of six were. I think it should be noted, here, that the 6th is a soldier and with the burgeoning situation in the Middle East spiralling rapidly out of control, it would be completely unreasonable to expect a serving military man to be at the beck and call of four loonies from the CFZ. Serendipitously, we were able to stay at a house owned by Davie Curtis. He and his wife Joanne were absolutely fantastic all the way through our sojourn in the North. The only sad thing about our stay with them, was that Davy had to work most of the time and was not able to join us during most of our adventures.

This is not the time nor the place to give a long, imaginative, travelogue style description of what was essentially a very tedious journey up the M1. However, we arrived in Seaham late on the Thursday night, and after a few pints at the Dawdon Miner's Welfare Club across the road from our lodgings, we collapsed into our beds and prepared ourselves for the first proper day of our adventure.

However, Davie not only made his *quondam* house available to us, but he had another surprise up his sleeve. His new house had a medium sized garden, and in that garden there was a slightly dilapidated shed.

Like many men, Davie Curtis took one look at his garden shed and immediately knew what he was going to use it for. Unlike most men, however, he did not decide to grow tomato plants in it, use it as a workshop for his motorbike, or even use it to store home-brew. No, he had much bigger plans. He decided immediately that he was going to turn it into a Jamaican theme bar, and furthermore that he was going to donate this edifice as a gang hut for the CFZ whenever we happen to be in the area. By the time we arrived in early January 2003, *Winston's* (as he christened it), was looking magnificently tacky.

From somewhere, he had managed to get hold of a 1970s era Formica bar, and a number of gloriously tasteless artifacts. A portrait of the Queen (the Annigoni one from the 1950s), hung in a broken frame on one wall, and a picture of Bob Marley on the opposite one. There were plastic fruit everywhere and reggae music played melodiously in the background. All four of the visiting members of the CFZ felt immediately at home. On our first proper night in the North (the first night doesn't really count), all four of us, plus Davie, Joanne and their little girl Rosy found ourselves crammed inside *Winstons*, drinking champagne, and toasting the success of our venture.

After a series of fairly dull misadventures, we met Geoff Lincoln, and Gail-Nina Anderson (a member of the CFZ Board of Consultants), and we made our way in convoy to Bolam Lake itself. It would be nice to say that we were overwhelmed with a spooky feeling, or that the *genius locii* of the location was in some way redolent of Fortean freakiness. But it wasn't. It was just what one would expect from a heavily wooded country park in the North of England in the middle of January - cold, wet and grey.

Geoff showed us three of the locations where these things had been reported. We carried out a thorough series of photographic mapping exercises, whilst Jon stayed back at the main car park and did his best to fend off the incessant inquiries from the local press. Just after lunchtime a TV crew from Tyne-Tees Television turned up and filmed interviews with the investigation team. It was only after they had gone that we realised that something rather strange was happening.

Although we had tested all of our electronic equipment the night before, charged up batteries where necessary, and put new batteries in all of the equipment which needed them, practically without exception all of our equipment failed. My laptop, for example, has a battery, which usually lasts between 20 and 35 minutes. It lasted just three minutes before conking out. Admittedly, I received an enormous number of telephone calls during our stay at the Lake, but not anywhere near enough to justify the fact that I had to change handsets four times in as many hours. The batteries in both Geoff's and our tape recorders also failed. It seemed certain that there was some strange electromagnetic phenomenon at work here.

Late afternoon we drove to a local pub where we met our first witnesses. Like all the other people we were to meet over the next few days they requested anonymity, and therefore in accordance with our strict confidentiality policy, we have respected this. Naomi, and her son had been visiting Bolam Lake only a few days before. Not believing any of the reports that had appeared in the local media, they were both appalled and frightened when - whilst walking across the car park itself - they had seen a huge creature standing motionless in the woods. They described experiencing an intense feeling of fear and trepidation, and rapidly left the area.

They were incredibly co-operative, and agreed it to come back to the lake with us the next day to stage a reconstruction similar to those done on the BBC television programme *Crimewatch*.

Then we drove to South Shields where I gave a briefing to a detachment of volunteer foot-soldiers from the *Twilight Worlds* Group who had kindly agreed to help us in our investigations on the next day.

I had a call time of 5.30 the next morning, and a taxi took him to a lay-by 500 yards up the road from the Bolam Lake car park, where I did a two and a half minute interview for the BBC Radio 4 Today programme. One thing of great importance happened during the half-hour or so he spent shivering by the side of road waiting to speak to the 'Beeb'. Just before dawn, the rooks which live in a huge colony in the woods, started the appalling row which is presumably the corvid equivalent of the dawn chorus. Suddenly the noise stopped. I heard a brief succession of booming noises-like a heavily amplified heartbeat from a *Pink Floyd* record - before the rooks started up again. It is unclear whether these noises came from the vicinity of the lake itself or were made by the incredibly Heath-Robinson set-up of satellite dishes, and recording equipment which was loaded in the back of, and on top of the BBC man's car.

During the taxi journey back to Seaham the driver remarked on the peculiar behaviour of the rooks, and said it that although he was a countryman himself and had spent his whole life living in this area he had never heard anything quite like it.

No sooner had I arrived back at base, than it was time for the entire CFZ expeditionary force to drive to the outskirts of Newcastle where, we met Geoff and a second witness in a cafe attached to a garden centre. The witness, Neil, had been fishing at Bolam Lake one night four or for five years previously. Together with two companions he had been making his way back to the car-park when they encountered a huge, dark man shaped object about 8 ft in height with what he described as sparkling eyes. The three fishermen did not stop to investigate but ran back to the car. However, this was by no means the only encounter that Neil had got to report to us. Together with one of his companions from the first adventure he had again been night fishing at Bolam Lake during the summer of 2002. They had been camped out on this occasion, and had heard noises, which they assumed, were from an enormous animal moving around in the bushes outside their camp. Deciding, that, discretion was the better part of valour they decided not to investigate but when they broke camp the next morning they found that fish in a bait tin had been taken, and there were signs that something very large had been moving around in the vicinity of their camp.

Possibly the most astounding story that he had to recount had taken place a couple of summers before our visit. He had been in the woods at the opposite side of the Lake with his girlfriend. They had been making love, when his girlfriend told him that that she could see we what she thought was a man in a monkey suit watching their sexual adventures intently from behind a bush. Neil, unsurprisingly looked around the area, but could find nothing.

We then continued to the lake. Neil had been amazingly co-operative, and had, like Naomi, agreed to stage a reconstruction with us. At the lake we liaised with the team from *Twilight Worlds* and began a series of exercises, which but would take up the rest of the day. Geoff had noted, the previous week, a series of apparently artificial tree formations similar to those "Bigfoot Teepees" noted by researchers in the United States.

Together with a team from *Twilight Worlds*, Geoff and Graham went off to map these formations and make a photographic record. They also took with them a *Twilight Worlds* member trained in using their EMF meter, together with a dowser. After our electrical mishaps of the previous day, we wanted to find out whether there were, indeed, any abnormal EMF fields in the area. Neither investigator found any unusual readings.

Our next task was to stage a reconstruction of Naomi's a sighting. Again a full photographic and video record was made, and EMF readings were also taken. Again no unusual readings were made either by the EMF meter or the dowser. We then repeated the exercise with Neil and reconstruct his first sighting.

At about half-past four, one of the members of *Twilight Worlds*, reported seeing something large, human shaped and amorphous in the woods directly in front of the car park.

As the dusk gathered at about 5 o'clock, I again heard the raucous noise of the rooks that he had reported. just before dawn. Suddenly, once again, they fell silent and one of the *Twilight Worlds* members shouted that she could hear something large moving around amongst the undergrowth. I ordered all of the car drivers present to switch on their headlights and to put them on to full beam. He did not hear any noise in the undergrowth although other people present did. Eight people were watching the woods and five of them, including Jon saw an enormous man shaped object run from right to left, disappear, and then a few moments later run back again.

It was an incredibly weird experience. I have been playing it back in my mind over and over ever since. It wasn't the first time that I had seen a cryptozoological creature. I had, after all, seen the Beast of Bodmin back in 1997, another mystery cat 10 years before, and I had even held the Mystery Lamprey of Puerto Rico in my hands. However, although I had encountered things which I had been unable to explain using strictly zoological and scientific terms of reference at secondhand before, for example the animals that had been killed by the chupacabra, this was the first time I'd encountered a monster for real.

What I saw was an incredibly flat and angular figure, which appeared to be two-dimensional. It is here that I have greatest difficulty in describing my encounter because what I saw were so far out of the normal run of human experiences that there simply are not adequate words to describe it. I will do my best, but even now - over a year after the expedition was done and dusted - I still find it almost impossible to describe with any semblance of a coherent description.

As far as its shape is concerned, the nearest analogue that I have been able to come up with is the angular metallic running man which can be found in certain levels of the computer game *Doom II*. However, this "thing" (as Ivan T Sanderson would undoubtedly have called it), was a matt-black. It was so black, in fact, that it was a quasi-human piece of nothingness, which had somehow become projected upon the Northumbrian landscape. It moved far too sharply and far too fast to be a living thing - at least in the ways that we know it. Again I have to resort to another unwieldy and fairly inadequate analogue. It was as if somebody had filmed this humanoid shaped piece of nothingness, and then projected it back on to the landscape using the fast-forward facility on the video recorder. The whole experience lasted only a second, but it has been with me ever since.

When the expedition returned on Monday, we conducted experiments to find out exactly how far away the creature - if it was a creature - was from the excited onlookers. Using Richard as a model, I made a fairly accurate estimate that the creature had been a hundred and thirty four feet away from him at the time of his sighting. I also estimated or that the creature had run along a distance of between 12 and 18 feet.

About five minutes after the sighting still dazed - I wandered across the car park to the location when Naomi had reported seeing the creature. There, I too, felt a sensation of intense fear and quickly returned to my companions.

But then something incredibly strange happened. I do not make any secret in the pages of this book that on occasion I have resorted - at various times and places - to medicating myself with various prescription and recreational drugs. You may have wondered why I have confessed in a relatively public forum to the abuse of of various opium derivatives from codeine phosphate to heroin. It is not something to be proud of, and, indeed, I believe that under current UK legislation I could even be prosecuted for these admissions.

However, apart from the fact that this book is in many ways my exegesis and as such I intend to tell the truth, the fact that I'm aware of the effects of opium derivative drugs upon the central nervous system is very important when one discusses what happened next. All opiate drugs work by mimicking the production of endorphins - the body's pleasure centre chemicals, comforting, glow which makes you feel like you have had a hot bath are, a belly full of chocolate, and have been tucked up in bed swathed in a shroud of pink, fluffy, cotton wool. In everyday life, the two things that promote the production of endorphins are sex and chocolate. Heroin or morphine produces the same effect as the afterglow of good sex without the necessity of having to talk to the woman afterwards.

Away from the car park I had been overwhelmed by a feeling of intense terror, but as I approached the car park again my body was flooded with endorphins the most amazing feeling of well-being that I have ever had in my life. It was like all the sex, all the drugs, and all the rock and roll (as well as all the chocolate), rolled into one, incredibly satisfying whole. I've never felt anything like it, and I doubt whether I ever shall again.

After an incident like that, anything else would have been an anti-climax. However, Geoff Lincoln took the CFZ team to interview two further witnesses. The first was a young man living in the suburbs of Newcastle. Geoff and Richard visited him at his home and he told of his encounter with an enormous man shaped being next to a hollow tree in the woods, some months previously. The incident had taken place whilst he had been walking his dog. He had been so frightened by his experience that he refused to ever go near the lake again.

Finally we went to another pub where we met another man called Neil. He had been with the first Neil at the time of his initial sighting. We were all impressed by his sincerity and by the way that he corroborated his friends' testimony in what seemed to us, at least, to be a very natural and uncontrived manner.

On Saturday we took a day off, and that lunchtime went to Davy and Joanne's for lunch, where an inordinate amount of alcohol was served. For some reason best known to him Davy insisted on playing *Apeman* by *The Kinks* whilst grinning at me maniacally. We then spent the afternoon in Winston's getting royally drunk. However, whatever it was that was pumping through my veins as a result of my encounter the previous day had a remarkable effect when mixed with for the amount of alcohol that seems to be *de rigueur* during Sunday lunch *chez* Curtis. My psyche went into a strange shutdown procedure and I had what can only be described as an enormous panic attack. I got immensely paranoid and began to question my own grasp of reality, and - unfortunately - decided that the best thing that I could do was to telephone everybody that I knew in the Cryptozoological community and to tell them what had happened. Unfortunately I continued to drink heavily as I did so, and - aided and abetted by Joanne Curtis - I undertook a series of weird, self-examining telephone calls to Nick Redfern, Loren Coleman and others. I told them what had happened, and dictated a press release to Nick. In my defence, I would say to anybody who criticised me for my behaviour that day, that if a they had seen a zoologically impossible monster, and then had an incredibly boozy lunch with David Curtis then they might well have acted in an even more bizarre fashion than I did. I am incredibly grateful to Loren Coleman for not having been judgmental about what I did and said that day.

After our day off (and nursing huge hangovers), we returned to the lake on Monday morning. We carried out a photographic survey of the final two sighting locations. We also carried out the aforementioned experiments to ascertain - as far as is possible - the size of the thing that had been seen on Saturday night, and also its distance from the eyewitnesses. As in both the dowsing and EMF scans had been remarkably unsuccessful, Mike Hallowell from *Twilight Worlds*, together with Graham Inglis and Richard Freeman tried to scan the era for magnetic anomalies using a pocket compass. Mike registered a strange magnetic anomaly at the location of the fisherman's first sighting. However, it must be reported, that when the team tried to replicate this later in the day, they were unsuccessful.

That evening, together with Gail and Geoff, we interviewed a final witness. A woman in her late fifties, who had been visiting the lake about five years before with her son who was then 11 years old. Like Naomi, and Jon, she reported intense feelings of - not exactly hostility, but what she interpreted as a message not to investigate a peculiar tree formation any further. She discussed these tree formations at some length. Like Geoff, she had been surprised to find them at several locations throughout the woodlands.

Our work finished, after a further days R&R in Newcastle and at the Dawdon Miner's Welfare Club, we returned home. We would like to thank the management, the staff and the members of the club from the bottom of our hearts. Not only had they made us welcome, and been friendly and kind, but they even gave us gifts of food and allowed us in nearly every evening to make use of their telephone for the purposes of carrying out radio interviews. There is a little bit of the corner of the collective heart of the CFZ, which will forever be in Dawdon.

When we returned to Exeter, I did what I always do, and wrote up an account of our expedition for our website. I also posted the account on various Internet newsgroups. I was completely unprepared for the hail of vitriol that I was to attract. Despite the unarguable zoological fact that the there was no way that an unknown species of higher primate could exist living in a country park only 40 miles from Newcastle city centre, I was vilified left right and centre for insisting that the "thing" that I saw could not have been a flesh-and-blood animal.

At no time have I ever publicly stated that the Bigfoot reports in North America are of zooform creatures. Some - especially those seen in conjunction with UFOs - undoubtedly are, but following my visit Texas in late autumn of 2003 I am convinced that an unknown species of higher primate does lurk undiscovered in the forests of North America. However I am equally convinced that such an animal could never exist in the UK. What I saw was definitely not an animal, and I said as much in public forums during the weeks following our return to Exeter. However, my statements to this effect resulted in me being banned from several Bigfoot newsgroups, receiving a level of hate mail, which I had never foreseen, and even a veiled death threat.

I had a pretty well had enough of the whole affair, and would have quietly let it lie if it wasn't for an email I received from a young man whom I have always referred to as 'Gavin'. It read:

"Now you know what it feels like to see a monster. Just be prepared for the fact that your life can never be the same again!"

Dude. It hasn't been.

Chapter Fourteen

A sort of conclusion

Three months later we were back in Seaham on Sea. We were revisiting Bolam woods with a TV company to make another in a long line of what Richard describes as "Mickey Mouse" documentaries, which are - sadly - the bread-and-butter of the day-to-day funding of the CFZ. It will come as no surprise to learn that we were staying, once again, with Davey and Joanne. I had a laptop with me, and I had written the first three or four chapters of this book, and I looked forward to hearing Davey's comments.

In the evening after we had filmed our slot for the documentary, Joanne had gone to bed and the three of us were sitting in Winston's. I was reasonably sober, though Richard and Davey were in a bizarre and somewhat surreal world of their own. Richard was particularly vacant that night, and somehow the conversation came round to the fact that Mars was nearer the Earth than it had been for any time in the past 30,000 years.

Richard wanted to have a look at it, and was not at all put off by the fact that the only thing that he would see was a tiny red speck in the night sky - a speck that was only minutely bigger than it would have been on any other night of his life. In a facetious moment I suggested that if he was to go out and look at the planetary manifestation of the God of War he should scream abuse at it, threaten it, and maybe buzz a few half bricks in its general direction. Much to my surprise he disappeared - shambling somewhat - out of the door of the garden shed, and apart from hearing a few muffled cries of "Take that you green skinned Martian bastards!" and a thud which sounded suspiciously like a half-brick landing on the roof of the shed, we saw nothing else of him that evening.

Davey and I cracked open another beer or three, and set down to discuss this book. He loved the first three chapters, and asked me what was going to be in the rest of it.

"Well, basically, dude," I slurred, "It is the story of my life as a cryptozoologist. Over the years people have asked me to write a textbook of Cryptozoological theory, but to be quite honest I just couldn't be bothered. When I first thought up the concept of Fortean Zoology, I wanted to call it Anarchozoology precisely because there weren't any text books, much of it works to its own laws, and those laws are not readily definable within a purely scientific framework..."

David grinned. "Bollocks," he said, " you just couldn't be arsed to write a text book could you?"

"Yeah", I grinned. "There's something to that, but there is more"...

and for the first time ever I told somebody else about my encounter with Rueben, late on the night of my 40th birthday. I also told him that as well as wanting to go back and re-examine my theory of Odylic life-form energies that I had first postulated in *The Rising of the Moon*, I'd been in therapy for nearly seven years and I thought that the only way I could put the past behind me was to write it down. I started to get into my theme, but before I could go too far down the road of turgid self-analysis, David interrupted. He had adored *The Rising of the Moon*, and was somewhat perturbed to find that I was re-evaluating my findings.

And then we both laughed. We have been friends for many years now, but it is always magical when two people start thinking the same thing at the same time. With Davey's encouragement I began to expound upon Richard's and my new theory. As Richard writes in his *magnum opus 'Dragons: More than a Myth'* (2005):

"Several million years ago, on the plains of East Africa, our remote ancestors were struggling to survive. Australopithecus had an existence fraught with peril. In moving down from the trees, and onto the grassland to exploit untapped food-sources, he faced new and deadly enemies. The crocodile was - and is - the biggest killer of mankind. The rock-python would also have found our ancestors easy prey. Australopithecus was small enough to have fallen victim to large raptors, and fossil evidence from South Africa supports this. Lions and leopards would have certainly preyed on our ancestors, and hunting-dogs may have also given them sleepless nights. Australopithecus and its descendents would have been in direct competition with other primate species. Some were smaller than itself - other, including the horrific giant baboon Dinopithecus - were larger.

Think about it. Here we have the genesis of mankind's monsters, the beginning of our species' bugbears. The dragon, the giant bird, the mystery big-cat, the phantom dog, the little people, and the hairy giant."

He continues:

"Perhaps our fossil memories can be triggered by certain things in our surroundings. Maybe some kinds of electromagnetic-interference coupled with the right person, with the right brain chemistry, in the right place, at the right time, can create a monster. If the brain - an electro-chemical computer - is "shorted" it "re-boots" like an mechanical computer, and for a while switches to its most primitive "operating-systemm" In this condition, our m-field kicks in, and together with our fossil-memories, creates a defence mechanism - the primal fear, 'flight or fight', taken to its extreme in the creation of something visible and (for a time at least), tangible."

Davey said:

"The links between what people like to call paranormal phenomena, including many monster sightings, and electromagnetic fluctuations been written about all over the place. Some silly buggers have suggested that UFOs or ghosts create these electro-magnetic glitches. Are you saying that it is the other way round?"

I grinned.

"Exactly. But there's more. Going back to my original theory about Orgone energy, and the way that some very psychicly powerful people seem able to form tulpas, can you imagine how powerful the psychic energy produced from the collective subconscious of every human being alive today would be? Also, all the evidence from my own experiences points to some sort of link between the electromagnetic fluctuations and some major changes in my own brain function. I was so flooded by endorphins after I saw the Bolam "beast" that something strange had obviously happened. Other witnesses, both at Bolam, and other locations across the world reported the same thing. Like Doc Shiels says, there ain't no such thing as a conincidence."

Davy sat bolt upright, and then had to refresh himself from his beer bottle before he was able to reply.

"So this could make some of the weirder monsters - those which cannot be explained within conventional zoological frameworks - achieve some level of objective reality for a while at least? Yeah it makes sense. But it's a pity - I really liked the '*Rising of the Moon*' theory.."

I grinned and remembered my conversation with Rueben.

"I'm not saying that that isn't the truth. It just isn't all of the truth. I'm not saying there are new theory covers it all either. Probably both are true. However, I prefer the new one because it is more hard science and less mumbo-jumbo. I have been uncomfortable with my work on Zooform Phenomena ever since I coined the term. People seemed to think that I was hypothesising entire races of phantom creatures which had their own the objective reality. To be quite honest, I have no idea whether there are independently 'real' demons and spirit animals. I have seen no evidence for, nor any real evidence against. I feel much more comfortable with these two theories, and although I am certain that they are not the only two mechanisms at work, I think both of them work to a certain extent".

Davey grinned. "Fuckin' A, pal", he said, " you've given me a lot to think about. Now hoy us a tab you fat bastard".

Knowing enough Geordie to realise that a 'tab' was a cigarette and not something out of my travelling pharmacy upstairs in my suitcase, I tossed a packet of Benson and Hedges over to him. It missed, ricocheted off the shelf, and knocked a three inch, dayglo, plastic rasta figurine to the floor.

"Wayay man," he said, " you throw just like a girl. Wor lass throws better than you. Wor fuckin' bairn throws better than you - and she's only eight !"

We joked around for a few minutes and then Davey looked at me with a serious look in his eyes.

"So this is your life story, warts and all?"

I nodded agreement.

"So you are telling all the crap stuff that happened as well as the good stuff?"

Again I nodded, and took a swig from my bottle of beer. I had been drinking slowly that evening, but had reached one of those strange plateaus of lucidity that sometimes happen at the end of an all night drinking session. Outside the dawn was beginning to break and a lone cock blackbird was beginning to sing. I was reminded of Pete Townshend's theory   in Lifehouse that the reason that they sang so sweetly was because they had managed to survive the terrors of another night. At that moment I knew precisely what he meant and would have joined in the blackbird's melody if I hadn't suddenly been overcome by a beautiful and all encompassing tiredness.

"The one thing I have always wondered," Davey began, looked thoughtful and then stopped.

Go on," I said.

"The one thing I have always wondered is why you do this. You work incredibly long hours, the money ain't very good and you get fuck all recognition for what you do".

I took a deep breath. Believe it nor not, I don't like talking about myself. Therapy was incredibly difficult for me, and most of the time I like to keep my motivations private. However this book and in many ways even more importantly, this conversation was the culmination of seven years of therapy, during which I had tried my best to come to terms with over forty years of good, bad, and sometimes extremely ugly experiences, and I had come so far that it would have been stupid not to finish.

"I do this because I have to", I said. "This is my mission in life, and if I am honest about it I have known this since I was a little boy. When I was a kid I fell in love with the mystery and majesty of the natural world. My mother showed me how wonderful the world was, and while other kids were doing the normal kid things I was falling in love with nature.

Then as I grew up I found that I was the only person that I knew that felt quite so strongly about things like this. The idea that there could be real monsters out there to be discovered just blew me away. As I grew older, I tried to live a conventional life.

I got a job. I got married, and all the time I was desperately miserable. It took me years to discover it, but essentially I believe that I am a very damaged person. A couple of years ago one of the leading forteans emailed several colleagues expressing concern about my drinking (which has always been exaggerated). 'Why was it', he asked, 'that people take Jon Downes seriously? He obviously has a problem.'

Of course I've got a fuckin' problem. But it's not booze. Like Ozzy Osbourne said once. 'Drink? Of course I drink. Spend five minutes in my head and you would be drinking as well'. I'm like that, except I've found another way to keep the demons away. Nowadays, instead of drinking myself into oblivion I try to do something positive with my life, and the search for unknown animals works fine for me…"

I looked over at Davey, but he had gone to sleep. But I carried on anyway.

"I honestly think that what we are doing is important. The search for mystery animals tells us as much about ourselves as it does about the natural world. I think that if the CFZ does the stuff I am planning for it over the next twenty years then we shall really have accomplished something important.

"Not only are we the only organisation in the world who actually goes out and looks for these things on a full-time basis, but we are fighting a rear guard action for freethinking naturalists. On one side you have the orthodox zoologists who on the whole are so hide bound by the strictures of their research grants and their budgets that they cannot even think about approaching anything as left field as cryptozoology, but on the other side we have the pathetic remnants of the once proud fortean publishing world. Apart from *Fortean Times* and a few others, everyone is so determined to make a fast buck that they refuse to publish anything which isn't immediately commercial. That's why you find that for every decent paranormal or fortean book there are a couple of dozens full of crap about crystal healing and angel therapy. Even the few good books that are published find themselves shoved in the corner of the 'Mind, Body and Spirit' section next to a book about astrology for pets.

"There you have us. We publish books that no-one else will publish, go to places that no-one else will go, and study things that no-one else is intersted in. It may be the only way that I can keep myself sane, but I think that what we do is vitally important and I am damn well gonna carry on doing it for the rest of my life. What's more I have written a charter for the CFZ that should ensure that when I finally leave this godforsaken planet, the CFZ will continue long after I am dead and forgotten."

There was a quiet snore from Davey's corner of the shed. I sat back and lit a cigarette. I had said what I wanted to say (even if nobody was listening), and it felt like my journey was almost over. I opened the door and watched the early light of dawn wash over the Co. Durham countryside.

Emboldened by my speech, I continued to lecture a non-existent audience about my hopes and fears for cryptozoology, forteana, the planet and myself. I told them how I wanted the CFZ to be more and more involved in conservation work. I told them how I was appalled that fewer and fewer kids were becoming interested in natural history, and stated my hope that we could rekindle a spirit of adventure into a subject that generations of schoolteachers had made increasingly more boring. I told them how I was afraid that after a string of failed relationships that I would never find a proper soulmate who would understand me and live with me in a mutually satisfactory and emotionally symbiotic relationship. I told them whilst this was sad, I still had a wonderful job, which meant I could travel the world, drive a Jaguar, pay the mortgage and never have to get out of bed in the early morning to work in a mind numbingly boring job in a factory. I told them how I miss my wife and my dog, but that I adore my daughter and have found a new and fulfilling relationship with my father. And I told them how, although I had resigned myself to the fact that I would probably never be truly happy, and that I knew that my own personal daemons would haunt me for however much longer I had to live on this planet, I had found a kind of contentment and fulfilment in the knowledge that I was doing something in my own little way that made a difference.

Then I became lyrical and even poetic. I told my unseen audience about the magickal things I have seen. Not the monsters, but the *truly* magickal things. I have seen the sun rise over the South China Sea, for an instant turning the ocean into a glorious cauldron of burnished gold. I have sat on a red sandstone mesa in the middle of the Nevada desert watching the clouds drift by in a sky so un-naturally blue that it looked as if it had been painted on in a Hollywood soundstage. I have seen the great granite tors of Dartmoor, and the sweeping Canadian forests in the fall when all the maple leaves are a rich scarlet. I have seen the last remnants of the rainforest in Puerto Rico, and I have flown over the Greenland ice floes. I may have had a lot of crap happen to me over the last four and a bit decades, I may suffer from a string of mental and physical ailments that will one day kill me, and I may have, on occasion, been so lonely and miserable that I have been compelled to try and take my own life, but on the whole I have lived a remarkable and very priveliged existance, and for that every day I thank God for having given me life.

Suddenly a realised that I had a 'real' audience again. An audience of two; a scruffy and unkempt black and white cat and an equally scruffy and unkempt Davey Curtis. The cat gazed at me in silence before putting its tail in the air and walking away. Davey broke the silence.

"Fuckin' hell, Jon. You don't half talk some soft shite at times. Have another beer".

So we did.

EPILOGUE

FEAR AND LOATHING 12 MILES EAST OF LAS VEGAS

Baal can spot the vultures in the stormy sky
As they wait up there to see if Baal will die
Sometimes Baal pretends he's dead, but vultures swoop
Baal in silence dines on vulture-soup

When the dark womb drags him down to its prize
What's the world still mean to Baal, he's overfed
So much sky is lurking still behind his eyes
He'll just have enough sky when he's dead

Once the Earth's dark womb engulfed the rotting Baal
Even then the sky was up there, quiet and pale
Naked, young, immensely marvellous
Like Baal loved it when he lived with us

Berthold Brecht   "Baal's Hymn"

And that was where this book was supposed to end in a garden shed that one of my madder and most loveable friends had converted into a Jamaican Theme Bar, not to mention the CFZ gang-hut. However fate has a habit of playing tricks on you, and no matter how hard authors like me like to pretend that events happen in easy, bite-sized chunks (each a chapter long), real life doesn't work like that. In November 2003 I was back in Nevada in a hotel a few miles outside Las Vegas - as a guest at another UFO convention.

Night falls quickly in the American desert. The sun, which for twelve hours had scoured the baking red earth below, had vanished behind the grim, unyielding mountains. In that strange time of the twilight, which the people in Devonshire call the dimpsey, the desert creatures (that had stayed hidden for the hottest parts of the day) began to stir, and what, to the casual visitor, seemed to be a barren wilderness soon became a haven of activity. The rats, mice and frogs emerged from their holes, secure in the knowledge that for a few hours, at least, they would be relatively safe from the larger animals like racoons and coyotes, and blissfully unaware that in the sky above them circled the night-birds searching for supper!

However, sadly I wasn't out with them. I always make sure, each time that I am at one of these bashes, that for at least one afternoon during the proceedings I manage to get out into the countryside and commune with nature. I had already made arrangements to go to the 'Valley of Fire' national park with Nick Redfern and a few others on the Sunday afternoon, and go we did, and very beautiful it was. But at the time I am writing about it was the Friday evening and one of those 'meet and greet' cocktail parties at which the Americans excel. It was an even more turgid event than usual and Nick Redfern and I were getting incredibly bored. We were sitting at a table in the middle of the seating area and were already cursing our lack of forethought. Our prime position meant that the conference organisers would notice immediately if we tried to sneak away, and so as we didn't want to offend them we were stuck there for the duration.

Sadly, although the drinks downstairs in the casino bar were incredibly cheap, there was a 'cash bar' in operation in the conference area. This meant that the drinks were expensive and overly watered down, so as neither 'Redders' or me were made of money, we had to forego even the pleasure of getting drunk. There were thirty-two different types of pie, however, and we had both eaten as much as we could of the sweet gloppy stuff without getting billious, and we were essentially counting the minutes until we could get away with leaving.

Then I saw him.

It was a skinny man with a big nose and piercing blue eyes. He looked like an uncanny cross between an ageing cowboy and the bass player in *Quicksilver Messenger Service*. It was Rueben!

In the intervening four years, Davey Curtis was the only person that I had ever told about my meeting with the strange old man on my fortieth birthday. Although it had been the meeting which was to provide my apotheosis, and which eventually inspired this book, I had treasured it and considered it to have been an intensely private encounter.

I wondered if he had remembered me. I wanted to rush up to him and tell him how he had set me on a journey that had finally come full circle. How he had inspired me to take a proper stock of my life and work, and that although he had only meant to question my findings in *The Rising of the Moon*, he had in fact set me on a path which had led me to discover myself and to come to terms with many of my personal demons. Shit. I wanted to hug him and tell him how he had possibly saved, and certainly enriched my life a thousandfold. But he was standing next to the trestle table of pies, and he was talking to one of the other delegates. I went up to get another slice of pie and surreptitiously listened in to the conversation.

I recognised it all.

"You need to go back to where you started, man," he said with a smile. "You gave a good talk. It's a good book. You're a nice guy; but until you go back to the beginning and make sure that you believe what you are writing, you'll never be happy".

I went back to the table and casually asked Nick if he knew *who* the stranger was?

"Christ-on-a-bike," he exclaimed. "It's that idiot Rueben. He's a homeless racist junkie who lives on the street somewhere in Vegas, and gate-crashes all the UFO conferences, trying to set the speakers onto some asshole spiritual path. He's a weirdo white supremacist and always ends up trying to get money from people for some hare-brained scheme or other. As soon as the security people notice him they'll sling him out! I'd be careful about having anything to do with him if I were you."

I took another mouthful of pie and tried to look innocently as if I was not a person who had undergone a major life-journey, and a thorough re-examination of his whole existence on the word of a homeless, racist junkie (who almost as an afterthought was completely mad). There didn't seem to be anything constructive that I could say, so I went up to the counter and helped myself to another piece of pie.

It's a funny old world innit?

FINismo

THE CENTRE FOR FORTEAN ZOOLOGY

The Centre for Fortean Zoology is the world's only professional and scientific organisation dedicated to research into unknown animals. Although we work all over the world, we carry out regular work in the United Kingdom, investigating accounts of strange creatures in the British countryside.

THAILAND 2000
An expedition to investigate the legendary creature known as the Naga

MARTIN MERE 2002
The hunt for the biggest and oldest fish in England

SUMATRA 2003
Project Kerinci - In search of the Orang Pendek

Led by scientists, the Centre for Fortean Zoology is staffed by volunteers and is always looking for new members.

To apply for a <u>FREE</u> information pack about the organisation and details of how to join, plus information on current and future projects, expeditions and events. Send a stamp addressed envelope to:-

The Centre for Fortean Zoology
15 Holne Court, Exwick, Exeter
Devon, EX4 2NA.

or alternatively visit our website at: w w w . c f z . o r g . u k

Life President: Colonel John Blashford-Snell OBE

Printed in the United Kingdom
by Lightning Source UK Ltd.
102762UKS00002B/55-92